For a moment they stood looking at each other, and he felt as if they were sixteen years old again.

How was it that the past ten years had disappeared so quickly and the link between them remained?

"Susannah, I hope—" He stopped, not sure he wanted to go on.

"What?" Her eyebrows lifted, her green eyes open and questioning.

He sucked in a breath, determined to get the words out before he lost his courage. "I just hope my return isn't…well, difficult for you…after the way we parted."

After the way he'd panicked as their wedding date grew closer, bolting in the night with only a short note left behind to explain himself.

All the vitality seemed to leave Susannah's face.

"Of course not." Her voice was that of a stranger. "I'm sure everyone in Pine Creek will be happy to *wilkom* you home."

Toby carefully smoothed the papers he'd clenched in his hand. Susannah didn't need words to spell out what she felt. It was only too clear.

She hadn't forgo

D1052121

A lifetime spent in rural Pennsylvania and her Pennsylvania Dutch heritage led **Marta Perry** to write about the Plain people, who add so much richness to her home state. Marta has seen nearly sixty books published, with over six million books in print. She and her husband live in a centuries-old farmhouse in a central-Pennsylvania valley. When she's not writing, she's reading, traveling, baking or enjoying her six beautiful grandchildren.

After thirty-five years as a nurse, **Patricia Davids** hung up her stethoscope to become a full-time writer. She enjoys spending her free time visiting her grandchildren, doing some long-overdue yard work and traveling to research her story locations. She resides in Wichita, Kansas. Patricia always enjoys hearing from her readers. You can visit her online at patriciadavids.com.

Carrie Lighte lives in Massachusetts, where her neighbors include several Mennonite farming families. She loves traveling and first learned about Amish culture when she visited Lancaster County, Pennsylvania, as a young girl. When she isn't writing or reading, she enjoys baking bread, playing word games and hiking, but her all-time favorite activity is bodyboarding with her loved ones when the surf's up at Coast Guard Beach on Cape Cod.

MARTA PERRY

USA TODAY Bestselling Author

PATRICIA DAVIDS

*An Amish Family
Christmas*

&

CARRIE LIGHTE

*Amish Triplets
for Christmas*

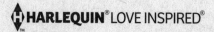

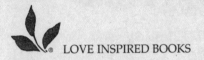 LOVE INSPIRED BOOKS

Recycling programs for this product may not exist in your area.

ISBN-13: 978-1-335-47016-4

An Amish Family Christmas
and Amish Triplets for Christmas

Copyright © 2019 by Harlequin Books S.A.

An Amish Family Christmas
First published in 2014. This edition published in 2019.
Copyright © 2014 by Harlequin Books S.A.

Heart of Christmas
First published in 2014. This edition published in 2019.
Copyright © 2014 by Martha Johnson

A Plain Holiday
First published in 2014. This edition published in 2019.
Copyright © 2014 by Patricia MacDonald

Amish Triplets for Christmas
First published in 2017. This edition published in 2019.
Copyright © 2017 by Carrie Lighte

CONTENTS

HEART OF CHRISTMAS

Marta Perry

This story is dedicated to the wonderful editors at Love Inspired, who have taught me so much. And, as always, to Brian.

Jesus said, "I am the light of the world. Whoever follows me will never walk in darkness, but will have the light of life."
—*John* 8:12

Chapter One

Susannah Miller stood behind the security of her teacher's desk, watching the departure of school board member James Keim and his wife, and wondered if her annual Christmas program was going to spell the end of her job as teacher at Pine Creek Amish School. The hollow feeling in her stomach brought on by Keim's complaints lingered even after the door had closed behind him.

Too worldly? What would make the Keims think there was anything worldly about the Amish school's Christmas program? The program celebrated typical Amish values and attitudes toward the birth of Christ. It had always been the highlight of the school year for her scholars and their families in this small, valley community in central Pennsylvania.

Susannah stiffened her spine. It still would be, if she had anything to say about it. She glanced around the simple, one-room schoolhouse that had become so precious to her over the past twelve years. Everything from the plain, green shades on the windows to the sturdy, wooden desks to the encouraging sayings posted on the wall declared that this was an Amish school, dedicated to educating *kinder* for life in an Amish community.

Becky Shuler, Susannah's best friend since childhood, abandoned the pretense she'd adopted of arranging books on the bookshelves. She hurried over to put her arm around Susannah's waist.

"*Ach,* Susannah, it wonders me why you don't look more upset. I'd be throwing something if I had to put up with James Keim's criticisms. The nerve of the man, coming in here and complaining about your Christmas program before he's even seen it."

Susannah shook her head, managing a smile. "I'm not upset."

Or, at least, she had no intention of showing what she was feeling. Becky was her dearest friend in the world, but she knew as well as anyone that Becky couldn't keep herself from talking, especially when she was indignant on behalf of those she loved.

"Well, you should be." Becky's round cheeks were even rosier than usual, and her brown eyes snapped with indignation. "The Keims have only lived here less than two years, and he thinks he should tell everyone else how to live Amish. How he even got on the school board is a mystery to me."

Shrugging, Susannah closed the grade book she'd been working on when the Keims had appeared at the end of the school day. "*Komm,* Becky. You know as well as I do that folks don't exactly line up to volunteer to be on the school board. James Keim was willing, even eager."

"That's certain sure." Becky's flashing eyes proclaimed that she was not going to be talked out of her temper so easily. "He was only eager to serve because he wants to make our school into a copy of the one where they lived in Ohio. All I can say is that if he liked Ohio so much, he should have stayed there instead of coming here and bothering us."

"Becky, you know you shouldn't talk that way about a brother in the faith. It's not kind."

Becky was irrepressible. "But it's true. You of all people know what a thorn in the side he's been. *Ach,* you know I wouldn't say these things to anyone but you."

"It would be best not to say them at all. James Keim has his own ideas of what an Amish school should be like. He's entitled to his opinion."

Based on his disapproving comments, Susannah suspected that Keim's previous community had been more conservative than Pine Creek, Pennsylvania. Amish churches varied from place to place, according to their membership and their bishops. Pine Creek, being a daughter church to Lancaster County, was probably a bit less stringent than what Keim had been used to.

"You're too kind, that's what you are," Becky declared, planting her fists on the edge of the desk. "You know perfectly well that he'd like to see his daughter Mary take your place as teacher, so he could boss her around all he wanted."

Susannah shook her head, but she had to admit there was some truth to what Becky said. As a thirty-year-old *maidal* who'd been teaching for a dozen years, Susannah wasn't easily cowed, at least not when it came to her classroom and the young scholars who were like her own children. Young Mary would probably be easily influenced by her father's powerful personality.

"I don't think Mary Keim has much interest in teaching, from what I've seen," she said, determined to deflect Becky's ire. Picking up the cardboard box that held Christmas program materials, Susannah set it on the desk. "If we're going to work on the program this afternoon, we'd better get started."

Becky shook her head gloomily. "Mary might not want to teach, but she'd never stand up to her *daad*. You're not going to let her help with the Christmas program, are you? She'd just be spying on you and reporting back to him."

"I'll cross that bridge when I come to it," she said. "Maybe she won't offer." Susannah pulled the tape from the box lid, sure that would divert Becky's attention.

"Just one more thing, and then I'll stop, I promise," Becky said. "You're not to pay any heed to Keim's nasty comment about you not understanding the *kinder* because you're unmarried, all right?"

"All right." That was an easy promise to make. One thing she'd never had cause to question was her feelings for her scholars.

"After all, it's not as if you couldn't have married if you'd wanted to." Becky dived into the box and pulled out a handful of paper stars. "Even after Toby left—" She stopped abruptly, her cheeks flaming. "Susannah, I'm sorry, I—"

"Forget it." Susannah forced her smile to remain, despite the jolt in her stomach at the mention of Toby's name. "I have."

That was a lie, of course, and one she should repent of, she supposed. Still, the *gut* Lord could hardly expect her to go around parading her feelings about the childhood sweetheart who had deserted her a month before their wedding was supposed to take place.

"Have you? Really?" Becky clasped her hand, her brown eyes suddenly swimming with tears.

"Of course I have," she said with all the firmness she could muster. "It was ten years ago. My disappointment has long since been forgiven and forgotten. I wish Toby well."

Did she? She tried to, of course. Forgiveness was an integral part of being Amish. But saying she forgave hadn't seemed to mend the tear in her heart.

"Well, I wish Tobias Unger was here right now so I could give him a piece of my mind," Becky declared. "He left so fast nobody had a chance to tell him how *ferhoodled* he was being. And then his getting married out in Ohio to someone he barely knew... Well, like I said, he was just plain foolish."

News of Toby had filtered back to Pine Creek after he'd left, naturally, since his family still lived here. Everyone knew he'd married someone else within a year of leaving, just as they'd heard about the births of his two children and about his wife's death last year. His mother had gone out to Ohio to help with the children for a time, and she'd returned saying that Toby and the *kinder* really ought to move back home.

But he hadn't, to Susannah's relief. She wasn't sure how she'd cope with seeing him all the time.

"Forget about him," she said. "Let's talk about how we're going to arrange the room for the Christmas program. I have some new ideas."

"You always have ideas," Becky said, apparently ready to let go of the sensitive subject. "I don't know how you keep coming up with something new every year."

"*Ach,* there's always something new to find in Christmas." Susannah felt a bubble of excitement rising in her at the thought of the much-loved season. "Maybe because we all feel like *kinder* again, ain't so?"

"I suppose so. Thomas and the twins have been whispering together for weeks now. I think they're planning a Christmas surprise for me." Becky smiled.

"Of course they are. That's what Christmas is, after all. God's greatest surprise of all for us." Susannah swung away from the desk, looking around the room. "What do you think about making the schoolroom itself surprising when folks come in? Maybe instead of having the scholars standing in the front, we could turn everything sideways. That would give the *kinder* more space."

She walked back through the rows of desks, flinging out her arms to gesture. "You see, if the audience faced this way—"

The door of the one-room school opened suddenly, interrupting her words. Susannah's heart jolted, and she felt as if she couldn't breathe.

Surely she was dreaming it. The man standing in the schoolhouse doorway wasn't…couldn't possibly be…Toby Unger.

Toby found himself standing motionless for a little too long, the words of greeting he'd prepared failing to appear. He'd known he would see Susannah, after all. He shouldn't be speechless.

William, holding on to his left hand, gave him a tug forward, while little Anna clung to his pant leg. Toby cleared his throat, feeling his face redden. He could only hope Susannah would think his flush was from the chill December air.

"Susannah. It's nice to see you after so long."

Susannah's heart-shaped face seemed to lose its frozen look when he spoke. She glanced from him to the two children, and a smile touched her lips.

"*Wilkom* to the school, Toby. These are your *kinder*?"

She stooped to Anna's level. "I'm Teacher Susannah. What's your name?"

For an instant, he thought his daughter would respond, but then she hid her face against his leg, as she always did with strangers these days.

"This is Anna," he said, resting his hand on her shoulder. "She's six. And this is my son, William."

"I'm eight," William announced. "I'm in third grade."

"You're a big boy, then." Something about the expression in Susannah's green eyes made Toby wonder if she was seeing him at that age. People often said William was very like him, with his gray-blue eyes and the chestnut-colored hair that was determined to curl.

When Susannah returned her gaze to his face, there was no longer any trace of surprise or shock in her. Her heart-shaped face had maturity and control now, although her soft peachy skin and the delicate curve of her cheek hadn't changed in the ten years since he'd seen her last.

"How nice that you could come to visit," she said. "I'm sure your *mamm* and *daad* are happy to see you and the *kinder,* especially since your father has been laid up with that broken leg from his accident."

Of course that was what she'd assume—that he was here to visit, maybe to help out after his father's fall from the barn loft. He'd made his decision so quickly there wouldn't have been time for word to spread, even though the Amish grapevine was probably still as effective as ever. Which meant he had to tell her the news that he assumed Susannah would find very unwelcome.

"We're not here to visit." He sent a quick, reassuring glance at the *kinder.* "We've come home to Pine Creek to stay."

"You're moving back?"

The question came from behind Susannah, and Toby belatedly realized there was someone else in the schoolroom. He must have been so absorbed in seeing Susannah again that he hadn't looked beyond her face. It took him a moment to recognize the woman who came quickly toward them.

"Becky Mast." He might have known that's who it would be. Becky and Susannah had been best friends since the cradle. He could just imagine how furious Becky had been at him for jilting her dearest friend all those years ago.

"I'm Becky Shuler now." She stood glaring at him, hands planted on her hips. Becky wasn't as good as Susannah at hiding her feelings, it seemed. "Are you serious about moving back to Pine Creek? Why would you?" The edge in her voice made no secret of her opinion.

"That means I'll have William and Anna in my classroom," Susannah said quickly, sending a warning look at her friend. "I'll be wonderful glad to have two new students in our school."

Becky, apparently heeding the stern glance from Susannah, seemed to swallow her ire. She smiled at the *kinder.* "Anna, are you in first grade? My twin girls are in first grade."

Anna didn't speak. He didn't expect her to. But she nodded slightly.

"The twins will enjoy having a new friend," Susannah said. "You can sit beside them, if you'd like. Their names are Grace and Mary."

"Where do the third graders sit, Teacher Susannah?" William pulled free of Toby's restraining hand. "Are there lots of boys?"

"Third graders sit right over here." She led him to a

row of desks somewhere in size between the smallest ones for the beginners and the almost-adult-sized ones for the eighth graders. "We have three other boys in the third grade and four in the fourth, so you'll have lots of boys to play with at recess."

William grabbed one of the desks and lifted the top. Before Toby could correct him, Susannah had closed it again, keeping her hand on the surface for a moment.

"That is someone else's desk. We don't look through other people's things unless they say we may." Susannah's quiet firmness seemed to impress William, because he nodded and took a step back.

The confidence of her response startled him. The Susannah he remembered hadn't been capable of correcting anyone. But they were both ten years older now. They'd both grown and changed, hadn't they?

"I hope it's not a problem to add two new scholars into your classroom in the middle of the year," he said.

His mind wandered to the things he'd have to tell Susannah about the *kinder,* sooner or later. Things that had made him return home, seeking help and stability from his parents.

There was William's talent for mischief making. And Anna's shyness, which seemed to be getting worse, not better. But something in him balked at the thought of confessing his failings as a parent to Susannah, of all people.

With her hand resting on the nearest desk, Susannah seemed very much at ease and in command in her classroom. "Becky, would you mind taking William and Anna out to join the twins on the swings? I have some papers their *daadi* must fill out."

Becky nodded and held out her hands to the children. "*Komm.* I'll show you the playground."

To his surprise, Anna took Becky's hand and trotted alongside her with only one backward glance. William, of course, raced ahead of them. After a pause at
the door to allow Becky to grab a jacket against the
winter chill, they went outside.

"*Denke,* Susannah." He turned back to her. "I wanted
a chance to talk without the children overhearing."

"Of course." Her tone was suddenly cool and formal.
She walked to the teacher's desk and retrieved a folder
from a drawer, not speaking. Then she turned back to
him. "Here are some forms you can fill out and return
when you bring the *kinder* to class. Will you want them
to start tomorrow?"

He nodded as he took the papers, hesitating in the
face of her frosty demeanor. It was as if all Susannah's
gentle friendliness had left the room with his *kinder.*

Still, he could hardly expect her to welcome him
back, not after what he'd done. Groping for something
to say, he noticed the Christmas stars strewn across her
desk, and the sight made him smile.

"Is it time for the Christmas program already? Some
things never change, ain't so?"

Susannah nodded, her expression brightening. "It
wouldn't seem like Christmas if we didn't have the
school Christmas program to look forward to. Becky
and I were just saying that the challenge is to come up
with something new every year."

"It's not possible, is it?" He felt a sudden longing to
keep her smiling, to keep her from thinking about their
past. "Except that someone usually makes a new and
different mistake each time."

Susannah leaned against the desk, her face relaxing
just a little. "I seem to remember a few mistakes that
might have been intentional. Like a certain boy who

mixed up the letters in the word the class was supposed to be spelling out, so that our Merry Christmas greeting didn't make any sense."

He grinned at the memory. "Don't mention that to William, or he'll try to outdo my mischief making."

"I'll keep your secret," she said, the corners of her lips curving, making the words sound almost like a promise.

For a moment they stood looking at each other, and he felt as if they were sixteen years old again, knowing each other so well they hardly needed words to communicate. How was it that the past ten years had disappeared so quickly and the link between them still remained?

"Susannah, I hope—" He stopped, not sure he wanted to go on with what he'd impulsively begun.

"What?" Her eyebrows lifted, her green eyes open and questioning, just like they used to be before he'd given her cause to regard him with wariness and suspicion.

He sucked in a breath, determined to get the words out before he lost his courage. "I just hope my return isn't...well, difficult for you...after the way we parted."

After the way he'd panicked as their wedding date grew closer, bolting in the night with only a short note left behind to explain himself.

All the vitality seemed to leave Susannah's face. She turned, taking a step away from him. The moment shattered as if it had never happened.

"Of course not." Susannah's voice was colorless, her voice that of a stranger. "I'm sure everyone in Pine Creek will be happy to *wilkom* you home."

Toby carefully smoothed the papers he'd clenched in

his hand. Susannah didn't need words to spell out what she felt. It was only too clear.

She hadn't forgotten, and she hadn't forgiven.

Chapter Two

Susannah held her breath, fearing her denial hadn't been very convincing. If she wasn't bothered by Toby's return to Pine Creek, why did she find it necessary to hide her expression from him?

Because he'd always been able to read her emotions too clearly, answered a small voice in her thoughts. Because she was afraid that the feelings between them might still be there.

Grow up, she told herself fiercely and swung around to face him. She touched her desk with the tips of her fingers, and the reminder of who and where she was seemed to steady her.

"It's been a long time." She hoped her smile was more natural now. "I'm sure people will chatter about us, remembering that we planned to marry. But if we show them that we are nothing more than old friends, that should silence the gossip, ain't so?"

If he believed her only concern was what people might say, so much the better. And it was certain sure the grapevine would wag with this tale for a time.

"If you can stand it, I can." Toby's smile was full of

relief. It relaxed the tight lines of his face, making him look more like the boy she remembered.

As for the rest… Well, Toby had changed, of course. Maybe men changed more between twenty and thirty than women did. Toby seemed taller, broader, even more substantial in a way. He looked as if it would take a lot to move him.

His hair, always the glossy brown of horse chestnuts, might be a shade darker, but she'd guess it still had glints of bronze in the sun. His eyes were a deep, deep blue, but there were tiny lines at the corners of them now, no doubt because of the difficult time he'd been through with his wife's death. His curly dark beard hid his chin, but she had no doubt it was as stubborn as ever.

Realizing she was studying his face too long, Susannah said, "Tell me a little about your young ones. Have they had a difficult time adjusting to their *mammi*'s death?"

Toby nodded. He perched on one of the first grader's desks, looking like a giant amid the child-size furniture. "It hasn't been easy. It's been over a year, you know. I suppose I thought her loss would become less hurtful for them after a time, but that doesn't seem to be happening."

"I'm sorry." Her heart ached at his obvious pain. Poor children. Poor Toby, trying to deal with them and cope with his own grief, as well. "There isn't any timetable for grief, I'm afraid. For a child to lose his or her mother is devastating."

"It is." He rubbed the back of his neck in a gesture so familiar that it made her heart lurch. "I feel like a pretty poor substitute for Emma in their eyes."

"They need you to be their father, not their mother,"

she said gently. "Was your wife's family not able to help?"

Toby hunched his shoulders. "They had moved to Colorado to help start a new settlement before Emma became sick. Her mother came for a time, but I can't say it helped a lot. She was so sad herself that it seemed to make the pain even worse for the *kinder*."

"So that's why you decided to come back home." It was growing easier to talk to him with every word. Soon it wouldn't bother her at all, and she could treat Toby just as she would any other friend of her childhood.

"That's so. I knew I needed more help, and my folks kept urging me to come. Then *Daad*'s accident seemed to make it more crucial." Toby shifted a little, maybe finding the small desk not well suited for sitting on. His black jacket swung open, showing the dark blue shirt he wore, which nearly matched his eyes. "*Daad* has always wanted me to work with him in the carriage-building business." He abruptly stopped speaking, leaving Susannah to think there was more to his decision than he'd admitted.

"Is that what you want, too?"

Toby's face lit up. "More than anything. Working with *Daad* was always the future I'd planned for myself, before I…left."

Susannah had been so wrapped up in her own loss ten years ago that she'd never thought about what Toby had given up when he'd run away from their impending wedding.

"Well, it's *gut* that you can join him now." She forced a cheerful note into her voice. "Especially since he's laid up. Although I don't suppose he's as busy in the winter, anyway, is he?"

"No. *Daad* says if he had to fall out of the hayloft, he picked the best time to do it. He'd intended to keep working over the winter, but all he's been able to do is supervise some repairs with Ben doing the work. And constantly criticizing, according to Ben." He chuckled.

Ben, Toby's younger brother, had been one of Susannah's scholars only a few years ago.

Susannah hesitated, but there was a question she wanted answered, and since they were talking so freely, maybe it was best just to get it out.

"I hope you didn't delay your return all this time because of what happened between us." That was as close as she could come to asking him outright.

Toby's eyes widened. "No, Susannah. Please don't think so. The truth is that Emma didn't want to move away from her family and the community she'd always known." He shrugged. "I didn't much like working in a factory, but I couldn't bear to tear her away from her family."

No, she could imagine that Toby hadn't been well suited to factory work. He'd always wanted to do things his own way and at his own pace. "You made the best decisions you could, I'm sure."

Toby's face tightened, and she had a sense of things unsaid. "Well, I'm here now, anyway. I thought Ben might resent me joining the business, but he seems wonderful glad to have someone else for *Daad* to blame when things go wrong." His face relaxed in a grin. "*Daad*'s a little testy since he can't do things on his own."

"I'm sure. Your *mamm* mentioned that she had her hands full with him."

"That she does. I'm afraid it's an added burden, me

returning with the two *kinder*. But I didn't know what else to do."

"*Ach,* don't think that way." She nearly reached out to him in sympathy but drew back just in time. She couldn't let herself get too close to Toby, for both their sakes. "You know your parents want nothing more than to have you and their grandchildren with them. Your *mamm* is always talking about the two of them."

"She may not be so happy when she realizes what she's got herself into." He stared down at his hands, knotted into fists against his black broadfall trousers. "The truth is, William and Anna are both…difficult."

Susannah had the sense that this was what Toby had been trying to say since the *kinder* had left the room, and she murmured a silent prayer for the right words.

"Difficult how?" She tried to smile reassuringly. "You don't need to be afraid to confide in me, Toby. Anything you tell me about the *kinder* is private, and as their teacher, I can help them best if I understand what's happening with them."

He nodded, exhaling a long breath. "I know I can trust you, Susannah." A fleeting smile crossed his face, then was gone. "I always could."

No doubt he was remembering all the times she hadn't told on him when he'd been up to mischief. "Just tell me what troubles you about them," she said.

"My little Anna," he began. "Well, you saw how she is. So shy she hardly ever says a word. She was never as outgoing as William, but she used to chirp along like a little bird when it was just the family. Now she scarcely talks even to me."

Susannah's heart twisted at his obvious pain. "Is it just since her *mammi* died?"

He nodded. "That's when I started noticing it, anyway. She hasn't even warmed up to her *grossmammi* yet, and I know that hurts my mother."

"She'll be patient," Susannah said, knowing Sara Unger would do anything for her grandchildren. "What about William? He's not suffering from shyness, I'd say."

"No." Toby didn't smile at her comment. If anything, he looked even more worried. "William has been a problem in another way." He hesitated, making her realize how difficult it was for him to talk about his children to her. "William has been getting up to mischief."

"Well, he probably takes after his father. You shouldn't—"

He shook his head, stopping her. "I'm not talking about the kind of pranks I used to play. I'm talking about serious things. Things where he could have been badly hurt." He paled. "He tried to ride bareback on a young colt that was hardly broken to harness. He challenged one of the other boys to jump from the barn window, and it's a wonder he wasn't hurt." Toby's jaw tightened. "He started a fire in the shed. If I hadn't seen the smoke—" He broke off abruptly.

Susannah's thoughts were reeling, but she knew she had to reassure him somehow. Say something that would show she was on his side.

"I'm so sorry, Toby." Her heart was in the words. "But you mustn't despair. William is young, and he's acting out his pain over his mother in the only way he can think of. This is going to get better."

"I want to believe that." The bleakness in his expression told her he didn't quite mean what he said.

"There's a way to reach William, I promise you. I'll do everything I can to help him. To help both of them."

Wanting only to ease the pain she read in Toby's

face, she reached out to clasp his hand. The instant they touched, she knew she'd made a mistake.

Their eyes met with a sudden, startled awareness. His seemed to darken, and Susannah felt her breath catch in her throat. For a long moment, they were motionless, hands clasped, gazes intertwined.

And then he let go of her hand as abruptly as if he'd touched a hot stove. He cleared his throat. "*Denke,* Susannah." His voice had roughened. "I knew the *kinder* could count on you for help."

She clasped her hands together tightly, feeling as if she'd forgotten how to breathe. "That's why I'm here," she said. She managed a bland smile and retreated behind her desk.

Toby rose, and for the life of her, she couldn't think of anything else to say. But one thing had become very clear to her.

She wasn't over Toby Unger at all, and somehow, she was going to have to learn to deal with it.

Toby sat at the kitchen table by lamplight with *Daad* while *Mamm* put dishes away. He felt as if he'd jumped backward in time. He and *Daad* used to sit like this in the evening when the chores were done, hearing the life of the household go on around them while *Daad* planned out their next day's work.

The two sisters who'd come after him were married now, with families of their own, but his youngest sister, Sally, was upstairs putting William and Anna to bed for him. Sixteen, and just starting her *rumspringa* years, Sally had developed into a beauty, but she didn't seem aware of it. Maybe she thought it was natural to have all the boys flocking around her the way they did. It didn't turn her head, at any rate. She was sweet and loving with his children—an unexpected blessing upon his return.

And Susannah? Would she be a blessing, as well? He still felt that jolt of surprise he'd experienced when their eyes first met. How could he still feel an attraction for the woman he'd jilted ten years ago?

Mamm leaned across him to pour a little more coffee into *Daad*'s cup. "Did you have a chance to talk to Susannah today about the *kinder?*"

He nodded. He had to keep his mind on his children. Any flicker of attraction he felt for Susannah was surely just a result of seeing someone again he'd once been so close to.

"It wasn't easy to tell her," he admitted. "But I figured she needed to know about my worries if she's going to be their teacher."

"You don't need to worry about Susannah. She's not one to go blabbing about private things." *Daad*'s voice was a low bass rumble. He shifted position on the chair, and Toby suspected the heavy cast on his leg was troubling him.

"She's a fine teacher," *Mamm* said warmly. "Look how patient she was with that boy of Harley Esch's when he had trouble learning. And now he's reading just as well as can be, his *mamm* told me. She can't say enough about Teacher Susannah."

"I'm glad to know it. I hope she does as well with William and Anna." Toby raised his gaze to the ceiling, hoping that William wasn't upstairs giving his young aunt any trouble.

"*Ach,* you're worrying too much." His mother patted his shoulder, fondly letting her hand rest there. "You'll see. Just being here with family is going to do them a world of good. And Susannah will help them, too."

Toby nodded, smiling, and wished he could share her confidence. The thing he couldn't talk about, never even thought about if he could help it, reared its ugly head.

If he hadn't rushed into marriage with Emma, if he had been a better husband, if he had been able to love her as much as he should have...

Once started, that train of thought could go on and on. He had to stop before the burden of guilt grew too heavy to carry.

"We've been fortunate to have Susannah settle in and teach for over ten years," *Mamm* said. "It's not often that a teacher stays so long. Usually just when they have experience, they up and get married—" She stopped abruptly, maybe thinking she was getting into rocky territory.

Was he the reason Susannah had never married? If so, he'd done even more harm than he'd known.

"I hear James Keim is saying she's been there too long," *Daad* commented, stretching his good leg.

Toby frowned. "Who is James Keim, and why would he be saying something like that?"

"*Ach,* I'm sure he means no harm," *Mamm* said quickly. "He and his family moved here from Ohio a couple of years ago, and he's certain sure interested in the school. He was even willing to serve on the school board."

That didn't really answer his question. "Why would he say something negative about Susannah?"

"Well, now, we don't know for sure that he did," *Daad* said in his calm way. He sent a quelling glance toward *Mamm*. "It was gossip, when all's said and done. But supposedly he thinks the school would be better off with a new, young teacher, someone closer to the students in age."

"That's nonsense." Toby's tone was so sharp that both his parents looked at him. He shrugged. "I mean, it seems silly to think of getting rid of a good teacher for a reason like that. Like *Mamm* said, the more experience a teacher has, the better."

Toby wondered to himself, where had that come from, that protective surge of feeling for Susannah? And more important, what was he going to do about it?

Chapter Three

When Susannah took her scholars outside for recess, she had a moment to assess William and Anna's first day of school. It would be hard to forget, since Anna was still clinging firmly to her skirt.

Normally, Susannah might opt to stay inside during recess and prepare for the next class, but her helper today was Mary Keim, and she suspected Mary wasn't ready to be left alone with the *kinder* yet. She studied the girl's face for a moment, searching for some sign that Mary actually wanted to be helping at the school. She couldn't find one. Mary stood pressed against the stair railing, not venturing toward the swings and seesaws, which occupied most of the children. She seemed afraid to move.

Susannah bit back a wave of exasperation. She rather expected this withdrawal from shy little Anna on her first day at a new school. She would think that sixteen-year-old Mary might have a bit more confidence.

"You don't need to stay here with me, Mary. Why don't you play catch with the older children? Or you can push some of the young ones on the swings."

Mary showed the whites of her eyes like a frightened horse. "I…I'll try," she said and walked slowly toward the swings.

No, not a horse, Susannah decided, watching the girl's tentative approach to the smaller children. Mary was more like a little gray mouse, with her pale face, pointed chin and anxious, wary eyes. She feared making a mistake, Susannah decided, and so she took refuge in doing nothing. If her father thought a few weeks as the teacher's assistant was going to turn the girl into a teacher, he was mistaken.

Well, parents were often the last to realize what their children were best suited for. She'd certainly seen that often enough as a teacher. But she had more immediate problems to deal with than Mary Keim's future.

Sinking onto the step, Susannah drew Anna down next to her. "You did very well with your reading this morning, Anna. Do you like to read?"

The child nodded, her blue eyes showing a flicker of interest, but she didn't speak.

"I'd guess somebody reads stories to you before you go to bed at night. Am I right?"

Again a nod, this time accompanied by a slight smile.

"Let's see if I can guess who. Is it *Daadi?*"

A shake of the head answered her.

"Grossmammi?"

"Sometimes." The word came in a tiny whisper.

"Who else, besides *Grossmammi?*" Why wasn't Toby doing it? Was he that busy with the carriage business at this time of the year? Maybe he considered that a woman's job, but…

"Aunt Sally likes to read stories."

That was the longest sentence she'd gotten from the child, and Susannah rejoiced.

"I know your aunt Sally. Once she was one of my scholars, just as you are. She liked to read then, too."

Anna's small face lit up. "She makes all the noises in the story when she reads."

Susannah couldn't help chuckling. "She did that in school, too. Do you giggle when she does it?"

And there it was—an actual smile as Anna nodded. Susannah put her arm around the child and hugged her close. All Anna needed was a little time, patience and encouragement. She would—

A sudden shout jolted Susannah out of her thoughts. She turned her head, her gaze scanning the schoolyard for trouble. And found it. Two boys were engaged in a pushing match, and even as she ran toward them, she realized that the smaller one was William.

"Stoppe, schnell," she commanded in the tone that never failed to corral her students' attention. It didn't fail now. Both William and Seth Stoltzfus, a sixth grader with a quick temper, jerked around to face her.

"This is not acceptable. Into the schoolroom. Now. Both of you." With a hand on each one's shoulder, she marched them toward the school.

Mary stood watching, openmouthed.

"Mary, you are in charge on the playground until I ring the bell. Try to get Anna to go on the swings with the twins, please."

Mary nodded and scurried to do her bidding, and Susannah sent up a quick prayer for guidance. After what Toby had confided to her, she'd expected trouble with William, but she hadn't thought it would flare up so quickly.

"Now then." Leaving them standing in front of her desk, she took her place behind it. "What did you think you were doing?"

"He started it," Seth said quickly.

"Did not," William retorted. "He did."

"Did n—"

"Stop." She halted the repetition of blame. "Were you arguing over the baseball?" Some of the older boys had been tossing it around before the trouble started.

Seth nodded. "It went toward him, and he wouldn't give it back."

"I *was* going to throw it." William glared belligerently. "You didn't need to grab."

"So, you were both wrong," she said. "That is not how we settle disputes in our school. You know that. You'll both stay after school and wash the boards for me today." She knew that would make an impact. While the girls vied for the opportunity to clean the chalkboards, the boys hated the job. For some reason she didn't understand, they'd decided it was unmanly.

"*Yah,* Teacher Susannah." Seth edged backward, and when she didn't say anything more, he hurried back to his interrupted recess.

William took a few steps, his expression hostile, then stopped. "Are you going to tell my *daadi?*"

Susannah's heart softened. "I don't think that's necessary."

The expression that swept across his face couldn't be missed. Disappointment. Why was the boy disappointed? Relief would be more natural, wouldn't it?

Jaw set, William turned away, contriving to knock the books off the nearest desk as he did so.

"Perhaps I *should* ask your father to come in," she said, watching for his reaction.

William shrugged. "He can't. He's busy working all the time."

Susannah surveyed the boy thoughtfully. That surely

wasn't true, but she had a feeling William thought it was. Possibly this attitude was a hangover from what must have been very difficult times. Toby had been working in a factory, he'd said, so he wouldn't have been able to take time off during the day very often.

Most Amish, if they could manage it, preferred to farm or run a home-based business so that the family could work together. Toby apparently hadn't had that choice, and with a sick wife and no relatives close at hand, he'd probably had little time for anything else.

"It might be different here," she suggested, concerned that she might be venturing too far into personal territory.

William shook his head, pressing his lips together. "Can I go?"

She nodded, feeling helpless, and watched him leave the room with a swagger probably designed to tell anyone who saw him that he didn't care about getting into trouble with the teacher.

She really didn't want to have any further private conversations with Toby, but she was afraid she'd have to.

The opportunity arose when Toby came to pick up his children from school. After a look at his son, busily washing the chalkboards, he walked out of the schoolhouse and approached Susannah where she stood on the steps, waving goodbye to her scholars.

"I take it William is in trouble already." He stood at the top of the steps, looking down at her.

Susannah went up a step. Toby had quite enough of a height advantage on her already, without adding any more. "I'm afraid so."

He looked as if he was bracing himself for the news. "How bad?"

"Not bad at all." She smiled to lessen the sting he was undoubtedly feeling. No parent wanted to hear that his child hadn't behaved properly. "I thought a session of washing the boards together might be good for both Seth and William."

Toby put one hand on the porch post, looking as if he'd like to pull it loose and throw it. "Fighting?"

"Just pushing each other. There's no need for you to say anything more to him. I can deal with what happens at my school."

"I'm sure you can." His glance held a hint of surprise. "You've changed, Susannah."

"I've grown up," she corrected. "We both have."

He blew out a sigh. "I don't know. Grown-ups are supposed to have the answers, aren't they? I don't seem to have any."

"No one does. We just muddle along and do our best to live as God wants."

She'd had every intention of keeping her conversations with him cool and impersonal, and here they were, talking like old friends again. Like people who'd known each other so long that they barely needed to use words.

"What can I do, Susannah?" He was looking at her, his eyes so honest and pleading that she knew she had to help him, no matter the risk to her heart.

"I've been giving it some thought," she said carefully. "It seems to me that Anna just needs a bit of time and patience to ease her transition to her new life. As for William…" She had to proceed slowly. She didn't want to add to Toby's burdens, but he seemed to be the key to the boy's difficulties. "Perhaps if you could spend more time with him—"

"Do you think I don't know that I'm to blame?" The quick flash of anger seemed to be directed more at himself than at her. "That's the main reason I moved back here. I want William to have the kind of relationship with me that I had with my *daad,* working together, enjoying each other...." His voice trailed off.

"I know," she said softly. "I thought perhaps if you volunteered to help with the Christmas program, it would be a start. William could work with you building the props and getting the classroom ready. And Anna would find reassurance in having you close at hand during part of her school day."

And what would she find in having Toby in her classroom, seeing him often, trying to manage her rebellious heart?

But Toby's face had already brightened at her suggestion. "That's a fine idea, Susannah. If you're sure you can stand having me around so much, that is."

She couldn't force a smile no matter how hard she tried, but she nodded. "*Gut.* That's settled, then. We'll start work on the program on Monday afternoon."

"I'll be here," he said. He started to turn toward the classroom and his *kinder,* and then stopped, looking into her face. "You're a kind person, Susannah. I won't forget this."

His fingers brushed her hand, and awareness shimmered across her skin. No. She wouldn't forget, either.

Susannah sat beside Becky in the buggy on Saturday, struggling to find the best way of telling her friend she was going to be working with Toby. There didn't seem to be any.

Becky was bound to disapprove, and Susannah could hardly blame her. After all, it was Becky who'd seen her through that terrible time after Toby left.

Back then, Susannah had managed to keep her calm

facade in place with other people. That had been prideful, most likely, but it had seemed necessary. She hadn't wanted to burden her parents or Toby's with her hurt. It was only with Becky that she'd felt free to expose her inner grief and pain.

They were pulling into the parking area at Byler's Book Shop, and she still hadn't managed to bring up the subject. Byler's, like most Amish businesses, was located right on the family farm—a square, cement-block building to house the store, run by Etta Byler, with the help of various sisters and cousins.

Becky parked the buggy at the hitching rail, and they both slid down. "I love having a reason to visit the book shop." Becky was smiling in anticipation. "I think I'll get a book for each of the twins for Christmas. After I help find the materials for the program, of course."

"You can do all the browsing you want," Susannah said, leading the way to the door. "That's the best part of coming to the book shop, ain't so?"

Susannah paused inside the door, taking in the sections devoted to children's books, history and the ever-popular Amish romance novels. Several women were already browsing through books by their favorite authors. Becky cast a longing look in that direction, but she followed Susannah to the area devoted to aids for teachers.

Susannah paused in front of a display of bulletin-board materials. "I was thinking that we might work the whole program around the idea of light. Jesus came to be the light for the world, and then there's the Christmas star and the idea of letting your light shine...."

"But not blinding your neighbor with it," Becky finished the familiar Amish phrase, grinning. "That's a great idea, if we can find enough things that relate to it."

"I can write some of the pieces myself, if I need to." The youngest scholars were usually the most difficult to find parts for. They needed roles that didn't require too much reading and would allow them to move around, if possible. They'd be fidgeting, anyway, unused to being the center of attention for all the parents and grandparents and siblings who would pack the schoolhouse for the event.

"Stars, candles," Becky said, musing. "Or even lanterns. We have some in the barn."

"I've been thinking of having two or three large cardboard candles on each side of the area where the scholars will perform. They'd enjoy that, I think."

Becky nodded, quick to jump on the idea. "We can get some of the fathers to make them, ain't so? Who do you want to ask?"

Susannah couldn't put it off any longer. At least no one was close enough to hear Becky's inevitable reaction.

"I already have a volunteer." She kept her voice casual and her eyes on the shiny cutouts she was leafing through. "Toby is willing to help."

It took so long for Becky to respond that Susannah thought she hadn't heard. She grabbed Susannah's hands and pulled her around to face her.

"Toby? What is wrong with you, Susannah? Why would you let Toby anywhere near you after what he's done?"

"Shh. Becky, his children are my students. I can't keep him away from the school." She had no hope that Becky would accept that as a reason.

"I know what he's doing." Becky's eyes narrowed. "He's volunteered to help because he wants to get close to you again."

Her voice had risen, and Susannah shot a quick look around. "Hush. Do you want someone to hear?" At least in a public place, she had a reason for trying to mute Becky's protests. Unfortunately she knew she'd have to listen to them all the way home.

Becky dismissed her words with a quick gesture. "Why didn't you tell him no? Say you already had enough help?"

"It wasn't that way." She found she was trying to avoid her friend's eyes. "Toby didn't suggest it. I did."

Becky was silent for a moment, clasping her hands tightly. "*Ach,* Susannah, what were you thinking? You're surely not falling for him again."

"It's nothing like that," she protested. "William is troubled, and he needs attention from his father. I thought if they worked together on the project, it might help him."

Becky pressed her lips together in disapproval. "Let him do that outside of school—far away from you."

"You don't have to worry about me. My only interest in Toby is as his children's teacher. I'm not going to get involved with him again."

Becky studied Susannah's face for a moment and shook her head. "I'm not sure if you actually believe what you're saying or not. But I am sure of one thing. If you let Toby get close to you, he'll only hurt you again."

Susannah felt her throat tighten as she considered the words. Becky was only saying what she herself knew was true. But her commitment to her students came before her own feelings. Somehow, she'd have to get through working with Toby without exposing her heart.

Chapter Four

Toby felt more than a little out of place when he arrived at the school Monday afternoon for his first stint helping with the Christmas program. Susannah had seemed confident that this would be good for his children, but he couldn't deny it made him self-conscious to think of trying to build bridges with his children under her gaze.

Well, Susannah wouldn't be critical of him. That wasn't in her nature. He'd turned his *kinder* over to her with complete confidence in her abilities, so the least he could do was follow her advice.

The schoolroom was already humming with activity when he stepped inside, and Toby paused for a moment, hefting his toolbox in one hand, while he tried to make sense of what was going on. One group of children seemed to be reading their parts out loud, while in another corner, some older girls were working on poster-size sheets of paper.

Becky was there, directing a group that was decorating a bulletin board. She gave him a cool nod, making him wonder what she'd said when she'd learned he'd be helping. Nothing complimentary, he imagined.

Susannah greeted him, wearing her usual composed

smile. "You're right on time. I have the materials over here for the big candles, and I thought you and some of the boys might start on those first."

He nodded, following her to one side of the room where some desks had been pushed out of the way. She'd described what she wanted, and it seemed simple enough, although time-consuming, especially since Susannah expected him to be working with the children instead of doing it himself. Still, that was a typically Amish way of learning—doing a task alongside someone who had already mastered it.

Almost before he had gathered his thoughts, Susannah left him alone with a group of boys that included his son. William wore a wooden expression that suggested he wasn't sure if he liked having his father here in the schoolroom.

"Suppose you all gather 'round, and I'll show you what Teacher Susannah wants us to build." He spread out the drawing he'd made for them. "The candles will be supported by a base and a diagonal, wooden brace on the back, where it won't show." He pointed with his pencil, and several of the older boys nodded.

"We'll be painting them when they're finished, ain't so?" One of them, a tall kid with a shock of wheat-colored hair brushing his eyebrows, asked as he leaned over the sketch.

Toby nodded. "We've got a lot of work to do before then, so let's get started."

To his relief, several of the older boys immediately caught on to what was required. They had obviously done some carpentry before. He was able to set them to work on one candle while he tackled another with the younger ones, and soon the tap of hammers joined in the chorus of children's voices practicing their lines under Susannah's direction.

"You started school here at the right time," he told William. "Putting on the Christmas program is one of most fun things you'll ever do in the Pine Creek school, ain't so?"

His son shrugged. "I guess."

Toby inwardly sighed. If he got discouraged every time William gave him a two-word answer, he'd be done before he started. He had to persevere.

"My *daadi* says you went to school here with him." The boy working next to William had a face spattered with freckles and a gap-toothed smile.

Memory stirred. "Is your *daadi* Paul Broder?"

The kid's grin widened as he nodded. "I'm Matthew Broder. Do you remember my *daad*?"

"I sure do. Ask him if he remembers the time we ate the green apples from the apple tree in the schoolyard and were sick all afternoon."

The memory brought a smile to his face. Paul had often been his partner in crime, as he recalled, but he hadn't trusted Toby's judgment quite so much after the green-apple affair.

William made a pretense of ignoring them, but he suspected his son was more interested in the conversation than he let on.

"Teacher Susannah was in school here with us, too," he said. "Did your *daad* tell you that?"

Matthew nodded. "Everybody knows that."

Of course. Everybody knew everything there was to know about people in this isolated community. Funny how he'd once been so eager to leave, when now he just wanted to fit in again.

Holding a crosspiece for the base while his son hammered a nail in, Toby realized he hadn't felt this content in a long time. It was good to be back in the familiar schoolroom, feeling again the sense of order and purpose that permeated it.

And it was especially satisfying to be working next to his son, watching William's small hands mimic his actions. This was what they could have had all along, if he hadn't been stuck working in the factory all day and getting home so late that he hardly saw his *kinder*.

But he'd known what to expect when he got married. Emma hadn't made any secret of her feelings. He just hadn't expected their marriage to turn out the way it had.

By the time Susannah rang the bell signaling the end of the school day, they'd made good progress on the first two candles. He glanced over to catch Susannah's eye.

"I'll stick around for a few more minutes to finish up, if that's okay."

She nodded, supervising as her scholars lined up to leave, obviously preoccupied with seeing that they had coats, jackets, books, lunch pails and so forth. In a moment the schoolroom had emptied, but Becky lingered, her jacket in her hands and the twins tugging at her skirt.

"I told my mother we'd pick her up right after school," she was telling Susannah, sounding unduly concerned about something so simple.

"Of course. Go ahead." Susannah picked up a pencil that had dropped on the floor.

"Are you sure?" Becky paused with a meaningful glance at him.

"Go." Susannah made a shooing motion with her hands.

Despite her doubts, Becky went out the door with her twins.

Once the door had closed behind them, Toby grinned at Susannah. "Is Becky worried about my reputation or yours?"

A faint color came up in Susannah's cheeks. "I... neither, I'm sure."

Her reaction took him aback. Maybe this was more than just a matter of Becky disliking him for jilting Susannah. He thought of what *Daad* had said about the school board member. Was Susannah's position really so precarious that she couldn't be in the schoolroom with a man she'd known all her life? Or was Becky afraid Susannah still had feelings for him? Either way, he'd best be careful.

Anna tugged at Susannah's apron. "Teacher? Were you really in school with my *daadi?*"

Apparently Anna's curiosity had overcome her shyness. He was so relieved he rushed to answer. "She was. And so was the twins' mother."

Anna blinked, absorbing this news.

"Your *daadi* grew up here in Pine Creek," Susannah explained. "So this was his school. When we were in first grade, like you, I sat here." She led Anna to the desk she'd occupied in the first row. "And he sat right across from me, where you sit now."

"Really?" Anna seemed to look at her desk with fresh eyes. "Did you really sit here, *Daadi?*"

"Teacher Susannah is right as usual," he said solemnly. "In fact, if no one has sanded it out, my initial might still be under the seat." Crossing to them, he turned the seat over and showed her. "See?"

Susannah looked at him with amusement in her eyes. She bent to run her fingers over the letters he'd dug with the point of a compass, bringing her face close to his. "I can see I'll have to have these refinished."

Her nearness brought a treacherous memory to mind. He'd taken Susannah home from a singing for the first time—*Daad* had let him take the two-seater buggy. He'd been so determined—and so nervous—to kiss her, it was a wonder he'd ever got up the courage.

He'd stopped the buggy just beyond the glow from her parents' kitchen window. Turned to her, just able to make out the soft curve of her lips. She'd smiled at him and then, maybe reading his intent in his face, her smile had trembled. Their lips had met—an awkward kiss that carried with it all the sweetness of first love.

Maybe the memory showed in his face too clearly. Susannah's eyes met his, and they darkened. Her lips trembled, and for a moment, he was transported back to that buggy on a spring night....

The schoolroom door clattered open, and heavy footsteps sounded. Fear flared in Susannah's eyes.

Moving deliberately, he righted the desk, setting it squarely upright. Then he turned to meet James Keim's unfriendly scrutiny.

"James Keim, isn't that right? I'm Tobias Unger."

"I know who you are." Keim glanced from Susannah to him. "What are you doing here?"

The question was almost openly hostile.

Anger flared, but before he could speak, Susannah did.

"Toby has two *kinder* in our school." Her tone was perfectly cool, and Toby wondered what it took to keep it that way.

Keim's face settled into a disapproving frown. "It's after school hours."

Toby clenched the edge of the desk hard enough to

turn his knuckles white. Susannah flashed him a look that spoke volumes.

"We are working on preparations for the Christmas program." Susannah gestured toward the half-finished candles. "Toby generously volunteered to work with the boys on some carpentry. We always need parents to help." She looked at Keim expectantly, and Toby had to suppress a smile. Obviously the man didn't want to help. Just as obviously he didn't want to admit it.

Keim cleared his throat. "You know how I feel about this program of yours. But I'll have Mary come help you. It will be more suitable than having the teacher alone in the schoolroom with a man."

Clutching the desk wasn't helping as his temper flashed, but he somehow managed to keep it under control. He had hurt Susannah once. The last thing he wanted was to cause trouble for her now. So he would say nothing, regardless of how much the man annoyed him. There was little he could do to make amends to Susannah, but at least he could do this.

Several days had passed, and although Susannah was pleased with the effect Toby's presence had on his children, she still couldn't entirely dismiss the implication of James Keim's words. Were other people coming to similar conclusions about her and Toby? She'd hate to think so.

Mary Keim was staying after school to help every day, and Susannah suspected she had orders to report to her father everything that was said. Still, the girl seemed to be responding to the small responsibilities Susannah gave her, and when Mary relaxed, she had a nice way with the children.

Susannah drew her buggy to a halt at the back porch

of Becky's home and tried to dismiss the worries from her mind. It was time for the monthly get-together of the girls who'd been in her *rumspringa* group, an occasion for eating, talking and much laughter. She knew these girls as well as she knew anyone, and with them, she could relax and be herself. Even the fact that she was teaching many of their children didn't seem to disrupt their bond.

Giving her buggy horse a final pat, she headed inside, already hearing the buzz of women's voices, interrupted by laughter. They were all married with children, happy for an evening away from responsibilities, eager to chatter about everything that had happened in Pine Creek since they'd last met.

Susannah paused, her hand on the door. What were the chances they'd heard about Keim's outrage over finding her working alone in the schoolroom with only a child to chaperone them? She shivered, as if a cold snowflake had landed on her.

With an annoyed shake of her head, Susannah opened the door. She would not let herself start imagining things. She stepped inside and was engulfed in a wave of warmth and welcome.

Over the supper Becky had prepared, the talk stayed general, and Susannah was able to join in the chatter about Christmas plans and holiday baking. She glanced around the table at the smiling faces. The eight of them hadn't changed all that much since their younger days, had they?

Sara Esch caught her eye. "What are you thinking that makes you smile so, Susannah?"

"*Ach,* she must be smiling because Toby Unger is back in town." Silence fell after Sally Ann's comment.

She'd always had a gift for blurting out what other people might think but not say.

"No, I was remembering the day we snuck off and had our picture taken. Sally Ann, you were so nervous you dropped your share of the money three or four times."

Sally Ann grinned, her good nature never letting her take offense when teased. "I was imagining the bunch of us getting hauled in front of the church to confess. I was sure my parents would have a fit if they found out."

"It was pretty hard to keep them from finding out." Rachel Mast commented, sensible as always. "After all, there *was* the photo."

It had been a fad for a time among Amish teens to have a professional photo made of their group during *rumspringa,* before any of them joined the church. The practice was frowned on by the older folks but generally accepted as part of growing up.

"*Ach,* the boys did far worse than that during their *rumspringa,*" Becky said. "They were no doubt glad that was all the mischief we got up to." She rose from the table and moved to the oak cabinet against the wall, opening a drawer. "And here it is. We were a pretty good-looking bunch, ain't so?" She passed the picture around the table.

"I don't think we've changed all that much," Susannah said, accepting the picture. She glanced down at the smiling faces.

The photographer had taken the picture of the group in a park, arranging the eight of them in various positions on and around a weathered picnic table. She'd thought it odd at the time, and it was only later that she realized what an artist he had been.

The eight of them looked so much more natural than

they would have lined up in a row. She studied their youthful faces. They'd all been eighteen then.

Her gaze was arrested by her own face gravely smiling back at her, and her heart gave an odd thud. She'd said they hadn't changed much, but the face of the younger Susannah had had a sweetness and an innocence that she wouldn't find if she looked in the mirror now. She'd been a girl then, looking forward to marriage, secure in Toby's love. She handed the photo on to the next person, happy not to spend any more time staring at her younger self.

Rachel pushed her empty pie plate away, sighing. "The *kinder* seem happy to have two new students in the school. Although from what I hear from Simon, young William is a bit of a handful."

"Just like his *daadi* was." Sally Ann grinned. "Remember when he put a whoopie pie on the teacher's chair and she sat on it?"

The resulting laughter had a slightly nervous edge, as if her friends weren't sure how she'd react to mentions of her old love.

Well, she had to let them see that it didn't bother her in the least. "Luckily for me, William hasn't thought of that trick. I just hope nobody mentions it to him."

"We won't tell," Becky said. "More *snitz* pie, anyone?" She held the knife poised over yet another dried-apple pie, but she didn't get any takers.

"So I hear Toby is spending a lot of time at the schoolhouse." Sally Ann's blue eyes twinkled, but there was an edge to her voice. Clearly there had been talk.

Well, maybe she could use the Amish grapevine to her advantage. "Toby's *kinder* are finding it difficult to adjust to losing their mother and then moving to a new place. I thought it would help them feel more comfortable if their *daad* was around for a week or so, and helping with the Christmas program seemed a perfect way of doing so."

There was a general murmur of approval. Good. The reason for Toby's presence would be passed along, and hopefully, other people would be equally understanding.

"And it gives the two of you time together, too, ain't so?" Sally Ann was irrepressible. "Take advantage of it, and you might have Toby falling for you all over again."

Susannah's smile froze. Several women started up their chatter again, obviously thinking Sally Ann had gone too far this time.

It wasn't malicious, Susannah knew, glancing at Sally Ann's ruddy, cheerful face. But it hurt, anyway, and the way her stomach was twisting made her think she shouldn't have had that last piece of dried-apple pie.

Which was worse—to have people thinking, like Keim, that she was acting improperly? Or to have them assume she was trying to snare Toby into marriage again?

Chapter Five

After a week of having Toby working at the school-house every afternoon, Susannah had begun to feel that all her fretting had been foolish. Whatever the girls from her *rumspringa* gang thought, she hadn't noticed that people were gossiping about her and Toby.

The previous day, during Sunday worship and the simple lunch served afterward, she'd been on alert for any hint of interest. But she hadn't intercepted any knowing glances or been asked any awkward questions. Surely, if folks were gossiping, she'd have sensed something.

Susannah forced her attention back to her younger scholars, who were rehearsing their part in the program. Apart from an inability to hold up their battery-powered candles and recite their lines at the same time, they were improving. As was Mary Keim, who was directing them. To Susannah's surprise, Mary had come through, once she was trusted with the responsibility for a task.

The *kinder* came to the end of their recitation, and Mary glanced anxiously at Susannah.

"*Gut* work, all of you." There were grins and waving

of candles at her words. "Now put your candles in the box on the desk. It's almost time to go home."

As the young ones hurried to obey, Susannah touched Mary's shoulder. "You are doing very well with the young ones. I'm pleased with your work."

Mary's thin face flushed with pleasure. "*Denke,* Teacher Susannah." She hesitated for a moment. "I...I just try to do what I think you would."

The words touched her. "That's how we learn, ain't so? Keep this up and you can be a *gut* teacher, if that's what you want."

The girl looked away. "I'm not sure," she muttered. Before Susannah could respond, Mary scurried away to help the younger ones with boots and jackets.

Now, what was that about? Perhaps Mary didn't share her father's intent for her, although despite her earlier doubts, Susannah felt that the girl had begun to show an aptitude for teaching.

When Mary opened the schoolhouse door, Susannah saw a light snow was falling. She had to smile at the children's reactions. They walked sedately at first, double file, across the narrow porch and down the steps as they'd been taught. When they reached the ground, they erupted like young foals, prancing and running delightedly through the white flakes.

Mary pulled on her own jacket, looking as eager as the *kinder*. "I'll go out and watch until they're picked up."

"*Denke,* Mary." Susannah closed the door after the girl, shutting out the chill December air, and then had to open it again as Anna came scurrying from the cloakroom with the twins, always the last to get their coats on.

"We're going to make a snowman," Anna announced.

"Will you come and look at it when we're done, Teacher Susannah?"

"I surely will," she said, doubting that they'd have time to finish before Becky came to collect her daughters.

She closed the door again and realized that Toby was watching her, a tentative smile on his lips.

"Anna is doing better, ain't so?" He seemed to want reassurance, as any worried father would.

"Much better." Susannah touched the last of the tall candles he'd been constructing with the older boys. A coat of paint and they'd be ready. "She put her hand in the air this morning when I asked for volunteers to read aloud. That's real progress from the first few days, when I couldn't get her to say anything."

Toby's expression eased. "You've been wonderful *gut* with her, Susannah. *Denke.*"

"It's my job." Yet she couldn't help sharing his pleasure. "As for William..."

Toby's eyes darkened. "What has he done now?"

"Nothing so bad." She hastened to assure him. "A few scuffles on the playground, that's all."

"I was afraid of that." Toby's shoulders hunched, and for a moment, he looked like an older version of his son. "I was hoping you'd be able to get through to him. I'm certain sure not doing it."

The bitterness in his voice shook her. "I'm sorry, Toby. You and he seemed to be talking while you were working together. I prayed things were better."

Toby shrugged, running his hand down the plywood candle. "Sometimes we start talking like we used to. But then it's as if William puts a wall up between us." His jaw tightened. "He's my own son, and I can't reach him."

Susannah longed to deny it, but she'd seen it for herself. William was holding his father at arm's length, and she didn't have a guess as to why. Pity stirred in her heart.

"When did things change between you and William?" The question might seem prying, but if Toby wanted her help, she had to ask it, even if it touched on the subject of his wife.

Toby frowned. "It's related to Emma's death. It must be. He's older, so he understood a little better what was happening."

Her heart twisted. "*Ach,* Toby, you couldn't protect him from the pain of his mother's dying, no matter how much you wanted to." Any more than he could control his own grief at the loss of his wife.

An unexpected rush of resentment washed over her, and Susannah was horrified. Toby had jilted her and married another woman, and now he expected her to help him deal with the aftermath of her death. She shouldn't let the resentment have sway—it was unkind and unchristian.

Toby swung away from her with an abrupt movement. "Sorry." His voice roughened with emotion. "I shouldn't be talking about Emma, not to you, of all people."

Shame engulfed Susannah. How could she think of herself in the face of his grief and that of his children?

A prayer formed in her thoughts. *Father God, forgive me. Give me a heart clean of pain and jealousy so that I can help them.*

She drew in a long, steadying breath. Then she reached out to touch his arm. "Toby, don't think that. You can talk to me. No matter what else happened between us, we have been friends from the cradle. You can tell me anything." Her fingers tightened on his arm. *"Anything."*

For a long moment she thought he wouldn't respond. Then his gaze met hers, and she felt as if his expression eased just a little. *"Ach,* how many mistakes I've made in my life. Mistakes other people had to pay for." He shook his head, as if trying to shake off the pain. "William... I'm afraid that somehow William felt I didn't love his *mammi* the way I should."

Susannah tried to absorb the impact of his words. That was the last thing she'd expected to hear. Hadn't Emma been the love he'd been looking for when he'd left Pine Creek?

"I don't understand." She took a breath, knowing she needed to hear the truth. "Is William right?"

Toby's jaw tightened. "You thought I left because of you, ain't so?"

She could only nod, bewildered.

For a long moment, Toby was silent. Then he spoke. "I should have told you this years ago. You deserved to hear the truth from me, and instead I ran away." He grasped the plywood candle so hard that his knuckles whitened. "I panicked, that's the truth of it. The closer our wedding came, the more it seemed to me that I was missing out on something." He frowned down at his hands. "I don't even know what I expected to find. I longed to experience something more than Pine Creek—to see other places, meet other people."

She felt the sudden urge to shake him. "Toby, you could have told me. Don't you know I would have understood? I would have given you whatever time you needed."

His lips twisted. "I could always be honest with

you, Susannah. I know. I didn't want to face it. I was ashamed to tell you—to see the hurt in your face."

He sounded almost angry. At himself? At her? She wasn't sure, and she'd always thought she could read his every mood. He'd been feeling all these emotions, and she'd never even had a hint of it at the time. Had she been too busy filling her dower chest and giggling with her girlfriends at the time?

She tried to zero in on what was important now. "We were young, maybe too young. We both made mistakes. The *kinder* are what's important now."

He nodded, seeming to look past her at something she couldn't see. "At first all I could think after I went West was how different everything was. There were all these people, and I hadn't known them from the day I was born. Everyone was a mystery to me. Including Emma."

"You loved her." Susannah willed her voice to be steady.

"I fell in love." His lips twisted in a wry smile. "That's how it felt. I had grown into love with you, but with Emma it was more like falling from the barn roof and landing with a thud. So we got married, and then I realized that we hardly knew each other at all."

"You were married." That was the important thing. The Amish married for life, not like the English world, where people seemed to change mates as often as they changed clothes.

"We tried. I think Emma was happy. But then she got sick. It should have brought us closer together, but it didn't."

She knew, without his putting it into words, what he felt. Guilt. He accused himself of not loving Emma enough, and her dying made his guilt all the heavier.

"Toby—"

He cut her off with a sharp movement of his hand. "William was devoted to his *mammi*. Nothing has been right between us since she died."

"I'm sorry, Toby." Focus on the child, she ordered herself. "Have you talked to William about his mother?"

"I've tried." Anger flashed in his face, and she suspected he was glad to feel it after opening his soul to her. "I've tried so many times. But William won't talk about it. He's slipping away, and I can't seem to hold on to him."

She couldn't be angry with him when she knew the depth of his pain. "I understand. We'll keep trying, ain't so? It will get better." The words sounded as hollow to her as they must to him.

"*Ach,* Susannah, you sound as if I'm one of the *kinder,* coming to you with a scraped knee." His tone was harsh. "This is big and real, and you tell me it will get better."

Her own anger spurted up. "What else can I say, Toby? You have to have hope. There's no magic answer. Just keep loving William, that's all."

He swung toward her, grasping her wrists. "You…" Whatever he was going to say seemed to get lost as his eyes met hers. She could feel her pulse pounding against his palms.

"Susannah," his voice deepened. "I'm such a fool, spilling all this to you. You ought to tell me to go away and solve my own problems."

"I couldn't do that." She tried to smile but failed.

"No." Everything changed in an instant. His gaze was so intense it seemed to heat her skin, and the very air around them was heavy with emotion. "You couldn't." He focused on her lips, and her breath caught in her throat.

She couldn't breathe, couldn't think, couldn't speak. She could only wait for his lips to find hers.

His kiss was tentative at first. Gentle, then growing more intense as her lips softened under his. His hands slid up her arms, and he drew her closer. She was sinking into him, unable to feel anything but his strong arms, his warm lips—

Then the schoolroom door flew open, letting in a blast of cold air. Toby let go of her so abruptly she nearly staggered. She turned toward the door.

Mary stood there, her face scarlet. Her mouth worked, but no words came out. She took a backward step and pulled the door shut with a bang.

Susannah could only stand there, aghast. Of all the things that could happen…

"I've done it again." Toby's mouth twisted as if the words had a bitter taste. "I've messed up your life again, haven't I?"

"Don't," she said quickly. "It's no more your fault than mine. I'll talk to Mary. I'll explain."

But how exactly was she going to explain being caught in an embrace in her own schoolroom? She was afraid she'd just handed James Keim all the ammunition he'd need to get rid of her.

Chapter Six

Toby strode across the narrow schoolhouse porch and down the steps, almost without seeing them. What had he been thinking? How had he let that kiss happen?

Susannah had deserved to hear the reason he'd left her before their wedding, pitiful as it was. At least maybe now she wouldn't go on thinking it was her fault. It had been his, with his longing to see more of the world. Not that that hadn't been wrong, but when he'd let his needs hurt others, it had been. He'd acted as if all that was important had been his happiness.

The church was right to teach that happiness wasn't the goal of life. The goal was to live in obedience to God, with happiness or sorrow coming to everyone at one time or another.

Well, he'd certainly brought Susannah an added measure of sorrow she didn't deserve. If only Mary could be persuaded not to speak about what she'd seen…

That was probably a futile hope, but he ought to try. Mary was standing by the swings, and she turned away when he approached.

"Mary." He kept his tone gentle. "Please let me speak to you for a moment."

Seeing him, William and Anna came hurrying over.

"*Daadi,* listen." William tugged on his coat. "I have an idea for the program."

"Wait, William." That came out more sharply than he'd intended, and he softened his tone. "Go over to the buggy and wait for me. I'll be there in a minute."

"But, *Daadi,* listen." William was nothing if not persistent, and Mary had taken several steps away already. In a moment he would lose her.

"Now, William." He pointed to the buggy.

William's small face set, but he went, closely followed by Anna.

"Please, Mary, wait."

She stopped, looking like a bird arrested in flight. Her face was turned away from him, but he caught a glimpse of red cheeks. For sure she'd be embarrassed.

"About what you saw…" He fumbled for words. "It wasn't Teacher Susannah's fault. It was mine. I'm to blame. I don't want her to lose her job over it."

Mary had to know what he was asking her, but she gave no sign that she understood. He took a step closer, searching for words that might make a difference. But then Mary fled, running across the snow-covered schoolyard to the shed, where her buggy horse was stabled with Susannah's.

Too late. He wouldn't have another chance. Approaching Mary again would just make things worse. Frustrated, he stalked toward his own buggy.

Anna and William were perched on the seat, a wool lap robe pulled over them. He swung himself up and took hold of the lines.

He sent one last glance toward the schoolhouse. It went against the grain to drive off and leave Susannah there alone and upset. But anything he said or did now wouldn't help. He clucked to the horse.

The icy lane crunched under the buggy wheels, and the mare tossed her head, as if expressing her opinion of the cold. The children sat silent under the lap robe. He turned onto the paved road, the mare's hooves striking the blacktop, already cleared of snow by the cars that had gone by.

Toby made an effort to shake loose the worry that pressed on him. There was no point in making the *kinder* think something was wrong. If the worst happened, they'd know soon enough.

"It's looking like Christmas, ain't so?" He nodded toward the spruce trees along the road, their deep green branches weighed down with a coating of white.

William didn't respond, but Anna nodded. "*Gross-mammi* said she would make a batch of *pfefferneuse*. Do you think she'd let me help her?"

"I think she'd be very pleased to have a fine helper like you."

Anna's smile lit her face, and she gave a little nod. "*Gut.* I want to take some to Teacher Susannah."

His heart lurched at the mention of Susannah, but he managed to smile. "She'll like it, that's certain sure."

William squirmed. "Move over, Anna. You're taking up the whole seat."

"Am not," Anna retorted. "You are."

Glad as he was to hear Anna standing up for herself, the seat of a moving buggy wasn't the right place for a scuffle.

"Stop it, both of you." They turned into the farm lane, the mare's steps quickening as the barn came into view. "We're almost there."

"She's hogging the seat." William gave his sister a shove.

Anna cried out, slipping from the seat. Dropping the lines, Toby grabbed her, pulling her to safety. The mare, feeling the lines go slack, picked up her pace, and for a moment, Toby had his hands full holding on to his daughter and groping for the lines. Finally he found them and pulled up.

"Hush, Anna. You're fine." He snuggled her against him and focused on William. "What is wrong with you? Your sister could have fallen under the buggy wheels."

William hunched forward, not looking at him. "She's not hurt."

"No thanks to you. You're big enough to know better than to act that way in a moving buggy. I'm ashamed of you."

"You're always ashamed of me." William flared up so quickly, it was as if he'd set a match to dry tinder. "You wish you didn't have to be bothered with me."

"That's nonsense." Toby pulled in a breath. This wasn't the time for anger. "You are my son, William. It's not a bother to be with you. Why do you think I'm helping with the Christmas program if not to spend more time with you?"

"Not me." William's face twisted. "You want to be with Teacher Susannah."

It was like being hit in the stomach. For a minute Toby couldn't catch his breath. Before he could speak, William jumped down from the buggy and took off, running toward the barn.

Toby could only stare after him and feel the taste of failure sour in his soul.

Susannah's first instinct when she'd left the school had been to flee to Becky. She had to talk to someone about what had just happened. She couldn't talk to *Mamm* and *Daad* about it, at least not until she had to.

Despite Becky's reputation as a chatterbox, Susannah knew she could trust Becky to keep silent when it was something really important. She couldn't count the number of secrets they'd shared over the years.

But now, sitting in Becky's warm kitchen, she couldn't seem to find the words to begin. Fortunately, Becky didn't find anything strange about Susannah stopping by after school. Smiling, she set a mug of hot chocolate in front of Susannah.

"That's what we need on a snowy day, ain't so?" She sat down opposite her. "Did you see the greens we brought in?"

Susannah nodded, hoping her smile looked natural. "How could I help it? You have all the windowsills decorated. It looks so nice."

Becky nodded, smiling in satisfaction at the greens and candles on the kitchen windowsill. A few red berries from the winterberry bush had been tucked around the pine, too, making a daring spot of color.

"After the last time we went to town, the twins were asking why we don't have Christmas trees. I explained that we want to keep our Christmas centered on God's gift of Jesus, and I think they understand. But I thought it wouldn't hurt to do a little more with the decor this year. And we set up the *putz* in the living room, too."

The *putz,* or manger scene, was an old tradition in Pennsylvania Dutch homes, including those of some Amish. The children told the Christmas story over and over with the figures.

"They told me all about it when they got to school today." She hesitated, thinking of how the school day had ended. Maybe she was wrong to burden Becky with her problems. Becky had warned her, but she hadn't listened.

Becky reached across to touch her fingers. "Susannah, what is it? I can see that something is wrong, and here you are, letting me babble away about evergreens."

"I don't…" Susannah stopped before she could deny it, knowing her voice was already shaking. "*Ach,* Becky, I am in such trouble."

"*Komm* now." Becky clasped both her hands warmly. "It can't be that bad, can it? Tell me what is wrong."

She spoke as if she were talking to one of the twins, and Susannah was reminded of Toby's anger when he said she was speaking to him as if he were a child.

She took a deep breath. Best just to say it, and quickly. "After school let out, Mary went outside with the *kinder.* Toby and I were alone in the schoolroom."

Becky drew in a sharp breath, as if knowing worse was coming, but she didn't speak.

"We were talking about how William and Anna are doing. He is worried about William, saying the boy doesn't talk to him. He thinks it has to do with Emma's death."

"He shouldn't be talking to you about the woman he married after he left you," Becky declared. "It's not right."

"That doesn't matter. And it's important, if it helps me understand William and find a way to help him."

Becky snorted. "Are you sure it's not Toby you're trying to help?"

"It's the same thing," she said. "If something is wrong between William and his father, it affects both of them."

"I suppose." Becky sounded reluctant to admit it.

"Goodness knows it's a hard thing for a child to lose a mother at that age."

"It is," she said softly, remembering Toby's words about not loving Emma as he should. "But we started talking about what happened when he left, and I guess maybe we touched those feelings we used to have for each other." She tried to swallow the lump in her throat. "Anyway we…we kissed."

"*Ach,* Susannah, how could you be so foolish?" Becky's voice was loving and scolding at the same time. "Isn't it enough that he broke your heart once?"

"That isn't the worst of it. Mary Keim came back in. She saw us."

"Oh, no." Becky's fingers tightened on hers, and Susannah could see her mind scrambling from one possibility to another. "I suppose there's no hope that she won't tell her father."

"I don't think so." Susannah rubbed her forehead with her free hand, trying to will away the tension that had gathered there. "Word will get out. It always does."

"I'm so sorry. Didn't I tell you to stay away from him? Now look what he's done. You'd think he'd be satisfied with jilting you once, and now, here he's back again, causing more problems. Kissing you as if you were teenagers again."

It hadn't been the tentative kiss of a teenager, but it was probably best not to admit it to Becky. "It's not only Toby's fault. I'm a grown woman. It's just as much my responsibility. I should never have put myself in that position."

"And it wouldn't have happened if you'd listened to me," Becky declared, indignant all over again. "I hate to say I told you so, but…"

"Go ahead, you can say it if you want." Worst of

all, she couldn't really bring herself to regret that kiss. Maybe she was destined to be a *maidal,* an old maid, but that didn't mean she hadn't yearned for Toby's kiss.

"Well, there's no point in crying over spilled milk." Becky seemed to have lost her urge to repeat her strictures once Susannah had told her she should. "We have to think what to do next."

Susannah spread her hands in a gesture of helplessness. "I don't see that there's anything I can do. I doubt Mary will be able to keep from telling her father what she saw."

"Maybe, but you can't just lie down and die. You have to fight." Becky's eyes flashed, and her hot chocolate sloshed dangerously when she pounded the table. "You have to start talking to folks, getting them on your side before Keim can sway them. After all, people here have known you since you were born. They'll listen to you."

True enough. But… "Becky, I can't turn the schoolhouse into a battleground. That is not right."

"It can't be wrong to defend yourself," Becky retorted. "Besides, you'd be doing it for the *kinder.* They need you. Think where they'd be with Mary Keim for a teacher."

"Mary's not as bad as we thought," she murmured. "Anyway, it might not come to that. But I can't start campaigning against James Keim."

Becky frowned. "Well, then, the least you can do is make sure Toby isn't spending time at the schoolhouse any longer. Maybe then the talk will die down."

"How can I do that? How would I explain it to the scholars? It would look as if he'd done something wrong. It might make things worse between Toby and his children."

"Well, if you don't, Toby Unger is going to destroy your life again," Becky snapped.

Susannah could only stare at her for a moment, her lips twisting wryly. "You agree with Toby, then. That's exactly what he said."

Chapter Seven

As soon as her scholars filed into the schoolroom the next morning, Susannah knew that the news of her misdeed had spread. The younger children seemed unaware of anything different, but several of the older boys refused to meet her eyes, and she heard embarrassed giggling from the girls.

"Settle down and take your seats, please." She frowned toward the older ones, and they slid into the desks, making it clear that some of those desks were empty. Susannah quickly checked the row of seats. All of the Keim children were missing, including Mary, who had been coming regularly to help.

Well, that made a statement, didn't it? How many other families would be following their example by tomorrow?

Wrenching her mind into its normal track, she began the day's routine with a reminder of upcoming events. "Don't forget that tomorrow we'll have a final rehearsal for the Christmas program. I expect all of you to be letter-perfect in your parts."

"*Ja,* Teacher Susannah," they chorused in unison.

Tomorrow was the last rehearsal, and Thursday, the

Christmas program. After that, school would close for a two-week winter break. If she could just keep going until then, she'd have breathing space to make a decision about the future. Surely she'd have that much time.

She walked slowly between the desks of the first graders, checking as they printed the alphabet. Each child looked up at her with a smile as she passed, and her heart filled with joy. Surely it wasn't God's will that she lose her role here.

Somehow she got through the morning, but it seemed a very long time until the *kinder* were settled with their lunches and a gentle hum of conversation buzzed through the room. Susannah walked into the small back room, which was a combination storage room and coat room. She was taking her lunch down from the shelf when she heard a tapping at the back door.

Her heart gave a little lurch, but when she opened the door, it wasn't Toby. It was Mary Keim, her face red from the cold.

"Mary, you look frozen." She grasped the girl's hands and pulled her inside. *"Was ist letz?"*

"Shh." Mary sent an anguished glance toward the classroom. "I can't let anyone see me," she whispered.

"But you're chilled through. You must come in and stand by the stove."

Mary quickly shook her head. "It's nothing. I had to walk so *Daadi* wouldn't know I was coming."

"Ach, no." Susannah put her arm around the girl. "You shouldn't have."

"I had to." Mary turned away for a moment and then swung back, clutching Susannah's hand. "I had to tell you. I'm so sorry." Tears spurted from her eyes, and her voice shook. "I didn't want to talk. I meant to keep it secret. But *Daadi* saw that something was wrong, and he kept asking me and asking me. He always knows when we're hiding something. I'm sorry. But I told him about you and Toby Unger."

"*Ach,* Mary, don't be upset." How could she blame the girl? She was the one who had done wrong. "I would never want you to get into trouble with your father because of me."

Mary sniffled and wiped away tears with the back of her hand. "I can't stay, but I didn't feel right, not speaking to you myself. And there's something else. I heard *Daadi* talking. He's called a meeting of the school board for Friday. I'm afraid he…"

She let that trail off, but Susannah knew what she was going to say. Keim was going to press for her dismissal. Friday. Well, at least she'd present her last Christmas program before she was told to leave. She drew in a deep, calming breath.

"Listen to me, Mary. None of this is your fault. I don't want you to blame yourself." She touched the girl's shoulder. "You have the makings of a *gut* teacher, if that's what you want to be. But don't let anyone push you into something you don't care about."

Mary looked away from her, and they both knew how unlikely it was that Mary would hold out against her father's wishes.

The girl stared down at the floor. "I wish I was strong, like you. But I'm not."

Susannah didn't feel particularly strong at the moment. Still, it was nice to know someone thought she was.

"I think you'd better go now, before your *daad* realizes you've left." She squeezed Mary's hands. "*Denke,* Mary. Don't worry too much. Whatever happens, it's God's will."

Nodding, Mary buttoned her jacket and pulled her bonnet into place, tying it securely against the wind. She looked for a moment as if she would say something more. Then she shook her head, blinking back tears, and scurried out.

Susannah grabbed the broom and swept out the snow Mary had tracked in. She was just closing the door again when she heard someone behind her.

"Who was that?" William stood in the classroom doorway, his face tight.

She looked at him steadily for a moment. "Is that the proper way to speak to your teacher, William Unger?"

He flushed, looking down at his shoes. "No, Teacher Susannah. I just… I thought maybe it was my *daad*."

"Your *daad* never comes in this door," she said. "I'm sure he'll come in the front like always when he arrives to help. Why?"

William shrugged. "Nothing."

Susannah studied the face that was so like Toby's had been at that age. "Is something wrong, William?"

He shrugged again, not answering.

"Because if there is something wrong, you can tell me. Or even better, talk to your *daadi* about it."

He looked up then, his blue eyes filled with misery. "I can't."

Susannah longed to pull the boy into her arms, but instinct told her that would be the wrong course of action. Something was troubling the boy, and if it was something involving his father, she shouldn't interfere. Still, she had to do something.

Susannah touched William's chin, tipping his face up so that she could see it. "Whatever is wrong, you can trust your father. I've known him since he was younger than you are, and I know you can tell him anything. When he comes this afternoon…"

William shook his head abruptly. "I forgot I was s'posed to tell you. He isn't coming today. My *gross-mammi* will pick up me and Anna after school."

Susannah felt as if someone had doused her in cold water. Toby wasn't coming. She hadn't realized until that moment how much she'd counted on talking to him.

She straightened, lifting her chin. Very well. She couldn't rely on Toby. She didn't even want to. She would handle this situation on her own.

Mary's words slipped into her mind. *Strong like you.* Never mind that she didn't feel it. A strong woman wouldn't just sit back and let someone take away the job she loved. She'd do something. But what?

"Are you coming to school to help today, *Daadi?*" Anna looked up from her oatmeal on Wednesday morning to pose the question. "Teacher Susannah says we have our last practice today."

Just the mention of Susannah hit Toby like a slap. He'd done enough damage to her for one lifetime. Surely the best thing he could do for her now was to stay away.

"Not today, Anna. I have too much work to do."

Toby glanced at his son. What was William thinking, staring so intently at his wedge of shoofly pie? He'd tried to talk to the boy, but he hadn't gotten anywhere. William seemed to have a talent for avoiding even a direct question. And Toby feared that pressing him too much would make matters worse.

"But *Daadi*…" Anna's small face crumpled. "You have to come. Who will set up the big candles for our program if you don't?"

"I'm sure someone else can do it." He exchanged

glances with his mother as she reached across to set the coffeepot on the table. *Maam* was looking about as stoic as William this morning. No doubt she'd heard all about her son's misdeeds already.

"Nobody will do it like you do." Anna was on the verge of tears. "Please, *Daadi*."

He clenched his teeth. It seemed he was destined to hurt someone no matter what he did.

"Hush, Anna." His mother patted Anna's head. "*Daadi* and I will both come to help this afternoon. Ain't so, Tobias?" She gave him a challenging look.

Well, at least if his mother was there, that would deflect any gossip. "You're right," he said. "We'll both go."

Once the *kinder* had scurried out into the snow, where his brother waited with the buggy to take them to school, Toby carried his dishes to the sink.

"Denke, Maam."

His mother turned to face him, her lined face stern, her hands clasped together over her apron. It was the pose she always took when she was about to say something you didn't want to hear.

"You're a grown man, Tobias. I don't want to tell you what to do with your life. But I think highly of Susannah."

"I think highly of her, too." His jaw clenched. "I hate that I've done something to hurt her."

His mother winced slightly. "It's true, then. You were seen kissing Susannah in the schoolroom."

"It's true." He felt as if he were ten and about to be sent to *Daad* for a well-deserved spanking. But this was a misdeed that couldn't be resolved so easily. "I never meant it to happen."

"You can't undo it now." Her disappointment in him was obvious. "But I hope you will do whatever you can to mend this situation for her. It's not right that Susannah lose what's most important to her because of you." She might have added "again," but she didn't.

He felt it, anyway. "I know. I will." If only he could think of something that would help.

Toby spent the morning in the shop, working on a carriage, finding some comfort in the craft. It gave him silence and solitude in which to think, but unfortunately that didn't seem to help. He could see no way to undo the trouble he'd brought on Susannah.

By the time he and *Mamm* reached the school that afternoon, the classroom was at the high pitch of excitement that always seemed to accompany the annual Christmas program. His gaze automatically sought out Susannah.

She seemed the same as always, her oval face serene as she tried to keep the *kinder* under control, but he knew her well enough to see the strain in her eyes.

His mother elbowed him. "I'll see if I can help Susannah. You should get the stage set up, ain't so?"

Nodding, he pulled his attention away from Susannah. *Mamm* had it right. He was here to help with the props, nothing else. Enlisting the aid of some of the older boys, he began moving the giant candles into place along the side of the schoolroom.

While he worked, he became aware of the looks some of the older scholars directed at him. So they had heard. Useless to hope they wouldn't, he supposed. But at least they were still in school. As far as he could tell, the Keim children were the only ones who were missing. No doubt James Keim had been very vocal about having his *kinder* in Susannah's school. A totally un-Amish anger gripped Toby, and he had to force it down.

After a few minutes, Toby had all the candles set up

in a row, along the side of the schoolroom. They would form a backdrop for the children as they recited. Becky moved along the windows behind the candles, trimming the sills with live greens. She carefully avoided looking at him while she worked, and he was grateful that she'd curbed her outspokenness for the moment. No doubt she was boiling inside with all the things she'd like to say to him.

"Looks *gut,* ain't so?" He clapped the nearest boy on the shoulder and got a grin in return. "We should start setting up the chairs next."

Folding chairs had been borrowed to accommodate all the parents and grandparents who were expected to attend the program. The schoolroom would be overflowing with people by this time tomorrow. At least, he hoped it would. Surely folks wouldn't stay away because of the rumors. The school Christmas program was one of the few opportunities an Amish child had to do something that might be considered performing.

Moving chairs brought him closer to where Susannah stood, directing the placement of the classes on the makeshift stage. He bent to open a chair, not looking at her.

"I'm sorry, Susannah." He kept his voice low, under the clatter of chairs and the sound of the children. "I've brought you trouble, and I never meant to."

"I know." Her voice was cool, her gaze never leaving the *kinder.*

Obviously she didn't want to hear him. He could hardly blame her for that. He went on setting up the chairs, listening to the children reciting as he did. The poems they spoke were typical of Amish school programs, expressing Amish values—humility, faithfulness, meekness, forgiveness.

Forgiveness. Could Susannah forgive him? He didn't know.

He paused, a chair in his hands. No one else was near enough to hear him. This might be his last chance. "I would do anything to make this right," he said quietly. "Anything. I hope you can forgive me."

That brought her gaze to his face. "Don't think that, Toby," she said quickly. "It was as much my responsibility as yours. There is nothing to forgive."

Their eyes met for a long moment. He thought she was speaking the truth—that she wasn't blaming him. But he couldn't excuse himself so easily.

"I want—" His words broke off at a clatter and the sound of raised voices. He swung around in time to see William shove the boy next to him.

"You're in the wrong place. Move over."

"Am not." The boy returned the shove. "You are."

"William," he began. But before he could get the warning out, his son had given the other boy a push that sent him stumbling into the end candle.

It swayed dangerously. He lunged toward it, a warning shout caught in his throat. But he was too late. The candle toppled, hitting the next one. Then, like a row of dominoes, they were all falling, one after another, and the room was filled with the clatter and the squeals of the children as they scrambled out of the way.

Toby reached them in time to catch the last candle and lower it to the floor. Susannah had already waded into the fray, trying to see if anyone was hurt. Then *Mamm* and Becky were there, as well, pulling children away from the mess that had been the stage for Susannah's Christmas program.

"Stop it!" The male voice was loud enough to silence the most high-pitched squeal. James Keim slammed the schoolroom door behind him like a punctuation mark. "What is the meaning of this?"

"An accident…" Susannah began.

"This is not acceptable." Keim didn't wait for her explanation. "I came here today because the bishop urged me to meet with you to resolve our difficulties, and I find the schoolhouse in chaos."

"It's not—" Toby began, but Keim shouted over him.

"Disgraceful!" He glared at Susannah, then the rest of the schoolroom. "The Christmas program is cancelled. The school is closed until a new teacher is hired. You will all go home. Now."

"Wait a minute." The anger that shook him startled Toby. "You can't—"

But Keim was already stomping out the door, as if he had no doubt that his orders would be obeyed.

Hands curling into fists, Toby lunged after him, but Susannah quickly put a restraining hand on his arm.

"Don't, Toby. Don't. It's over." Her voice broke on the words.

All Toby could do was stand there, looking at the despair in her face and know that it was his fault.

Chapter Eight

Susannah struggled to hold herself together. Her students were clustering around her, some of them crying. She had to stay strong for them.

"Hush, now." She drew a couple of weeping children close against her. "There's no reason to cry. It's not your fault."

"We should have behaved better." Zeke Esch, one of her eighth graders, looked at the other children as he spoke. "All of us should." He sent a firm look at William and Thomas, whose quarrel had ignited the trouble.

William studied the tips of his shoes, while Thomas wiped away a tear with his sleeve.

"It startled all of us when the candles fell," Susannah said. She didn't want William and Thomas to be the target of anyone's blame, whatever they'd done. "Right now we must concentrate on cleaning up."

"But, Teacher Susannah, what's going to happen?" Sarah Esch, Zeke's twin sister, had blue eyes bright with tears. "Can't we have our Christmas program?"

Zeke nudged her. "It's worse than that. We're going to lose Teacher Susannah."

There was a fresh outburst of sobs at his words.

Susannah tried to smile, fighting down her own despair as she looked for the right words. If nothing else, she owed the children honesty, as always. "I'll pray that we can work out this trouble so that I can still be your teacher. But if not, then we must accept it."

And that would be a bitter pill to swallow. How much easier it would be to blame others for this grief.

She had to suck in a breath before she could continue. "If you have a new teacher—"

"No," Sarah said, the word echoed by others.

"If you have a new teacher," Susannah said again firmly, "I know you will behave in a way to make me proud of you."

Several of the older students looked solemn at that, but they nodded.

"Now." She couldn't keep going much longer without breaking into tears. "If you are walking home, you may get your books and your coats and be dismissed. If you are waiting to be picked up, I want you to help with the cleaning."

She glanced at Becky. She looked shaken, but she responded with a quick nod. "Come along now," Becky said, shepherding children away from Susannah. "You heard Teacher Susannah. Sarah, will you help organize the walkers? And, Zeke, you can start that cleanup, ain't so?"

Both of them nodded, looking gratified at being singled out as the oldest scholars in the school. In a moment the *kinder* had moved away reluctantly.

But she'd barely had time to take a breath before Toby appeared, holding William with one hand and Thomas with the other. He gave them each a shake, his face grim.

"What do you have to say to Teacher Susannah?"

"I'm sorry, Teacher Susannah." Thomas couldn't get the words out fast enough, and tears welled in his eyes. "I shouldn't have done it."

"*Denke,* Thomas." She touched his shoulder lightly, and Toby let him go. He scurried off, obviously eager to disappear.

Toby gave his son another little shake. "Well, William?"

"Sorry," William muttered, his gaze on the floor.

She could see that Toby wasn't satisfied with the apology, and she shook her head in silent warning. It might only make the boy's behavior worse to push the point.

"*Denke,* William." She said the words quietly, hoping he'd look at her.

But he didn't. He wrenched himself free of his father's grip and darted off.

Muttering something, Toby started to go after him, but she caught his arm.

"Let him go. Talk to him later, after you both calm down. And listen to him."

"It hasn't done too much good so far," he said. "As if I haven't done enough harm to you, and my own son—"

"Don't, Toby." She really couldn't listen to any more. "Just get him and Thomas to help clean up. That's the best thing right now."

He gave a curt nod and stalked off to help clear away the mess.

It seemed to take forever, but the schoolroom was finally neat again. And empty, with all the children gone. Susannah stood for a moment, looking around, trying to create a picture in her mind of the schoolroom as it looked at this moment. If she never saw it again—

Stop, she ordered herself. Moving stiffly, she went

to her desk and sank down on the chair. Maybe she should take her personal belongings home with her, just in case, but she couldn't seem to summon the energy to do so. She felt empty. Drained. All she wanted was to be home, with the door closed, free to indulge in the tears that kept threatening to overflow.

The schoolroom door opened, and she barely had time to put her defenses in place before Toby had come in. He strode toward her with the air of a man who'd made up his mind about something.

"Susannah, we have to talk." He planted his hands on her desk.

"Not now." She pushed herself to her feet, feeling as if she was weighed down by a heavy load. "Later."

"This can't wait." His lips twisted. "What happened is my fault. I have to do something."

She couldn't cope with his feelings, not when she could barely manage her own. "There's nothing you can do." *Please, Toby, go away and leave me alone.*

"There has to be. If I hadn't given in to impulse and kissed you, you wouldn't be at risk of losing your school."

Her heart winced at his casual mention of their kiss. She could never let him know how much it had affected her. "We were both to blame."

He shook his head, jaw set, brows lowering, making her think how little he'd changed from the boy she'd loved. "No."

"You were always impulsive," she said. "And always sorry afterward, too."

He stared at her for a moment and then, quite suddenly, he smiled.

The smile traveled straight to her heart, bursting there like fireworks and illuminating all the dark corners.

He caught her hands in a typically impulsive movement. "Marry me, Susannah," he said. "I know it doesn't solve all your problems, but at least then you wouldn't have to worry about teaching or dealing with a man like Keim." He seemed to warm to his theme even as she struggled to process it. "Think about it. We have always been friends. We could have a good life together, couldn't we?"

His hands tightened on her fingers, and in that moment, she saw two things very clearly. She had never stopped loving him. And she couldn't marry him.

Her breath caught in her throat. Perhaps a few weeks ago she'd have said yes. She'd have taken what he offered her, thinking half a loaf was better than none.

But not now. If this trouble had taught her anything, it was that she was stronger than she'd thought. She would not take second place in anyone's heart, not even Toby's.

"No." She said it with a finality she hoped he'd recognize, and she pulled her hands free. "I can't take that way out of my troubles, Toby." She walked away quickly before he could stop her. "Losing my job is not a good enough reason to marry you." She grabbed her coat and hurried out the door.

"Wouldn't you like a little piece of shoofly pie?" Susannah's mother hovered over her, a plate in her hand. She had been forcing food on her ever since Susannah got home from school the previous day. She'd eaten something to please *Mamm,* though even her mother's delicious baking tasted like ashes in her mouth.

"Leave the girl alone," her father said, correctly interpreting her expression. "Eli will have a piece. He's always hungry."

The family, gathered around the kitchen table, smiled at the reference to her next older brother's notorious appetite. Eli grinned.

"Give it here, *Mamm*. I'll have Susannah's share." He accompanied the words with a wink, reminding her of their childhood, when the two of them had always paired up against their two older brothers.

She tried to smile, but her face felt stiff. Much as she appreciated the support they'd come to offer, she longed for nothing more than to be left alone to nurse her wounds.

That was a useless hope, she knew. In the close-knit Amish community, there was no such thing as struggling with your problems alone.

Becky, who'd shown up before her brothers, refilled coffee cups around the table before sitting down next to Susannah. "What are we going to do?" she said, resuming the discussion that had been interrupted by *Mamm*'s determination to feed all of them. "We certain sure don't want our *kinder* taught by anyone but Susannah. Maybe the other school board members—"

"I spoke to them already," *Daad* said. At Susannah's look of surprise, he nodded. "Went over to see them last night, that's what I did." He frowned. "They want to support our Susannah, but it's no use expecting much from them. Harley Fisher works for Keim, after all, and Matthew Busch is too ill to get into a wrangle."

"Well, I still say we should go to the school board meeting," her oldest brother insisted. "Make Keim come right out in the open with his accusations."

Susannah shuddered at the thought, thinking of what Keim was likely to say. Still, was there anyone in the church who hadn't heard it already? Her already-sore heart twisted.

"I say we go to Keim's house and have it out with him," Eli said, his eyes bright and his big hands curling into fists. "He's got no right to dictate to the rest of the church. And maybe we should have a talk with Toby while we're at it."

Daad reached across the table to clasp Susannah's hand in his, an unusual demonstration of affection for someone usually so taciturn. "What do you think, Susannah? You know how we feel about this, but it's for you to say."

She looked around the table, and the love and caring in each face eased her pain. She glanced at the candles and greens *Mamm* had placed on the windowsills and thought of her scholars' faces, and the answer seemed to grow clearer.

"*Denke.* It helps so much to know you care. But how can we do something that could divide the church? It would be a poor way of honoring the birthday of the Prince of Peace."

They objected to the idea of giving in so readily, of course, but fortunately before they could wear Susannah down with their arguments, there was a knock at the door.

Eli, who was closest, rose to answer it and drew back to usher in John Stoltzfus, the bishop. The clatter of voices ceased abruptly at the imposing figure.

Bishop John was tall and lean, stooped a little after years of bending over in his work as a farrier. His beard was more white than gray, but his eyes were still bright with the energy needed for the two church districts under his care.

"*Wilkom,* Bishop John." *Daad* eyed him warily, but there was nothing very frightening in the bishop's expression. He smiled and greeted everyone, and when his keen eyes rested on Susannah, she felt as if he looked right through her and still found reason to smile.

"We should have a little talk, ain't so, Susannah?"

She nodded. There was bustling around the table as everyone found some reason to be elsewhere. In a few minutes, with warm hugs and murmurs of support, they were gone, leaving her alone to talk with Bishop John.

He pulled a chair over so that they sat facing each other, and she gave him a quick, apprehensive glance before lowering her gaze to her hands, folded in her lap.

"There's no reason that I know of for you to look so worried," Bishop John said, his deep voice gentle. "I didn't come with two ministers to confront you with wrongdoing. It's *chust* the two of us, wanting to talk about the problem."

Susannah blinked back a rush of weak, foolish tears. "*Denke,* Bishop John." She took a steadying breath. "I don't know what to do."

"That is a *gut* place to start," he said, and she thought she detected a trace of amusement in his voice. "Too many folks think they already know what the Lord wants them to do."

She risked a glance. "James Keim says I have given the board cause for dismissal."

"*Ja,* I have heard from James. What do *you* say?"

Of course Keim would have gone straight to the bishop with his accusations. She should have anticipated it. "I was wrong to let Toby kiss me in the schoolhouse. That was inappropriate, and I don't blame anyone for being shocked. But the problem at the rehearsal for the Christmas program—"

Her voice shook a little as she remembered that scene. "It was an issue with two boys misbehaving, and I would have dealt with it as I have with countless problems in the past ten years. There was no good reason to cancel the Christmas program and disappoint the students and their families."

"I should tell you I have talked to Toby Unger," he said. "He is very quick to blame himself for what happened between you. He says that he took you by surprise, and he is truly grieved that he's caused you such trouble."

She was shaken at the thought of Toby discussing her with the bishop, and her cheeks flamed. Naturally the bishop would put this incident first, concerned as he was with the hearts and souls of his people.

"The guilt belongs to both of us," she said firmly. "I'm a grown woman, not a foolish teenager, and I am… was…the teacher."

"True, the schoolhouse is not the place for kissing." Slight amusement sounded in his voice. "But there is not anything wrong with a kiss between a single man and a single woman that I know of. Toby tells me he has asked you to marry him."

Her hands clenched. "I have told him no." She could feel the bishop's gaze on her face, and she didn't dare look up.

"Do you love him, child?"

She felt her cheeks grow hot. She might try to lie to herself, but she certain sure couldn't lie to the spiritual leader of the church.

"I do love him," she said softly. "I always have. But he…he doesn't feel the same way toward me."

To her relief, Bishop John didn't pursue it further. "As to this other matter, my feeling is that James Keim acted in haste." He paused, and Susannah could almost feel him choosing his words. "I will continue to pray for guidance, and I'll speak to James again." He didn't sound as if he expected much from that conversation.

"*Denke,* Bishop John. I'm grateful." She met his gaze then and saw the sorrow there. Bishop John truly lived the command to bear one another's burdens, and she could almost see them weighing on his shoulders.

"If nothing else," he said, "I think the Willow Run School will need a teacher next fall. I'll speak with them. I'm sure they would be eager to have you."

"*Denke,*" she said again. "It's very *gut* of you."

So why didn't she feel more joy at the thought of having a school again? The truth sank in. Losing her school was a terrible thing.

But losing Toby was even worse.

Chapter Nine

Stretching out next to the carriage he'd been working on, Toby squirmed his way underneath to check the axles. The owner had complained of a squeaking noise he hadn't been able to account for, so he'd brought it back to the workshop, probably hoping Toby's father would be fit for work again. Well, he'd have to settle for Toby.

Even Toby's persistence in keeping busy hadn't been enough to keep his mind occupied. Bishop John had accepted his version of things without much comment, other than to say that he'd be seeing both Keim and Susannah and hoped to straighten matters out. But so far Toby hadn't heard anything else. Nearly twenty-four hours had passed since Toby had stood with Susannah in the schoolroom and watched the destruction of her dreams.

He frowned absently at the axle just above his face. A dozen times he'd nearly gone over to the Miller place to try to speak to Susannah, but what could he say that hadn't already been said?

Again and again he saw Susannah's face when he'd suggested marriage. He could kick himself. No won-

der she'd refused him. She'd known it was an impulse
of a moment.

If only Bishop John succeeded with Keim...

The shop door opened, letting in a blast of cold air
and a flurry of snowflakes. It closed again quickly,
and he recognized William's shoes and pants He stiffened. He still hadn't gotten a satisfactory explanation
of William's actions. He seemed to hear Susannah's
voice telling him to keep trying, to be as calm and patient as she always was.

"I'm under here, William."

William bent over, peering beneath the carriage, his
face inverted. "Can I come under, too, *Daadi?*"

Toby patted the floorboards next to him in answer.
In a moment William had rolled under the carriage and
moved next to him, staring into the underbelly of the
vehicle.

"What are you doing?"

"The owner says it's making a funny noise, so I'm
trying to figure out why. I thought it might be the axle,
but the fittings are fine." He patted the sturdy axle just
above his face.

"What else could it be?"

Toby suspected William hadn't come out to the shop
in the snow just to ask him questions about the buggy
business, but if it helped ease him into what he wanted
to say, that was okay by him.

"I'm thinking, maybe the springs." He indicated
them with the pliers he held. "They're what give you a
comfortable ride, and one of them might be rubbing."

William nodded solemnly. "You like to work with
tools, *ja, Daadi?*"

"I do." *Give me the right words for my boy, Father.
Help me to find out what troubles him.*

William was silent for a moment. "I liked building the candles with you. I hope they're not broken."

"I hope so, too. But if they are, maybe we can fix them." He breathed another silent prayer. "Most broken things can be fixed, if you know what's wrong with them."

William nodded, his forehead furrowed.

Treading cautiously, he went on. "It seems to me that something's broken between you and me. We're not as close as we used to be."

He paused, but William didn't respond. His gaze was fixed on the springs.

"I don't know why," Toby said. "If I did, maybe I could fix it. Was it something to do with your *mammi*'s dying?"

William's lips pressed together. He shook his head. "Look, *Daadi*. That spring is crooked. Maybe that's making the noise."

Toby's heart sank. But he tried to infuse some enthusiasm into his voice. "I believe you're right. Let's see if I can fix it."

He eased the pliers along the spring, trying to grasp the kink that had formed. It might have to be replaced.

"I heard you," William said suddenly. "You were talking to *Grossdaadi* and *Grossmammi* about sending me and Anna out West with them after *Mammi* died."

Toby's hand jerked, and the twisted spring snapped. He dropped the pliers. He knew perfectly well what conversation William had overheard. He'd thought both children safely asleep when Emma's parents had brought up their idea.

Toby's heart thudded in his ears. He wanted to set William straight, but he'd better try to find out exactly what the boy had been imagining. "What did you think that meant?"

"You wanted to send us away." A tear trickled down William's cheek.

Toby shifted to his side so that he could see his son's face more clearly, his shoulder brushing the axle. "Then I think you didn't hear the beginning of the talk. Or the end. Because if you did, you'd know that it was *Gross-mammi* and *Grossdaadi* who brought up the idea. They wanted to take you with them. And you know what I told them?"

William's gaze met his, wide-eyed, and he shook his head.

"I said I knew they wanted to help, but I couldn't even think of being parted from my children. I said I loved you and Anna more than anything, and I couldn't let you go." He looked steadily into his son's eyes. "That's exactly what happened. You can write to them and ask them, if you want."

William just stared at him. Then he rolled right into Toby's arms. Toby squeezed him close, his heart swelling, caught between laughter and tears. What a place for a father-and-son talk!

But at last they had cleared the air between them. What difference did it make where it happened?

William snuggled against him the way he had when he was younger. "I'm sorry, *Daadi*." His voice was muffled. "I'm sorry I was mean to you."

"It's okay. I love you even when you're mean to me."

William sniffled a little. "And I'm sorry I messed up the Christmas program. I shouldn't have got mad at Thomas and pushed him and wrecked the candles we made. We worked so hard on the Christmas program, and I messed it up."

"All of us worked hard on it," he said. The faintest glimmer of an idea seemed to light up Toby's mind. So many people were involved with the program. Maybe, just maybe...

He moved, sliding himself and William across the floor.

"What are we doing?" William seemed to sense his urgency.

"You know how I said that broken things could be fixed? Well, maybe the Christmas program can be fixed, if we all work together."

And maybe, if his idea worked, even more than the Christmas program.

Everyone in Susannah's family seemed to have somewhere to go on Friday afternoon. She wasn't sorry that even her mother had taken off to go shopping, but she was a little surprised *Mamm* hadn't insisted on Susannah accompanying her. Maybe her mother realized Susannah wasn't ready for casual encounters with any church families yet.

At last she had the solitude she'd been longing for, but oddly enough, she didn't find it as peaceful as she would have expected. She found herself aimlessly wandering around the house, looking for something to do. Each time her thoughts slid toward Toby, she ruthlessly reined them in.

She had been right to turn down his proposal, she told herself firmly. He hadn't really meant it, and a marriage founded on guilt wouldn't stand much chance of happiness.

The Willow Run School was a far better subject for her to concentrate on. She'd been there several times when the local Amish teachers got together for meet-

ings. It was always helpful to share ideas, and Susannah
had picked up more than one useful tip that way. The
school building was much like the Pine Creek School,
with maybe a few more scholars. She'd think of it as
a challenge.

All of her teaching materials and books were still
at school, of course. She'd been so numb after everything that happened, she hadn't been able to bear the
thought of packing them up. Maybe after Christmas,
it would be easier.

The whole extended family would be here for Christmas Day, and the following day, Second Christmas,
they'd be making the rounds, visiting other relatives.
Several gifts were already tucked away in the dower
chest in her bedroom, but she was still working on a
muffler for her brother Eli. Sitting down in the rocking
chair, she took it from the workbasket and smoothed it
out across her lap. The variegated brown yarn was soft
to the touch but sufficiently masculine, she thought,
and the half-double crochet stitch was easy enough that
she could do it and carry on a conversation at the same
time. In the evenings, she and *Mamm* sat on either side
of the lamp to work, their tongues going as fast as their
hooks or needles.

Smiling a little, she began a new row. This was better. She hadn't thought about her troubles in at least a
minute or two.

Susannah had barely reached the end of the row before she heard a buggy driving in the lane. Sticking the
hook into the yarn ball to hold her place, she went to the
kitchen window to see who was back already.

But it wasn't any of the family. It was Becky. She
stopped by the back porch, jumped down from the
buggy and trotted toward the door.

Susannah hurried to open it. "Becky, I wasn't expecting you. I'll put the kettle on."

"No time for that." Becky yanked Susannah's wool jacket from the hook by the back door. *"Komm, schnell."*

Susannah resisted Becky's efforts to push her arm into the sleeve. "I'm not one of the twins. You don't have to dress me. Where are we going in such a hurry?"

"Don't you trust me?" Becky's eyebrows lifted.

"Not when I think you're up to something." Susannah took the jacket firmly into her own hands. "I'm not taking another step until you tell me where we're going."

"All right, stubborn. I'm going with you to get your things at the school. You don't think I'd let you do it by yourself, do you?"

Susannah blinked back a rush of tears. Becky knew her so well. She must have guessed that was preying on her mind.

"That's wonderful kind of you. But we don't have to do it today—"

"Better sooner than later, otherwise you'll just be stewing about it."

"I'm not stewing."

"You're moping then, and that's worse. *Komm.* We'll get it over with, and if you want to have a good cry, no one will see you."

Susannah recognized the look in Becky's eyes. She was determined, and when Becky was determined, she wouldn't let you have a moment's peace until you did what she wanted. Susannah might as well get it over with.

"All right. We'll go." Susannah pulled on the jacket. "But only because I know you'll nag me to death if I refuse."

Though she didn't relish the purpose of the expedition, Susannah found her spirits lifting a bit once the buggy was moving down the road. The crisp air seemed to blow away the cobwebs in her mind, and sunlight sparkled on the snow-covered fields where ice had formed.

Becky gave her a searching glance. "So, how are you, really?"

Susannah shrugged. "Better, I guess. I'm starting to feel enthusiastic about teaching at a new school. And I do need my materials so I can sort through them, if nothing else. Maybe it is best just to clear my things out of the Pine Creek School." She tried not to let her voice quaver on the words.

"I'm sorry." Becky's voice mirrored her grief. "I know how hard this is. That school has been your life."

True enough. Odd, that the school had fulfilled her all these years, and yet now, she longed for more. But the gift she wanted wasn't going to be hers.

"I'll miss the school. The memories. The children." She made an effort to swallow the lump in her throat. "But I can move on. Really. Now that the worst has happened, I can deal with it."

"I never doubted it for a minute," Becky said. "But what about...well, Toby? I know you'd probably rather not talk about him, but he did ask you to marry him."

For once Susannah couldn't tell from Becky's voice what she was thinking, and the brim of her black bonnet hid her face. "He asked me," she admitted. "And I refused him."

"But—"

Susannah shook her head and hurried on. "It wouldn't be right. Toby doesn't care for me that way, not anymore, and I...I guess I'd rather be a good teacher than somebody's second-choice wife."

"You're sure about that?" Becky turned a concerned face toward her as they approached the turnoff for the school.

Susannah nodded. "It's for the best. All of this has made me realize that I truly have forgiven what happened between us. I can let it go and trust that God has a plan for my life."

"I'm sure the *gut* Lord does have a plan." Becky negotiated the turn into the school lane, where the snow was banked high on either side by the snowplow. "But you know, maybe Toby is part of that plan. And if he is, don't let your pride stand in the way."

Susannah was still trying to adjust to that startling statement when she saw something equally surprising. The lane was lined on either side with buggies, all the way up to the schoolhouse, where still more ringed the building, giving it the air of being surrounded.

Her stomach clenched. "Becky, what's going on? If there's going to be a school board meeting, I don't want to have anything to do with it."

Becky ignored her, driving the buggy straight up to the door. "It's not the school board meeting. It's your scholars. They have a surprise for you."

Susannah gripped the edge of the buggy seat. "I don't want any more surprises."

"Now, don't be foolish," Becky chided. "You can't disappoint the *kinder*. Look, here's Eli to take you in."

Sure enough, her brother was already reaching up to seize her waist and swing her down before she could find words to refuse.

"Just come along," Eli said. "There's nothing to worry about."

Becky had already slid down, and she grasped her other arm. "That's right." Together they propelled Susannah across the porch and into the school.

Chapter Ten

Susannah's mind seemed to stop working for an instant when she walked inside her classroom. The room was filled with people—so many it seemed the walls would burst from the pressure. Family, neighbors, Bishop John, parents and former students, so many of the scholars who had gone through the Pine Creek School in the past decade. And everyone was smiling.

Eli and Becky swept her up to her own desk chair, pushed her into it and turned her to face the makeshift stage at the side of the room. It was then that she saw her students, lined up in front of the tall candles Toby had made. The metallic gold paint that formed the flames of the candles seemed to glow, but not more than the faces of the children…the boys in their black pants, white shirts and suspenders, the girls with pristine white aprons over a colorful array of dresses.

Suddenly the room grew still. Not missing a beat, her scholars spoke together. *"Wilkom,* Teacher Susannah."

She could only smile at them, her eyes misted with tears, as her heart swelled in her chest. For this moment, at least, she was at home.

Mary Keim stepped forward, her smile seeming perfectly confident. With a quick glance at Bishop John, she spoke.

"We *wilkom* all of you, our dear visitors, to the Pine Creek School, for our Christmas program." She turned, nodded, and the children moved quickly and quietly to their places. Mary slid into a chair placed at the side of the stage, probably so she could prompt anyone who forgot a line, and the program began.

It was her own program, of course, with every word familiar to her, and yet it seemed to Susannah that it had taken on a special dimension. It was hard to imagine Mary taking control, standing up in front of everyone and looking so composed. She had found the strength she'd been seeking.

But how had Mary dared to go against her father this way? Surely James Keim didn't support this idea after he'd expressly forbidden the Christmas program.

Susannah took a quick glance around the room, searching for Keim, and found him standing at the back corner, his arms crossed over his chest, his expression forbidding. No, he didn't look as if he'd changed his opinion.

The first graders came forward, grouped nervously close together, with the twins and Anna holding hands. Their recitation was a simple poem wishing everyone a merry Christmas, and they made it through without a single glance at Mary for help. They closed by inviting everyone to join them in singing Jingle Bells, and the resounding chorus seemed likely to lift the roof off.

Songs, poems, recitations, skits were done, interspersed with the singing of familiar Christmas carols. The morals were the simple ones that were reiterated year after year in Amish school programs, celebrating the gift of love, the joy of giving, the humility of the believer honoring the birth of Jesus, the Light of the World. Susannah glanced around as the program moved forward, seeing the rapt faces, the pleased smiles, some apprehension when a child began and the glow when he or she finished.

Some things never changed. Most of the people in this room would have heard every one of these thoughts expressed at countless Christmas programs, and yet, like the Christmas story itself, they were fresh and new each year.

The final presentation involved ten students with lighted candles—a process that always filled Susannah with lively apprehension. Becky and Mary moved quickly along the row of children, lighting the white candles they held.

The poem began, with the ten lights symbolizing ten young Christians. As the words were recited that showed how each one fell short from his or her Christian duty, a flame was extinguished, until only one was left—the one held by young William. His solemn face was pale in the light of his candle as he held it firmly. The rest of the scholars gathered behind him as they spoke of how one person could shine his light so that it reached the world and brought others to Christ. Then William, intent on his task, went to each child, lighting the candles one by one until the room was aglow with their light.

Mary's voice lifted in the first line of "This Little Light of Mine," and the children soon joined in. Susannah suspected there wasn't a dry eye in the room by then. As they reached the end of the song, they lifted their candles so that the light spilled out over the whole room.

Zeke, the oldest of the scholars, stepped forward.

"We just want to add one more thought to our program before it ends. Teacher Susannah has been a light to us. We don't want to lose her." He sent a challenging look around the room.

For an instant there was silence. Then the schoolroom erupted with the sound of applause and murmurs of agreement that became louder and louder.

Bishop John stepped out to stand by the children. "*Denke*. We thank you, boys and girls, for showing us so much today. I think we all agree that we don't want to lose Teacher Susannah because of a foolish misunderstanding." He looked directly at James Keim.

Susannah's breath caught. It was the public confrontation she'd longed to avoid, and yet it had been accomplished in such a lovely and loving way. How would Keim respond?

James Keim stood stiffly, hands at his sides. His gaze was locked with that of the bishop. Susannah found she was holding her breath.

At last Keim nodded. "I agree. It was a misunderstanding."

Thank you, Lord. Susannah's heart filled.

The room began to hum with excited conversation. Mothers started uncovering the trays of cookies and cakes set out on a long table at the back of the room. And Susannah's students rushed to her and enveloped her in their love.

It was nearly an hour until the schoolhouse emptied enough that Susannah could look for answers to the questions that bubbled through her mind. She found Mary Keim in the midst of taking down Christmas decorations.

"That can wait until later." She caught Mary's arm

before she could climb up on the step stool. "Tell me how this came about. I couldn't believe my eyes when I saw you standing up there leading the *kinder*."

Mary flushed. "I could hardly believe it myself. But it was important to the little ones, ain't so?"

"I'm sure it was." She still felt a little overwhelmed at the love her scholars had showered on her. "But your father..." She let the question die out, not sure she wanted to know if Mary had openly defied her parents.

"It was the bishop," Mary said, a smile lurking in her eyes. "Bishop John came to the house and talked about how important the Christmas program was to the whole community. And when he asked me to help right in front of my *daad,* well, *Daadi* just couldn't say no."

"I guess he couldn't." She had to suppress a chuckle at the thought of that conversation. Bishop John had been wily, it seemed. "So the bishop was the one who thought of all this?"

Mary shrugged. "I guess. Anyway, he's the one who spoke to us." She hesitated, and then she went on in a rush. "I really wanted to do it. No matter what."

Touched, Susannah patted the girl's arm. "When school starts again, will you be back as my helper?"

Mary flushed again, with pleasure this time. "If you want me."

"That's certain sure." Her first impression of Mary Keim had certainly been mistaken. "You're going to make a fine teacher, if that's what you want."

"More than anything." Again she hesitated. "Teacher Susannah, I hope you can forgive my father. I want to learn from you, not replace you."

"Of course I forgive him." She gave the girl a quick hug. "And who knows? You might end up doing both."

Letting Mary get back to her work, Susannah cor-

nered Bishop John before he could slip away with the
last group of parents and children.

"*Denke,* Bishop John. I don't know how you thought
of this, but I'm truly grateful for all the trouble you've
gone to for me." She blinked back a fresh set of tears
at the thought.

"*Ach,* Susannah, you owe me no thanks. It was important that you know how much we value you, no
matter what you decide to do in the future." His eyes
crinkled with a smile. "Besides, the idea wasn't mine.
This was all Toby Unger's doing. He's the one you must
thank."

"Toby?" Her voice shook a little on his name.

Bishop John nodded. "He came to me with it all
thought out. Seems he and that boy of his were determined to make things up to you." He gave her a little
push. "I think I saw him carrying things into the back
room."

Warmth spread through her. No matter how much
she regretted losing what might have been between her
and Toby, at least she now understood that their friendship was solid and unbreakable, just as it always had
been.

Bishop John was right. She owed Toby her thanks,
and she'd best do it now, before she lost her nerve.

When she reached the back room, she found Zeke
and William helping Toby store the program props on
the wall shelves. All three looked around at the sound
of her steps.

"Toby, I… May I have a minute?"

Zeke grinned and clapped William on the shoulder.
"Let's go grab some cookies. We deserve it after all
this work, ain't so?"

William glanced from her to his father, and she

thought she read hesitation in his face. Then he nodded, and the two boys headed back into the schoolroom.

When they were alone together, Susannah found herself suddenly tongue-tied. "Toby, I…I… Thank you."

"Forget it." He grinned, and for an instant he was a mischievous boy again. "It wasn't just me. I talked to Bishop John, and then the two of us talked to Becky and your parents, and it just snowballed."

"But it started with you." She took a step closer, her embarrassment slipping away. This was Toby, after all. She had always been able to say anything to him. "We didn't exactly part on the best of terms, and I—"

"Don't, Susannah." A spasm of pain crossed his face, wiping away his smile. "Every chance I get, I just end up making a mistake and hurting you."

"You didn't hurt me by asking me to marry you." She was as close as she dared get to him without risking him seeing how deeply he affected her. "I know that you were only trying to be helpful."

"Helpful." He grimaced. "All I've done is make your life a shambles since I came back, but I never meant for that to happen."

"Toby, I…" She was trying to find the words that would reassure him when his hands shot out and grasped her arms. His warmth penetrated the fabric, heating her skin, and her mouth went dry.

"Whatever else you might think, at least know that I meant it when I said our friendship was a solid foundation for marriage." His grip tightened. "But that's not all, and I didn't even realize it until I thought I'd cost you everything."

He took a step closer, and her heart was beating up in her throat so hard that she couldn't have spoken to save her life.

"I know you, Susannah Miller. I know you better than I've ever known anyone else in my life. The more I see of you, the better I understand. You're honest and good all the way through. No matter how I tried to kid myself, I know now that you have always held first place in my heart. I love you, Susannah. I always have, and I always will."

The rapid rush of words stopped, and he looked at her with his heart in his eyes. He lifted her hands, holding them close to his lips, so that she felt his warm breath on them when he spoke again.

"What about it? Do you think you could possibly take a chance on me again?"

Susannah was caught between laughter and tears. "*Ach,* Toby, you know me so well. Can you possibly doubt the answer to that question?"

Relief seemed to wash over his face. She knew he really had been uncertain, and her heart leaped. She raised their clasped hands so that she could touch his lips with her fingertips.

"I know we're in the schoolhouse," she said softly. "But I think this occasion merits a kiss, don't you?"

She could feel his smile as his lips claimed hers, and then she was lost in the warmth and tenderness and belonging that bound them one to the other. She slipped her arms around him, holding him close. *This time, forever.* The words seemed to form in her mind. Despite all the grief and pain, they'd found their way back where they belonged.

A thought hit her, and she drew away an inch or two. "We mustn't rush. The *kinder*... We have to think of them. We must give them time to get used to the idea."

Toby nodded. "We will, but I think they won't find it hard." A smile tugged at his lips. "Maybe, by the time you're ready to quit teaching for a family of your own, you'll have Mary trained to step into your place."

Blushing at the thought of the children they might have together, she nodded. If he was right about William and Anna, this really might have been her last Christmas program as teacher at the Pine Creek School.

But whether it was or not, she knew for certain what her future Christmases would be like. She and Toby would be celebrating together for the rest of their lives. As the children had said in their program, love was the best Christmas gift of all.

* * * * *

A PLAIN HOLIDAY

Patricia Davids

It is with heartfelt love that I dedicate this story to my brothers, Greg, Bob, Mark and Gary. I'm sorry for the grief I gave you as your spoiled-brat sister. You guys made me tough. You taught me to throw a ball like a boy and not like a girl, and you allowed me to share many adventures. Thanks for that and for your lifelong love and support. Merry Christmas, from Sis.

And suddenly there was with the angel
a multitude of the heavenly host praising God,
and saying, Glory to God in the highest,
and on earth peace, good will toward men.
—*Luke* 2:13–14

Chapter One

"This is the worst Christmas ever."

Sally Yoder bit the corner of her lip and glanced over her shoulder at her young charge. She shouldn't have said that aloud. It made her sound ungrateful. She wasn't. She was happy to have a good job as a nanny for the Higgins family. Most days.

Eleven-year-old Kimi wasn't paying attention so Sally stared out the window again. In her hand, she held the most recent letter from her mother. It had arrived last week. Sally kept it in her pocket and took it out whenever she was missing home. Like now.

Traffic clogged the street below her employer's Cincinnati apartment building. It was rush hour, although she saw scores of cars no matter what time of day she looked out. The view was cold and depressing. The holiday lights and Christmas decorations didn't improve it much. Piles of dirty snow lay melting into gray slush along the sidewalks where pedestrians wove in and out of the mess as they hurried along.

Sally's upbringing among the serene Amish farms in Hope Springs, Ohio, had ill-prepared her for the noisy bustle of life in the city.

This is my rumspringa, *my time to experience the outside world and discover if I wish to remain Amish. I should be eager to see and do everything here in the* Englisch *world.*

But she wasn't, and she knew why. It was hard to enjoy the adventure when her heart remained in Hope Springs. Rather, the broken bits of it remained behind, scattered at Ben Lapp's feet. It was awful to love someone who didn't love her back.

She glanced at her letter again. It wasn't possible to be more homesick than she was at this second. She reached for the ties of her Amish prayer *kapp*. She often twirled the ribbon around her fingers when she was deep in thought, but she realized her head was bare. She had been dressing English for three months now and it still felt odd. Would she ever put a *kapp* on again?

"If I don't get a new iPod, it *will* be the worst Christmas ever." Kimi proved she had heard Sally's comment, after all. Kimi was sprawled on her bed with her smartphone, that ever-present accessory, clutched in her hands. It giggled and shouted "Text message!" in a cartoon voice that Sally found increasingly irritating.

It was the first day of winter vacation for Kimi's private school. The girl had been complaining all morning about missing her friends and being bored.

Kimi suddenly sat bolt upright. "Jen got blue diamond earrings from her stepdad? No way. That is so awesome. I should let Grams know I want a pair. She likes to buy me cool stuff." Kimi flipped her long black hair out of her face and began typing furiously on her phone.

"Christmas is not about expensive gifts." Sally used her stern "nanny voice" to deliver the message.

"Whatever."

Sally shook her head and returned to contemplating the dreary world outside. If Kimi were this materialistic at eleven, what would she be like as an adult? The answer was easy. She would be like her mother.

Michele Higgins rarely had time for her children. Shopping and lunch with her friends took up most of her day. Sally was just the latest in a long string of nannies to raise the children. The family's money came from the huge real estate business Michele's workaholic husband managed. The contrast between this family and Sally's simple Amish roots was glaring.

"Christmas is about our Savior's birth. It is a time to reflect on our salvation. A time to give thanks for the blessings God has bestowed on us. A time to visit family and friends who are dear to us."

"I don't know how you people live without electricity. I'm so glad my grandmother left the Amish when she married Grandpa McIntyre. Ugh! How can Christmas be fun without shopping and holiday lights?"

"The beauty of the season doesn't come from lights and store displays. We enjoy going to see them in town, but God decorates the land in His own way this time of year. The snow lies like a pristine white blanket over the Amish farms and countryside. Sometimes, the snow glitters so brightly in the sun that it hurts my eyes, but it's so beautiful that I can't stop looking."

"Okay, it's pretty, but what do you do for fun?"

"Many things. At Christmastime, my mother's kitchen is filled with the smell of wonderful baking things. The youngest *kinder,* my brothers and sisters, will start pestering *Mamm* to make her delicious peach cobbler with snow ice cream. Someone will host a cookie exchange and my married sisters will come over and help *Mamm* bake all day."

"Sounds like work."

"*Nee,* it's not. The kitchen is full of laughter and happy chatter. We have such good times together." And she was going to miss it all this year.

"What's a cookie exchange?" Kimi asked, while at the same time answering a text, leaving Sally to wonder how she could do two things at once.

"A cookie exchange is a kind of party. Each family that's invited will bring a big container, sometimes even a bucket, filled with all kinds of cookies and baked goods. The hosting family has hot chocolate, coffee and cider for everyone. There's sure to be singing and game playing and lots of cookie sampling. Then, when it's time to go home, each family fills their bucket with everyone else's delicious baked goods to enjoy all week long."

"Sounds boring. No wonder you left." Kimi plopped on her stomach to read another text message.

Sally's spirits plunged. A Plain Christmas was the best kind of Christmas, but she might never be a part of one again. She was at a crossroads in her life. For a long time she had been wondering if she truly belonged among the simple, devout people. She didn't possess a meek spirit, and she couldn't pretend any longer that she did.

She turned her mother's letter over to read the back. With all the news her mother relayed, Sally found herself reading the same small tidbit again and again and wishing there was more. Some of the ink was blurred where her tears had fallen on the paper.

We heard Ben Lapp has taken a job at the McIntyre horse farm and likes working there. His mother says he'll be home for Christmas though.

Ben would be home, but Sally wouldn't. She was here to get over him, but it didn't seem to be working.

Kimi had caught Sally crying the day the letter arrived. In a moment of weakness, Sally had told her why. Kimi's advice was to go out and buy something nice. At her age, Kimi couldn't understand that material things didn't mend hearts.

The door to Kimi's room burst open, startling Sally into dropping her letter. Ryder, Kimi's younger brother, came charging in. "You'll never guess what," he shouted.

Kimi slapped her phone facedown on the bed. "Can't you learn to knock, you idiot!"

Sally scowled at her. "Don't call your *bruder* names."

"It's pronounced *brother,* and tell him he should knock."

Ryder rolled his eyes. "If I knocked, you'd just tell me to go away. Guess what?"

Ryder, an eight-year-old bundle of energy, was Sally's secret favorite. Maybe it was because they shared the same red hair and overabundance of freckles. His parents had placed him in a special program for hyperactive children. Because of that, he only went to school in the mornings. He and Sally spent every afternoon alone together and they both enjoyed it.

Kimi sat up cross-legged on the bed. "Okay, I'll guess your news. Mom and Dad have decided it's better for me to be an only child so they're giving you to a needy family for Christmas."

Sally crossed the room and snatched up the phone. "I'm keeping this."

Kimi's mouth dropped open. "Why?"

"That was a mean thing to say. Until you apologize to your…brother…I keep the phone."

"Oh, for real!" Kimi crossed her arms and glared at Sally.

Smiling, Sally slid the phone in the pocket of her jeans.

Kimi caved. "This is so unfair. I'm sorry...*bruder*."

"That was not a sincere apology." The girl's imitation of Sally's Amish accent didn't offend her. It made her more homesick. She picked up her mother's letter.

Kimi huffed and threw herself back against her headboard.

Ryder held his hands wide. "Doesn't anyone want to hear my news?"

"I do," Sally said.

"Dad's taking Mom to Paris for Christmas."

Kimi screamed and leaped off the bed. "We're going to Paris?"

Ryder dropped his hands to his sides. "You didn't let me finish. Dad is taking Mom to Paris and we are going to Grandma's. Yay!"

Kimi's face fell, but brightened again quickly. "New York isn't Paris, but it's still better than Cincinnati. Grams will take me shopping at all the best places."

Ryder folded his arms, a gloating expression on his face. "Not that grandmother, Kimi-Ninny. We're going to Ohio to spend Christmas vacation with Grandma McIntyre on her farm."

"No! Not there!" Sally said.

The two children turned shocked faces toward her. She quickly recovered her composure and tried to look unaffected. "I mean, I'm sure you'll have a wonderful time."

"On a horse farm in the middle of nowhere? Not likely," Kimi snapped.

Ryder tipped his head to the side. "I know why Kimi

doesn't want to spend Christmas with Grandma Mc-Intyre, but why don't you? I thought the Amish liked horses."

"I want to experience a non-Amish Christmas in the city. I'll talk to your mother about it. I don't think I'll be needed."

Kimi looked at Sally with an odd expression. "Grandma McIntyre broke her leg last week. She can't keep an eye on Ryder, and I'm not going to babysit him for two weeks."

Sally pressed her lips together tightly. What did God have planned for her? Not to be the wife of Ben Lapp, that was sure and certain. So why was He sending her to the very place where Ben had a job?

"Did you know our grandmother used to be Amish?" Ryder asked.

Sally smiled at the boy. "I do. My father is a contractor. He built the new stables on your grandmother's farm. That's how I learned your mother was looking for a nanny. Your grandmother put in a good word for me and I got the job." Sally hoped her odd reaction would soon be forgotten.

A malicious gleam sprang to Kimi's eyes. "I know why you don't want to go. It's because *he* is there."

Sally closed her eyes. She would never share another confidence with Kimi. No matter how lonely she was or how much she needed to confide in someone.

"Who are you talking about?" Ryder asked.

Kimi's grin bordered on evil. She held out her hand. "His name starts with a *B*. Shall I tell my blabbermouth brother more, or can I have my phone back?"

"The grandbrats are coming for the entire Christmas break. Somebody shoot me now."

Ben Lapp smiled at Trent's gloomy tone and continued brushing the mare he had just finished exercising. Trent Duffy, the head groom at the McIntyre Stables, had a way of making any little problem sound dire. "Mrs. McIntyre will be happy to have her grandbabies here for the holidays."

"I'm not talking about her son Sam's kids. I'm talking about her daughter Michele's two brats."

Ben fumbled and dropped his brush in the straw.

Sally Yoder worked as a nanny for Michele Higgins. She wouldn't come along on a Christmas family gathering, would she? Surely not.

Snatching up the brush, he checked to see if Trent had noticed his reaction. Trent was busy unwrapping Lady Brandywine's front legs. Ben resumed his work. "So the whole family is coming. That's nice."

"No, Michele and her *über*-rich husband are going to Paris. Just the kids and their nanny are staying. Hey, didn't I hear the nanny is a friend of yours?"

Ben closed his eyes and bowed his head. Sally Yoder had managed to make his life miserable for two solid years. "*Nee,* she's not a friend."

"That's right. She left the Amish or something, and now she is shunned or whatever you people call it."

Ben ran the brush along the mare's sleek brown neck. "Sally is not shunned. She never took the vows of baptism. She is free to choose the *Englisch* life. I've known her since the first grade, but we're not friends."

"Englisch?"

"It means English. What we call people who aren't Amish."

"Someday you'll have to explain to me about the shunning stuff. Would you hand me that curry comb?"

Ben stopped brushing and slipped under his horse's

neck to hand the metal comb to Trent. Maybe he could arrange to be gone while Sally was here. Mrs. McIntyre had been good about giving him time off in the past for weddings and such. The loss of salary would be a small price to pay to avoid seeing Sally. "When did you say they were coming?"

Trent looked out the open stable doors. "If I'm not mistaken, that's their car pulling up to the house now."

Ben's faint hope evaporated. So much for making his escape. Still, the McIntyre horse farm was a good-sized facility. He could stay out of sight if he tried.

Trent led his horse to her stall and closed the lower half of the door. "They'll want help carrying in the luggage. Michele won't lift anything heavier than a hundred dollar bill. Must be nice to have all the money in the world."

"I'll finish up here for you," Ben offered.

"No way. I'm not going to be the only one getting yelled at for scuffing her expensive bags. Come on."

Ben looked out the stable doors toward the black SUV parked in the drive. A woman with bright blond hair, a fur-trimmed coat and tall leather boots got out of the driver's seat. A boy about eight charged out from the backseat and came running toward the stable.

"Ryder, get back here," his mother yelled. He stopped. Ben could see the indecision on his face.

A young woman in jeans and a short leather jacket with a long braid of fiery red hair hanging over her shoulder got out next. She held out her hand to the child. "Ryder, come greet your grandmother first."

Ben looked closer. Dark glasses obscured her face but he knew that voice, and it didn't belong to a woman who looked so...*Englisch.*

The boy ran back to her. "But I want to see the horses, Sally."

"They will still be there after you say hello to your grandmother."

She glanced around the yard. Was she looking for him? Ben stayed where he was. For two long years, Sally Yoder had made a complete fool of herself running after him. She never understood that he wasn't interested. She wasn't the kind of woman he was looking to settle down with. Still, he had been shocked when she took a job in the city.

Trent slapped him on the back. "Let's go. The bags won't get any lighter."

There was no point in putting it off. He would have to endure two weeks of Sally throwing herself at him at every turn, but then she would leave with the family. It wouldn't be fun, but he would manage. He stepped out of the barn and walked toward the car in resignation.

A second, younger girl with black hair got out and stood huddled against the cold beside her mother. "Please, don't make me stay here. I will die of boredom. Let me come with you."

Her mother patted her cheek. "Your dad and I need some alone time. You'll have a wonderful two weeks with your grandmother."

"No, I won't."

Michele walked toward the house, leaving the children standing beside the car.

Ben approached the group. "Would you like some help with the bags?"

Sally pulled her sunglasses off. The stare she gave him dropped the temperature by ten degrees. "Hello, Ben. Come along, children. Let's get out of this awful weather."

She shepherded the children into the house without a backward glance. Ben watched in stunned surprise as she walked away. Sally hadn't gushed about how glad she was to see him or how much she had missed him. Had she really changed so much? He wouldn't have thought it possible.

How could she go from mooning over him for years to ignoring him?

He honestly hadn't expected her job in the city to last this long. To begin with, he thought she'd left because she hoped he'd realize he couldn't live without her. She was wrong on that score. He enjoyed his Sally-free time. Until today, he thought the only thing that would stop her foolishness for good was for him to marry someone else. Unfortunately, he hadn't found the right woman. Yet. But he sure wasn't going to settle for a wild-spirited redhead with no *demut*.

Sally suffered from a serious lack of humility. When he chose a wife, it would be someone who knew the meaning of meekness and modesty. Someone who didn't question the old ways at every turn and didn't make him feel like a trophy buck in a hunter's sights each time she looked at him.

He pulled a pair of suitcases from the back of the SUV and headed for the front door. He knew what he wanted in a wife and Sally Yoder wasn't it. Somehow, he would avoid her for the next two weeks if he had to hide in the haystacks.

Chapter Two

I can't do this.

Sally caught her lower lip between her teeth to stop it from trembling. She couldn't spend two weeks pretending she didn't care that Ben was here, too. How could she hide her feelings for so long?

"Welcome, everyone, and Merry Christmas." Velda McIntyre, an elegant woman with piercing blue eyes and gray hair cut in a short bob, rolled forward in her wheelchair. She was dressed in a pink jogging suit. A cast covered her left leg from hip to toe.

The Higgins family stood in the large foyer in an awkward group. Sally remained in the background, willing the suddenly shy children to show their grandmother some affection. She heard the door open behind her. She didn't have to look to know it was Ben.

He was the last man on earth she wanted to see. No, he was the only man on earth she wanted to see. She wanted to drink in the sight of him. She wanted to gaze into his beautiful brown eyes and apologize for her abrupt manner outside and for so much more. Instead, she focused on her hostess.

Mrs. McIntyre's face glowed with excitement. She

clapped her hands like a child. "I'm so happy to see all of you. We're going to have such a wonderful old-fashioned Christmas. Come here and give me a hug, Ryder. You've grown so much."

"Does your leg hurt?" Ryder inched closer.

"It was silly of me to fall on the ice and break my old bones just before Christmas, wasn't it? It only hurts when I'm not getting a hug from my favorite boy." She held out her arms.

Ryder jumped forward and gave her an enthusiastic squeeze. Kimi, still pouting after two hundred miles, gave her a lukewarm embrace.

The elderly woman didn't seem to notice. "You children have no idea how much fun I have in store for you. We'll bake cookies the way my mother and I did when I was your age, Kimi. We'll make a real gingerbread house, too, and decorate it. Your grandfather always said it wasn't Christmas without one. How does that sound?"

"Totally awesome, Granny." Kimi couldn't have sounded more uninterested if she tried. She didn't want to be here and she didn't care who knew it.

"What do I get to do?" Ryder asked as he leaned on the arm of her chair. For him, a farm was the perfect place to spend Christmas vacation.

"I haven't forgotten about you. You can help with the cookies, too, but I'm giving you a special mission. I'm sending you to find us a Christmas tree. Your sister will go along with you, but you are in charge of finding the perfect one."

Ryder grinned. "I'll find the best one on the lot, Granny."

Mrs. McIntyre hugged him. "You can't find the perfect Christmas tree at a lot, dear. You have to take a sleigh ride up into the forest the way your grandfather and I used to do with your mother. You'll see dozens of trees to choose from, but you will know the perfect one when you spot it. Trent, you can take them up above Carson Lake tomorrow, can't you?"

He quickly shook his head. "I'm afraid I have too much work to do before the snow moves in, but I can spare Ben for a few hours."

"Will you take them, Ben?" she asked.

"Sure. I'd love to take the kids on a sleigh ride."

Just the sound of his voice brought tears to Sally's eyes. She furiously blinked them back. How pathetic was it to be head over heels for someone who didn't care about her? She studied the large painting of a horse on the wall instead of looking at him. She would just have to get over him.

Please, dear Lord, let it happen soon.

Mrs. McIntyre said, "You will have to cut the tree down with a saw, Ryder. It's hard work, but Ben can help you. He'll lash the tree to the back of the sleigh for the ride home, too. The harness bells sound so merry when you're dashing across the snowy fields. You'll never forget the sound. And on your way back, you will stop and visit my mother. She lives with my two brothers and their wives on a farm a few miles from here. They haven't seen you since you were a baby, Ryder. Mama was so excited when I told her you were coming. She'll have good things to eat and hot tea or cider to warm you before you start home again. I only wish I could come with you."

Sally saw Mrs. McIntyre's eyes mist over. She chanced a glance at Ben. He wore a kindly smile that told her he cared about his employer. Sally had missed his smile. When Ben looked her way, she focused on the painting again. She didn't want him to see how much she still cared.

Going away had been for the best. She was more certain of that now than ever. She didn't have an Amish heart. She tried hard to fool herself and everyone else into believing she belonged among the Plain people, but she always knew she would leave one day when she found the courage.

She had decided to make a play for Ben when she was eighteen because she knew he would never propose to a girl like her. She ran around with the wild group of teens. He stayed on the straight and narrow. She kept up the charade of being madly in love with him to discourage her family and other young men from pressing her to marry. Marriage would bind her to the Amish life forever.

Her plan worked. Until she made the mistake of actually falling for Ben. Soft-spoken, caring, always helpful, he was a wonderful fellow but she had been right. He had no interest in settling down with her. Her plan had one side effect she hadn't counted on. She learned there were several young women in her community who wouldn't go out with Ben because they didn't want to risk hurting her feelings. After making such a fuss about him for so long, she couldn't convince them she had suddenly stopped liking him.

That was when she found the courage to leave.

Ben deserved someone who embraced the Amish faith and way of life wholeheartedly. She wasn't that woman, but she wouldn't stand in the way of his happiness.

"Can we go get the tree now?" Ryder asked.

Mrs. McIntyre laughed. "Settle in your rooms first.

Ben will take you tomorrow. Ben is a groom here. He's Amish, Ryder. Do you know what that means?"

"Sure. Sally's Amish, too. They talk funny and only drive horses and buggies. Mom cussed a lot when we got stuck behind a buggy on our way here."

"Not a lot, Mother," Michele said quickly.

Mrs. McIntyre turned her attention to Sally. "You're from the Hope Springs area, too, aren't you? David Yoder's daughter, right? He did a fine job building my new stables. I suspect from the way you're dressed that you're enjoying your *rumspringa.*"

"Yes, ma'am. I'm grateful you told my father about this position and that you vouched for me."

"Your father said you were a fine, upstanding young woman. That was good enough for me."

"I don't know what I would do without you," Michele added quickly.

Mrs. McIntyre looked pleased. "Do you and Ben know each other, Sally?"

"We do." Sally gave him a cool smile. He dropped his gaze to his boots and didn't say anything.

Mrs. McIntyre patted the wheels of her chair. "I'm so grateful you agreed to come along and help me look after the children over Christmas vacation, Sally. We must make sure you get a chance to visit your people while you're in the area."

"I would love that," Sally said eagerly. A visit to her family would cheer her up and get her away from Ben. Maybe she could convince Mrs. McIntyre to let her stay for several days.

Michele stepped to her mother's side and bent to kiss her cheek. "I've got to run. I need to get back and finish packing. Our plane leaves at nine o'clock tonight.

Have fun with the children. Sally, I'd like to speak to you outside."

"You're not staying for supper, Michele?" Mrs. McIntyre's face fell.

"Wish I could, really. Merry Christmas, Mom. See you in two weeks. We'll have time to visit then, I promise." Michele kissed Ryder and Kimi on the cheeks and hurried out the door.

Sally glanced at Ben and saw he was watching her. Her heart lightened. His gaze slipped from her head to her shoes and back up again. Slowly. He seemed puzzled by what he saw. Her momentary satisfaction was quickly swallowed by cold reality. He was noticing her *Englisch* clothes with silent disapproval. No, she wasn't the woman for him.

After Sally followed Mrs. Higgins outside, Ben shook his head. How had she changed so much in such a short time?

"Can I go see the horses, now?" Ryder asked.

"After Ben takes your bags to your room," Mrs. McIntyre said. "Do you remember which one it is?"

"I think so. That way, right?" Ryder pointed to the hall leading to the west wing of the house.

"That's right. All the way to the end. Kimi, you and Sally will have the rooms on either side of his."

"Come on, Ben, let's put this stuff away. I want to see the horses." He took off at a run down the hall.

Mrs. McIntyre laughed. "I don't envy Sally trying to keep up with him. He's all go, go, go."

After depositing the luggage in their rooms, Ben followed Ryder outside. Michele was going over a list with Sally. When she saw Ryder, she pushed it into Sally's hands. "You'll figure it out."

"Bye, Mom." Ryder ran past.

"Bye, dear." Michele waved to him. When he was out of earshot, she turned back to Sally. "Make sure the presents are marked from us."

"I will. Have a nice trip."

Michele sighed. "Paris is wonderful, but I do wish they would learn to speak English there. I mean, how hard can it be? You learned Dutch and English."

"Pennsylvania Dutch," Sally replied quietly.

"It's the same difference, isn't it?"

"Almost." Sally's voice slipped lower.

"Pennsylvania Dutch isn't Dutch at all. It's Deitsh, a German dialect," Ben said as he stopped beside them.

Michele curled her lip. "Whatever. Make sure you get everything on the list, Sally."

"Yes, ma'am."

Michele got in the car and sped out of the yard. At least she was allowing the children to visit. Mrs. McIntyre's life hadn't been easy since she lost her husband to cancer. She deserved a chance to share her happy memories with her family and pass on the stories of her youth to her grandkids. She didn't deserve to be ignored.

Ben held out his hand for the bag Sally was clutching. "May I take that in for you?"

"*Nee.* I've got it."

"Don't let the *greilich Frau* get you down."

"She isn't abominable, and shame on you for saying it." Spinning around, Sally marched toward the house. Her thick, gleaming hip-length braid swayed behind her as if it had a life of its own.

He never expected to see her hair down. Even in a braid. An Amish woman did not display her crowning glory to anyone but God and her husband. It was true that Sally hadn't taken her vows of faith yet, but still, it was a disturbing sight, although he wasn't sure why. He'd seen *Englisch* women with their hair down. None of them made his pulse kick up a notch and his chest tighten until it was hard to take a breath.

What would Sally's hair look like unbound? He imagined a riot of fiery red ringlets and curls. It would be beautiful. He shook off the thought and shoved his hands deep in the pockets of his coat. It wasn't right to imagine such things.

At least she wasn't dogging his every move. Yet. What was her game this time? He'd find out sooner or later. He glanced toward the corrals where Ryder was climbing the white-board fence. There was someone he might be able to pump for information.

He sauntered up next to the boy and leaned his arms on the top rail. Inside the enclosure, a black horse with a white star pranced and tossed his head. "This fellow is Wyndham's Fancy. He's put in some impressive times on the track. Your grandmother thinks he'll be her next champion."

"He looks like a champion to me. What kind of horse is he?"

"Your grandmother raises Standardbreds, although we have a few ponies to keep some of the more nervous horses company, and a draft horse, too."

"Can I ride this one?"

"I'm afraid not. Wyn loves to pull a sulky, but he doesn't care to have a rider on his back."

"What's a sulky?"

"It's a two-wheeled cart that's used in horse racing. I'll show you one later."

"Can I see more horses?"

"Come this way." Ben led the excited boy toward

the new stables. The bright red building was trimmed in white. A central corridor divided the long rows of stalls. The place smelled of horses, hay and oiled harnesses. Ben loved it.

He introduced Ryder to a number of his grandmother's prized animals. When they had made the circuit and were at the last stall, the one that held Dandy, the farm's draft horse, Ben said, "I can see you are excited about spending Christmas on the farm. What about your sister?"

"I think it's tight, but Kimi thinks it's jacked."

Ben chuckled. "Could you *shvetza Englisch,* maybe *ja*?"

"What?"

"Talk English."

Ryder grinned. "I think it's great, but Kimi thinks it's terrible. She hates the farm. She would rather go to Paris with Mom and Dad. Or to New York and stay with our other grandmother."

"Was it Sally's suggestion for you to come here?"

"No. She about fell over when I told her. Kimi said Sally didn't want to come because she didn't want to see some guy she knew was here."

Ben perked up. "Are you sure?"

"I think so. Anyway, Mom said Sally had to come because Grandma can't look after us. I'm glad she came. I really like Sally. Better than any of our other nannies. She's cool. She doesn't think I'm stupid like Mom and Dad and Kimi do."

"You seem pretty sharp to me." Why would anyone call this energetic and charming child stupid?

"Sally says I'm brighter than a kerosene lantern at midnight."

Ben ruffled the boy's hair. "That's bright."

"I wish Mom thought I was smart, but I don't do so good in school."

Ben leaned closer. "I didn't do so well in school, either."

"Honest?"

Ben nodded. "Honest."

"Do you think Sally might marry someone who doesn't do well in school? I mean, if he was older. She's really smart."

It was clear the boy was taken with her. Ben tried to keep a straight face. "If Sally is as smart as you say, I reckon she knows there's more to a man than schooling."

Ryder looked up at Ben in relief. "Good."

"Is she dating anyone?" Ben asked, trying to sound casual.

Ryder shrugged his shoulders. "I don't know."

"Ryder, come in and unpack," Sally called from the doorway of the house.

The boy waved at her and turned to Ben. "I'd better go."

Ben nodded and digested the information Ryder had shared as the boy ran toward the house. Maybe Sally had finally come to her senses. Ben hoped and prayed that was the case. Maybe she was happy in the outside world. She was good for Ryder, that was certain.

Did she have an *Englisch* boyfriend? That would explain her rapid change of heart.

It should have cheered him to think Sally was interested in someone else…but for some odd reason it didn't. At least she seemed content to avoid him, and that was what he wanted.

Wasn't it?

* * *

"Are you seriously going to make me ride in a one-horse open sleigh with my pain-in-the-neck brother?" Kimi demanded.

It was early afternoon on the second day of their stay. Sally had managed to avoid Ben after their first meeting but that didn't mean she wasn't thinking about him. She looked out the bedroom window. Ben was already outside getting the sleigh ready for their tree-cutting expedition and the trip to the children's great-grandmother's home. The sky was overcast and it looked as if it could start snowing at any moment.

Sally turned to Kimi and said, "An old-fashioned sleigh ride is fun. Try to enjoy yourself today."

"Old-fashioned is right," Kimi groaned. "Nowadays, we don't think frostbite is fun."

"You won't get frostbite. Not if you dress warmly. Put on extra socks and wear your mittens. Make sure you take a scarf to cover your face. I'll have hot chocolate waiting for you when you get home. How does that sound?"

"Wait. You aren't coming with us? You get to stay here in a warm house and watch TV while poor little Ryder and I are freezing our toes off?"

"Yes."

"That is *so* unfair." Kimi flounced onto the bed.

"What is unfair?" Mrs. McIntyre asked.

Sally turned around. She hadn't heard the wheelchair approaching over the thick carpet. Kimi launched herself off the bed. "It's unfair that Sally doesn't get to join in our fun, Grandma. I know she's dying to come with us today. Tell her it's okay."

Sally shook her head. "I don't care to go along."

Kimi moved to stand beside Sally and slipped an arm

around her waist. "She's just saying that. She doesn't want you to think that she's trying to horn in on our fun, but Sally is practically part of the family. I feel terrible about leaving her here."

"Sally, I never meant to exclude you. By all means, accompany the children.

"*Nee,* I couldn't." Sally disengaged Kimi's clinging arm.

Mrs. McIntyre held up one hand. "It's settled. You are going with them, and I don't want to hear another word about it. I'll call the stable and tell Ben to expect one more on this trip. I know my mother will be delighted to have more company."

Sally's halfhearted smile vanished as Mrs. McIntyre rolled away. A whole afternoon with Ben. This would not be good.

Kimi leaned closer and muttered, "If I have to be miserable, you have to be miserable, too."

Sally looked at her sharply. "Why do you hate me so?"

"I don't hate you. I like you." Kimi smiled, as she waltzed out of the room.

Sally stood staring at the empty doorway. *Please, Lord, let Ryder find his tree quickly.*

Chapter Three

"This is her doing. I know it is."

Ben threw a heavy blanket in the back of the sleigh, still fuming after Trent delivered the last-minute news that Sally was joining them. So much for her change of heart.

Trent stood with his arms crossed. "Look on the bright side. You'll have someone to help you watch the brats."

Ben checked the stash of tools in a box fitted behind the backseat. "Why can't she get that I'm not interested in being her *boo-freind?*"

"Her what?"

"Boyfriend," Ben translated. It was harder to speak English when he was upset.

"Have you told her that?" Trent held out a silver thermos of coffee.

Ben took it and shoved it under the front seat. "Not in so many words, but I've made it clear."

"Apparently not."

Maybe Trent was right. Maybe blunt speaking was required. He'd avoided Sally, ignored her at singings and frolics when the younger crowd from their church got together. He'd told others he wasn't interested in courting her, but he hadn't told Sally to her face. He didn't want to hurt her feelings. He'd always liked her, even after she started running with the wilder crowd. But then she started telling her friends he was The One. He had no idea what caused her obsession with him, but enough was enough. He'd find an opportunity to tell her exactly what he thought of her pointless pursuit today.

He walked around the horse, checking to make sure the harness was secure and hitched properly. Dandy, the only draft horse on the farm, shook his cream-colored mane, making the harness bells jingle gaily. Satisfied, Ben checked over the sleigh. Painted a rich, dark mahogany color with yellow pinstriping, the sleigh was as pretty as they came. The two small bench seats in the interior were upholstered in thick tufted burgundy mohair, a material that was both warm and water resistant. A smaller box on runners had been added to the back to enable the estate staff to haul loads of firewood, bales of hay or other equipment when the roads were impassable. It would easily carry a Christmas tree. The sleigh wasn't Trent's preferred method of travel, but Ben was right at home in one.

Trent glanced at the gray sky. "The forecast is calling for snow."

"It's winter, Trent. It snows in the winter." There was already eight inches on the ground. By the end of March, there could be several feet, if not more. Ben wasn't concerned about a little snow. Dandy could plow through just about anything. Besides, if the *kinder* got cold, they'd want to come home more quickly, and he'd be rid of Sally that much faster.

"They're calling for a major storm. It could miss us, but it may move this way. Don't lollygag. Get a tree, visit Grandma Weaver and get back here. I wish Mrs. McIntyre wasn't so set on sending the kids out to get a tree. I know it's because that's what her husband loved to do, but these kids don't care. With you gone, I'll have to clean the stalls myself."

Ben swept his hand toward the driver's seat. "Say the word and I'll shovel manure while you go for a sleigh ride and a few hours of winter fun."

"Not on your life. I'll clean the stalls. You just get back in time to help me exercise those colts."

"Get going. Get a tree. Visit Granny. Get back. That's my plan."

Ben climbed into the sleigh and drove up to the front door to wait for his passengers. He didn't have to wait long. The front door burst open, and Ryder came flying out. He skidded to a stop when Ben held up one hand. "You can't come without a hat and mittens."

"It's not that cold."

Ben pointed to his own flat-topped, wide-brimmed black felt hat. "It's not that cold…yet. In an hour, you'll be telling a different story. Covering your head will keep you twice as warm as just a coat and that's a fact."

"Ryder, come put your hat and gloves on," Sally called from inside the doorway.

Ryder sighed. "Sally says the same thing. She always makes me button up and put a hat on, even if I'm not cold."

"We're not going anywhere till you are dressed properly." Ben was pleased to hear Sally looked after the boy so well. She had always been good with children.

Ryder charged back the way he'd come. He seemed to have two speeds. Fast and faster.

When he came out a moment later, he had his hat and mittens in his hands. "Can I sit up front with you, Ben?"

"Sure."

"Can I drive? What's your horse's name? Is it a long ways to the trees? How are we going to cut the tree down when we find the perfect one?"

"Put a sock in it," Kimi said as she came out the door and climbed in. "I don't want to listen to your endless questions this whole stupid trip. It was bad enough on the drive here yesterday."

Ryder stuck his tongue out at her, but fell silent. Ben smothered a grin. He had siblings, too. They didn't always get along, although they loved each other dearly. He looked forward to going home and seeing all of them on Christmas Day but Christmas was still a week away.

Sally came out with Mrs. McIntyre, who waved to them all. "Have fun. Give my mother and my brothers all my love."

"We will, Grandma!" Ryder waved wildly.

Sally kept her gaze down as she approached the sleigh. She was dressed in jeans, tall boots and a long black wool coat, the same style as his mother wore. Serviceable and sensible, a good Amish coat. Not like the short brown leather jacket she had on yesterday. She settled a red-and-white stocking cap on her head and wrapped a red-and-white-striped knitted scarf around her neck. The bold colors were not ones an Amish woman would choose.

Her clothes were a contradiction that mirrored Ben's confusion about her. Was she still Amish? Did she intend to return home after her *rumspringa,* or was she determined to become a fancy *Englisch* woman? If that was the case, he had nothing to worry about. As an *Englischer,* she was forbidden to him and she knew it.

Pulling on matching mittens, she paused beside Ben.

"I'm sorry about this. Mrs. McIntyre insisted I join you."

She spoke so softly that he could barely hear her. Was she trying to make him think she hadn't planned this? Should he believe her? He wanted to give her the benefit of the doubt, but he hesitated. He'd never known her to tell an outright lie, but Sally could bend the truth to suit herself. Especially where he was concerned.

After she got settled in the seat behind him, Ben flicked the reins to get Dandy moving. When they were out in an open pasture, he handed the reins to Ryder. With one arm around the boy, he explained how to hold the lines and how to give commands the horse would understand. After making wobbling tracks across the fresh snow for several hundred yards, Ryder began to get the hang of it. It gave Ben a chance to check on the passengers behind him.

A tiny muffled voice shouted, "Text message!" Kimi pulled her phone out of her pocket.

Sally leveled an exasperated stare at her. "You were supposed to leave your phone at the house."

"Ryder is having fun. Why can't I have fun, too?"

"Would you like to take a turn driving Dandy?" Ben asked.

Kimi arched one eyebrow. "That is not fun. Texting my friends is fun."

"Suit yourself, but you're not going to get much reception up in these hills."

"How far are we going?" Sally asked.

"The McIntyre family owns five hundred acres of forest above Carson Lake. It's about three miles as the crow flies. It will take an hour."

"An hour round trip? You've got to be kidding." Kimi looked ready to jump out and walk home.

"An hour there and an hour back," he clarified. "Plus, we have to stop in to see your great-grandmother. That will take at least another hour."

Kimi pointed off to the side. "There's a row of trees. They look great. Cut down one of them and save us two hours."

Ben caught a glimpse of Sally's smile and shared her amusement before he remembered the conversation they needed to have. He couldn't do anything to foster her mistaken impression that he wanted to be her boyfriend. "They have been planted to make a windbreak along the field. I don't think our neighbor would like it if we cut down one that belonged to him."

Ryder looked them over and shook his head. "I'll know the perfect tree when I see it, Kimi. I get to pick. Grandma said so."

"Fine. Just make it quick." She leaned back and snuggled under the blanket.

Sally said, "Relax, Kimi. Enjoy the ride. Your grandmother is right. You'll never forget this experience." There was a wistful, husky quality in her voice that Ben found strangely appealing. Everything about her seemed different, somehow. He glanced back and found her staring at him. She gave him a sad little smile and looked away.

It bothered him to see her sad.

Ben took the reins and pushed Dandy to a faster pace. The sooner they finished this outing, the better.

The ride through the open country was as pretty as Sally could have wished for. The horse carried them along an old logging road that gradually climbed a long ridge of hills. It ran between stands of thick forest with open breaks that afforded breathtakingly beautiful views of the Amish farms spread out across the wide, snow-covered valley below. She couldn't see her father's farm from here, but it was nice to be this close to home. If only Ben wasn't upset with her.

She stared at his broad back and admired the way he handled Ryder and the horse at the same time. He would make a good father someday.

A stab of sorrow shot through her chest. He would be a good father, but she wouldn't be the mother of his children. She forced herself to admire the scenery and not think about the man handling the reins.

A few smaller roads branched off the main track as the road climbed, but they all led deeper into the woods. None of them bore signs of recent travel. After nearly thirty minutes in the sleigh, a lone deer ran across the road in front of them.

"Do you hunt, Ben?" Ryder asked.

"I go hunting with my *daed* and my older brother Adrian every year."

"I didn't think the Amish touched guns," Kimi said in surprise.

Ben glanced back at her. "We do for hunting, but we can never raise a gun against a man."

"But you can shoot someone to protect yourself, can't you?" Ryder asked.

Ben shook his head. "No, never. We must pray for the wrongdoers. Our lives are in God's hands, not in our own."

"The Amish must submit meekly to those who would harm us," Sally said, failing to keep the bitterness out of her tone.

"That's messed up," Kimi said.

"Yes, it is," Sally agreed softly. She kept her eyes on

Ben's back, but he didn't turn around. She wasn't meek and she didn't have to pretend that she was anymore.

It started to snow a short time later. The flakes were small and light and added to the beauty of the ride. Sally relaxed and started enjoying the quiet stillness of the snow-covered woods. The only sounds were the hiss of the sleigh runners gliding over the snow, the jingle of harness bells and Ryder's occasional questions. It was never this quiet in the city.

At last, Ben drew Dandy to a stop. "This is it."

Off to the side of the road stretched a wide-open, gently sloping hillside with hundreds of trees that were only a few years old. Sally realized why Mrs. McIntyre had sent them here. About thirty acres of forest had been clear-cut. The replanted trees, mostly white pine and balsam fir, were just the right size for the Mc-Intyre's great room.

Kimi threw her lap robe on the floor of the sleigh and got out first. She took Ryder by the hand and led him to the closest tree. "This one is perfect. Get your saw."

"No, it's crooked."

"Okay." She led him to another. "This one is straight."

"But it's got a hole in the branches. See?" He ran down the row, stopping every few trees and then running on.

"Don't go far, Ryder," Sally called after him. It wouldn't take much for the energetic boy to get confused in the maze of green.

"I won't."

"Tell me what you do if you get lost," she said.

"I stay put and you'll come get me."

"That's right."

"Or follow your tracks back here if you can't see us,"

Ben said as he got down from his seat. Ryder waved and kept going.

"I should go with them," Sally stood up.

"We need to talk, Sally."

She decided to ignore his comment. She didn't want to talk to him. She just wanted the day to be over. "I'm going to follow the children."

He stepped in front of her to block her way as she tried to rush past him. Her feet tangled in Kimi's lap robe. She tripped and fell headlong out of the sleigh and into Ben's arms. The impact sent him backwards into the snow with Sally on top of him. Stunned, they lay face-to-face, staring at one another.

Chapter Four

Surprised, Ben lay in the snow with Sally clasped to his chest. Her face was inches from his. There were snowflakes caught on the tips of her thick lashes. He stared into her wide, startled eyes. Bright cornflower blue, they had tiny streaks of silver in them. He'd never noticed that before. The freckles scattered across her nose were downright cute. Her lips were parted ever so slightly.

What would it be like to kiss her?

She closed her eyes and his scattered wits returned. What was he thinking? He was not about to kiss Sally Yoder. Ever. She was doing it again. Throwing herself at him. This time literally.

He rolled to the side, depositing her in a fresh drift of snow as he scrambled to his feet. "Stop this foolishness, Sally. I'm not going to date you even if you throw yourself at me all day. If you were the last woman on earth, I'd still think twice about marrying you."

Her wide eyes filled with tears. Her bottom lip quivered pitifully before she bit down on it. Remorse sucked the air from Ben's lungs. He'd gone too far. It wasn't his intention to be hurtful. Sometimes, she brought out the worst in him. He extended a hand to help her up. "I'm sorry."

She blinked furiously and batted his hand away. "I wouldn't marry you, Ben Lapp, if you were the last man on earth and you begged me on bended knee. And I wouldn't have to think twice about it."

Jumping to her feet, she furiously brushed the snow from her clothes. "And I did *not* throw myself at you. I tripped."

"Well, excuse me for jumping to the wrong conclusion, but you've given me plenty of reason to expect such behavior."

Her chin came up as she faced him and blinked away her tears. She took a deep breath and shoved her hands in her coat pockets. "I admit that I may have behaved badly in the past, but I got over that teenage silliness ages ago. If you thought otherwise, that is your mistake."

She pushed past him and moved to stand beside the horse. Staring straight ahead, she said, "I did not want to come to the farm, but I couldn't talk Mrs. Higgins out of it. I *really* did not want to come on this outing today, but Mrs. McIntyre insisted. I'm not here because I'm dying to spend time with you, Ben. The truth is I'm dying to get back to the house. Go help Ryder find a tree so we can put an end to this painful situation."

He sighed. "I didn't say having you here was painful."

She turned around and glared at him. "Frankly, I don't care. It's becoming unbearable for me. Go make sure the *kinder* don't get lost."

He scowled. Now she was going to boss him around? "I thought watching the children was your job?"

"Fine. Stay here and watch the horse, stable boy."

As she stomped away, he could tell she was still fuming by the way she kept her head up. Better to have her mad at him than to have her in tears. He couldn't bear it when a woman cried.

Her forceful steps sent her braid swaying again and drew his attention to the curve of her figure in her jeans. She was an attractive woman, he had to admit that much. Maybe he hadn't noticed it before because he'd spent all his time trying to avoid her.

It wasn't until she vanished from sight behind a curtain of white that he realized how heavy the snow had gotten.

I'm not going to cry. Not over him.

Sally wiped the moisture from her eyes. She got it. He was not now, nor would he ever be, interested in her. Good, because she was done being interested in him.

Although it had felt amazing to be held by him, if only for a moment.

His words hurt, but she forgave him. She'd made a nuisance of herself in the past. She could hardly blame him for assuming she was up to her old tricks. This was exactly like something she would have done last year. Before she realized how much she cared for him. Before she realized her behavior might be hurting him.

Was he seeing someone now that she was out of his life? He hadn't mentioned that.

No, he just said he wouldn't marry her if she were the last woman on earth. Well, that was good because she wasn't staying Amish. She was a free woman who would control her own fate. She didn't need a husband.

She saw the children just ahead of her. She sniffed once more and composed herself. If she concentrated on her job, she wouldn't have time to think about Ben.

She was being paid to take care of the children. She called out, "Have you found the tree you want, Ryder?"

"Maybe. What do you think of this one?"

She came to stand beside him and give the fir due consideration. "It's nice, but since I have never had a Christmas tree before, it would be better to ask your sister what she thinks."

"It's fine." Kimi said with her shoulders hunched against the cold.

"You think they're all fine." He walked around the tree looking it over carefully.

Kimi held out her phone and snapped a picture. "If it will make you feel better, I'll ask my friends what they think. I'm posting this to my social media sites."

A few moments later, she held the phone out so he could read the text. "Jen says it's the prettiest tree she has ever seen. And you know she has great taste. Her mother is an interior designer."

Sally wasn't quite sure what an interior designer was, but it seemed to satisfy Ryder. "Okay, this one it is."

"Goot," Ben said, coming up behind Sally. She took a step to the side, crossed her arms and stared at her feet. She was afraid of what he might see in her eyes. He ignored her and handed Ryder a small saw. "Trim away the lowest branches while I get the chain saw."

Ryder started working with enthusiasm, but he had only one limb severed by the time Ben returned. Motioning for Ryder to stand back, Ben gave a quick pull of the starter rope. The chain saw roared to life and the stillness of the snow-covered woods was replaced by the whine of the blade slicing through the wood. The smell of fresh-cut pine scented the air, along with gasoline fumes.

Sally felt a moment of sadness for the small tree as

it toppled. "It seems sad to cut down a perfectly good tree."

"Why?" Ryder asked.

"Because birds will never nest in its branches. It will never tower above the landscape. It won't supply fuel to heat a family's home or be used as lumber to build something useful."

Sally noticed Ben was staring at her with an odd expression and she fell silent. A blush heated her cheeks. Would it be this way forever when she was around him? Would she always be so intensely aware of him? If so, it was a good thing she lived in the city now.

"The tree is being useful," Ryder declared. "It will remind us that it's Christmas and there will be lots of presents under it." He looked up at Ben. "Where do the Amish put their presents if they don't have a tree?"

"My parents put a present for each *kinder* on their plate at the kitchen table on Christmas morning."

Ryder's eyes widened in shock. "Only one present?"

Ben smiled at him. "Sometimes two. Nuts and candy, too. For us, Christmas isn't about getting gifts and such fancy stuff. It's about remembering our Savior's birth. He is God's greatest gift to us."

"Sally says the same thing," Kimi said.

"Does she?" Ben asked quietly.

Sally glanced his way and found him watching her with a soft look in his eyes that made her stomach do flip-flops. How was she going to get over him when he looked at her like that? "Just because I chose to live in the city doesn't mean I have forgotten the important things in life."

"I'm glad."

"Can we go now?" Kimi shifted from one foot to the other.

For once, Sally concurred with the girl's impatient attitude. The sooner they got back to the farm the better. Hopefully, today would be the last day she would have to spend in Ben's company.

"*Ja,* we should get going," Ben said as he took hold of the tree trunk.

"Finally." Kimi rushed toward the sleigh.

Sally should have followed her, but she found herself asking, "Do you need help, Ben?"

"*Nee.* Ryder and I can manage, can't we?"

"We sure can." The boy's chest puffed out and he grabbed the back end of the tree.

Sally followed the pair, noticing the way Ben shortened his long stride to allow Ryder to keep up with him. Kimi was already at the sleigh, brushing the accumulated snow off her spot in the backseat when they arrived. She plopped down and pulled the lap robe up to her chin. Sally cleaned off her spot and then the front seat while Ben and Ryder secured the tree.

"*Danki,*" Ben said as she finished. Sally took her place in the backseat.

"What does *danki* mean?" Ryder asked as he climbed up beside Ben.

"It means *thank you* in Pennsylvania Dutch," Ben picked up the reins and turned the horse toward Granny Weaver's home.

"*Danki.*" Ryder repeated the word. "How do you say horse?"

"*Gual,*" Ben replied. "Or if you have a horse in harness, like Dandy is, you could say, *fuah. Mie gual* or *mie fuah.* My horse or my harnessed horse."

Ryder repeated the words and then asked, "How do you say grandmother?"

"*Grossmammi.*"

"How do I say I'm having a wonderful time?"

"Are you?" Ben grinned at him.

"I sure am."

"Then wonderful is *wunderbarr.*"

Kimi kicked the back of the seat in front of her. "Enough with the questions, Ryder."

The boy leaned close to Ben. "How do you say my sister is a pain?"

Sally smothered a laugh at Kimi's outraged expression.

Ryder continued to quiz Ben about names for different things as they made their way down from the hills. He answered the boy patiently and even let him drive again. The snow continued to fall heavily. Sally noted with concern that the tracks they had made on the way up were almost completely filled in.

"I'm getting kinda cold," Ryder said from the front seat.

Ben pulled the horse to a stop. "Why don't you get in the back and get under the blanket with your sister. That way you'll be out of the wind."

Ryder jumped out and wedged himself into the back-seat beside Sally. He pulled the blanket his way and uncovered his sister in the process.

"There's not enough room back here for him," Kimi complained. She yanked the lap robe back and held on to it as she glared at him.

"But I'm cold," he wailed.

His teeth were beginning to chatter, but Kimi was right. The sleigh was built to carry two people in front and two in back. It wouldn't hold three of them comfortably, even though Ryder was small. Sally got up and let him have her place. He scooted close to his sister. Sally tucked them both in. Kimi lifted the corner of the lap robe and covered his head. "Is that better?"

"Much. Thanks, sissy," came his muffled reply.

"Whatever," Kimi shot back, but her usual sarcasm was missing. Sally knew Kimi did care about her brother, though she tried to hide the fact. It was a rare moment when she let her affection show.

Once Sally had the children settled, that left her with only one place to sit. Beside Ben.

Would he blame her for this situation, too? Perhaps she should suggest that Kimi ride up front. She glanced at the children. She doubted Kimi would agree. Both children were cold and tired. And they weren't getting any warmer while she stood there staring at the empty space on the front seat.

Ben jerked his head toward the spot beside him. "Come on, get in. I won't bite."

She hesitated for a second, then quickly climbed in. "I'm more worried about being growled at."

"I won't growl, either. I'm sorry I barked at you earlier. Am I forgiven?"

"I reckon."

"Goot." He flicked the reins to get Dandy moving.

Sally tried to stay as far away from Ben as she could on the narrow seat, but the track was rough. The jolting ride caused her shoulder to bump against his frequently. Each time, she jerked away from him and muttered, "Sorry."

He finally put his foot on the dash to brace himself against the rough going. "Relax. I'm not growling."

"Yet." She pitched into him again.

"Yet," he admitted, but the touch of humor in his tone made her feel better. Ben really was a kind fellow. It took a lot for him to lose his temper. She looked back and saw the children huddled together under the heavy cover. At least they weren't complaining.

Sally glanced at Ben's profile as he concentrated on driving. His hat was pulled low on his brow and his scarf was up over his chin, but she knew how handsome he was beneath the layer of wool. Some girl would be blessed when he set his sights on her.

Some girl, but not her.

She struggled to ignore the twist of pain in her chest. Would she have stood a chance with him if she hadn't behaved so foolishly?

At the time, pretending to be smitten with him had seemed like an easy way to keep other young men from trying to court her and to keep her parents and friends unaware of her struggles with her faith and her self-worth. Behind her bright smiles, endless questions and outspoken ways hid a frightened and confused young woman.

It hadn't always been that way. One horrible night, two *Englisch* men had changed everything. Changed her. Maybe if she had found the courage to confide in someone about what had happened, things would be different, but she had never told anyone.

"What?" Ben asked.

Jerked back to the present, Sally shook her head. "Nothing. Why?"

"You're staring at me."

"Sorry. I was lost in thought." She redirected her gaze to the horse. Dandy's breath rose in white frosty puffs as he trotted through the falling snow. He seemed eager to reach the warmth of the stable and the ration of oats that would undoubtedly be waiting for him. She should be as eager to see this day done, but suddenly she wasn't. Would this be the last time she got to sit beside Ben?

The wind picked up when they finally left the sheltering woods. The road was all but obscured in places where the drifts were creeping in from the fields. Ben drew the horse to a stop at an intersection of two rural roads. Sally sensed his indecision. She asked, "How much farther is it to Granny Weaver's place?"

"Half a mile, give or take."

"The weather is getting worse. Do you think we should go back to the farm instead of going on to see her?"

"I've been thinking about that, but she's expecting the children. I would hate to disappoint her. Besides, if we don't show up, she'll be worried. It's almost two miles to the McIntyre farm from here. All of us could use a warm-up before we head that way."

"I guess you're right."

"We won't stay long. Dandy can get us home through more snow than this. There's no need to worry."

It wasn't the snow that worried her; it was the wind. Even the big horse would have trouble lumbering through heavy snowdrifts if it got much worse. "All right. I trust your judgment."

Ben turned north and urged Dandy onward. The cold wind in her face made Sally pull her scarf higher on her cheeks and wish she could huddle close to Ben for warmth.

Wouldn't he hate that? It was better to freeze alone. She kept her eyes closed and her head down. She would turn into a block of ice before she asked Ben Lapp for a favor after today. Suddenly, Dandy stumbled and fell. The sleigh tipped forward as it jerked to a stop. Sally was thrown from her seat. She put her hands out, but knew they wouldn't protect her from the horse's huge thrashing hooves as he struggled to get up.

Her flight was cut short when she was jerked backward. It took her a second to realize Ben had grabbed her coat, saving her. She heard the children yelling in confusion but not in pain. Dandy recovered his footing and stood but took only two limping steps before he stopped.

Ben pulled Sally back onto the seat and held on to her. "That was too close. Are you okay?"

She clung tight to his arm. She took several gasping breaths before she managed to nod. "*Ja.* You?"

He studied her intently. "I'm fine. You have blood on your mouth."

She pressed a finger to her mouth. "I think I bit my lip."

"Let me see?" He put a hand beneath her chin and carefully examined her face. She could feel his fingers trembling, even through his gloves. She was trembling, too.

"What was that?" Ryder stuck his head out from beneath the blanket in the back.

Sally pulled away from Ben and turned to the children. "The horse fell. Are you kids okay?"

"Hello! I'm on the floor! Get off me, Ryder!" Kimi's muffled shout reassured Sally.

Ryder grinned. "She's okay. Her phone didn't break." Kimi surged to her feet with the device in her hand as proof and sat back with a huff.

Ben jumped out of the sleigh without looking at Sally. "I need to check on Dandy."

As he trudged forward, Sally realized she missed his strong arms around her. She needed comforting after her fright, but of course the horse was his main concern. He probably thought she would see his quick-thinking action as proof that he had feelings for her. She knew better.

If she wanted to be a strong, independent woman, she needed to start acting like one.

Ben lifted the horse's left front leg. When he put the animal's foot down, Dandy refused to put weight on it. He stood holding the leg off the ground with his head hanging low. Sally got down and joined Ben.

Snow swirled around them, leaving them in a white cocoon. They could have been alone in the world for all she could see of the countryside, but they weren't alone. They had two children in their care.

She stared at Ben's worried face. If Dandy's leg was broken, the patient animal would have to be destroyed. She didn't want the children to know it was a possibility. She kept her voice low. "How bad is it?

Chapter Five

Checking on Dandy gave Ben something to do as he willed his racing heart to slow and waited for his composure to return. He kept seeing Sally flying over the front of the sleigh and falling beneath the horse's flailing hooves. If he hadn't had his foot on the dash, if he'd lost his own balance, if he hadn't been quick enough… it could have happened.

God had been with him in that moment as surely as the snow was falling around him now. By His mercy alone, Sally had been spared a frightful fall…perhaps worse. Ben's heart thudded painfully at the thought. He glanced at her worried face. "Are you sure you're okay?"

Sally nodded. She pressed her hand to her chest and let out a deep sigh. "I thank God Ryder wasn't in the front seat."

"Amen to that. *Gott es goot.*"

"*Ja,* God is good. Ryder's first sleigh ride could have turned into a tragedy. I'm relieved to see he wasn't too scared by this. He's a very sensitive boy. Please tell me Dandy is going to be okay."

She was pale as the snow in the field around them,

but she was thinking about the children and his horse and not her own close call. Sally Yoder was made of sterner stuff than Ben had suspected. Her time away had been good for her. Or maybe being in charge of the children had matured her.

Whatever the reason, she had changed for the better. He couldn't sugarcoat their situation, although he wanted to spare her further worry. They had two children to keep safe, as well as his employer's injured horse to look after.

He should have turned for the farm when he had the chance. Now it was too far for Dandy to travel. They were stranded in open country in a snowstorm. Mrs. McIntyre had put her faith in him and entrusted him with the children. He would do whatever it took to get them back to her safe and sound.

He patted the big horse's neck. "I hope it's only a sprain and nothing worse, but I can't be sure. He must have slipped on some ice under the snow."

"Can he pull the sleigh with us in it?" Sally asked.

Ben shook his head. "I'll not ask him to do that. I don't want to make his injury worse."

Sally peered down the deserted road in both directions. "Should I stay here with the children while you go get help, or do you think we should walk?"

"The *kinder* will be warmer walking. It's less than half a mile to the Weaver farm. There's nothing closer."

Sally glanced at her charges. "I don't think they've walked that far in their lives, unless it was at the mall."

"They can make it. We'll leave the sleigh here. I'll come back with one of Granny Weaver's horses to pick it up and then take us home. Trust me. That's our best option."

She licked her lower lip and winced. Pressing a hand

to her mouth, she said, "I trusted your judgment ten minutes ago and look where that got us."

"That's hardly fair, Sally. The horse could have fallen anywhere."

Remorse filled her eyes. "I'm sorry, Ben. I shouldn't berate you when you just saved me from a nasty fall. I'm still a little shaken. I'll explain to the children what we need to do while you unhitch Dandy." She walked back to the sleigh.

She wasn't fawning over him for saving her the way he expected. A few months ago, she would have gone on and on about how strong he was and how much she admired his quick thinking. Maybe she was telling the truth when she said she was over him. He wasn't quite sure why that idea bothered him.

He set about freeing Dandy and listened to Kimi's rant at Sally about incompetent drivers and stupid horses. When Ben heard her say that she was calling a cab, he almost laughed. Sally took a step back from the sleigh. "Please, do call a cab for us."

"I will. What's our address?" Kimi held her phone higher, turning it one way and then the other.

"Somewhere near the middle of nowhere," Ben said.

Kimi scowled at him. "That's not funny."

Sally held her arms wide, "Look around, Kimi. Do you see a street sign?"

"I can't get a signal anyway."

Sally stepped back to her side. "Then we should get going before we all freeze to death."

Kimi stuffed her phone in her pocket. "I'll wait here for someone to come get us. I'm not walking."

Sally slipped an arm around her shoulder. "You will walk. I'm not leaving you here. If I have to be miserable, you have to be miserable. Maybe the good Lord is just giving you what you asked for."

"I didn't think it would be this bad."

"Everything will be fine when we reach your great-grandmother's house. Ben will get another horse and take us back to your grandmother's farm."

Ryder said, "Come on, Kimi. I'm getting hungry."

"Oh, fine. Let's go."

Ryder grinned. He was up for a new adventure. He walked beside Ben through the knee-deep snow without complaint. Sally was not so blessed by her companion. Kimi's tirade ran the gamut of complaints about the cold to assurances that her father would see both Sally and Ben fired for getting them into this situation in the first place. After a quarter of a mile, the physical exertion finally got the better of her and she fell silent. Unfortunately, her brother began to lag, too. Ben briefly considered putting the boy on the horse, but knew the animal's uneven gait and broad back would make it difficult for the child to hang on.

"Ryder, would you like a piggyback ride?" Sally asked.

"I guess." He looked uncertain.

She crouched so that he could wrap his arms and legs around her. Ben said, "I can take him."

Sally stood upright and shifted the boy to a more comfortable position. "When I get tired, you can carry him."

He nodded and looked at Kimi. "Are you doing okay?"

"Not really. I'm cold. I'm tired. I can't feel my toes or my nose." She had her mittens pressed to her face.

"Stomp your feet to get the circulation going," he suggested.

She tried it briefly but stopped. "It's not helping."

Sally tried to encourage her. "We are almost there, Kimi. Think how amazed your friends will be when you tell them about this vacation."

"I doubt they'll believe me, but I know one thing. This is the last time I will ever ride in a one-horse open sleigh. I'll never even sing that stupid song again."

Ben tried to make it easier going for them. He trudged ahead of them so that he and the horse could tramp a path through the snow. He was amazed at how quickly the white stuff was piling up. If it hadn't been for the mailbox at the end of the lane, he might have missed the turn altogether. He could barely see a dozen yards in front of them. Dandy limped gamely along, but Ben could tell he was struggling. If the big horse went down, Ben knew there was little he could do to save the animal.

He glanced back to make sure Sally and the children were keeping up. Sally's breath was coming in quick gasps. He stopped. "Are you ready for me to take him?"

She shook her head. "*Nee,* your bigger boots are breaking trail better than I could."

"Are you saying I have big feet?"

Her smile was halfhearted. "Keep walking."

If she was trying to impress him, she was doing a good job. Much better than in the past. Her flighty ways usually annoyed him, but she was serious and determined today.

"I see a house," Kimi shouted.

Ben turned to look down the lane. The outline of the white farmhouse and red barn could be seen just up ahead. Everyone surged forward with renewed energy.

Sally put Ryder down when they reached the porch.

He stomped up the steps ahead of Sally and his sister. "We made it."

"We did. God was looking after us," Sally said.

Ben gazed at her tired face and said, "I'm going to put Dandy in the barn. I'll be in as soon as I can. You did well. The children are blessed to have you looking after them."

Speechless, Sally stared at Ben's back as he walked away. Had he just given her a compliment? That was something she never thought would cross his lips. Wouldn't it be wonderful to hear more such things from him?

She gave herself a quick mental shake. No, it wouldn't, because when he was nice it made it harder to ignore him. The sooner they got back to the McIntyre farm, the sooner she could shut herself away and never spend time with Ben again. She quickly hustled the children across the porch and through the front door.

Just to be out of the wind was a blessed relief. Sally's teeth were chattering as she helped the children out of their wet coats and mittens and led them to the kitchen stove. Nothing had ever felt better than the warmth radiating from the large black kitchen appliance.

"Thank goodness you are finally here."

Sally turned to see a diminutive Amish woman wrapped in a huge black shawl enter the room. Her cheery round face was wreathed with wrinkles and a welcoming smile. She had thin, wispy gray hair parted in the middle and drawn back beneath her black *kapp*. Her sharp dark eyes belied her age. At the moment, they sparkled with delight.

"Good day, Mrs. Weaver. My name is Sally Yoder. I have brought your great-grandchildren for a visit. Your daughter sends her love to you and her brothers and their families."

"It's such a pity that Velda is laid up. I would love to see her. I must get over there when the weather clears, although my old bones are telling me we're in for a stretch of cold. And it's a pity that my sons are gone today, too. They and their wives went into Hope Springs this morning. My daughters-in-law had some Christmas shopping to finish. I expected them back before now, but perhaps the weather has delayed them. They said they might stay over with their cousins in town so I wasn't to worry."

"The roads are starting to drift. It's possible they won't get back tonight," Sally said. The children paid little attention to their great-grandmother. They were huddled close to the stove and holding their hands over it to soak in the warmth.

Sally quickly added, "Don't touch the stove, children. Everything on a wood burning stove is very hot."

Mrs. Weaver nodded and smiled at her. "You must be the *kinder heedah* Velda told me about? I'm so glad you have brought them here. Children, let me look at you. Now, you can't possibly be Ryder, for he is only a tiny baby."

Ryder stood straight and tall. "I'm not a baby. I'm eight years old."

"Where has the time gone? I see you have grown like a weed while I wasn't looking. And this pretty *maydel* is Kimi. I would know you anywhere for you look like your mother. Do you remember me?"

"Sort of. I think I met you at Grandpa McIntyre's funeral."

"*Ja,* that's right. My name is Constance, but everyone calls me Granny."

Kimi looked around and then shot Sally a sour look. "You told us there wasn't any electricity in Amish homes."

"There isn't."

"I see lights. I see a refrigerator."

Granny gave her an indulgent smile. "My lights and icebox run on propane, but we burn wood in the stoves."

Kimi frowned. "What's propane?"

"A form of gas. Like your father uses on his outdoor grill," Sally said.

Granny Weaver motioned to the children. "Come into the living room and sit down. The stove in there keeps it very warm."

Adjacent to the kitchen, the large living room contained four recliners in various dark colors, a blue sofa with a blue-and-white crocheted blanket over the arm, a glass-fronted china cupboard, a tall bookcase filled with books and a foot treadle–operated sewing machine in front of a large window. A small black cast-iron stove sat on a brick base near the back wall and radiated blessed warmth.

"What's a *kinder heedah?*" Ryder asked.

Mrs. Weaver frowned. "Let me think."

"A nanny," Sally answered.

"*Ja,* I could not remember the *Englisch* word. How was your trip in the sleigh? Did you enjoy it?"

"No!" Kimi said.

"I liked it," Ryder said. "Ben let me drive part of the way and I found a perfect Christmas tree."

"Then the horse tripped and we had to walk forever." Kimi dropped onto the sofa with a scowl.

"It was only half a mile," Ryder rolled his eyes.

Kimi shot him a derisive look. "You weren't walking. Sally was carrying you."

Granny's eyebrows rose over the top of her wire-rimmed glasses as she turned to Sally. "You carried the boy that far?"

Sally made light of her deed. "The snow was too deep for him and Ben had his hands full trying to keep our horse moving. The poor thing's foreleg was injured when he fell. Ben is putting him up in your barn. I hope that's okay. He may be here for a few days."

"Your Ben is free to use anything he needs. There is plenty of hay and oats. You *kinder* must be chilled to the bone. Let me get you something to eat and something hot to drink. How about some peppermint hot chocolate with marshmallow cream and poppy seed bread with butter?"

Ryder's eyes grew round. "Sounds *wunderbarr, grossmammi.*"

Mrs. Weaver chuckled. "Someone has been teaching you Pennsylvania Dutch. Was it Sally?"

"Ben taught him a couple of words so he's acting like hot stuff. You're not as smart as you think, Ryder."

"Kimi," Sally cautioned her with a stern look.

"What? He's not." She pulled her phone out of her pocket and sat up. "Finally, a signal."

Sally said, "I'm going to see if Ben needs anything." He should have come in by now and she was worried.

Granny Weaver began to bustle about in the kitchen. "You must tell me what you've been doing. Ryder, how do you like school?"

Sally collected Kimi's and Ryder's clothing and hung the coats over the backs of the kitchen chairs. She arranged them, along with the hats and mittens, around the stove so that they would dry before they left. She slipped her coat on again and went out. The snow was blowing sideways in the gusty wind.

She crossed the farmyard to the barn that was only a hundred feet from the house. The drifts were three feet high around the corners of the building and nearly covered a pair of low evergreens growing next to the walls. Pulling open the barn door, she stepped into the dark interior and waited for her eyes to adjust to the dim light. She saw a glow coming from one of the stalls toward the back and went toward it. She passed several stalls. Most were empty. One contained a black mare that looked as old as Granny Weaver. The next held a brown-and-white milk cow. Another held two brown goats that stood on their hind legs to get a better view of her. Overhead, she heard the clucking of chickens in the loft.

Inside the last stall, Ben was wrapping a length of cloth around Dandy's leg by the light of a battery operated lantern. The big horse turned his head toward her and whinnied.

"How is he?" she asked.

"It's too soon to tell. If it's an injury to the ligament, it could be serious. For now, all I can do is ice it several times a day and keep it wrapped for support."

Sally glanced around. "I only noticed one other horse."

Ben stood and patted Dandy's neck. "Mrs. Weaver doesn't live alone. Where is everyone?"

"Her family went into Hope Springs this morning and haven't returned."

"The black mare down there is too old and too small to pull the sleigh through this snow. Unless there is another horse on the property, we may be stuck."

"We can't be stuck." She stared at him in shock.

"Believe me. I'm even less eager than you are to spend the night here."

"I doubt that. We have to get the children home. I'm responsible for them." She did not want to spend time with Ben in the close quarters of the old farmhouse. She kicked a corncob across the dirt floor.

"I'm responsible for them, too. I know I got us into this. I'll get us out. I'll walk back to the farm and bring a team out to fetch you and the children. It should only take a couple of hours."

She rubbed her hands up and down her arms as she listened to the sound of the rising wind. "You don't have to hike."

One side of his mouth lifted slightly. "I can't very well fly."

His teasing tone was almost her undoing. She looked around for another corncob to kick before she blurted out how much she adored his smile. "We can use Kimi's phone to call Mrs. McIntyre and tell her what's happened and then wait here until Trent arrives with another horse."

Ben thought it over and nodded. "That's smart thinking. I forgot about Kimi's phone."

"You've had a lot on your mind. The children are safe now. You take care of Dandy and I'll go make the call. Come inside and warm up when you're done here." She turned away.

"Sally," he called out.

She stopped but didn't look at him. "What?"

"I'm sorry if I misjudged your motives in coming along today. You've been a great help. I'm not sure how I would have managed without you."

"It's good of you to say so." She kept her voice flat. She hated it when he was being nice to her. It was easier to keep her distance when he was angry.

"When I'm wrong, I admit it, Sally." He paused for a

long moment and then said, "Maybe we can start over and be friends."

Sally closed her eyes. She could never settle for friendship when she wanted so much more from him. The only way to get over him was to make a clean break. She knew that, but the crumb of affection he offered made it painful to say what needed to be said. "*Nee,* Ben. I don't think that's possible."

She started to leave, but the outside door opened and Mrs. Weaver came into the barn. She held a flashlight and a wire basket. "Ben, it's nice to meet you. You can call me Granny. I need to feed my chickens and the goats."

"Granny, do you have another horse I can borrow?"

"*Nee,* my Nellie is the only one here. My sons have the other horses. Nellie is getting a bit long in the tooth, but I can't bear to part with her. She has pulled my cart for twenty years. How is your horse?"

Ben left the stall and stopped beside Sally. "Dandy will be better for some rest. It took a lot out of him to hobble so far in the snow."

"It took a lot out of all of you. I had Kimi call Velda for me. I explained to her that you would be staying with me. She was happy to know all of you are safe. She'll send someone to fetch you when the weather breaks."

Sally crossed her arms and glanced his way. He shoved his hands in the pockets of his coat. "I reckon we can spend one night here."

"Might be more than that," Mrs. Weaver said cheerfully. "Velda said the weatherman is predicting a mighty blizzard. Could last three or four days. I knew we were in for a bad spell. My old bones have been aching something fierce. I can't tell you how happy I am that God sent you and the children to stay with me. What a blessing it is with my family gone. It will be just like a frolic, like an early Christmas party. We'll have a fine time together." She chuckled and turned to climb the steep stairs leading to the loft.

Had Granny said three or four days? This couldn't be happening, Sally thought, feeling the edge of panic creeping over her. How could she spend that much time with Ben and keep her feelings hidden? She had to find a way. She rushed toward the barn door and out into the snow.

Chapter Six

Ben stared at the barn door banging open and shut in the wind. Sally hadn't bothered to latch it in her haste to get away from him.

She'd said she couldn't be friends with him. What did that mean?

He had spoken roughly to her earlier that day, but she said he was forgiven. So why turn his offer of friendship down flat? Was she angry at him about something else? What had he done? He had complained bitterly about her to Trent, but she couldn't possibly know that.

He rubbed the ache in the back of his neck. He didn't understand why Sally pursued him in the past, and he didn't understand why she refused his friendship now.

If there was one thing that Sally Yoder could do well, it was confuse him.

"I like that young woman."

Ben looked up to see Granny Weaver coming down from the loft. She held a basket of eggs hooked over her arm.

"Sally is nice enough."

When Granny had both feet on the ground, she turned to him with a smile. "I know her family. They are good people. I hope she finds her way back to them. I pray that is God's will for her."

"I do, too." Ben took a pitchfork and tossed some hay in with the horse and milk cow. "What other chores do you need done?"

"If you will see that all the animals have water, they won't need anything else out here until morning. I like to gather the eggs a few times a day so they don't freeze while the hens are off the nests. I don't mind telling you that I'm happy to give over the chores to you. My old bones don't like going out in the cold."

"I'll take over the care of the animals. It's the least I can do in exchange for Dandy's room and board. He's a big eater." Ben went around to all the stalls and checked on each animal's water supply. He had to break the ice open on the tub for the cow, but the others had only a skimming of ice around the edges. By morning, they would all need to be chopped open.

Granny came out of the goat's stall. "I hear the wind howling like a wolf. It makes me happy the Lord has seen fit to give me a sound house to cover me and a good stove to keep me warm."

Ben took the eggs from her and followed her to the house, making sure the elderly woman made it across the yard without falling. Inside, Ryder was seated at the kitchen table. He had a white mug clasped between his hands and a chocolate mustache on his upper lip. A second mug with inviting steam rising above the rim sat across from him. Ben looked around but didn't see Kimi or Sally.

Mrs. Weaver hung up her coat. "I will take those eggs now. I have a lot of cooking to do. Christmas is just around the corner. I have gift baskets to make for a few of my *Englisch* friends and for a couple of elderly widows in my church. And I have a cookie exchange to get ready for. That cup of chocolate is for you. Get warmed up. I know you must be chilled."

He was. He crossed the kitchen to stand beside the stove and snagged the mug from the table on his way. After taking a sip, he let the warmth spread through his body and savored the rich sweet peppermint chocolate combination. "Ryder, where's your sister?" he asked.

"Pouting."

Granny Weaver looked surprised. "Pouting? Whatever for?"

"She's unhappy because we won't be back in time to watch her favorite TV show tonight. She's upstairs in one of the bedrooms."

"I reckon I will have to keep her busy so she doesn't get bored," Granny said with a wink for Ben.

Ryder licked his chocolate-covered lips. "What can I do?"

"I have a chore for you boys. I need a large bowl of pecans shelled. Can you do that?"

Looking perplexed, Ryder shifted his gaze to Ben. "Can we do that?"

"It's easy. I'll show you how it's done."

Grandma Weaver fisted her hands on her ample hips. "Do you mean to tell me that you have never cracked pecans?"

Ryder shook his head. Ben said, "The trick is not to eat them all."

"I'll be back in a minute." Granny took a large wooden bowl from the shelf, opened the door at the far end of the kitchen and went down into the cellar.

"Where's Sally?" Ben had already noticed her coat hanging by the door so he knew she had come in.

"She went upstairs to try to tease my sister into a better mood."

Ben thought of Kimi's stubborn, uncooperative actions earlier. "Does it work?"

"Sometimes. Sally is better at it than anyone."

"Maybe because they're birds of a feather."

Ryder tipped his head. "Huh?"

"Because they are a lot alike."

"Sally doesn't get into bad moods. She's almost always happy except when she gets a letter from home. Then she gets sad. She misses her home a lot."

Ben glanced toward the stairwell. "Maybe she will return there someday."

"I hope not. Sally's my friend and I would miss her."

So, Sally could be friends with this *Englisch* boy, but she wouldn't be friends with him. Ben was determined to find out why.

"I'm not going downstairs, and that's final." Kimi pulled the blue-and-white quilt over her head and leaned against the headboard. She would soon run out of air beneath the heavy fabric, so Sally folded her arms and waited.

The upstairs bedroom was chilly, even with the warm air rising from the kitchen below. Lacy frost coated the windowpanes, obscuring the view. Even if she could look out, Sally knew there wasn't much to see. Just a lot of blowing snow that was trapping her in the same house with Ben. Sitting upstairs in a cold bedroom had seemed like her only option to avoid Ben, but she realized she was being foolish.

Since God seemed determined to force them together, Sally had to ask herself why. What was His purpose in doing so?

Maybe it was time for her to confess her foolish past behavior and ask Ben's forgiveness. She had used him. In doing so, she had compromised her own integrity. She cringed at the idea of explaining why she had pretended to be head over heels for him, but if she had that embarrassing confession off her chest, perhaps it would be easier to deal with her current feelings.

Easier, but not easy.

Ben confused her. He made her feel breathless and frightened, yet wonderfully excited all at the same time. She wanted to be wrapped up in his arms the way Kimi was wrapped in Granny's quilt.

This wasn't what Sally imagined love would be like, so maybe it wasn't truly love. Maybe it was the kind of wild infatuation that would burn out in a few months, rather than the steady, gentle love shared by her parents for thirty years. Maybe if she allowed herself to know Ben better, she would see that he wasn't the ideal fellow she imagined.

If she told him the truth about her charade, he certainly wouldn't want to be friends with her.

Kimi flipped the quilt down. "It's too cold to be out from under these quilts, but I can't breathe under them."

Sally tucked her chilled fingers under her armpits. "Welcome to Amish living."

"Why can't the bedrooms be heated?"

"Our parents and grandparents lived like this. We value the old ways."

"Would it kill anyone to have an electric blanket?"

Sally ignored Kimi's question when she heard the sound of Ryder's and Ben's laughter below.

"Everyone is gathered downstairs. Ben and Ryder are doing something together with Granny. It might be work, but they are doing it together and having fun. Do you hear Ryder laughing? You are missing out. How many times will you miss out on what he does before he's grown? How will he remember his sister? As someone who laughed and worked beside him? Or as someone he only saw occasionally? Amish children know and love their brothers and sisters well. Oh, we fight and make up like all people do, but we spend time together as a family. It's very important to us."

Kimi pulled the covers to her chin. "Spending time with Ryder won't fix what's wrong with our family."

"Maybe not, but I guarantee that it would make him happy. You might find spending time with Ryder makes you happy, too."

"I doubt it."

"I'm going downstairs. I want to see what is making your brother laugh."

Kimi's phone giggled and shouted, "Text message." She pulled it out from beneath the covers. "Fine. Leave me up here to freeze all by myself. At least my friends want to talk to me. You just want to spend time with Ben."

"You should turn your phone off and conserve your battery. We don't have any way to charge it and we might need it. We don't have any idea how long we will be here."

"Whatever." She began typing a new message.

Sally shook her head sadly and admitted defeat. Down in the kitchen, she saw Ryder and Ben were cracking nuts. A piece of shell flew out of Ryder's nutcracker and landed in Ben's hair. Ryder dissolved in a fit of giggles. Ben removed the offending piece and dropped it in the trash can beside the table.

"I wondered what was so funny down here." Sally crossed to the table.

Ryder sat up straight. "Where is Kimi?"

"Texting."

"She should do this. It's fun." He squeezed a pecan between the jaws of a handheld nutcracker. The face he made while he was trying to exert enough force to break the shell made her turn away to keep from laughing. Ben had no such trouble. He laughed outright, which reminded her how much she loved his laugh. And his smile. And his kind eyes. Everything about him.

He operated a lever-action nutcracker mounted to a short board. He was able to crack five nuts before Ryder managed to split his. Once it broke open, Ryder promptly picked away the shell and ate the meat.

Sally grinned at him. "Are these for snacking or did Granny want some for cooking?"

"Both," Granny said from her place at the stove. She was smiling as she stirred something in a large pot.

Ben pushed an extra handheld nutcracker across the table toward Sally. "Want to help?"

"Come on, Sally, it's fun." Ryder gave her a big smile.

"I reckon I can crack more than you can. I know I won't eat as many." She took a seat across from Ryder and tried not to look at Ben. He was watching her. She could feel his eyes on her. She wished she were dressed Amish. It didn't feel right to be wearing jeans at an Amish table. It didn't feel right to have her head uncovered.

She sat working in uncomfortable silence while Ryder and Ben kept up a constant flow of friendly chatter. After a few minutes, Ben addressed her. "Do you like living in the city, Sally?"

"It's okay."

"You must miss your home and your family," Granny said.

"Sure I do. You must miss yours, too, Ben. Do you get home often?" The McIntyre farm was twenty miles from Hope Springs.

"Fairly often. I get back for church services every other week."

"So you get to some of the singings?" Would he mention if he were seeing someone regularly? How could she ask without sounding nosy?

"What's a singing?" Kimi asked from the foot of the stairs.

Sally kept her surge of joy hidden. Maybe her words had made an impression on the girl after all.

Granny answered before Sally could. "It's when Amish young people get together for a good time. We call it a singing, because they sing songs, but there is always food and games."

"Kimi, can you crack this one? I can't get it." Ryder held out his pecan.

"I guess." She took it from him, broke the shell easily and handed it back.

"Thanks. Can I play games on your phone since you aren't using it?"

"No." Kimi sat beside Sally. "So what kind of games do Amish kids play?"

"Volleyball is a game that we like in the summer," Sally said.

Kimi gave her a sidelong glance. "You play volleyball?"

"Kimi wants to make the volleyball team at school, but she isn't good enough," Ryder said.

Sally shook her head. "It isn't because she isn't good

enough. She's just younger than the other players on the team are. They're all eighth graders. When she's older, she'll make the team. She has skills."

Kimi's chin came up. "I do have skills."

Sally grinned. "Amish kids play baseball, all kinds of board games and lawn games."

"I like chess," Ryder said.

"Me, too," Ben said, looking surprised.

"He isn't very good," Sally winked at Ryder. "You should play him a game."

"What kind of songs do you sing, Ben?" Ryder asked, dropping his chin on his hands.

"All kinds of songs."

"Even rap?" Kimi asked with a sly grin.

Ben began to pound a rhythm on the table. "Do you know my face/I teach horses to race/I hate to roam/ but I'm a long way from home. Do you like it? I just made it up."

Sally giggled at the looks on both the kid's faces. "No, we don't sing rap songs. Ben has been listening to the radio too much."

Kimi frowned at him. "I thought you couldn't do that?"

He said, "From the time we reach our sixteenth birthday until the day we become baptized in our faith, we are free to do the same things non-Amish people do. It's called our *rumspringa.* It's a time when we get to decide if we want to remain Amish."

"Being Amish is not an easy life, but we live it to remain close to God and to each other," Granny said.

Ryder turned in his chair. "Did you have a *rumspringa,* Granny?"

"I did. But the temptations of the world were not so

great in my time as they are now. Young people now have a much harder decision to make."

"Were you mad at Grandma McIntyre when she left the Amish?" Kimi asked.

"*Nee,* I was not mad. Her father and I were very sad. It was her choice, we accepted that, but we worried that we would not be as close to her children and grandchildren as we would be to our others. In that, we were right. I see my other grandchildren all the time, but I don't see you enough."

Ryder stared at the pecan shells on the table and stirred them around. "Mom and Dad are always too busy to bring us here."

"I know, but I miss you nonetheless. I miss your mother, too. I think she is ashamed of her relatives who live without electricity and drive buggies."

Ryder looked up with a kind expression. "We're not ashamed of you, *grossmammi.* Are we, Kimi?"

Kimi looked at Ben. "You never said what kind of songs you sing."

"Most of them are from our songbooks. German songs and church hymns," Sally said quickly to cover the awkward moment.

Ben said, "We do sing some English songs. 'Amazing Grace' is one of my favorites. This time of year we sing Christmas carols but not modern ones."

"Let's have a little song while we wait for our supper to finish cooking," Granny said.

"Do you have a favorite, Granny?" Sally asked.

The elderly woman sat down beside Kimi and laid a hand on her shoulder. Sally knew it was a sign that she forgave Kimi for being ashamed of her, too. "I reckon my favorite Christmas carol will always be *'Stille*

Nacht.' Ben, you start us off. The German version first, and then the *Englisch* so the children can sing, too."

With Ben's hearty baritone voice leading the way, Sally was soon singing along with many of the Christmas songs she knew and loved. For the first time since meeting Ben again, she felt at ease in his company. This was something they had shared in the past. It was part of the fabric of her Amish life and she missed it.

After twenty minutes of songs, Granny said, "I reckon the stew is done."

Sally rose. "I'll set the table."

Before long, they were enjoying Granny's wonderful beef stew with hot, flaky biscuits and apple pie for dessert. Only Kimi picked at her food. It wasn't the fare she was used to. When the meal was done, Granny said, "Our singing has truly put me in the Christmas spirit. I have been remiss in not setting out my candles. Kimi, would you help me? Ben, can you bring in some greenery? There are some evergreens beside the barn. They donate branches each year to help celebrate our Lord's birth."

Kimi got up and headed for the stairs. "I should check my messages."

Sally's heart sank. She knew what was wrong with Kimi. The girl was afraid to admit she cared about others. She was trying to be as unconnected as her mother.

"I'll be happy to get some greenery." Ben rose from the table and went to put on his coat and boots. "I have to check on Dandy, anyway."

Ryder jumped down from his chair. "Can I come? I want to visit Dandy. He might be lonely out there by himself."

"Not right now."

Ryder accepted Ben's pronouncement with nothing

more than a slight frown. "Okay." He headed for the stairs. "Kimi, can I play a game on your phone? Please? It's my turn now."

Sally began to clear the table. She heard Ben go out, but less than a minute later, the door opened and he came back in. She looked up in surprise. Snow was plastered on his clothing. "Did you forget something?"

"No, but I can't find the barn."

"Are you serious?" Sally and Granny grabbed their coats and stepped out onto the porch. The house offered some shelter from the fierce wind, but it was bitterly cold. There was nothing visible beyond the porch steps but a curtain of white. The snow was blowing sideways. It was so thick nothing could be seen beyond the end of the steps.

"I've never seen a whiteout like this before." Ben had to shout to be heard over the wind.

Granny wrapped her arms around her middle. "You were smart not to try to make it to the barn."

"Dandy needs the wrapping on his leg checked to make sure it's not too tight if it has started swelling."

Sally remembered something she had read. "We can string a rope between the house and the barn so you can find your way."

The elderly woman started back into the house. "I have several lengths of clothesline in the cellar we can use. I'll get them."

Sally met Ben's gaze. "I'm not sure my idea is the best."

"It's a pretty good one. Tie one end to the porch and the other end to me. I'll head to where the barn should be. When I find it, I'll tie the rope to the door handle and come back once I check on Dandy. If I can't reach the barn, I follow the line back to the house."

"Are you sure you have to do this?"

"Dandy's my responsibility."

Granny returned with the thin white plastic coated rope. Ben measured off how much he thought he would need and then added another ten feet. He secured the rope and tugged on the knot "This should do."

Sally grasped his arm. "Be careful. Don't make me come after you."

"If I'm not back in fifteen minutes, you might have to do just that."

"Don't think for a minute that I won't, Ben Lapp."

"There's the bossy Sally I used to know. I wondered what had happened to her." He stepped off the porch and was gone from sight before she could think of what to say.

Chapter Seven

Waiting for Ben to reappear turned into the longest fifteen minutes of Sally's life. She and Granny huddled together out of the wind while they watched and prayed for his safety. Sally strained her ears trying to hear a cry for help over the wind if he should need her.

Just when she thought she couldn't stand it any longer, his dark figure emerged from the blizzard at the foot of the steps. In that instant, she realized how deeply she loved him and how foolish she had been. Foolish to turn aside his offer of friendship.

Just because he didn't love her the way she loved him was no reason to spurn him. On the wall at the small community church where she took Ryder on Sundays was a poster. She knew the meaning of the words came from Corinthians. Love bears all things, believes all things, hopes all things and endures all things. Nowhere did it mention that love had to be returned. She hadn't truly understood that until now.

It was childish and shallow to think Ben's friendship was a burden to her or that she couldn't return that friendship. She would treasure the love she held for him, but she would never turn her back on him again. She stood aside so that he could come up on the porch. "I was about to come get you."

He pulled off his hat and shook the snow from it. "I ended up in the evergreens, but once I realized what they were, I was able to find my way to the barn door. The rope is secure, Dandy's doing well, and I have your greenery and two more eggs for you, Granny." He pulled them from his pocket and handed them to her.

Granny chuckled. *"Danki."*

They followed her inside and left their coats and boots near the door. Granny put the eggs in the refrigerator and carried the evergreen boughs to the windowsill in the living room, where she arranged them around a thick red candle. The spicy smell of cedar filled the room. After lighting the candle, Granny stepped back. "This light will remind all who see it that Christ is the Light of the world as we celebrate his birth in this holy season."

The warm glow of the flame reflected on the frosty glass of the window and made the panes sparkle with multicolored points of light. Sally felt a deep peace settle in her heart.

Granny sighed heavily. "I think I'll go to bed now. It's been a long day for me. I'll bring in some wood from the back porch if you can stoke the small stove, Sally."

Ben said, "I'll bring in the firewood and take care of the stoves. You head to bed."

"All right, I will. Bless you both for looking after the *kinder* and for helping an old woman. *Gott* will reward your kindness." She walked with shuffling steps across the living room and entered a bedroom beyond.

Ben started down the hall that led to the rear of the house. Sally followed him. If he was surprised by her company, he didn't show it. The back porch was a small enclosed space with a large wood rack along the wall. Cut logs were stacked nearly five feet high. A ringer washing machine and storage cabinets lined the other wall.

Sally grabbed several logs from the high stack. Ben held out his arms. She began loading him down with wood. It took until his arms were full before she found the courage to speak. "I would like to talk to you, Ben. I owe you an apology."

"For what?"

"For a remark I made earlier, among other things."

"When you said we couldn't be friends?"

She nodded. He said, "Can we talk inside where it's warm? My feet are freezing."

She glanced at his stocking feet and held open the door for him. "Oh! Of course."

After he deposited the logs in the wood box and added one to the stove, he sat in a recliner and leaned back with a weary sigh. "I hope we don't have any more excitement on this adventure, because I'm beat."

"I know what you mean. We can talk tomorrow." She welcomed the reprieve and started to walk past him.

He reached out and caught her hand. "*Nee,* I'm not too tired to talk."

His hand was work-roughened, warm and strong and he held her slender fingers perfectly. As if he had been fashioned for that single purpose.

She withdrew her hand and missed his touch intensely. She took a seat on the sofa and clasped her hands together. "I'm sorry I said we couldn't be friends. We can. I would like that, but you may not feel the same when I tell you that my pursuit of you for the last few years was just a ruse. I wasn't madly in love with you."

Not like she was now.

"Why were you dogging me if you weren't interested in me?" Ben asked in amazement.

It was hard and painful to explain, but he deserved to know the truth. "I knew that you would never ask a girl like me to marry you."

"You aren't making sense, Sally."

"I made a fool of myself over you to discourage other boys from asking me out. It kept my parents and friends from pushing me to settle down and marry. I used you to avoid getting into any serious relationship."

"But why?"

"What does that matter? I didn't realize I was making your life miserable. I'm sorry for that."

"Sally, it does matter why. It matters to me. Not because you owe me an explanation, but because, odd as it sounds, I do care about you."

She stared at her hands. "You're just being kind."

"Isn't that what friends do?" he asked softly.

Her throat closed and she couldn't speak for the tears that threatened.

"I thought you meant you were leaving the Amish for good and that's why we couldn't be friends. Is that the case?"

She sniffed. "I truly don't know if I can come back."

"It isn't an easy decision, because it isn't an easy life."

Looking up, she asked, "Have you made your decision?"

"I always knew I would follow in the faith of my father."

"I wish I had your certainty. One way or the other."

"A man can easily straddle a fence, but he'll never get anywhere until he gets off. What's stopping you, Sally? I once thought of you as flighty and wild, but you are wonderful with the kids. You were a good friend to those close to you. Give me one reason why you should leave our faith?"

"I'm not meek."

He chuckled. "No, you aren't."

"Don't laugh at me."

"I'm sorry. That was wrong. I see meekness as accepting what God wills."

She rose and crossed to the window. Folding her arms tightly, she said, "I see it as a weakness that others can take advantage of."

"Who took advantage of you, Sally?"

She closed her eyes against the shame. She wasn't ready to speak of it. Turning around, she forced a smile to her stiff lips. "I meant our people in general. I didn't mean me in particular."

"You aren't a very good liar."

"I've fooled a lot of people for a long time."

He crossed the room to stand in front of her. He was so close she could feel his warmth. More than anything, she wanted to lean into his embrace. "You aren't fooling me anymore, Sally."

She gazed into his eyes, stunned by the compassion she saw there. "I've never told anyone."

"I'll never tell anyone, either."

Could she trust him? When she started to speak, all the words came out in a rush. "I was seventeen. I was driving home from a friend's house in my little open cart instead of the family buggy. It was a pretty Indian summer evening and I wasn't in a hurry. I was passing by the gas station outside Hope Springs when a man stepped out from behind a truck and held up a hand to stop me. I thought he needed help. The moment I slowed down, he grabbed my horse and a second man got out of the truck. They started laughing. The one holding my horse said I was prettier than the last few had been. The one from the truck came up and grabbed my wrist. He was so strong. I was scared." She pressed a hand to her lips and turned away from Ben.

She could see her reflection in the window and the way the light of the candle shone all around her. She could see Ben, too. He didn't say anything. He didn't move. He simply waited.

"I knew what was going to happen when the one holding me leered and said he liked Amish girls the best because they didn't fight back. None of us saw the third man. He came from around the back of the station and told them to stop. The one holding me let go and they fought. I couldn't accept my fate or wait to see who won. I grabbed my buggy whip and I struck the one holding my horse over and over again until he let go. Then, I whipped my poor horse until we reached home."

"I'm so sorry. Something like that should never happen. God will punish them."

"But how many meek Amish girls have suffered a fate worse than mine at their hands? I get sick when I think about it."

"Yet God saved you."

"I saved me. The buggy whip saved me. I'm not sure God was even there."

"God is everywhere, Sally. He did not abandon you."

She sighed heavily as she faced the truth. "No, He did not fail me. My entire life I have been taught to believe that I must submit to evil and never, ever resort to violence in return. When God tested me, I failed Him."

Ben stepped closer. "God knows we are not perfect, Sally. We're human. Our Lord will test us many times in our lives, but He does not require that we live a perfect life. He only requires that we try to live as He wills. The only way to fail Him is by giving up."

Ben's kind words were a balm to her wounded spirit. She longed to throw herself into his arms and weep, but she couldn't. He had spoken to her as a friend. She had to behave as a friend in turn, no matter how much she longed to tell him that she loved him.

Kimi came into the living room. "Is there anything good to eat?"

Sally welcomed Kimi's interruption and stepped away from Ben with relief. "I'll fix you some church spread. I think you and Ryder will like it."

Kimi looked around the room. "Where is the brat?"

Sally scowled at her. "I have told you not to call your brother names."

"I thought Ryder was upstairs with you," Ben said.

"He was bugging me so I sent him out."

Ben took a step closer. "What do you mean you sent him out?"

Kimi walked toward the kitchen. "I told him to go check on Dandy."

Ben grabbed her by the shoulders and spun her around. "He went outside? How long ago?"

Kimi shook off his grip, but she must've recognized the fear on his face. "I don't know. A while ago. He came back, didn't he?"

Sally shouted his name. There was no answer. She raced to the front door. Ryder's coat and boots were gone. "I didn't hear him go out."

"We must have been on the back porch. I'll go get him." Ben began pulling on his boots.

Sally held out a scarf. "Be careful. Don't let go of the rope."

It was a useless caution. Ben knew how dangerous

the whiteout conditions were. When he opened the door, a blast of wind almost jerked it from his hands. Sally stood beside him shivering in the icy draft. He shouted Ryder's name, but the boy wasn't on the porch. Did he know to keep hold of the rope? Ben went down the steps and disappeared into the chilling white.

"What's going on? Why are you yelling?" Granny came out of her bedroom dressed in her robe and slippers.

Sally closed the door against the storm. Kimi turned to her great-grandmother with wide, worried eyes. "I told Ryder to go check on the horse. I just wanted him to leave me alone. I didn't know it was so bad outside."

"Hush, child. He is in God's hands. The Lord is taking care of him." Granny caught Sally's eye. They both knew what this could mean. If Ryder hadn't held on to the rope, he could easily become lost in the blizzard. If that happened, the likelihood of his survival was next to none. Was it already too late?

Chapter Eight

The door opened and Ben stumbled in. Sally's heart dropped. He was alone.

"Ryder's not in the barn. I searched through the snow as far as I could reach without letting go of the rope between here and there. He could have been a foot away from me and I wouldn't have known it. You can't see your hand in front of your face out there."

Tears sprang to Kimi's eyes. "I just wanted him to stop bugging me. We have to find him. He's too little to be out in such bad weather." She started to pull down her coat.

Ben stopped her. "I can't let you go out there, Kimi."

Granny put her hands on Kimi's shoulders. "He's right. Getting yourself lost will not help your brother."

Kimi turned around and buried her face in her great-grandmother's robe. Mrs. Weaver's eyes pleaded with Ben to continue the search.

Sally said, "I'll go out."

"Not without me." He was shivering with cold but she knew he wouldn't stay inside.

"Do you have more of that rope, Granny?" Sally asked

"*Ja.* In the cellar."

"Ben, we can tie ourselves together and then tie one end of the line so it will slide along the main rope. That way we can search farther from the path without becoming lost ourselves."

"Good thinking. I'll get it. Put on more clothes. The wind cuts right through you." Ben raced toward the basement doorway.

Granny said, "My grandson has long underwear, pants and extra socks that will fit you. His room is at the top of the stairs on the right."

Sally charged up the steps two at a time. She pulled the extra clothing over her jeans as fast as she could. She knew every moment was critical. Downstairs, she met Ben at the door. He tied the rope around her waist and made a second loop around himself. "Hang on to me until I get this rope secured."

Sally checked the distance between them. It was only about three feet. "This isn't much line."

"We will make a first pass all the way to the barn if we don't find him. When we get there, we'll lengthen the rope and come back."

"How many times?"

"Until we run out of rope. After that…"

He didn't finish the sentence. He didn't have to. Sally understood. If Ryder had walked farther away than their rope could reach, he wouldn't be found in time.

Granny handed them each a flashlight.

"Are you ready?" Ben asked.

Sally nodded and followed him out the door. The wind almost pushed her off the steps. She had to grab hold of Ben to keep upright. When he had the rope looped over the guideline and secured, she leaned close to him so that he could hear her over the howling wind.

"Ryder couldn't walk into this. He would turn his back to it."

"You're right. We'll search along the downwind side of the rope."

At the bottom of the steps, Sally let go of Ben's hand and stepped as far away from him as the line would allow. She could barely make out his figure. Together they began struggling toward the barn, shuffling through the snow, searching with their feet. Sally was shivering within minutes. She had no idea how Ben could tolerate being out in this again so soon. Only the thought of what Ryder must be enduring kept her stumbling forward.

They reached the barn without finding the boy. Ben pulled her toward him and pushed her into the barn. To be out of the wind was a blessing. At least she could see and hear Ben now. He loosened the rope from around her waist and lengthened the distance. When he had it secured again, he brushed the snow off her face. "Are you ready? Do you need another minute?"

"Not with that precious child lost out there. I'm ready."

"You are a brave woman."

"*Nee,* I'm not. I'm frightened to death."

"Only a fool wouldn't be frightened. God gives us the strength to endure what we must. Let's go." He opened the barn door and they went back into the maelstrom.

Sally began shivering immediately. The brief time in the barn hadn't been enough to rewarm her. Again, they shuffled along the length of the rope, searching as they went. Sally called to Ryder, praying he could hear her, even though she knew it was hopeless. She searched with her hands and her feet, knowing she could miss him by inches. Her light was all but useless. When she came up against the porch railing, she almost broke down.

They had to find him. They had to.

Ben pulled her toward him. He pressed his mouth to her ear. "Go inside. I'll go back."

She shook her head. "I'm coming with you. We have a better chance of finding him together."

He nodded and retied the rope. "This is all the length we have."

"It will be enough." She had to believe that. She had faith. She would not meekly accept Ryder's loss. God made her stubborn for a reason.

Still shivering, they ventured away from the limited shelter of the porch and began their sweep. What if she was wrong? What if Ryder had walked into the wind? Were they searching in the wrong direction? Could he survive this long? Her feet and cheeks were growing numb already. The scarf around her face was frozen solid.

Suddenly, she caught a glimpse of something dark in the snow. She jerked on the rope to signal Ben. He stopped. She stretched out her arm, but couldn't reach whatever it was. Another few inches was all she needed. She slipped out of the rope and dropped to her knees knowing she had to keep her sense of direction. She crawled forward and touched something hard. It was Ryder's boot. She latched on to his leg. Ben came to the end of the rope. She held her hand toward him. He grabbed her and pulled. It took all her strength to bring Ryder with her. She couldn't tell if he was alive. He wasn't moving. Ben pulled them to his side and lifted the boy in his arms. Together, they struggled back to the house. On the porch, Sally threw open the door and stood back to let Ben inside.

He staggered in with Ryder in his arms, stumbled and fell to his knees. Shivers racked his body. Sally was chilled to the bone and Ben had been out twice as long as she had. Ryder had been out much longer.

Kimi stood plastered against the wall, her face white with shock. "Is he dead?"

"He's breathing," Ben managed to say through his chattering teeth.

Granny rushed in as Ben laid the boy on the floor. "Get his clothes off. I have blankets warming in the oven. I'll get them."

Sally pulled off her hat and scarf and tossed them to the floor, along with her coat. She used her teeth to pull off her frozen mittens. Her fingers were almost useless as she tried to unzip Ryder's coat. "Kimi, help me."

Kimi pushed away from the wall and dropped to her knees beside her brother. "I'm so sorry. I didn't mean for this to happen." She managed to pull his coat off. "What do we do now?"

Sally looked at Ben. He said, "I'm not sure. Warm him as fast as we can."

Sally grabbed Kimi's arm. "Get your phone. We can call 911. They'll tell us what to do."

Kimi shook her head. "It's dead. I know you told me not to use it, but I wanted to talk to my friends today. The battery died while I was trying to call Mom. She didn't answer. I was leaving a message for her and Dad to tell them what happened to Ryder when my phone cut off. I'm sorry."

Sally wanted to shake the child, but it wouldn't do any good. She could see that Kimi was upset enough. "It's okay, Kimi. Be strong for your brother."

Granny came back with the blankets. She gave one to Ben and one to Sally. "Wrap yourselves up. Dr. White said, 'Warm them little by little and start in the middle. Warm them too fast and the good won't last.' My grandson Marvin fell through the ice at a skating party. By God's grace, he was rescued and Dr. White was fetched to take care of him. God bless that good man. Get all Ryder's wet clothes off. Leave his underclothes on if they're dry. Wrap this blanket around his body, but don't cover his hands and feet with it just yet. Keep an eye on his breathing."

Kimi quickly did as she was instructed. Granny spread a quilt over Ryder. His face was deathly pale and his lips were an awful shade of blue. Sally helped Ben out of his coat. He was shivering violently. She wrapped one of the blankets around his shoulders. He closed his eyes in bliss. She squeezed his arm, offering him comfort and something more. His hand came out from beneath the blankets and captured hers, holding it tight. He opened his eyes and gazed up at her. *"Danki."*

It was more than thanks for the warm blanket. It was his thanks for her help, but it was something else, too. There was intense emotion in his eyes. Afraid of reading too much into what she saw, she pulled her hand away. She wrapped herself in the blanket Granny had given her. To be warm was the most wonderful sensation she had ever known. Her hands started stinging as the circulation returned to her icy fingers.

Although he was still shivering, Ben managed to stand. "We should get him into bed."

Granny said, "It is warmer in the kitchen. I have a cot that I use when I have more company than beds. I'll get it and put it near the stove. Rest a few minutes longer, Ben."

He nodded and huddled deeper in the blanket as she left the room. Kimi had Ryder's head in her lap as she knelt beside him. She looked up at Ben. "I didn't want this to happen. You believe me, don't you? I love him. I know I say mean things to him, but I'm never gonna say anything mean to him again. He's going to be all right, isn't he?"

"We are doing everything we can. It is up to God," Ben said.

"If I pray, God will listen, isn't that right? Sally, you said God always listens to our prayers."

Sally knelt beside Kimi and put her arm around her shoulders. "He does. God always hears our prayers. He gave Ryder back to us tonight. We must have faith in His goodness. He will not abandon us."

A tear slipped down Kimi's cheek as she gazed at her brother and brushed his hair back with her hand. "It's almost Christmas. God has to be listening."

Ben moved Ryder to the cot as soon as Granny had it set up in the kitchen near the stove. Following her instructions, Sally placed a warm blanket under him and wrapped warm towels around his body. Ryder's color began to improve and he started shivering. Color flowed back into his cheeks and his lips. What worried Sally was that the boy didn't rouse. Kimi couldn't be persuaded to leave him. She pulled a chair up beside his cot and sat talking to him and stroking his hair.

After the adults conferred in the living room, Granny decided to take the first shift with the boy, leaving the others to rest briefly. Ben agreed and went upstairs to lie down in one of the bedrooms. Sally was as reluctant to leave Ryder's bedside as Kimi was. Granny said, "You need to go get some rest."

"I don't think I can close my eyes."

Granny squeezed Sally's hand. "He is doing as well

as can be expected. You get some sleep, and I'll wake you in two hours."

"I would give anything if this hadn't happened."

"Bad things will always happen, my child. We endure them and wonder why, but *Gott* has a plan, even if we can't understand it. Sometimes we think we know the reason, but more often than not, we must rely on faith and simply trust our Lord. One day, when we stand before Him, we will see all that He has wrought. Until then, we are but the threads of the quilt He stitches and binds. We can see no further than the threads around us. Who could know that what I learned when my grandson fell through the ice ten years ago would be needed now? *Gott* knew and He gave me the knowledge."

"Having faith is not easy for me," Sally admitted.

"Holding true faith in your heart is harder than being Amish and that's difficult enough. Anyone who tells you differently is either lying to themselves or to you."

"Surely, it's not difficult for you, Granny?"

"Of course it is. I pray all the time that I may be worthy in the sight of God. I'm not as charitable as I should be. I resent that my *Englisch* granddaughter doesn't come to see me and keeps her children away. And I can't abide my neighbor, Ezekiel Knepp. His old cow is forever getting into my garden because he won't keep his fences in repair.

"Only God is perfect, Sally. The rest of us must struggle with our faults. We strive to overcome our shortcomings. Sometimes we fail. That is when we must accept that *Gott* loves us for who we are, faults and all. Our sins are forgiven. That knowledge inspires us to try harder to live a life pleasing to our Lord. Do you understand what I'm saying?"

"What if I don't think I can overcome my faults?"

Granny smiled. "With God's help, all things are possible. It may take a lifetime, but someday I'm going to like Ezekiel Knepp. Of course, I'll have to outlive that old cow of his. Go get some rest. Ryder will want to see your bright and smiling face when he opens his eyes."

Kimi ran into the room and grabbed Sally's hand. "He's awake. I think he wants you."

Ben threw back the quilt and shot out of bed when he realized that no one had come to wake him. He padded downstairs in his stocking feet and stopped at the entrance to the kitchen. The cot beside the stove was empty.

"We're in here, Ben," Sally called from the living room.

She was sitting in a recliner with Ryder wrapped in a quilt in her lap. She looked tired but happy. Ryder's color was pink and his lips were cherry red. His eyes were closed. Kimi was asleep on the sofa. Ben relaxed. Sleep was the best thing for both of them. He walked over to Sally and squatted beside her. "How is he?"

"He won't talk, but otherwise he seems okay. He whimpers if I'm out of his sight."

"That's not too surprising. It must've been a terrible fright for him."

Sally stroked the boy's hair. "For all of us. Four days ago, I was standing at the window looking out at the city and I said that this was going to be the worst Christmas ever. I was lonely and missing home. But I have to tell you, seeing Ryder's boot sticking out of the snow last night was the greatest Christmas gift I have ever received."

"I know what you mean. I'll put some coffee on and

take care of the animals, then I'll hold him for a while so you can get some sleep."

"The storm has not let up. It's still howling out there. There's no way Mrs. McIntyre can send somebody to get us. You won't get home today."

"I can get to the barn and back. Some smart woman told me to put up a rope."

"Make sure you use it."

"Are you going to start worrying about me?"

Her eyes softened and then she looked down. "Isn't that what friends do?"

As he gazed at her pretty face and the faint blush coloring her cheeks, Ben realized being friends with Sally wasn't enough. He wanted more. Was there any chance for them? Knowing it wasn't the time or the place for that kind of discussion, he rose and went out to do the chores.

When he came back in, Granny was cooking breakfast while Sally was setting the table. He could smell the coffee and bacon and it made his stomach rumble. He glanced into the living room. Kimi was on the recliner holding Ryder, just as Sally had done, except that she had an open book in front of them and was reading him a story.

"It's remarkable," Sally said softly. He hadn't heard her approach.

"What's remarkable?"

"The way Kimi takes care of him. Last night opened her eyes in a way a hundred lectures from me would never have done."

"I may be cynical, but we'll have to see if it lasts once she gets her phone battery recharged."

"I have a feeling that it will. He still isn't talking,

but he drank some water and took a few sips of hot chocolate."

"Sounds like he is on the mend." Ben smiled at her and she smiled back. His heart did a funny little flip.

After breakfast, Ben sat down with Ryder. The boy began to whimper when Sally went upstairs to lie down. Kimi came over to sit on the arm of the recliner and said, "She'll be back. Sally isn't leaving you."

Ryder quieted. Kimi asked, "Do you want me to read you another story?"

The boy shook his head.

"How about a game of chess?" Ben asked. "You said that you like to play."

Ryder considered the request and nodded. Ben left him propped up in the chair and brought a second chair over beside him. Then, he moved a table with an inlaid checkerboard on it between them. The chess pieces and checkers were inside a small drawer in the table.

Ben looked at Kimi. "I'll play him one game, you can play the next."

Kimi shrugged. "I never learned."

"Kimi, would you like to help me make some bread?" Granny called from the kitchen.

"Sure."

She went into the other room and stood beside Granny. The two were soon measuring flour, mixing dough and giggling. Glancing up from his game, Ben could see they were both enjoying themselves, although Granny's spotless kitchen was becoming something of a mess.

When Sally came down a few hours later, she went straight to Ben's side. Ryder was asleep again on his lap. She sat down in the chair Ben had vacated when the chess game was done. "How is he?"

"He still isn't talking. He points and grunts or whimpers if he wants something."

She chewed on her lower lip. "Why do you think that is?"

"I'm not sure, but his little mind is sharp. He almost beat me at chess."

She chuckled and the sound delighted him. "I've seen you play. It wouldn't take much to beat you."

"If that is a challenge, you're on. I know I'm good enough to take you."

"Careful, pride is a sin and it goes before a fall."

"Let's just say it will be a one-sided match."

Ben took Sally's hand. She didn't pull away and that gave him hope. "The boy is going to be okay."

"I pray that's true."

"God was looking after him. Especially when He sent you to be his nanny. You have been the answer to this young fellow's prayers, whether he knows it or not."

"I was looking for answers in my own life. I wasn't looking to be the answer to anyone else's prayers."

"And yet you are."

She slipped her hand out of his and looked into the kitchen. "What are Granny and Kimi up to?"

"They have been baking up a storm. Bread, cinnamon rolls, and now they are on to sugar cookies. I think we will all be decorating them this evening. Did you get some sleep?" She wasn't looking at him, she was still gazing into the kitchen.

"I did. This is what I have been missing about Christmas."

"Being snowed in?"

"*Nee,* I was missing the baking and the preparations and the anticipation of everyone coming for holiday visits."

"You should go join them. I reckon there's enough room in Granny's kitchen for one more cook."

She looked at him and shook her head. "I should hold Ryder and give you a break. Besides, I don't want to horn in on Granny's time with Kimi."

"Ryder and I are fine. Go. You know you want to. Granny will secretly welcome the help."

Sally grinned and left him. Even though his arm was growing numb from Ryder's weight, Ben didn't move. He had a perfect line of sight into the kitchen. Sally tied an apron around her waist, and then in a move that surprised him, she tied a white kerchief over her hair.

Her outfit wasn't particularly Amish, but he knew she was inching back toward her roots. And it gave him hope.

Chapter Nine

Although Ryder still wasn't speaking, he managed to eat a little bit of supper that evening. He developed a cough and a slight fever that put the worry back in Sally's eyes. He slept on the cot, with Kimi on the sofa beside him and Sally in the recliner.

By the next morning, he seemed better. Outside, the blizzard continued and Ben began to wonder if they would be rescued before Christmas.

He sat in the kitchen in the early afternoon pretending to read a book while he studied Sally. She was knitting at the table. She had borrowed some yarn and needles from Granny and was working on a pair of matching scarves. Her needles clicked softly as she worked. He had never seen her so still. So engrossed in something. Sally always seemed to be in motion. He liked that about her.

He liked a lot of things about her. Had he been ignoring the woman he should have been getting to know better? If she returned to the Amish, he wouldn't waste any time asking her out. Should he let her know that was his intention? Would it make a difference in her decision?

Kimi came out of the living room and sat beside Sally.

Sally stopped working and laid her needles down. "How is he?"

"He's sleeping."

"Why the long face? Your brother's doing okay."

"I want to make him something special for Christmas."

Sally smiled. "Kimi, that's a wonderful idea. I know he would treasure anything that you made."

"It's just that I don't know what he would like."

"There's plenty of yarn. Do you know how to knit?"

When Kimi shook her head, Sally said, "I will be happy to teach you."

"I want it to be something special from me."

Ben spoke up. "He likes to play chess. You could make him a chess set."

Kimi turned to look at him. "How could I do that?"

"You could carve them from wood, or you could use some of Granny's wooden bobbins with symbols of the pieces drawn on the tops.

Sally brightened. "Or we could make some out of bakeable clay. It would be easier than carving, and once they're baked, the pieces would be hard and durable."

Kimi's shoulders slumped. "We don't have any bakeable clay."

"We can make some. It's easy. We have everything we need in the kitchen. It takes two cups of flour and a cup of salt. You mix that in a big bowl and then you add a little cooking oil and just enough water to form soft dough. We can make them different colors by adding a drop or two of food coloring. Once you have the pieces shaped, I'll bake them."

"That's an awesome idea. Sally, you're the best."

The two of them got to work and were soon shaping pawns, horse's heads for knights and slender columns with crowns and hats for the kings, queens and bishops. One set they left white, and one set they made blue. Ben went in to check on Ryder and found he was still asleep.

"Sally, are you coming back to Cincinnati with us?" he heard Kimi ask.

Ben stayed in the living room. He wanted to hear Sally's answer.

"That was my plan. Why do you ask?"

"It's just that you seem happy here."

"I am happy here. It's like home to me."

"There's something nice about being here, isn't there?" Kimi asked. "It's so peaceful. I think this old house must be full of love. Did you know Granny has been teaching Ryder some prayers when she sits with him?"

"I didn't know that, but I'm not surprised."

"Do you think God left us here so that we could become a better family?"

"I can't speak for our Lord, but I think you might be right."

"I don't want Ryder to know this, but I think Mom and Dad are going to get a divorce."

"Why do you say that? They are on a fabulous vacation together."

"I heard Mom tell Dad that this was their last chance. If they can't work it out, it's over."

"That would be very sad for everyone."

"Granny says the Amish don't believe in divorce. Is that true?"

"It is. We must choose our husband or wife very carefully. We must pray about it and we must listen to what God desires us to do. Once we take the vows of matrimony, they can never be broken."

"Isn't it hard to find the right guy?"

"It can be very hard."

"So why don't you want to stay Amish, Sally?"

"I do want to remain Amish, but sometimes I feel that God has other plans for me. I must do as He wills, not as I want."

"I hope those plans include staying with us. Ryder needs you."

"I'm not so sure he does, when he has a wonderful older sister who loves him as you do, Kimi."

"If Mom and Dad split up, he's really going to need you, Sally. He's not like me. He's going to take it hard."

"Maybe your parents won't split up. Maybe they'll work things out in Paris."

"Maybe." Kimi didn't sound convinced.

Ben returned to the sofa and sat down with his book. He hadn't been thinking about how much the children needed Sally. He'd only been thinking about his own feelings. Ryder was as dear to him as any of his nieces and nephews. By urging Sally to remain Amish, he would be sending Ryder back into a family that didn't hold God and each other at the center of their lives. How could he do that to the child?

No, Sally had to make her decision without his interference.

Something awakened Sally. She sat up in bed listening to hear if Ryder was crying. She heard only silence. The wind had stopped. She got out of bed. Through the frosted glass of the window, she saw stars glittering outside. Relief was quickly followed by regret. Her time with Ben would soon be over.

She crept downstairs to check on Ryder and Kimi. Granny had moved the children into her room. Opening the door, Sally peeked in. Everyone was quiet. She pulled on her coat and went to the front door. When she opened it, she saw Ben standing on the front porch. She hesitated, but she could see that he was smiling. "Did I wake you?" he asked.

She pulled her coat tighter. It was still freezing cold. "I think it was the stillness that woke me. It's over. Praise be to God."

He looked out at the night sky. "Have you ever seen such beautiful stars?"

She moved close to him. They weren't touching, but she felt an intense connection with him she had never known before. She gazed up and marveled at the beauty before her.

The moon wasn't out, but the stars were as bright as she had ever seen them. The world was white below and sparkling with reflected starlight. The sky above was black with a million twinkling pinpoints of light, glittering as if in celebration that the storm had passed. There was something reverent about the hushed world spread before them. "It's so still."

He said, "The world in solemn stillness lay. This is what it must've been like on the night of our Savior's birth. A great hush of anticipation by the heavenly host as they waited for the moment."

With the words of her favorite Christmas hymn flowing through her heart and mind, softly, she began to sing. "It came upon a midnight clear, that glorious song of old."

Ben joined in with his beautiful baritone voice and their duet became a prayer of thanksgiving. As the last syllable died away, they gazed at each other and Sally began to hope that this wonderful man cared about her.

"I didn't expect to hear caroling at this time of night, but it is a wonderful way to welcome the spirit of Christmas." Granny Weaver came out to stand beside them. "Could we sing 'O, Holy Night'? It feels like a holy night, doesn't it?"

"It does," Ben agreed. He began to sing, and Sally and Granny joined in.

"What's going on?"

They all turned to see Kimi standing in the doorway. She had a quilt wrapped around herself and Ryder, who stood in front of her peeking out like an owl chick with his red hair pointing every which way.

Granny moved to drape her arm around Kimi's shoulder. "We are just giving thanks that the storm is done and that Christmas is almost here. Come join us. What Christmas song would you like to sing?"

Kimi looked skeptical. "Not the one about a one-horse open sleigh."

Ben and Sally looked at each other and smiled.

"'Silent Night,'" Ryder croaked.

Kimi dropped to her knees in front of him. "You spoke."

He nodded.

Kimi pulled him close in a big hug. "You can talk for as long as you like and I will never, ever tell you to be quiet and go away again."

"Yes, you will." He sounded like a little bullfrog.

Kimi pulled back to smile at him. "Okay, I might, but I won't mean it."

"Sing 'Silent Night,'" he said again.

"We'll sing, you rest your voice, froggy." Kimi wrapped the blanket around them both. She began to sing in a surprisingly sweet alto. Granny, Ben and Sally joined her. Although she didn't know the words to more than the first verse, Kimi joined in every chorus until they were done.

"All right, children, back inside. I'll make us something warm to drink and then I'm going to read you the Christmas story from my Bible so you will know what our hymns are all about." Granny made little shooing motions at them.

Sally was once again alone with Ben. The closeness she felt earlier began to fade. "How soon do you think we will be rescued?"

"I think we have a few more days yet. I find I'm not eager to leave," he said.

"Not eager to get away from me? That's a switch."

He stepped forward and put his hand beneath her chin to tip her face up. "*Nee,* Sally, I'm not eager to get away from you."

Sally held her breath as he leaned in and kissed her cheek. Her heart exploded with joy.

"It's too cold to be necking on the porch," Granny said from inside the door. "Leave it until tomorrow."

"Yes, ma'am," Ben said as he stepped back. His soft smile sent Sally's heart racing and she knew she wouldn't get a wink of sleep the rest of the night.

Ben was rewrapping Dandy's leg early the next morning when he heard a strange noise growing louder. He didn't realize what it was until he stepped outside of the barn. A red-and-white helicopter was flying low over the hills to the south. It dipped into the valley and came straight toward him. To his surprise, it stopped and hovered above the corral at the back of the barn.

The blades blew up a blizzard of snow as it slowly settled to the ground. Was the chopper in trouble?

He glanced toward the house. Everyone was out on the porch to see what was going on. When he looked back at the helicopter, the door on the side slid open and a man in a red-and-white outfit got out. Ben waited where he was as the man approached.

"Is this the home of Constance Weaver?"

"Ja," he answered.

"Are Kimi and Ryder Higgins here?"

"They are up at the house with their great-grandmother. What's going on?"

"Ryder is here? He's safe?"

"Ja. He is fine."

The man grinned widely, gave a thumbs-up sign to the pilot, and then pressed a hand to his throat. "The boy is safe. I repeat. Ryder is safe. Over."

The pilot returned a thumbs-up sign. The man in front of Ben held out his hand. "I'm Officer Jake Cameron. I'm with the Ohio Search and Rescue. We were dispatched by the children's parents to find them. They were under the impression that Ryder had been lost in the storm. As you can imagine, they were frantic when they couldn't reach anyone to confirm that."

"Kimi's phone battery went dead. We had no way to charge it. Please, come up to the house. The children are both fine."

"We are under orders to take them to a medical facility for evaluation. Their parents have insisted on it." Officer Cameron followed Ben to the house.

Ryder stood wide-eyed on the front steps. "This is so awesomely cool. A helicopter just landed in our yard. No one at school is gonna believe this." His voice was still hoarse, but he was grinning from ear to ear.

Jake introduced himself to the group and grinned at Ryder. "I am sure happy to see you, young man. We were afraid you were lost in the blizzard."

"I was. I let go of the rope and then I couldn't find it again. Sally always told me that if I got lost I was to stay where I was and she would find me. I was really, really cold, but I stayed where I was and she found me." He smiled at Sally.

"Then we all owe her a debt of gratitude."

"This is my sister, Kimi, and this is my *Grossmammi* Weaver. That means grandmother. She's Amish. Do you speak Pennsylvania Dutch?"

"I'm afraid I don't." The officer straightened to address Granny. "The children's parents are on their way back from Europe. They had trouble getting a flight out, but they will be in Cincinnati tonight. They have asked the children be taken to a hospital there for evaluation. Although they look fine to me, I have to follow my orders. I hope you understand."

Kimi spoke up for the first time. "Mom and Dad are coming back already? They were going to stay in Paris for two weeks."

"When they heard your message, they immediately started trying to get back. They are very concerned about you and your brother."

Kimi rolled her eyes "That's a switch."

Although the officer looked puzzled by her comment, he turned his attention to Ryder. "How would you like to ride in our helicopter?"

Ryder's excitement faded. He reached for Sally's hand. "I don't know."

"It's a little scary, but your sister will be with you and so will I and our pilot. It's very safe."

"What about Sally?" Ryder gazed at her with frightened eyes.

"I don't have any instructions to take Sally with us. Just you and your sister."

Ryder wrapped his arms around Sally. "I'm not going without her. Kimi, tell him we aren't going without Sally." Ben heard the panic setting in.

"I'm sorry, son."

"No. No. I won't go. You can't make me go!" He screamed and began sobbing wildly.

Jake glanced at Ben for help. "I can't authorize another person unless they are a patient in need of medical care. I can't reach the parents to get their okay for the added expense of transporting another passenger."

If Sally got on the helicopter, would Ben ever see her again or would she be lost to him in the outside world? He had grown to care about her deeply in these few days, but Ryder needed her desperately. She was the one anchor in the boy's life. She could help him become a man pleasing to God.

Ben's hopes to start a courtship with her crumpled beneath the onslaught of Ryder's tears. "Contact their grandmother, Velda McIntyre. She can make the decision and she will cover the cost."

"Great. What's her number?"

Sally comforted Ryder but she really needed someone to comfort her. She loved Ben. She loved him more than she had ever thought possible. She wanted to believe his kiss meant as much to him as it meant to her, but she couldn't be sure. Did she dare tell him of her love? If he gave her some sign that his affection was more than friendship, she might find the courage. For a woman who wanted to be independent and in charge of her own life, she was miserably inept at telling the one person who mattered most how she felt about him.

Officer Cameron went back to the helicopter and conferred with the pilot. She hoped she would be able to go with Ryder, but she desperately wanted a reason to return to Ben. Had their kiss last night meant anything to him? It meant everything to her. She gazed at him, but he avoided looking at her.

When Jake approached them again, he was all smiles. "Everything's been taken care of, Miss Yoder. You are to accompany the children and to stay with them until their parents arrive."

Ryder's sobs tapered off. He wiped his nose on the sleeve of his coat and sniffed. "Sally can come with me?"

"Sally can come with you," Jake replied. "You and your sister should go collect your things. We'll leave as soon as you're ready."

Kimi threw her arms around her great-grandmother. "Thank you for a wonderful time and for telling us the Christmas story. I want to come back and learn all about how to make bread and rolls with you."

"That may take a while."

Kimi looked up and Sally saw tears in her eyes. "I have three months off from school in the summer. Would that be enough time?"

Granny stroked Kimi's hair. "Three months would be exactly enough time."

"Can Ryder come, too?"

"Of course he can. You are welcome here whenever you want."

Sally took the children inside and they packed up their few belongings. Kimi gently wrapped the chess pieces she had made for her brother in the wool scarf her great-grandmother had given her. When she had the gift carefully tucked in the small box, she looked at Sally. "Mom and Dad are never going to bring us back here."

"You don't know that."

"I'm making an educated guess."

"You're a wise girl, Kimi. Someday, you will be old enough to do what you want and to visit whomever you want."

"Granny Weaver is pretty old. She might not be here then."

"If God wills it, your Granny will be here for a very long time. Her mother lived to be a hundred, and Granny is only eighty-one."

"You always look on the bright side, don't you, Sally?"

"If I do, it's because I know that when God made the heaven and the earth, he put the greater light to rule the day and the lesser light to rule the night. To me, that means he wanted us to see the bright side more than he wanted us to dwell in darkness."

"I have a lot to learn about God."

"You've made a good start. Just remember, he doesn't have a cell phone number."

Kimi grinned. "He might not, but my friends do."

Sally shook her head and followed Kimi downstairs where Ben and Ryder were waiting for them. As the children headed toward the helicopter with Jake, Sally hung back. She wanted to promise Ben that she would return to him. She wanted to speak of her love, but after behaving foolishly for so long, she knew she had to wait for him to speak of his feelings first. When he remained silent, she tried to prompt him. "It was quite an adventure, Ben. I will never forget it."

"Nor will I."

There was something odd in his voice. He wouldn't meet her gaze. She tossed caution to the wind. "I'm going to miss you, Ben."

He cleared his throat and said, "Ryder and Kimi will keep you busy. God knew what he was doing when he sent you to them. They need you, Sally. You have done them a world of good. Continue teaching them the important things in life."

She didn't want to hear that the children needed her. She wanted to hear that Ben needed her. She wanted to hear that he would wait for her. "They won't need a nanny much longer."

"Then you'll be free to decide on the life you want to live."

"And if that life is among the Amish?" Would he be waiting for her and rejoice at her decision?

"If that is where you believe you belong, I will be happy for you."

It was so much less than she wanted to hear. What was wrong? Had she misread his feelings, making his kindness into more because that was what she wanted?

"And if I wish to live *Englisch?*" She held her breath.

He straightened and smiled at her, but the smile didn't reach his eyes. "Then I will be pleased to say I have a friend who is *Englisch.*"

He thought of her only as a friend. Then that was what she must be. She looked away before he could see the tears she couldn't hide. "Goodbye, Ben."

With her head down, she rushed toward the helicopter.

Chapter Ten

Two days after Sally and the children left, Ben was able to leave, too. An Amish neighbor with a team of draft horses pulling a snowplow opened the lane for Mrs. Weaver's sons in their buggies. After promising to look after Dandy until he was fit to travel, Mrs. Weaver's grandson gave Ben a lift to the McIntyre farm.

Trent was overjoyed to see Ben return. "Finally. I hope you had a nice vacation while I was working myself to death."

"You look well enough to me."

"I managed. Mrs. McIntyre hired some temporary help yesterday. She knew you wanted to go home for Christmas. I heard you almost lost the boy. I'm glad I wasn't in your shoes."

"I wish I hadn't been in my shoes." No, that wasn't true. He wouldn't trade those remarkable days with Sally and the children for anything.

After packing a few things, he had Trent drive him home. Everyone in his family was delighted to see him, but he couldn't call up the delight he knew he should feel in return.

He wasn't the kind of fellow who would dwell on his

mistakes. When he messed up, he would admit it. He learned from his mistakes. What he learned was that life wasn't the same without Sally.

The day after he arrived home, he attended a Christmas Eve singing being held at the home of Eli Imhoff. It had seemed like a good way to get his mind off Sally, but it wasn't working. There were two dozen young men and women from Ben's church group present as well as a half-dozen visitors from a neighboring community.

He stood by the back wall with a glass of punch in his hand. He didn't feel like joining the game being played. A nearby table was laden with good things to eat, but he found he wasn't hungry, either. He eyed the group of girls across the way. There were some pretty girls and some plain ones, but none of them had ginger-red hair and amazing blue eyes with silver flecks in them.

"I can't believe you survived being snowed in with Sally Yoder."

Ben looked over his shoulder at the twins, Moses and Atlee Beachy. Moses said, "Will we hear the banns read in church this Sunday?"

Ben shook his head. "Sally is living *Englisch* now."

"That's a shame," Atlee said.

"A shame for us you mean." Moses took a sip of his punch. "Now that Ben is a free man, half the girls in here will be waiting for him to take them home in his buggy, and you and I will be riding home by ourselves."

Ben didn't put much stock in their banter. "The two of you like to exaggerate."

"Ha!" Moses turned his back to the room and leaned closer. "Don't look now, but Wanda Miller is coming over." He and his brother shared a chuckle as they moved away and left Ben as the lone target.

"The pastries look good." Wanda gave him a shy smile but kept her eyes down.

Humble, unassuming, easy on the eyes. There was a lot about Wanda that was exactly the kind of girl he was looking for in a wife. Except for one glaring problem. She wasn't Sally Yoder.

Bold and outspoken, Sally had a caring heart that was every bit as important as the modesty he thought necessary in a woman.

Wanda added a doughnut to her plate. "I heard about your adventure. I'm so glad you were able to save that little boy."

"It was Sally Yoder and Granny Weaver who saved him."

"Is it true that Sally has chosen to be *Englisch?*" Wanda still didn't look at him.

He sighed heavily. "Sally is taking care of two children who desperately need her. It is the path God has chosen for her."

"Our ways are not for everyone," Wanda said. Was that a smile twitching at the corner of her mouth? He wished that she would look up.

"*Nee,* they are not."

She glanced at him then. "She had quite a thing for you. She really made a fool of herself over you. People say she lacked *demut.*"

"Sally struggles with meekness but she is humble before God." He didn't repeat Sally's story. That was something that would remain between the two of them. He treasured the fact that she'd trusted him enough to confide in him. He treasured a great many of his moments with Sally.

No, that wasn't true. He cherished every hour he'd spent with her because he was in love with her.

The thought took his breath away. He loved Sally.

Wanda spoke again, "I'm sure that none of us are surprised she left, but it still must be hard on her family. I wonder if she even gave them a thought."

He frowned. "Sally cherishes her family."

The entire time they had been with Grandma Weaver, Sally had been trying to instill that same kind of love of family in Kimi and Ryder. Without her, they might never have understood the importance of caring for one another and having faith in God.

If he had spoken of his love, would it have made a difference to her? His mind told him that he had made the right decision. His heart told him he had made a terrible mistake.

Wasn't he guilty of assuming that he knew what God had planned for her? For all of them? When the children didn't need a nanny anymore, Sally might well return home. He could wait. She needed to know that. They were both young. Marriage was nothing to rush into. Sally had said that herself.

She cared for him, but did she care enough to come back when he hadn't given her an indication about the way he felt?

He loved her. She deserved to know that. He tossed his empty cup into the trash can next to the pastry table. "It was nice talking to you, Wanda." He started toward the door.

"Where are you going?" she asked.

"I forgot to tell someone something important." He ignored the puzzled look on Wanda's face and rushed out the door. Tomorrow was Christmas Day. He would spend it with his family, but the day after that, he would travel to Cincinnati and see the woman he couldn't get out of his mind.

* * *

Christmas morning arrived quietly in Ben's home. There was a small package on his plate when he came down for breakfast. He unwrapped a fine pair of calfskin gloves that were lined with fleece. He gave his mother a new teapot to replace the one she had chipped a few weeks before. He gave his father a book of woodworking plans. They were both delighted with their gifts. After breakfast, he went out to help his father with the chores. When they came in, his mother was already starting preparations for the feast they would enjoy with their extended family later that day. Now was the time to tell them of his plans, before more people arrived.

"*Daed, Mamm,* I'm going to Cincinnati after Christmas."

"To the city? Why?" His father began washing his hands at the sink.

Ben hesitated. There was nothing certain between himself and Sally. "I need to speak with…someone."

His mother stared at him for a long moment. "What could be so important that you have to go all the way to Cincinnati? It will cost a tidy sum to hire a driver to take you there."

His father turned around, drying his hands on a kitchen towel. "Will Mrs. McIntyre let you off work?"

"I have vacation time coming to me. Trust me when I say it's very important, even if I can't really explain right now." After complaining about Sally's behavior for two years, he didn't expect his parents to understand his sudden change of heart. Before he said anything about his new relationship with Sally, he wanted to make sure of her feelings.

His mother tipped her head to the side. "Very important?"

"It's vital to my future."

She struggled to hold in a smile and turned back to her cake. "You don't have to go all the way to Cincinnati to talk to her. I saw her mother in the store yesterday and she told me Sally's coming home today."

Ben wasn't sure he'd heard correctly. "She's home? She's here in Hope Springs?"

"Why would Ben need to see Sally Yoder, *Mamm?*" Ben's father looked confused.

"Because he's in love with her," his mother said with a soft smile.

"He is? Since when?"

She walked over and took the towel from him. "Oh, for ages now, Papa."

"Why am I always the last one to know these things?"

"Because you are too busy running a business, saying your prayers, keeping your wife happy and your children fed." She planted a kiss on his cheek.

"It's good someone notices all I do," he replied gruffly.

"Of course we notice, dear. Now, get changed out of your work clothes. Our children and grandchildren will be here soon. And bring in those pies I put on the back porch to cool."

Ben's father winked at him. "She's a bossy thing, isn't she?"

"*Ja,* she is. I just never noticed before."

Daed frowned slightly. "Sally Yoder, huh? She always said she wanted to marry you. I thought that was pretty bold of her."

Mamm went back to the stove to stir something. "I told all my friends I intended to marry you, Henry," she said. "When I was just twelve. Sometimes, a girl knows these things."

Daed chuckled. "When I was about that age, I told my brothers I was gonna marry Esther Chupp. Happily, she married Bishop Zook instead. I'm not sure I could live with a woman who doesn't know how to laugh. Reckon it proves your mother is the smart one in the family."

"It's good someone notices," she replied with a sassy smile. "Ben, you had better get going if you're going to get to the Yoder place and back in time to eat with us. I'll put dinner back an hour."

"Danki." He kissed her cheek and raced out the door.

Sally smiled brightly at her sisters and her parents. She chatted happily with her aunts, uncles and cousins who had arrived for Christmas dinner. She was determined that no one would know how truly miserable she was. She reached for the ribbon of her *kapp* and her fingers found it. She was back in her Amish clothes and it felt right.

She didn't question her decision to return to her Amish community and family. This was where she belonged. She knew that now with the certainty that she would never question again. She was miserable because she knew that she would come face-to-face with Ben Lapp one of these days and she would have to pretend that she didn't love him. She wasn't sure how that was possible, but it was something she would have to do.

She prayed God would give her the strength she needed.

"Is that another buggy I hear?" her mother asked, glancing out the window. "I'm not expecting anyone else, but what a joy to have more company. See who it is, Sally, and make them welcome."

Her mother scurried away with a tray of vegetables.

Sally pasted on her fake smile and opened the door.
"Merry Christmas and wel..." Her voice trailed into
nothing. Ben stood hat in hand on her front porch.

He was every bit as handsome as she remembered
and her heart turned over with love. She pressed a hand
to her chest to stop the wild thumping. It wasn't fair.
She wasn't ready to see him so soon.

"Hello, Sally. Merry Christmas to you."

She wrapped her arms tightly across her chest.
"What are you doing here?"

"I came to see you. Actually, I was leaving for Cincinnati tomorrow, but then I found out you were here.
Is there somewhere we can talk, just the two of us?"

She stared at her feet. "I'm not sure I..."

He grabbed her hand and pulled her along behind
him toward his buggy. "Ben Lapp, what do you think
you're doing?"

"I need to talk to you, and you need to listen to me."

She glanced back at the house and saw several of her
family members watching them. "All right, but I don't
like to be manhandled."

He stopped and spun around to face her, shock written on his face. "Oh, Sally, I'm so sorry. I didn't mean
to frighten you. Please forgive me."

"I'm not frightened of you, Ben. You didn't hurt me."

He took a step away from her and shoved his hands
in his pockets. "Would you please take a ride with me
in the buggy?"

Once Sally got in, he climbed in beside her. He took
off his coat and wrapped it around her. "Are you warm
enough?"

"I'm fine. What is so important that you have to drag
me away from my family's Christmas dinner?"

He steered the buggy down the lane and out onto the highway. "How are Kimi and Ryder?"

"Fine. Happier than I've ever seen them. Spending three days not knowing if their son was dead or alive while they tried to get back home was an incredible wake-up call for Mr. and Mrs. Higgins. They decided they would all go to Paris together, and then they will come back and spend New Year's with Mrs. McIntyre and Granny Weaver. I think their family is on the mend."

"God moves in mysterious ways, His wonders to behold. So does this mean you are going back to them after the New Year?"

She looked out the window. "I resigned."

He turned the buggy onto a narrow lane that ran between towering trees. Their bare, arching branches interlaced overhead and cast intricate shadows on the snow-covered road. When they were out of sight of the highway, he stopped.

"But why? Ryder needs you."

"He needs his mother and father more."

"I'm sure you could have found another job in the city."

"I knew it wasn't where I want to be. It was where I needed to be for a little while, but it is not the life for me. I will be joining the church in the spring."

"I planned to talk to the Bishop about doing the same thing. I'm ready to settle down and start a family."

"I'm happy for you. That you found someone."

He placed a hand beneath her chin and lifted her face so that she had to look at him. "Are you happy for me? Because you don't sound happy."

Tears filled her eyes. Her throat closed and she couldn't speak.

"Do you want to know who has captured my heart?"

She shook her head.

"We shared so many confidences in our time together at Granny Weaver's that I feel I can tell you anything, Sally. The woman I've fallen in love with is a wonderful Amish maiden. She loves her family. She tries to live her life in a way that is pleasing to God. I'm not sure if she is a good cook, but I suspect that she is. What I don't know, what I'm afraid to ask is, does she love me?"

Tears slipped down Sally's cheeks. "She's a fool if she doesn't."

He let out a sigh of relief. "I know for certain that you are no fool, Sally Yoder. Do you love me? I pray that you do, because I don't think I can wait another minute to kiss you."

Sally looked at him in shock. "You love me?"

"I think I have for a very long time. I just didn't know it."

"Oh, Ben, I've loved you for so long. You have no idea." She threw herself into his arms and kissed him with all the gladness in her soul.

When the most wonderful kiss in the world ended, Sally snuggled against Ben's side, content to be near him. Knowing she had a lifetime of bliss to look forward to, if God willed it.

Ben kissed the top of her *kapp*. "You are a wonderful woman, Sally. I feel so blessed to know you. I'll spend my life giving thanks to God."

"A week and a half ago I thought I was facing the worst Christmas season. If Mr. and Mrs. Higgins didn't decide to go to Paris, if Dandy hadn't fallen, if the blizzard hadn't happened and Ryder hadn't been lost, I wouldn't be here in your arms."

Ben chuckled. "I reckon God knew it would take a lot to get us together."

She cupped his cheek, her heart soaring at the love she saw in his eyes. "It took a lot, but He has given me the most wonderful Christmas ever."

* * * * *

AMISH TRIPLETS
FOR CHRISTMAS

Carrie Lighte

To my family, who always supports
my creative endeavors, with thanks also to
the Love Inspired team, especially Shana Asaro,
for helping this dream become a reality.

And my God will meet all your needs according to the riches of his glory in Christ Jesus.
—*Philippians* 4:19

Chapter One

Hannah Lantz rose from her desk, smoothed her skirt and forced her pale, delicate features into a smile. She didn't want the little ones to know how distraught she was that she would no longer be their teacher once harvest season ended. Positioning herself in the doorway, she waited to greet the scholars, as school-aged children were known, when they climbed the stairs of the two-room schoolhouse where she herself had been taught as a child.

Doris Hooley, the statuesque redheaded teacher who taught the upper-grade classes, stood on the landing, fanning herself with her hand. "It's so hot today, you probably wish Bishop Amos and the school board decided to combine your class with mine immediately instead of waiting until late October."

"Neh," Hannah replied, thinking about how desperately she and her grandfather needed the income she earned as a teacher. "I'm grateful they extended my position a little longer. It's been a blessing to teach for the past eleven years, and I'm truly going to miss the scholars."

"Jah," Doris agreed. "Such a shame so many young

women from Willow Creek left when they married men from bigger towns in Lancaster County. Otherwise, enrollment wouldn't have dwindled. Not that I blame them. Willow Creek isn't exactly overflowing with suitable bachelors. That's why I'm so eager to meet John Plank's nephew from Ohio. Not only is he a wealthy widower, but I've heard he's over six feet tall!"

Hannah cringed at her remarks. Thirty-six-year-old Doris never exercised much discretion about her desire to be married, a trait that eventually earned her the nickname of "Desperate Doris" within their small Pennsylvania district. As an unmarried woman of twenty-nine years herself, Hannah thought the term was mean-spirited, although if pressed, she had to admit it was fitting in Doris's case.

"I believe John's nephew is coming here to help with the harvest—not to meet a bride," Hannah contradicted as a cluster of children trod barefoot across the yard, swinging small coolers in their hands.

"That kind of pessimistic attitude is why you're still unmarried," Doris retorted, craning her neck to spy the first buggies rolling down the lane. "It isn't every day the Lord brings an eligible man to Willow Creek, and I, for one, intend to show him how *wilkom* he is here."

Hannah gave her slender shoulders a little shrug. "*I* intend to show his *kinner* how *wilkom* they are," she emphasized. "It can be difficult for young ones to start school in a new place. Besides, if it weren't for their increasing the size of my class, there would have been no need for the school board to keep me on. You could have managed the rest of my scholars yourself."

As the children approached, Hannah considered whether Doris was right. Was she being pessimistic about the prospect of marriage? Or was she merely accepting God's provision for her life? After all, she'd scarcely had any suitors when she was a teenager; her grandfather had seen to that. So what was the likelihood she'd find love in their diminishing district now, at this age?

Even if she did meet someone she wished to marry, her grandfather was incapable of living alone and too stubborn to move out of his house. She couldn't leave him, nor could she imagine any man being willing to live as her husband under her grandfather's roof and rule.

To her, it seemed only realistic to accept that no matter how much she may have yearned for it, her life wasn't meant to include the love of a husband. And she had come to believe God wanted her to be content with teaching other people's children rather than to be bitter about not having children of her own.

In any case, she figured she had more urgent priorities than pursuing a stranger who was only visiting their community—like figuring out what she'd do to support her grandfather and herself once her teaching position ended.

She shook her head to rid her mind of worrisome thoughts. *The Lord will provide*, she reminded herself. When Eli and Caleb Lapp said good-morning, a genuine smile replaced Hannah's forced one.

"Guder mariye," she returned their greeting enthusiastically as they clambered up the steps.

After all the older students were accounted for, Doris sighed. "I guess the wealthy widower isn't showing up today after all. Perhaps tomorrow."

She ducked into the building while Hannah waited for the final student to disembark her buggy. It was Abigail Stolzfus, daughter of Jacob Stolzfus, one of the few men Hannah had briefly walked out with when they were younger. But when he proposed to her almost nine years ago, she'd refused his offer.

"One day, your pretty face will turn to stone," he had taunted. "You'll end up a desperate spinster schoolmarm like Doris Hooley."

She knew Jacob's feelings had been hurt when he'd made those remarks, and she had long since forgiven his momentary cruelty. But this morning, she was surprised by how clearly his words rang fresh in her mind. Watching Jacob's daughter, Abigail, skip along the path to the schoolhouse, Hannah couldn't help but imagine what her life might have been like if she—instead of Miriam Troyer—had married him.

Granted, she never felt anything other than a sisterly fondness for Jacob, so a marriage to him would have been one of convenience only, which was unacceptable to her, even if her grandfather had permitted it. But might it have been preferable to being on the brink of poverty, as she was now? Thinking about it, she could feel the muscles in her neck tighten and her pulse race.

She chided herself to guard her thoughts against discontentment; otherwise, it would be her heart, not her face, that turned to stone. God had brought her through greater trials than losing her classroom. She trusted He must have something else in store for her now, too.

She reached out and patted Abigail on the shoulder, smiling reflexively when the child grinned up at her and presented a jar of strawberry preserves.

"*Denki*, Abigail. You know I have a weakness for strawberries!" she exclaimed, bending toward the girl. "Did you help your *mamm* make this?"

"*Jah,*" Abigail replied. "I picked the berries, too."

"I will savor it with my sweet bread."

As the girl continued toward her desk, Hannah reached to shut the door behind her.

"Don't!" a deep voice commanded.

Startled, Hannah whirled around to find a tall sandy-haired man holding the door ajar with his boot. His broad shoulders seemed to fill the door frame, and she immediately released the handle as if she'd touched a hot stove.

"Excuse us," Sawyer Plank apologized in a softer tone. He stepped aside, revealing three towheaded children who each looked to be about seven years old. "Sarah, Samuel and Simon are to begin school today."

He watched the fear melt from the woman's expression as she surveyed the triplets. "*Wilkom.* I'm Hannah Lantz," she said, as much to them as to him.

"*Guder mariye,*" the three children chorused.

"I'm Sawyer Plank," he explained. "Nephew of John Plank."

"Of course." She nodded, tipping her chin upward to look at him. He couldn't help but notice something sorrowful about her intensely blue eyes, despite her cheerful tone. "We've been expecting you."

"I apologize for being late," Sawyer said. Then, so quietly as to be a whisper, he confided, "I had to fix Sarah's hair myself, and it took longer than I expected."

Hannah narrowed her eyes quizzically.

"I'm afraid my hands are better suited for making cabinets than for arranging a young girl's hair." He held out his rough, square hands, palms up, as if to present proof.

Hannah's eyes darted from them to Sarah's crooked part. "You've done well," she commented graciously, although he noticed she was biting her lip. "Sarah, please take a seat next to Abigail Stolzfus, at the front of the class. Samuel and Simon, you may sit at the empty desks near the window."

Sawyer thrust a small paper bag that was straining at the seams in Hannah's direction. "It's their lunch," he explained, still speaking in a low tone so as not to be heard by the children.

"My *onkel* made it because, as you may know, my *ant* is deceased, so I'm not sure what the lunch consists of. Ordinarily my youngest sister, Gertrude, takes care of such things in Ohio. She would have accompanied us here, too, but shortly before my *onkel* broke his leg, it was nearing time for my eldest sister, Kathryn, to deliver her *bobbel*, so Gertrude traveled to Indiana to keep her household running smoothly."

Although he was usually a private man of few words, Sawyer couldn't seem to stop himself from rambling to the petite, dark-haired teacher whose eyes were so blue they nearly matched the shade of violet dress she wore beneath her apron.

"I'm not much of a farmer, but as soon as I heard John needed help, I put my foreman in charge of the shop," he continued, neglecting to add that the timing couldn't have been worse, since he had just lost one of his carpenters to an *Englisch* competitor who constantly threatened to put Sawyer out of business. "The *kinner* and I immediately set out for Pennsylvania. We only arrived on Saturday evening."

He was quiet as he wiped the sweat from his brow with his sleeve.

"It was *gut* of you to come help your *onkel* during harvest season," Hannah commented. "If there's nothing else, I will see to it the *kinner* divide the lunch evenly between them."

Sawyer sensed he was being dismissed, and he was only too relieved for the opportunity to end the conversation. "I won't be late picking them up," he muttered as he turned to leave.

Once he was in his buggy, he flicked the reins with one hand and simultaneously slapped his knee in disgust with the other. What was wrong with him, babbling on about Sarah's hair and his work as a cabinetmaker? No doubt Hannah Lantz thought he was vain as well as tardy.

He hadn't meant to sound boastful about dropping everything in Blue Hill in order to help his uncle, either. John was family and family helped each other, no matter what. Just like when John came to Ohio and kept the shop running smoothly after Sawyer's mother and father died six years earlier, and again when he lost his beloved wife, Eliza, three years later. It was an honor—not a burden—to assist his uncle now. He only wished Gertrude hadn't gone to Indiana, so the children could have stayed in Ohio with her. Sarah had had nightmares ever since Gertrude left, and the boys had grown so thin without her cooking.

But he knew there was no sense focusing on the way he wished things were. In all these years, no amount of regret had ever brought his Eliza back. He trusted God's timing and plans were always perfect, even if they were sometimes painful to endure. His duty was to accept the circumstances set before him.

But that didn't mean he couldn't try to make a difficult situation better. As the horse clopped down the lane to his uncle's farm, Sawyer devised a plan so he could spend as many hours as possible in the fields. If the weather and crops cooperated, he'd help finish harvesting in six weeks instead of eight or more, so his family could return to Ohio at the first opportunity.

As the children barreled outside for lunch hour, the paper bag Simon was carrying split down the middle, spilling the Planks' unwrapped cheese and meat sandwiches onto the ground, so Hannah invited the children to join her for sweet bread inside the classroom. She marveled at how quickly they devoured the bread and preserves.

"Do you have such appetites in Ohio?" she inquired, aware the children seemed thinner than most.

"*Ant* Gertrude doesn't bake bread like this," Samuel said, his cheeks full. "She says it's because her *mamm* died before she could learn her the best way to make it."

"Before she could *teach* her," Sarah corrected.

"Our *mamm* died, too," offered Simon seriously. "She's with the Lord."

"As is my *mamm*," Hannah murmured.

"Did your *mamm* teach you how to make bread before she died?" asked Samuel.

"*Neh*, but my *groossmammi* did. See? *Gott* always provides."

"I wish I had a *groossmammi* to teach me." Sarah sighed. "*Daed* said *Groossmammi* died when we were as little as chicks that didn't even have their feathers yet."

"I'm happy to share my bread with you," Hannah told Sarah. "Eating it is better than baking it anyway. Now that you're done, why don't you go outside and play with the other *kinner*."

Doris passed them as they exited. "What darling little things," she remarked to Hannah. "They must be triplets."

"*Jah.* Their names are Samuel, Sarah and Simon Plank," Hannah replied.

"So you've met the wealthy widower?"

"He has a name, too. It's Sawyer. We spoke briefly this morning."

"What did you think of him?" wheedled Doris. "Give me your honest opinion."

"Well, I didn't have my tape measure with me, so I can't confirm whether he's over six feet tall," Hannah answered evasively, although she knew exactly what Doris was getting at.

"*Schnickelfritz!*" Doris taunted. "I meant, what did you think of him as a potential suitor?"

"I *didn't* think of him as a potential suitor," Hannah emphasized. "I thought of him as the *daed* of my scholars, a nephew of John Plank and a guest in our district."

"He's not to your liking, then?" Doris persisted.

"I didn't say that!" Hannah was too exasperated to elaborate.

Fortunately, she didn't have to, as Eli opened the door at that moment, yawping, "Caleb got hit with a ball and it knocked his tooth out."

Doris covered her mouth with the back of her hand. "You'll have to handle it," she directed Hannah. "You know that kind of thing makes me woozy."

"Of course," Hannah calmly agreed. "But you'll need to get used to it soon, since *kinner* lose their baby teeth all the time. It's all part of caring for 'darling little things' at that age."

After they'd eaten lunch, John urged Sawyer to join him on the porch before returning to the fields.

"It's never too hot or too late for coffee," he said,

hobbling toward him with a crutch under one arm and a mug sloshing precariously in his other hand.

Sawyer accepted the strong, hot drink. Brewing coffee appeared to be his uncle's only culinary skill; from what Sawyer had tasted so far, the food he prepared was marginally palatable, although there was certainly a lot of it.

"I've been thinking," Sawyer started. "I'd like to hire a young woman to watch the *kinner* after school. She can transport them home in the afternoon and cook our supper, as well."

"Our meals don't suit you?" joshed John.

"*Jah*, the food is ample and hearty," he answered quickly, not wanting to insult his host. He launched into an earnest explanation. "But since you can't get into and out of the buggy without an adult to assist you, it would be easier to have someone else pick them up from school in the afternoon. This way, my work will only be interrupted in the morning, not in the morning and afternoon both. If the woman I hire is going to care for the *kinner* in the afternoon, she may as well fix us supper, too."

John chortled. "Trust me, Sawyer, I understand. The boys and I haven't had a decent meal since my Lydia died five years ago. But they're teenagers and they'll eat anything. How did you get on without Gertrude these last few weeks in Ohio?"

"I hired their friend's *mamm* to mind the *kinner* with her own while I was in the shop during the day, but evenings were chaotic," Sawyer admitted. "You can guess what the cooking was like by how scrawny the *kinner* are."

"You need a full-time wife, not a part-time cook,"

John ribbed him. "Someone who will keep you company, not just keep your house."

"So I've been told," Sawyer replied noncommittally. His uncle was only a few years older than he was, and they good-naturedly badgered each other like brothers. "I imagine you've been given the same advice yourself?"

"*Jah*, but I live in withering Willow Creek, not in thriving Blue Hill. Isn't there a matchmaker who can pair you with one of the many unmarried women in your town?"

Chuckling self-consciously, Sawyer confessed, "After a dozen attempts, the matchmaker declared me a useless cause, much to Gertrude's dismay."

He'd found his lifetime match when he'd met Eliza, the love of his life and mother of his children. But rather than try to explain, he offered John the excuse he'd made so frequently he half believed it himself. "I can't be distracted by a woman. I have a cabinetry shop to run, employees to oversee. Their livelihood depends on me, and business is tough. But Gertrude is at that age where her mind is filled with romantic notions about love and courting, probably more for herself than for me."

"My sons are at that age, too," John said. "It's only natural."

"Perhaps," Sawyer agreed. But he wanted to protect his sister from the risk that came with loving someone so much that losing the person caused unimaginable grief. She was too young to experience that kind of pain.

Besides, as long as Gertrude lived with them, he didn't have to worry about the children being raised without a female presence in the house. His sister tended to their every need, as much like their older sibling as their aunt.

Aloud he said, "I'll arrange to hire someone as soon as possible. Do you have any recommendations?"

"Most of the women in Willow Creek are married with *kinner* and farms of their own, and they live too far from here to make transporting your *kinner* worth anyone's while. Either that, or the younger *meed* need to watch their siblings," John replied. "But Hannah Lantz, the schoolteacher, lives nearby and she's unmarried. She's very capable to boot."

Sawyer suppressed the urge to balk. There was something about the winsome teacher that unsettled him, although perhaps it was only that he hadn't gotten off on the right foot with her by showing up late to school.

"Are you sure she's the only one?"

"Not unless you want Doris Hooley fawning over you."

"Who's she?"

"She's the upper-grade schoolteacher. You haven't met her yet?"

"Neh," Sawyer answered. "Not yet."

"Consider yourself fortunate." John grinned. "I don't know her well, but it's rumored she can be very…attentive. Especially toward unmarried men."

A woman's amorous attention was the last thing Sawyer wanted. Deciding he'd present his employment proposition to Hannah that afternoon, he downed the last of his drink.

"If only I were half as strong as your coffee," he joked, "the fields would be harvested in no time."

But the work was so grueling that Sawyer lost track of time and returned to the schoolhouse nearly an hour after the rest of the students had departed. The boys were tossing a ball between them and Sarah was sitting on the steps, her head nestled against Hannah's arm as Hannah read a book aloud to her.

When he hopped down from his buggy and started across the lawn, Hannah rose and the children raced in his direction.

"I told Sarah not to worry—there was a *gut* reason you were late," Hannah said.

Her statement sounded more like a question, and whatever vulnerable quality he noticed in her face earlier was replaced by a different emotion. Anger, perhaps? Or was it merely annoyance? Whatever it was, Sawyer once again felt disarmed by the look in her eyes—which were rimmed with long, thick lashes—as if she could see right through him.

"Forgive my tardiness," he apologized, without offering an explanation. He didn't have a valid excuse, nor did he want to start rambling again. He needed to make a good impression if he wanted her to consider becoming a nanny to his children.

"I notice there's another buggy in the yard," he observed. "Is it yours?"

"It's Doris Hooley's," she responded curtly. "She's the upper-grade teacher."

"In that case, may I offer you a ride home?"

"*Denki*, but *neh*. I have tasks to finish inside. Besides, it seems as if your horse trots slower than I can walk," Hannah answered in a tone that was neither playful nor entirely serious. "Samuel, Simon and Sarah, I will see you in the morning, *Gott* willing."

She turned on her heel, gathered her skirt and scurried back up the steps into the schoolhouse. Inside the classroom, she quickly gathered a sheaf of papers and stuffed them into her satchel.

She knew she hadn't acted very charitably, but Sawyer Plank seemed an unreliable man, turning up late, twice in one day, without so much as an explanation or excuse for his second offense. Did he think because he was a wealthy business owner, common courtesies didn't apply to him? Or perhaps in Ohio, folks didn't honor their word, but in Willow Creek, people did what they said they were going to do. Not to mention, Sarah was fretting miserably that something terrible had happened to detain her father. It was very inconsiderate of him to keep them all waiting like that.

As Hannah picked up an eraser to clean the chalkboard, Doris sashayed into the room. Although she lived in the opposite direction, she had volunteered to bring Hannah home. Hannah suspected Doris wanted an excuse to dillydally until Sawyer arrived so she could size him up. But whatever the reason behind Doris's gesture, Hannah was grateful for the transportation home on such a muggy afternoon.

"Where have the triplets gone?" Doris inquired. "I thought they were with you."

"They just left with their *daed.*"

"Ach! I must have been in the washroom when he came to retrieve them," Doris whined.

They were interrupted by a hesitant rapping at the door—Sawyer hadn't left after all. He removed his hat and waited to be invited in. Hannah hoped he hadn't heard their discussion.

"You may enter. I won't bite." Doris tee-heed. "I'm Doris Hooley."

She was so tall her eyes were nearly even with Sawyer's, and Hannah couldn't help but notice she batted her lashes repeatedly.

"Guder nammidaag," he replied courteously.

She tittered. "You remind me of a little boy on his first day of school, so nervous you forget to tell the class your name."

Apparently unfazed by Doris's brash remark, Sawyer straightened his shoulders and responded, "I am Sawyer Plank, nephew of John Plank, and I'm sorry to interrupt, but I need to ask Hannah something concerning the *kinner.*"

"Of course," Hannah agreed. Although she had no idea what he wanted to request of her, she felt strangely smug that Sawyer had sought her out in front of Doris. "What is it?"

"As you may have guessed, my work on the farm makes it inconvenient for me to pick up the *kinner* after school," he began. He continued to explain he considered delivering the children to school to be a necessary interruption of his morning farmwork, but that he hoped to hire someone to transport them home and oversee them after school through the evening meal.

"She also would be expected to prepare a meal for all of us, but I would pay more than a fair wage. Of course, she would be invited to eat with us, as well."

He hardly had spoken his last word when Doris suggested, "I'd be pleased to provide the *kinner's* care. I have daily use of a buggy and horse and could readily bring them to the farm when school is over for the day. I think you'll find I'm a fine cook, too."

Sawyer opened his mouth and closed it twice before stammering, "I'm sorry, but you've misunderstood. I—I—"

"I believe he was offering the opportunity to me,

since I'm the *kinner's* teacher and they'll be more familiar with me," Hannah broke in. Despite her initial misgivings about Sawyer, she was absolutely certain this was the provision she'd been praying to receive. She didn't give the matter a second thought before adding, "And I agree to do it."

"I see," Doris retorted in a frosty tone directed at Hannah. "Well, I'll leave the two of you alone to discuss your arrangement further."

"*Denki.* I will stop by your classroom as soon as I'm ready to leave," Hannah confirmed.

Before exiting, Doris turned to Sawyer and brazenly hinted, "With Hannah watching the triplets, I hope you find you have time for socializing with your neighbors here in Willow Creek."

No sooner had Doris flounced away than Hannah confessed, "I was being hasty. I shouldn't have accepted your offer. I'm terribly sorry, but I can't possibly help you."

"Why not? If it's a matter of salary, I assure you I'll pay you plentifully and—"

"*Neh*, it isn't that," Hannah insisted. "It's…my *groossdaadi*. I have a responsibility to him. I must keep our house, make our supper… He is old and deaf. He can't manage on his own. And unlike Doris, I don't have daily transportation. Our buggy is showing signs of wear and the horse is getting old, so we limit taking them out for essential trips only."

Sawyer was quiet a moment, his eyes scanning her face. She looked as downcast as he felt.

"Suppose the *kinner* come home from school with you and stay until after supper? Would your *groossdaadi* object? I would collect them each evening. They could help you with your household chores and they wouldn't make any—"

"Jah!" she interrupted, beaming. "I will have to ask *Groossdaadi*, but I don't think he'll object. I'll need a few days to confirm it with him and make preparations. Perhaps I could begin next Monday?"

"Absolutely." Sawyer grinned. "Now, would you please permit the *kinner* and me to give you a ride home? I'll need to know where you live in order to pick them up on Monday."

She hesitated before saying, *"Denki,* but Doris has already offered."

"Are you certain?" he persisted.

Just then, a flash of lightning brightened the room and Hannah dropped the eraser she was holding, effectively halting their conversation. "I'm certain," she stated. "You mustn't keep your *kinner* waiting any longer. They've been so patient already."

Sawyer was taken aback by the sudden shift in Hannah's demeanor. As he darted through the spitting rain, he thought that her countenance was like the weather itself; one minute her expression was sunny and clear, but the next it was clouded and dark. He wasn't quite sure what to make of her at all, but at least his worries about the children's care had subsided for the time being.

Chapter Two

Because Doris gave her a ride home from school, Hannah arrived early enough to prepare one of her grandfather's favorite meals: ground beef and cabbage skillet and apple dumplings. Making supper kept her distracted from the peals of thunder that sounded in the distance, and so did thinking about Sawyer and the children.

She supposed she could have accepted his offer to bring her home, instead of imposing on Doris. But what kind of example would she have been to the children—a grown woman, afraid of a storm? Hadn't she reminded Sarah several times that day to trust in the Lord when she was worried about her father? Yet there Hannah was, trembling like a leaf because of a little thunder.

She realized there was a second reason she hesitated to ride with Sawyer: she worried what kind of foolish thing she might say. She didn't know what had caused her to joke about his horse's speed, but she couldn't risk offending him, especially as he might be her new employer. Thinking about the slight smile that lit his serious, handsome face made her stomach flutter. She retrieved her satchel from its hook in search of a piece of bread, but then remembered she'd given her last crust to Simon, who gobbled it up in four bites.

When her grandfather entered the kitchen, his first words were not unlike those she had cast at Sawyer, but his tone was much gruffer.

"What is your reason for being so late?" he barked.

Because her grandfather had lost his hearing years ago, he had no sense of the volume of his voice—at least, that was what Hannah chose to believe.

"I'm sorry, *Groossdaadi*. I was helping my new scholars." She looked at him directly when she spoke. Although her grandfather was adept at reading lips, she knew from experience a brief answer was the best reply, especially when he seemed agitated.

"Is dinner going to be late again?" he complained, despite the early hour.

Please, Lord, give him patience. And me, too, she prayed.

"*Neh.* It is almost done."

"*Gut,*" he grunted. "You left me here with hardly a morsel of bread."

Hannah knew the claim was preposterous; she fixed him a sizable lunch before leaving for school, and there was always freshly made bread in the bread box. Thinking about it made her remember Sarah's desire to learn how to bake bread. Hannah hadn't been exactly accurate when she'd said it was more fun to eat than to bake. Eating freshly baked bread was a pleasure, but smelling it baking was equally appealing.

She realized because her grandfather was deaf, he probably looked forward to having his other senses stimulated. Adding a little extra garlic to the skillet to enhance the aroma, she began to sing, and by the time she and her grandfather were seated, the storm had blown over.

After saying grace, she touched her grandfather's arm to get his attention. He dug into his meal, chewing as he watched her lips.

"*Gott* has provided us help with our income," she said, knowing that if she prefaced her proposal by indicating it was from the Lord, her grandfather would be less inclined to say no. "I have been asked to watch the *kinner* of Sawyer Plank. He is John Plank's nephew, the one who is helping him harvest until his leg heals."

Her grandfather shoveled a few forkfuls of meat into his mouth. When he looked up again, Hannah continued.

"I will need to bring them home with me after school—"

"*Neh,*" her grandfather refused, lifting his glass of milk. Unlike most Amish, they had always been too poor to afford their own milk cow, but for generations the Zook family had made it a faithful practice to deliver a fresh bottle—often with a chunk of cheese—to their milk bin.

As her grandfather took a big swallow, Hannah finished speaking, undaunted. "They will stay here through supper time. Then Sawyer will pick them up."

"*Neh,*" her grandfather repeated. "I will not have *kinner* in my house."

Hannah curled her fingers into a fist beneath the table, digging her fingernails into her palm. She knew how much her grandfather disliked having children around—after all, he'd reminded her and her younger sister, Eve, of that fact repeatedly when they were growing up. She waited until he'd had a second helping of beef and cabbage, and then she dished him up the biggest, gooiest apple dumpling before she attempted to persuade him again.

"Groossdaadi," she pleaded, her eyes expressing the urgency he couldn't hear in her voice. "I promise to keep them outside as much as possible. They will help with the chores. The boys will stack wood and clean the coop and do whatever else you need them to do. I will see to it they don't disturb you in your workshop."

This time her grandfather merely shook his head as he cut into the tender dumpling with the side of his fork. The crust oozed with sweet fruit.

"I know how hard you've worked to provide for us," Hannah said, tugging on his sleeve to make him read her lips. "But I've stretched our budget as far as I can, and it will only get worse when I am no longer a teacher. Please, *Groossdaadi*, let me do my part and earn this income."

As he ate the rest of his dessert, Hannah sent up a silent prayer. *Please, Lord, let him agree to what I've asked.* When he pushed his chair back across the floor, the scraping sound sent a chill up her spine, but she remained hopeful.

"They'd better not make too much noise," he warned crossly before retiring for the evening.

Hannah had to bite her tongue to keep from retorting, "But, *Groossdaadi*, how would you know if they did?" Having grown up under his thumb, she understood what he'd meant: he wouldn't permit them to make nuisances of themselves.

She threw her arms around his neck and looked him in the eye. "I will see to it they don't," she promised.

"Bah," he muttered, but he didn't pull away from her embrace until she let him go.

* * *

On the way home, when Sawyer asked the children how their first day at school was, they all spoke at once.

"We made friends with some other boys," Samuel said.

"Eli and Caleb. They said they have a German shepherd, and it had six puppies," Simon announced. "Can we have a puppy, *Daed*?"

"It's '*may* we.' Teacher says we're supposed to say '*may* I,' not '*can* I.' A *can* is something you store food in," Sarah corrected him. "I made a new friend, too, *Daed*. Her name is Abigail, but she said I can call her—I *may* call her—Abby."

Distracting the children from their request for a puppy—Gertrude was allergic—Sawyer commented, "It sounds as if you've already learned something from your teacher, too?"

"Jah," Samuel agreed. "We learned how to bat a ball after lunch hour! The teacher can hit it farther than anyone else, even the boys from the upper classes!"

"And she fixed my hair, see?" Sarah twisted in her seat to show him where her hair was neatly tucked into a bun. "It didn't hurt a bit, even the snarled parts. The teacher said her *mamm* taught her how to brush them out when she was a girl my age. Her hair is dark like a crow's and wavy, but mine is light like hay and straight, but she said her secret brushing method works on all colors of hair and all sizes of tangles."

As minor of a matter as grooming was, even Gertrude complained about how much Sarah always wiggled when she was combing her hair. During Gertrude's absence, Sawyer often had to refrain from using a harsh tone to make Sarah sit still. The small but important empathy Hannah demonstrated to his daughter by carefully fixing her bun seemed like a promising indicator of the care she'd provide as their nanny.

After they arrived home, the children helped with chores around the farm: Sarah swept the floors and sorted and washed vegetables, and the boys cleaned the chicken coop, stacked firewood and helped in the stable. Their chores in Ohio were similar, but because they lived on a modest plot of land in a neighborhood instead of in a large farmhouse on sizable acreage, their new assignments in Pennsylvania took them much longer to complete. Simon and Samuel usually had boundless energy, but by supper time, they were too weary to lift their chins from their chests at the table.

"Try a second helping of beef stew," Sawyer urged them.

"I'm too tired to chew," Samuel protested.

Simon asked, "May we go to bed?"

"Look," Sawyer pointed out. "*Onkel* bought special apple fry pies from Yoder's Bakery in town. You may have one if you eat a little more meat."

"*Denki, Onkel.* That was very thoughtful of you," Sarah said, imitating a phrase Sawyer knew she'd learned from Gertrude. "But I couldn't eat another bite."

"No promises the pies will be here tomorrow," Sawyer's cousin Phillip warned.

"We survived for five years without our *mamm* here to cook for us," Jonas, Sawyer's other cousin, scoffed. "You shouldn't coddle them, Sawyer, particularly the boys."

Sawyer got the feeling Jonas resented the children's presence, but he couldn't fault Simon, Samuel and Sarah for being too tired to eat; he, too, was exhausted from the day's events.

Still, he didn't believe in wasting food, and when

Simon chased a chunk of beef around his bowl with his spoon, Sawyer directed, "Sit up and eat your meal. *Waste not, want not,* as your *mamm* always said."

"I'm not hungry." The boy sighed.

Sawyer warned, "You need to eat so you can do well in school tomorrow."

"He'll just ask the teacher for a piece of sweet bread instead," Sarah said. "Like she gave him today."

"Sarah, it's not kind to tattle," Samuel reminded her. "Besides, the teacher gave us *all* a piece of bread."

"*Jah*, but she gave Simon an extra piece in the afternoon," Sarah reported. "The very last piece, smothered in strawberry preserves. Teacher says strawberries taste like pink sunshine."

"Sweets in the afternoon before supper," Jonas scoffed. "No wonder they turn up their noses at meat and potatoes. Pass me his serving. My appetite hasn't been spoiled and neither have I."

Simon ducked his head as he handed over his bowl. He had a small freckle on the top of his left earlobe, whereas Samuel had none. It was how Sawyer could tell the two boys apart when they were infants. Watching Simon's ears purpling with shame, Sawyer felt a small qualm about Hannah. Well-intentioned as the gesture may have been, Sawyer wondered if it represented her common practice. He couldn't allow her to continue to ply the children with sweets instead of wholesome meals if he expected them to grow healthier under her care, and he decided to speak to her about it when he saw her next.

After supper, Hannah's grandfather retired to his room to read Scripture as she washed the dishes and swept the floors. She folded the linens she had hung out to dry that morning before leaving for school. As she was putting them away, she passed the room that used to be Eve's. Spread on the bed was one of the quilts her younger sister had made. Although it was darker and plainer than those she fashioned to sell to tourists, there was no mistaking her meticulous stitching and patterns.

Hannah had never developed the superior sewing abilities Eve possessed. As the eldest, she was tasked with putting supper on the table, gardening, caring for Eve and meeting her grandfather's needs. Not that she minded; she felt indebted to her grandfather for raising her and Eve, and she knew the Lord provided everyone with different talents. She admired her sister's handiwork a moment longer before closing the bedroom door with a sigh. How Hannah missed Eve's chatter ever since she moved to Lancaster to set up house with her husband last year.

But at least now that Hannah would be watching the Plank children and she had lessons to plan and students' work to review, the evenings wouldn't seem to last forever, as they did during the summer months.

Kneeling by her bed, she prayed, Denki, *Lord, for Your providing for* Groossdaadi *and me, as You have always done. Please help me to be a* gut *nanny to Sarah, Simon and Samuel.*

She removed her prayer *kapp* and hung it on her headboard before sliding between the sheets. A loud rumble of thunder caused her nightstand to vibrate, and she closed her eyes before lightning illuminated the room. No matter how hard she tried to push the memory from her mind, the metallic smell in the air always brought her back to the night her mother and father perished when lightning struck the tree under which they'd sought shelter during a rainstorm. She had been such a young girl when it happened that the memory of the storm itself was more vivid than almost any recollection she had of her parents prior to their deaths.

She rolled onto her side and buried her face in the pillow, much like Sarah had buried her face in Hannah's sleeve when Sawyer failed to show up on time. Hannah wondered if Sarah was insecure because Sawyer was an unreliable parent or merely because she was anxious about being a newcomer. The boys seemed to be more outgoing than their sister was. They adjusted to their lessons magnificently and joined the games during lunch hour. But Sarah seemed uncertain, trying to say and do everything perfectly and in constant need of reassurance from Hannah. She supposed the girl might have been feeling at a loss without any other females on the farm, and she decided to do her best to serve as a role model for her.

Raindrops riveted the windowpane, and although the air was sultry, Hannah pulled the quilt over her head, mussing her hair. She recalled how Sarah's bun had come undone during lunch hour. Hannah giggled, imagining Sawyer struggling to pin his daughter's hair in place. Then, as she thought of his large, masculine hands, a shiver tickled her spine. The suddenness of it surprised her, but she attributed it to the change in air temperature.

Before drifting off, she anticipated showing the children the shortcut home from school and studying insects and birds along the way. She imagined teaching Sarah how to make sweet bread and chasing squirrels with Samuel and Simon. They would grow sturdy from her meals and smart from her tutelage. She would sing hymns and read stories to them on rainy afternoons. It would be like teaching, only different: it would be, she supposed, more like being a mother than she'd ever been. Now that she actually had the opportunity, she had to admit, she could hardly wait!

Sawyer felt as if a huge burden had been lifted from his shoulders. As he knelt beside his bed, he prayed, *Thank You, Lord, for Hannah's willingness to care for the* kinner. *Please work in her* groossdaadi's *heart to agree to it, as well. Bless Kathryn and her family, especially the baby, and keep watch over Gertrude. Please keep the crew safe and productive in Ohio.*

Praying about his employees, Sawyer exhaled loudly. Upon returning to the farm that afternoon, he had discovered a soggy express-mail letter in the box from his foreman reporting that one of his crew members severed his finger the day Sawyer left for Pennsylvania. *Due to being short staffed already, we are falling even further behind on orders*, the note said. It was another urgent reminder to Sawyer that he needed to hasten his work with his cousins so he could return home as soon as possible. At least being able to work longer days without interruptions would help with that.

He was relieved that Hannah, in particular, possibly would be watching the children. He owed her a debt of gratitude for rescuing him from Doris's clutches. He had known women like Doris in Ohio, who seemed to use the children's welfare as an excuse to call on him and Gertrude. At least, that was what Gertrude had claimed on a few occasions.

"I thought you wanted me to marry again," he teased one afternoon after Gertrude was irked by a female visitor who stopped by with a heaping tray of oatmeal whoopee pie cookies *and* an entire "sawdust pie." (When the woman found out Sawyer wasn't present, she took the sweets home without allowing the children or Gertrude to sample so much as a bite.)

"I *do* want you to marry again," Gertrude insisted. "But I want you to marry someone genuine, like Eliza."

There will never be anyone as genuine as Eliza, he thought.

Take Hannah, for instance. Whereas Eliza was soft-spoken and reserved, Hannah seemed a bit cheeky, which made it difficult to discern how sincere she was. Sawyer supposed Hannah was used to teasing men for sport; someone as becoming as she was no doubt found favor with the opposite gender, especially because she appeared competent and helpful, as well. Yet, surprisingly, she was unmarried—Sawyer ruefully imagined her suitors probably were tardy arriving to court her, so she turned them away.

Lightning reflected off the white sheets on Sawyer's bed and thunder shook the walls. He stretched his neck, listening for Sarah's cries, but there were none. He figured she was too exhausted to stir.

Sawyer's thoughts drifted to the dark tendrils framing Hannah's face that afternoon. They had probably come loose when she was playing ball with her students. He supposed someone who earned the affection of his daughter and the admiration of his sons in one day deserved his high regard, too. It wasn't her fault she was so pretty; he recognized he shouldn't judge her for that.

He remembered how Hannah suddenly hurried him out the door that afternoon. Despite her authority in the classroom and her outspoken joshing, there was something unmistakably vulnerable in her eyes. But he had no doubt she'd take excellent care of Simon, Samuel and Sarah—especially once he restricted the amount of treats she served them—for the short time they were visiting Pennsylvania.

As the sky released its torrents, Sawyer's contented sigh turned into a yawn and he rolled onto his side. He slumbered through the night, waking only once when he had a dream of bread smothered in strawberry jam that was so real, he almost thought he could taste its sweetness on his lips.

The next morning, Hannah rose early to prepare a hearty breakfast for her grandfather, and she set aside an ample lunch, too. If Sawyer Plank was tardy again after school, she didn't want her grandfather to accuse her of neglecting his appetite. She ate only a small portion herself in order to stretch their food budget, but she took the bread crusts with her. At lunch, she'd spread them with the preserves Abigail had given her, an indulgent treat these days.

She scuttled the mile and a half to the school yard from her home. Built on the corner of the Zook farm, the tiny house and plot of land were all her grandfather had ever been able to afford. But Jeremiah Zook had always granted Hannah and Eve access to the rolling meadow, thriving stream and dense copse of trees on the south side of the property. The setting provided the young sisters a serene and spacious haven from their grandfather's unrelenting demands.

As an adult, Hannah still chose to zigzag across the acreage on her way to and from school instead of taking the main roads. She always felt she could breathe deeper and think more clearly after strolling the grassy and wooded paths she knew by heart.

The weather was still unseasonably warm, and her upper lip beaded with perspiration as she picked her way across the final damp field. From a distance, she could see a single buggy in the lane by the school, which was strange since Doris was usually the last to arrive and the first to leave. As she drew nearer, she spotted three familiar blond heads, bobbing in and out from behind the trees during a game of tag. Sawyer was perched on the steps.

"Guder mariye," she greeted him, before adding, "Your horse's legs must have healed. You're early."

A peculiar look passed across Sawyer's face, and Hannah immediately regretted her comment. She had meant it to be playful, not vexing. There was something so solemn about his demeanor she couldn't help but try to elicit a little levity.

"If we're too early, I will wait with the *kinner* until you're ready for them to come inside," he replied seriously.

"Neh, you mustn't do that," she said by way of apology, but then recognized it seemed as if she were dismissing him from the yard. She quickly explained, "You are free to leave the *kinner* or to stay with them as long as you wish. You're free to stay with them outside, that is—not in the classroom. Unless you also need help with your spelling or mathematics."

There she went again! Insulting him when she only meant to break the ice. This time, however, a smile played at the corner of his lips.

"My spelling and mathematics are strong," he said. "It's only my time-telling that suffers."

"Your time-telling is already improving," Hannah said generously. "I notice you're working on your daughter's grooming skills, as well. I don't mean to intrude on your efforts, but if Sarah's hair should need additional straightening, would you allow me to complete the task?"

"Allow you? I would *wilkom* you," he insisted. "It's no intrusion. Especially if you are to become the *kinner's* nanny."

His enthusiasm delighted Hannah, who tipped her head upward to meet his eyes. "I'm glad you mentioned that," she trilled. "Because my *groossdaadi* has agreed that I may watch the *kinner* after school, beginning Monday."

"That's *wunderbaar*!" Sawyer boomed, and again Hannah was warmed by his unbridled earnestness.

Just then, Simon skidded to a stop in between them and thrust his fist up toward his father.

"Look! Have you ever seen such a big toad?"

"It *is* huge," Hannah acknowledged, studying the boy's catch. "It's the same color as the dirt. You must have keen eyesight to be able to spot him."

The little boy modestly replied, "I didn't know he was there at first, but then I saw something hopping and that's when I grabbed him."

Samuel and Sarah circled Simon to get another look.

"Not too tight, Simon. You're squeezing him," Sawyer cautioned. "You must be careful not to harm it."

As he spoke, Hannah felt his warm breath on the nape of her neck as she bent over the amphibian. She hadn't realized Sawyer was standing in such close proximity, and she was overcome with a peculiar sensation of dizziness.

She stepped backward and announced, "You ought to release him now, Simon. Be sure to wipe your hands, please."

With that, she darted up the steps and into the classroom. *"Mach's gut,"* she said, bidding Sawyer goodbye over her shoulder.

* * *

As the horse made its way back to the farm, Sawyer rubbed his forehead. Hannah had ended the conversation so abruptly he didn't have a chance to speak to her about not giving the children treats. He had no idea what caused her brusque departure, although he noticed she visibly recoiled when he scolded Simon; had she thought him too strict?

Eliza at times had grimaced when he'd corrected the children as youngsters. They had spoken about it once toward the end of her illness, after the triplets were asleep and Eliza herself was lying in bed.

"Of course, *kinner* must be disciplined to obey their parents," she said when he asked for her opinion. "It is our greatest responsibility to train them in what is right and to keep them safe."

"But?" he questioned.

"But, my dear Sawyer." Eliza sighed. "You are so tall and the *kinner* so small—sometimes it seems you don't realize the strength of your own voice. I know how gentle you are, but to *kinner* or to strangers, a single loud word may be perceived as threatening as the growl of a bear."

She had been right: Sawyer admitted he hadn't realized the intimidating effect of his size and volume. He'd raised his hands like two giant paws and let out a roar to make Eliza laugh, which she did, as weak as she was. After that, he made a concentrated effort to speak in a low but firm voice, but perhaps this morning his volume had been too loud?

Then he asked himself why he should be bothered about what Hannah Lantz thought of him. She was a virtual stranger. Besides, *Gott* knew the intention of his heart, just as Eliza had always known.

Troubled he'd found himself comparing Eliza and Hannah, Sawyer was glad for the heavy field work that lay before him, which allowed him to pour all of his energy into the physical labor and sufficiently rid his mind of memories of Eliza and notions about Hannah.

By late afternoon, the air was oppressive with humidity, and as Sawyer rode toward the schoolhouse, a line of clouds billowed across the horizon. He was neither early nor late for dismissal; as he approached, several children scampered across the yard and climbed into buggies parked beneath the willow. After waiting a few minutes without seeing Sarah, Samuel and Simon, he jumped down and strode toward the building. A few hot raindrops splashed against his skin before he tentatively pushed the door open.

Inside, the children were paying rapt attention as Hannah read aloud to them from a book opened in her lap. He had never seen the boys sit so still. When Sawyer cleared his throat, she glanced up in his direction, her eyes dancing.

"Here is your *daed* now, Sarah," she said. "Didn't I tell you he'd arrive on time?"

"I was waiting outside," he explained, removing his hat. "You told me earlier I wasn't to come indoors."

She tilted her head and pursed her lips in the curious manner she had a way of doing, and then recognition swept over her expression. "Not during lessons, *neh*, but you are allowed—indeed, you are *wilkom*—to come in after school. It's no intrusion."

Her repetition of the same phrases he'd used earlier that morning gave him pause. Did he dare to think she was deliberately being facetious? If so, it was difficult to tell; her quips were far subtler and more amusing than Doris's overt coquetry.

His mouth was so dry, all he could muster was *"Denki,"* and this time he was the one who departed abruptly without saying another word.

Chapter Three

The warm weather caused the yeast to rise quickly. As Hannah kneaded the dough the following morning, she racked her mind for recipes she could make once Simon, Samuel and Sarah arrived. She had been so thrilled that she'd convinced her grandfather to allow her to watch the Plank children that she'd neglected the practical details involved in the arrangement. Every month, she budgeted their meal allowance down to the penny; she didn't know where the money would come from to feed her grandfather and herself as well as the children. As it was, she wouldn't receive the next installment of her teacher's salary until the first of October.

"I should bring your toys to the shop on Saturday," Hannah mouthed to her grandfather when he looked up from his plate of eggs and potatoes at breakfast.

It wasn't too early for tourists to begin shopping for Christmas during their excursions through the countryside. The sooner Hannah's grandfather put the wooden trains, tractors and dollhouses on consignment, the better. She also hoped one of the toys her *groossdaadi* put on consignment last month sold, which would help supplement the cost of groceries for the upcoming week.

"I'll take you," he shouted, wiping his face with a napkin.

She had hoped to go alone; his handling of the buggy made her nervous. He couldn't hear passing traffic and many a car had to swerve to avoid hitting him when he should have yielded. Also, he bellowed so loudly to the shopkeeper, the poor man cringed and shrugged, which frustrated her grandfather. Hannah inevitably had to translate.

"Are you certain? I expect it will be a very hot and busy day."

"Am I certain?" he repeated. "I am certain of this— my toys put food on the table. If I am to get the best price, I must accompany you. Unless you wish us to starve as I nearly did yesterday?"

Even if her grandfather had been able to hear, she wouldn't have pointed out that her teaching salary—and soon, her temporary income from watching the Plank children—also helped put food on the table. Compared with his provisions over the years, she felt her contribution was meager at best.

"Of course not, *Groossdaadi*," Hannah replied. "I'm sorry you were hungry yesterday. I sliced extra bologna for you today."

Please, Lord, continue to provide my groossdaadi *and me our daily bread*, she prayed as she wrapped a few bread crusts to take to school for lunch. *And allow the loaf to rise big enough to feed Samuel, Sarah and Simon, as well.*

Come sunrise, Sawyer woke the children to get dressed for school. As the boys pulled their shirts over their heads, he noticed how prominent their ribs and shoulder blades were becoming. How had this happened during the few weeks Gertrude was away? It emphasized the need for them to return home and establish their normal routine as soon as possible.

He was grateful his uncle prepared a substantial breakfast of ham and eggs, but it was so early the children hadn't any appetites, especially not for a meal fit for grown men. Sawyer bundled fruit and bread with slices of meat into separate sacks for each of them for lunch. After instructing them to complete their morning chores, he strode to the barn with his cousins.

His body ached as he walked. Farming required him to use a different set of muscles from those he exercised at his cabinetry shop. The leftover stew they'd eaten for dinner the night before sat like a rock in his gut. No wonder the children were unable to finish their portions. As he groaned from the effects of nausea and the stifling morning air, he remembered he needed to discuss the children's dietary needs with Hannah. Yet he couldn't imagine how he might broach the subject or what her reaction would be.

There was something—not necessarily mysterious, nor distrustful, but definitely skittish—about Hannah that caused him to want to measure his words with her. Or at least, that caused him not to want to offend her. Yet he seemed to do exactly that.

The dilemma occupied his mind as he performed the morning chores, and he tried to recall how he and Eliza settled their differences concerning the children. Funny, but he couldn't remember having many. Without speaking about it, they tended to naturally agree on what was best for Simon, Samuel and Sarah. Their mutually shared perspective about raising the children was a strength he missed terribly. Even when they disagreed about some small aspect of the children's care,

Eliza's opinion was invaluable to Sawyer and they always reached a reasonable compromise. He wished she were there to guide him about what to do now.

By the time he had hitched up the horse to take the children to school, he concluded being forthright about the sweets was the best approach. Hannah undoubtedly would understand and honor his requests concerning the children, but unless he made them clear, how would she know what they were? After all, she was no Eliza.

Hannah was still so excited about the prospect of becoming a nanny that she hadn't been able to eat when she sat down with her grandfather for breakfast. So when she arrived half an hour early to school, she settled behind her desk and peeled the shell from a hard-boiled egg.

Still trying to come up with inexpensive meals she could make for the children, she realized as long as the chickens were laying, eggs were plentiful, a good source of protein and cost nothing. Likewise, the garden was still going strong with tomatoes and corn, but she brooded about their limited dairy supply, knowing how important milk was for growing children.

When she finished her egg, she smeared a dab of preserves over a crust of bread. She was wiping the corner of her mouth with a napkin when the heavy door inched open.

"Guder mariye, Teacher," the triplets said in unison. With their pink cheeks and blond hair backlit by the sun streaming in behind them, they looked positively adorable, and Hannah couldn't help but smile at their appearance.

"Guder mariye," she replied. "Is it just the three of

you today, or have you brought your friend, the toad, inside?"

She was referring to the toad they'd caught the previous morning, but as soon as she finished her sentence, Sawyer crossed the threshold.

"Guder mariye," he stated apprehensively. "Might I have a word with you outside?"

She followed him to the landing and squinted up at him. Against the sunshine, he appeared aglow, with the light rimming his strapping shoulders in golden hues and bouncing off his blond curls. But when she noticed his austere expression, she worried he might have thought she was referencing *him* when she'd asked the children about the toad.

"Is something wrong?" she questioned.

"Neh..." Sawyer objected slowly. "But there's something I'd like to bring to your attention."

Hannah thought whatever it was he wanted to discuss, it must have been a grave matter—he could hardly look at her.

"How may I be of assistance?" she asked, hoping to put him at ease.

"You are already of assistance. Perhaps too much so," he began hesitantly. He glanced away and back at her. "It is my understanding that you gave sweet bread and preserves to Simon the other afternoon?"

Oh, then, it wasn't a serious matter at all. He simply wanted to thank her; how kind.

"It was a trifling. I'm happy to share with any child who may be hungry."

"But it wasn't a trifling," Sawyer countered. "It ruined Simon's appetite for more substantial food. I recognize many Amish families consider pastries and other treats to be part of their daily bread—especially in Willow Creek. But, as you probably noticed, my *kinner* are a bit thin and it is important for their physical health that they receive adequate sustenance. I trust the meals you will prepare as part of the *kinner's* daily care will be nutritious and substantial, with limited sweets?"

Hannah felt as if the air had been squeezed from her lungs. Here she had sacrificed her entire noonday meal and Sawyer was acting as if she'd tried to *poison* the boy. She felt at once both foolish and angry, and her face blazed as she struggled to keep her composure.

"Of course," she agreed. "*Kinner*—all *kinner*, whether they are from Pennsylvania or Ohio—do need sustenance, which is why I often bring extra eggs or a slice of meat to school. Two days ago, I had only brought bread enough for me. Your Simon upended the lunch sack into the dirt, so I gave bread and jam to him as well as to Sarah and Samuel. But Simon later complained of a headache and I thought it was because he was still hungry, so I permitted him another piece. But I apologize for ruining his appetite for *adequate sustenance*. I assure you it won't happen again, and I most definitely will prepare healthy recipes while they are under my care."

She stomped up the stairs and into the classroom, leaving Sawyer alone on the stoop.

Sawyer was so abashed, he didn't know whether to follow Hannah and apologize or flee as quickly as he could. As he was hesitating, an approaching buggy caught his eye and he decided to leave.

He tried to shrug off his interaction with her as being an unfortunate misunderstanding, but despite his efforts, throughout the morning he couldn't shake her expression from his mind. She looked as if she'd been stung. And no wonder—he'd been such an oaf, criticizing her when she was only looking after Simon's welfare.

"Are you watching the clouds or napping with your eyes open?" Jonas ribbed him when he drifted into thought.

He wiped his hands on his trousers without saying a word and continued to work. He decided there was only one thing he could do—apologize to Hannah. He needed to be as forthright now as he'd tried to be this morning. He completed his tasks with a new vigor, motivated by his resolve to set things right.

But when he arrived at the schoolhouse, Samuel, Sarah and Simon were playing tag with a girl Sawyer recognized from the first day of school.

"Where is your teacher?" he called to them.

"She's inside, speaking to my wife, Miriam," a voice from behind him answered. The dark-haired man was short and stout. "I'm Jacob Stolzfus and that girl your son is chasing around the willow is my daughter, Abigail. You must be Sawyer Plank, John's nephew."

"I am," Sawyer responded. "Those are my *kinner*, Sarah, Simon and Samuel, the one who just tagged your daughter."

"Abigail has told us about your Sarah," Jacob commented. "She already is very fond of her."

"Sarah is pleased to have a girl her age for a friend, as well," Sawyer acknowledged. "Usually her brothers are her primary playmates. She's happy not to be outnumbered."

As they spoke, the door to the schoolhouse swung open and Miriam and Hannah emerged. Miriam was stroking her swollen belly and chatting animatedly. A breeze played with the strings of Hannah's prayer *kapp*, and Sawyer was distracted by the sight of her lifting a slender hand to cover her bright pink lips, as if to contain a mirthful gasp.

"How about you?" Jacob was saying.

"Pardon?"

"How do you find Willow Creek so far?"

"It's to my liking," he answered absentmindedly, still watching as Miriam and Hannah descended the staircase. "It is unique, to say the least."

"You might consider staying beyond the harvest, since you wouldn't be leaving behind a farm of your own in Ohio," suggested Jacob. "Our district is shrinking. Any relative of John Plank's would be *wilkom* to take up residence here permanently. We could use a young family like yours in our district."

At the bottom step, Hannah glanced up and Sawyer caught her eye. He noticed a slight dimming of her countenance before she continued to amble with Miriam toward their buggy.

"Neh," Sawyer replied definitively. "I am only here for a short while to help my *onkel,* as you apparently have heard. Everything I have is in Ohio—my business, my home, my family. People there depend on me and I on them. It's true I don't own a farm, but the Lord gave me responsibilities there I wouldn't soon abandon."

He sharply called to the triplets, who sprinted across the lawn and piled into the buggy. The children waved to Abigail, her family and Hannah as they rode away, but Sawyer kept his eyes locked on the road ahead of him.

That night when supper was served and they each asked for second helpings—Simon even requested a third—he decided no matter Hannah's reason for feeding his children, he had been right to prohibit her from giving them sweets before supper as a general rule. An apology to her wasn't necessary after all.

Hannah wiped her forehead with the back of her hand. She hoped the hot spell would break, but it still seemed more like the dog days of summer than nearly autumn. She was grateful Jacob and Miriam had given her a ride home from school on their way back from town, but standing over the gas stove cooking supper in the tiny kitchen caused her to sweat almost as much as if she'd walked home.

"It's dry," her grandfather said disgustedly about the chicken she'd prepared. "Bring me a different piece."

Since she had served the only meat they had, Hannah took both of their plates to the stove and covertly switched her piece with his, slicing off the ends so he wouldn't notice. While her back was still turned toward him, she practiced an old trick she and Eve sometimes used to communicate with each other.

"Just once I wish I had someone to talk to in the evening who had something pleasant to say." She spoke aloud, knowing he couldn't see to read her lips. "Either that, or I wish *I* were the one who was deaf, so I couldn't hear your surly remarks."

Without Eve's sympathetic ear, expressing herself in such a manner did little to defuse Hannah's frustration, and she remained feisty until bedtime, rushing through her evening prayers before crawling into bed. She kicked off her sheets as a drop of perspiration trickled down the side of her cheek and into her ear. Or perhaps it was a tear. Despite her best efforts to please everyone, the day had been plagued with upsetting events.

First, Sawyer had shamed her for sharing her bread

with Simon. Then Miriam had shown up at the school-house at the end of the day and her effervescent glee emphasized how bereft Hannah felt.

Although Amish women were reluctant to discuss such matters—sometimes not even mentioning they were carrying a child until the baby was born—Mir-iam confided that earlier in the morning, she had con-sulted a midwife.

"I'll soon give birth to a healthy *bobbel*, *Gott* will-ing," Miriam tearfully divulged. "After losing three unborn *bobblin*, I can't tell you how joyful we are."

"I am very joyful for you," Hannah said, squeezing Miriam's arm. "I will keep you in my prayers."

"*Denki.* The midwife warned me that meanwhile I must limit my physical activities. Abigail is a help, but with her at school, it's difficult for me to keep up the house and garden."

Judging from how full-figured Miriam had become, Hannah guessed she had merely a month or two before she delivered, but that was an unspoken subject, some-thing only God knew for certain.

She was truly glad for Miriam and Jacob, and she wouldn't have dreamed of begrudging them such fulfill-ment. Nor did she envy Miriam's marriage: she'd always known Jacob wasn't the Lord's intended for her. But Miriam's news made her all the more aware that soon she'd have to bid her students goodbye—and teaching them was the closest she'd ever come to having *kinner* herself. What was she going to do without their daily presence in her life?

It didn't help that just as Miriam was telling her about the *bobbel*, Hannah glimpsed Sawyer conversing with Jacob, and his chastisement burned afresh in her mind.

It almost seemed as if neither man nor God believed she was fit to care for children!

Her hurt was further magnified by the letter she had received upon arriving home.

Dearest Hannah, her sister's familiar penmanship said. *I am so ecstatic I will burst if I have to keep it to myself any longer: I am with child!*

Of course, Hannah was elated that God had provided such a blessing for Eve, and she was exuberant she would soon be an aunt. But her joy was tinged with envy. Not only had her sister managed—at twenty-four years of age, which was considered late in life by their district's standards—to meet and marry a good man who thoroughly loved her, but soon she'd experience motherhood, too.

Every time Hannah thought she'd finally accepted that her prime responsibility was to care for her grandfather and her life wouldn't include marriage or children, the desire for both manifested itself again, like symptoms of a virus she couldn't shake. Would she ever be cured of the longing to have what it seemed she wasn't meant to? *And why can't I have it?* she lamented. It wasn't as if she longed for something sinful: the Bible described children and married life as being gifts from God.

She eased out of bed, donned her prayer *kapp* and knelt in the darkness. *Please, Lord, show me Your provision for my life, especially once my teaching job ends,* she beseeched. *And help me to be content with it, whatever it may be.*

When she awoke the next morning, her pillow was still damp and her eyes were swollen, but her spirit was inexplicably peaceful. She didn't know how it would happen, but she did know one way or another, God would provide for all of her physical, emotional and spiritual needs. She donned her *kapp* and knelt again.

Lord, please forgive my envy and lack of faith. Help me to spend this day in glad service to You, she prayed.

Despite the heat, she felt refreshed as she hiked through the fields toward the schoolhouse, listening to the birds and inhaling the scent of wildflowers. After Sawyer's visit the previous morning, she had distanced herself from Sarah, Simon and Samuel for the rest of the day, fearing their father might interpret any kind attention she paid to them as spoiling them.

But this morning, she realized she hadn't responded maturely to Sawyer's misunderstanding or given him a chance to acknowledge his mistake. She saw why he was concerned about his children's health, and she'd certainly respect his wishes regarding their diet. As long as she didn't give them treats, she didn't believe he'd fault her for being nurturing and warm.

The thought of a treat caused her mouth to water. Yesterday she was so out of sorts that she barely swallowed five bites of supper, and suddenly she felt ravenous. When she reached the classroom, she unwrapped a piece of sweet bread from her bag and pulled the preserves from the cooler. She bit into a thick slice, closing her eyes to enjoy the flavor in quiet solitude.

"*Guder mariye*, Teacher," several small voices squeaked merrily, interrupting her thoughts.

Her mouth was too full to reply, but she reflexively stashed the remaining food into her bag, embarrassed to be caught eating at her desk again.

"*Guder mariye*," Sawyer echoed his children.

Hannah chewed quickly and then swallowed before replying. "*Guder mariye.*"

"Is that the bread your *groossmammi* learned you how to make?" Samuel pointed.

"*Teached* you," Sarah corrected. "And it's not polite to point."

"Hush," Sawyer instructed them both. "We disrupted your teacher's breakfast. *Kumme*, we'll wait outside until she is finished."

"*Denki*, but I wasn't really eating," Hannah protested.

Sawyer noticed a smudge of preserves at the corner of her mouth. She must have sensed him looking at it, because she traced her lips with her finger, her cheeks blotching with color.

"I mean, I wasn't eating breakfast," she faltered. "It was only a treat. I have eggs for breakfast. Sometimes ham. That is, despite what you may think, I don't ordinarily just have treats for breakfast. Or for snacks. Or at any time of the day. Not every day, anyway, or not without eating something else, as well. But I was terribly hungry, you see, because—"

"I am terribly hungry, too," Sawyer interrupted. His resolve not to apologize suddenly dissipated, and he felt nothing but a desire to ease Hannah's discomfort, which he knew he had caused with his comments the day before. "The *kinner* are hungry, as well. Last night, my *onkel's* dinner sat like bricks in our bellies, so this morning we were unable to eat breakfast. What we wouldn't do for a piece of bread and strawberry preserves…"

Cocking her head to one side, Hannah narrowed her eyes at him for what seemed an interminable pause. Rather than speaking, she again removed the jar of preserves from the cooler and pulled the bread apart in chunks. After spooning a dollop onto each piece, she directed the triplets to eat theirs at their desks. She gave the biggest piece to Sawyer, who stood next to her while he devoured it.

When he was finished, he wiped his mouth with the back of his hand. "I must apologize," he began. "I fear I misjudged you."

"Say no more. I accept your apology." She smiled readily. Then she asked, "Are your *onkel's* meals really like bricks in your bellies?"

"Unfortunately, they are. In fact, I have a hunch Simon dropped their lunch bag on purpose. I know I would have, if it meant I'd get to eat a piece of your sweet bread instead."

Hannah's giggle reminded him of a wind chime. "It tastes alright, then?"

"Better than a dream," Sawyer replied.

Hannah's face again flushed. "That's a kind thing for you to say," she replied modestly and busied herself putting the lid on the jar before meeting his eyes again.

"I want you to know I *do* understand and respect your concerns about your *kinner's* health," she said somberly. "I have noticed they are thin, but it's possible they're going through a growth spurt, and their width hasn't caught up with their height yet. In any case, in Willow Creek, we like to think our *gut* farm air has a way of working up healthy appetites, and I'll feed those appetites with wholesome, hearty suppers."

Sawyer blinked and ran his hands over his head, pushing back his curls. Until that instant, he hadn't realized how much he'd needed reassurance that the children would be alright. He was so often in the position of instructing and comforting his children, encouraging Gertrude and guiding his crew at work that he rarely received a word of consolation himself. Her sentiment was as heartening as something Eliza may have said, and he was touched. His silence allowed Hannah to continue speaking.

"My intention is to help relieve your concerns, Sawyer, not to add to them. I hope you won't worry about Simon, Sarah and Samuel while they're under my care. But if you have a concern, please tell me—I promise not to have another tantrum like a *kind* myself, as I did yesterday."

Sawyer broke into a huge grin. "Hannah Lantz," he replied, "you may be slight in stature, but you most certainly are no child!"

When Hannah looked perplexed, he rushed to explain, "I mean that you're every bit a woman."

Her forehead and cheeks went pink and her eyes widened. Clearly he was embarrassing her.

"An adult, that is," Sawyer clarified. "Someone I wholeheartedly trust to mind my *kinner*."

As he stood there feeling every bit the fool, two boys shuffled up the stairs into the classroom.

"*Guder mariye*, Caleb and Eli," Hannah greeted them. To Sawyer she said, "Those are friends of Samuel and Simon's."

"Ah, Caleb, whose bloody mouth you tended to—the *kinner* told me about it."

"High drama in the school yard," Hannah said with a giggle, and Sawyer knew any awkwardness between them had passed. "It's all in a day's work."

"Speaking of work," Sawyer remembered, "I should be going now."

"Me, too." Hannah nodded. "I hope you have a pleasant day."

The day was already far more pleasant than Sawyer could have hoped for himself.

Chapter Four

"Be careful!" Hannah's grandfather commanded as she helped him hoist the dollhouse into the buggy Saturday morning. "This could fetch a pretty penny, but not if you crack it."

Hannah dismissed his harsh admonishment as concern about their income. The dollhouse was larger and more detailed than any he'd ever made before—clearly he had designed it to appeal to *Englisch* tourists—so it was no wonder he wanted to be certain it arrived without a nick. She mopped her brow and took her place beside him in the buggy, uttering a silent prayer for travel mercies.

As they sped past the fields and into town, Hannah let her mind wander to her conversation with Sawyer, as it had often done in the past hours, making light work of wringing and hanging the clothes and scrubbing the floors. *Better than a dream*, he had said about her sweet bread. She knew pride was a sin, but being given a compliment was such a rare occurrence she couldn't help but treasure his words. They weren't merely flattery, either—his bright green eyes had shone with genuine earnestness as he'd spoken the phrase.

A driver honked his horn, jarring Hannah from her thoughts. She touched her grandfather's sleeve to warn him of the approaching vehicle so he could move to the shoulder of the road, but he jerked his arm away. She was relieved when they finally pulled into the lane behind the mercantile. So many tourists' cars filled the lot that Hannah and her grandfather had to tie their horse at the designated horse and buggy plot nearly a quarter of a mile away.

They purchased their groceries and returned to the buggy to secure them there before heading to Schrock's Shop, which was located three doors down from the mercantile. Hannah helped her grandfather unload the dollhouse first; they'd come back to retrieve the other toys later. She was aware of but not bothered by the curious stares of the *Englischers* as they trudged down the long street toward the shop.

Hannah's grandfather had been apprenticed as a carpenter—he once owned a small furniture shop that eventually closed for lack of business. After that, he reluctantly went to work in the *Englisch*-run factory on the edge of town. Ever since the company retired him some eight years ago, he had been consigning wooden toys at Schrock's, where his work was highly prized among tourists. Eve's quilts were equally appreciated. However, sometimes it seemed the *Englisch* were willing to *praise* more than they were willing to *pay*, so the income generated from the sales was nominal at best.

Still, the sales had been a provision from the Lord, and Hannah thought about how thankful she was for that as she pulled open the door to the back entrance.

"Guder nammidaag," she said, wishing a good afternoon to Joseph Schrock, Daniel Schrock's son, who

was in charge of making consignment arrangements for new merchandise.

He looked up from where he was sitting at his desk, a pinched expression on his face. "Good afternoon, Hannah, Albert," he greeted them in *Englisch.*

As they placed the dollhouse carefully on the floor, Hannah expected Joseph to fuss over it more than he usually did, since the dollhouse was especially handsome. Instead, Joseph slid his pencil behind his ear and offered them a chair.

Her grandfather refused. "I am not so old I need to sit after a stroll down the lane."

Hannah's cheeks grew hot, but out of respect for her grandfather, she remained standing, too. Joseph excused himself to close the door leading to the main gallery where the customers browsed.

"The news isn't good, Albert," Joseph acknowledged. He mouthed the words toward Hannah's grandfather, but his eyes shifted to Hannah. He held up two fingers. "Only two of your items sold since you were last here. The *Englisch* are less inclined to buy wooden toys any longer. They spend their money on electronic devices, I am told."

Hannah chewed her lip, nodding.

"I'm afraid we have to limit the amount of shelf space we can devote to your items, Albert. Until what you have here already sells, we cannot accept more toys. Especially not something as large as that dollhouse."

Hannah's grandfather pounded his fist against the desktop, causing Hannah and Joseph both to jump.

"I made the cradle you slept in, Joseph Schrock!" he shouted. "Your own sons have slept in it, as well. Now, are you to tell me you're turning away my goods?"

"My father made the decision, and it is final," Joseph stated, nervously pushing his glasses from where they'd slid down the bridge of his nose.

"What is final," Hannah's grandfather thundered, "is that we will never darken your doorstep again!"

He grunted as he bent to heave the dollhouse from the floor, and Hannah leaped to his aid.

"I'm sorry," Joseph apologized to her. "I hope you understand."

Hannah felt pulled between being loyal to her grandfather and being polite to Joseph. She dipped her head so her grandfather wouldn't see her lips move but replied in their German dialect so Joseph would remember whom he was dealing with. "*Mach's gut*, Joseph."

Although he spent Saturday morning working in the fields with his cousins, Sawyer cut his work short to take a trip into town in the afternoon for groceries. John was learning to navigate around the house on his crutches and to provide minimal assistance on the farm, but he still couldn't climb into and out of the buggy without another adult helping him. Rather than having two adults make the trip, Sawyer volunteered to go.

Samuel, Sarah and Simon were apt contributors to the daily chores around the house and with the farm animals. The boys also wanted to participate however they could in the fields, but Sawyer's cousins generally treated them more like hindrances than helpers, and often sent them on errands to fetch tools that were impossibly heavy for the boys to carry on their own. Sawyer thought it best to keep the children from being underfoot.

He also figured by doing the shopping he'd have a bit of input into what kind of meals John prepared for breakfast and dinner. But his main objective was to stock up on staples for Hannah and her grandfather, who surely weren't equipped to feed three more mouths.

Sawyer and the children were toting packages toward their buggy when Simon hooted, "Look, there's Teacher!"

Across the street, an old man and Hannah were struggling to lug a cumbersome object along the sidewalk.

"They have a dollhouse!" Sarah marveled.

"Kumme," Sawyer directed. "Follow closely."

He led them across the street through a clearing in traffic.

"Hannah," he beckoned. "Hannah Lantz!"

She came to a halt but the old man continued, nearly losing his balance. The dollhouse teetered between them. Sawyer dropped his parcels where he stood and lunged to steady their burden.

"Please, allow me," he said as he deftly pulled the dollhouse to his chest. In the process, his arm brushed Hannah's, and heat rose to his face. The touch was unintended, but he hoped she didn't think his gesture was impudent or resent him for interfering.

"Denki," she replied and greeted the children, but she didn't introduce the old man, who had pivoted and swooped up Sawyer's packages from the sidewalk.

"My sons can carry those," Sawyer began to say, but the man walked on without acknowledging him.

"My *groossdaadi* is deaf," Hannah reminded him quietly, so the children wouldn't hear. "He is also stubborn, so please let him carry the bags. We are just down there, on the other side of the lot."

Sawyer nodded and they continued walking side by side. In his peripheral vision, he noticed her expression was so forlorn, he wondered if she was ill. Was this the same woman whose lilting laughter had filled the schoolroom only days before? He tried to think of something conversational to say, but he drew a blank.

At the buggy, Hannah's grandfather handed the packages to the boys and Sawyer helped him secure the dollhouse into the back. The old man untied the horse from the far end of the hitching rail and repositioned the carriage. Then he climbed inside next to Hannah and took the reins in his hands.

Only then did he pause to acknowledge Sawyer, who looked him squarely in the eye and enunciated exaggeratedly, "I am Sawyer Plank, whose *kinner* Hannah will be caring for after school."

"Albert Lantz," the man yelled back.

"That is high-quality workmanship," Sawyer stated, nodding toward the dollhouse.

"Hmpff," the man snorted, but his eyes seemed to brighten.

"Your granddaughter Hannah is a fine teacher," Sawyer said. "The *kinner*—"

But before he could finish his sentence, the old man broke eye contact and slapped the reins against the horse's back.

"Giddy up!" he shouted, and Sawyer hopped back, his legs buckling beneath him as the wheels rolled forward and the buggy pulled away.

Hannah clenched her fists on her lap, fighting back tears. It was bad enough that her grandfather had demonstrated such an unbridled temper to Joseph Schrock, but he had been deliberately rude to Sawyer Plank, as well.

Joseph knew what her grandfather was like, but Sawyer met him only today. Perhaps Sawyer might have believed her grandfather didn't hear the words he spoke, but there was no mistaking the fact that her grandfather nearly rolled over his foot with the buggy! Why did he behave that way, especially toward someone who was being as helpful as Sawyer was?

By the time they returned home, carried the dollhouse back to his workshop and Hannah had set supper on the table, her grandfather's mood seemed to have lightened. Hannah's burden, however, had intensified, as she wondered how to stretch out their meals. If only her grandfather hadn't left the store in such haste— they hadn't collected what was due them from the two toys that sold, and they desperately needed the money.

"You are not eating?" he asked when Hannah took only a scant amount of pork and sauerkraut.

"The heat," she mouthed simply, waving her hand in the air to indicate the warm weather even though she doubted it was the humidity that tied her stomach up in knots.

"I'll have another helping," he ordered, thrusting the dish toward Hannah.

She knew his request meant he enjoyed the food more than usual, and she served him an ample scoop. At least the next day she wouldn't have to worry about providing their dinner, since they'd eat following church service. She only needed to be certain to have a light meal on hand in the event they received unexpected visitors for Sunday night supper, as was the practice in their district.

After she dried the last dish, she sat adjacent to her grandfather, who was silently reading the weekly newspaper, *The Budget*. Out of the corner of her eye, Hannah could see the man's profile fringed by the gray of his sideburns and beard. His lips moved as he read to himself, and she was instantly filled with compassion.

She supposed the way he saw it, the shopkeeper's son might as well have told him his life's work was meaningless. Her grandfather once had a reputation for being one of the most skilled furniture makers in the district, and now he couldn't even peddle his toys to *Englisch* tourists, who weren't exactly esteemed for their eye for craftsmanship.

He was old, deaf and near penniless, and she realized he deserved more respect than certain people— including herself, if only in her thoughts—had given him. Hadn't he raised her and provided for her all these years? And didn't she know how troubling it was to feel as if you'd lost your purpose? She might have lashed out the same way if she were in his shoes.

Before folding back her sheets that night, she silently prayed, asking God to forgive her own anger and allow her to mend the rift with Joseph Schrock her grandfather had created by his. She ended by asking once again, *And please, Lord, give us our daily bread.*

"Daed, Daed!" screamed Sarah.

Before his eyes were even open, Sawyer leaped out of bed and scrambled for her room. He propelled himself forward so quickly that he slipped and crashed against the door. He managed to brace himself against the frame with his hands, but not before his forehead made contact with the knob.

I'm getting hit at both ends today, he thought as he staggered down the hall.

"Hush, Sarah, hush," he quieted her. "It's only a dream."

"Giant black horses were circling me," she cried. "I was all alone. I kept calling you and calling you, but you couldn't hear me."

"I am here now," he said soothingly. "I heard you calling me and I came. But you must remember, the Lord is always with you, so you are never truly alone."

After Sarah finally dropped back to sleep, Sawyer stretched out in his bed and put his arms behind his head, which by that time was throbbing from his fall. It was little surprise that Sarah had such a vivid dream; the day had been filled with unpleasant experiences.

First, she had witnessed him narrowly springing clear of Albert Lantz's buggy, only to land on his backside. His dignity had been the only part of him that was injured, but the near-accident frightened Sarah to tears.

Then, an hour after dinner, Sarah and Samuel were both sick to their stomachs. The only reason Simon didn't throw up was because he barely took two small bites of the undercooked fish John served, filling up instead on potatoes and broccoli.

"When my brother and I were their age, we ate what our *mamm* served or we went to bed hungry," Jonas said gruffly, and Sawyer hadn't pointed out that their mother's cooking was undoubtedly better than their dad's.

Rubbing his eyes, he prayed, *Lord, please help Sarah to sleep through the night.* When he took his hand away, his fingers felt sticky. He realized he'd broken his skin during the fall and knew he should get up to rinse it off, but before he could give it a second thought, he drifted into dreamland himself. The next thing he knew, it was time to rise and milk the cows before church services.

"What happened to you?" Phillip asked as they headed to the barn in the light from the rising sun.

"I tripped in the dark last night and whacked my head on the doorknob."

"You're as clumsy as the boys," Jonas ridiculed.

"I heard the ruckus and assumed they were horsing around."

Sawyer counted to three so he wouldn't respond defensively. Although the boys engaged in horseplay during the day, they'd never been disruptive of anyone's sleep, so Jonas had no reason to suspect they caused the late-night commotion.

"*Neh*, it was me. Sarah had another nightmare, so I was rushing to her room when I fell."

"If you ask me," Jonas advised, "she shouldn't be so afraid of her own shadow by now. She's a *scholar*, not a *bobbel*."

Sawyer didn't know how to take Jonas's remark. Perhaps he and Phillip weren't used to the ways of small children because they didn't have younger siblings. Or, because it had been several years since Lydia died, maybe they couldn't remember how their *mamm* nurtured them when they were youngsters.

That was yet another reason he appreciated Gertrude's—and now Hannah's—presence in the children's lives: he wanted them to have a maternal influence, especially Sarah. Sawyer knew how to raise boys, but girls were a different matter. Still, he wondered if Jonas was right and he was being too soft. Eliza would have known better what to expect of a girl Sarah's age.

He changed the subject, teasing his cousins about a topic he knew was at the forefront of their teenage minds.

"I'm looking forward to the services today," he said. "I want to see if it's true, that there are no young women in Willow Creek to capture your fancy. Although, Jonas, if you usually show up wearing that scowl on your face, it's no wonder they go into hiding."

Jonas joked back, "The sight of your forehead is the

only thing that would make a woman go into hiding, *dopplich*!"

Sawyer didn't mind his cousin calling him clumsy. "*Kumme*, we'd both better wash the 'ugly' from our faces, then," he agreed, affectionately clapping Jonas on the shoulder as they headed back to the house to get ready for church.

That Sunday, services were held at Miriam and Jacob Stolzfus's home. Afterward Sawyer surveyed the young women setting the long, makeshift lunch tables the men had set up in the yard. Most of the females wore black *kapps* to church, indicating they were unmarried, but they appeared so young as to be children themselves.

He was just thinking he could understand why Jonas attended singings in a neighboring district when he spotted the black *kapp* of a *maedel* delivering a pitcher of water to a freshly set table. From behind, Sawyer couldn't distinguish her age for certain—she was small enough to be a teenager but something about her posture suggested the poise of an adult.

He craned his neck to peer over a row of men taking their places at the table. The woman glanced over her shoulder at that moment and Sawyer recognized it was Hannah. His pulse quickened when she gave him the briefest of nods before turning forward again.

He'd have to wait for her to finish serving before telling her he'd bought a surplus of items for her pantry so she wouldn't worry about having three extra mouths to feed in the coming weeks. Just as she didn't want their arrangement to add to Sawyer's concerns, he didn't want it to add to hers. But meanwhile, when he spotted Hannah's grandfather voraciously wolfing down a helping of bread, cold slices of ham, cheese and pickled beets, he deliberately took a seat at the farthest end of the table. He already had two bumps too many to risk getting a third.

Although lunch at the women's table was a rushed affair—everyone knew there were more people after them waiting for a seat, so they ate quickly and then vacated the space—Hannah welcomed the opportunity to visit with the other ladies afterward while they did dishes.

"Have you heard the news?" Doris Hooley hissed, nodding toward Miriam.

"You mean about Miriam being with child?" Hannah asked, realizing she was spoiling Doris's gossip. She was surprised Miriam had confided in Doris, too, but perhaps she was too exuberant to exercise prudence. "Isn't it *wunderbaar*?"

"Jah," Doris agreed and directed her next question to Miriam. "Did you know that John Plank has a nephew visiting for harvest season? We have a wealthy widower in our midst—and he is six foot two if he's an inch!"

"His name is Sawyer Plank," Hannah confirmed to Miriam. "He was chatting with Jacob when you visited the schoolhouse recently."

"I think I recall seeing him," Miriam said. "My Abigail talks about his Sarah incessantly. They've become fast friends. She enjoys his sons, as well."

"Jah, they're all very eager scholars and—"

"Enough talk about the *kinner*," Doris interrupted. "Let's talk about their *daed*. I found him to act a bit stiff initially, but perhaps he's the silent, brooding type. He needs a little loosening up. Hannah, you've had many conversations with him. What do you think?"

Hannah was so flabbergasted by Doris's assessment

that she didn't know quite how to respond. "I hold him in high regard as the *daed* of my students."

Doris rolled her eyes and commented to Miriam, "She has to say something formal like that—he's also her employer. She's taking care of his *kinner* after school."

"That's not true!" Hannah protested.

"You're not caring for his *kinner* after school?" Doris smirked mischievously.

"I think what Hannah means," Miriam interjected, "is that her primary focus is on her scholars, not on their *daed*, even though she finds him to be a very decent man."

Hannah shot her a grateful look, but Miriam's words were wasted on Doris, who retorted, "Well, while you're focusing on the *kinner*, I'm going to focus on Sawyer. I would have thought that someone in your financial situation would have been leaping to stake a more, shall we say, *permanent arrangement* with him. But if not, just don't complain that I didn't give you every opportunity. You, of all people, should know not to let an eligible bachelor pass you by, lest someone else snatch him up."

Hannah was doubly embarrassed. First, because Doris drew attention to how strapped she was financially and implied that Hannah would use Sawyer to improve her future status. Secondly, Doris's remarks included a direct reference to Hannah's rejection of Jacob, and she felt so mortified that Doris had brought up the subject after all these years that she couldn't even look at Miriam.

"Excuse me, please. I'm finished here and I need some air," Hannah calmly stated, wringing out the dishcloth.

She found a quiet place in the yard beneath an apple

tree. Picking up a stray piece of fruit, she rubbed it against her skirt and paced in small circles. There was a third reason for Hannah's agitation: it annoyed her that Doris was intent on pursuing Sawyer.

It wasn't that Hannah had a romantic interest in him herself, but she resented how easy Doris assumed it would be to win his affections and perhaps even become his wife. Or perhaps she resented the fact that in Doris's case, marriage *could* have been simply a matter of falling in love and getting wed; Doris had no other responsibilities or obstacles standing in her way. Even her advanced age didn't seem to discourage her. Hannah supposed she could have drawn inspiration from her friend's attitude, but on this roasting afternoon, she just felt irritated.

The longer she waited for her grandfather to finish his meal, the more agitated she became, and she was so consumed by her own impatience that when she heard her name called from behind, she twitched, dropping the apple.

"I'm sorry—I didn't mean to startle you," Sawyer said.

He had been trying to remember to use a softer tone, especially around Hannah, but he had been so keen to talk to her, he couldn't contain his eagerness. He bent to pick up the fruit that had rolled toward his feet. Before straightening to his full height, he noticed she avoided meeting his eyes, and he thought she was angry at him for his trespass. Had she been praying? Did she wish to have a quiet moment alone?

"Better a bruised apple than a bruised foot," she said, her fingertips grazing his as she accepted the fruit. She seemed almost embarrassed to look at him.

"Pardon me?" he questioned. She was so quick-witted that he sometimes was puzzled by her turns of phrase.

"I mean, I am the one who is sorry. Please accept my apology for my *groossdaadi's* reckless steering yesterday."

Sawyer waved his hand in dismissal. "Your grandfather was concentrating on the horse, not on me. I shouldn't have been standing so close to the wheel. After all, he is deaf."

"Deaf, *jah*, but blind, *neh*." Hannah's white smile brightened her face, and when she finally peeked upward at him, she gasped. "Oh, *neh*! Your forehead! Was that from yester—"

Sawyer's hand flew to his eyebrow. He'd forgotten all about it. *"Neh,"* he assured her. "Your *groossdaadi* may be a poor driver, but I am even a worse sleepwalker. I got this when I collided with a doorknob trying to comfort Sarah last night. She has nightmares, you see."

"How upsetting," she commented, scrunching her forehead.

"Some people think I should let her calm herself at night. They say she's too old to be so frightened by her dreams."

"Nonsense!" Hannah declared. "I recall suffering from terrifying dreams after my *mamm* and *daed* died when I was a child. They worsened again when *Groossmammi* passed, and during other times of adjustment. Sarah is fortunate to have you to comfort her. She'll outgrow the nightmares in due time."

Once again, Sawyer found Hannah's insights to be reassuring. He was about to thank her for her encouragement when she added comically, "Of course, you might want to wear your hat into her bedroom at night, lest you scare her all the more with that wounded forehead of yours."

Their laughter was interrupted by Doris's shrill voice.

"Yoo-hoo," she called. "I hear there's a patient in need of nursing."

She waved a vial and cloth as she promenaded in their direction.

"Hello, Sawyer. Jonas told me you had an accident."

"Did he, now?" Sawyer grimaced. "It's nothing, really."

"I'll be the judge of that," Doris ordered. "Here, let me clean it off with witch hazel."

Sawyer put his hands up defensively as Doris approached. No woman had tended to his wounds or touched his face since Eliza died.

Suddenly a man bellowed from the distance, "Hannah! Hannah!"

"I must go. I'll see you both in the morning, *Gott* willing." Hannah excused herself before Sawyer had the chance to mention the groceries.

"Why must you flinch?" Doris chastised. "You're a big strong man, not a *bobbel*, so stop squirming. This won't hurt a bit."

As she dabbed witch hazel onto Sawyer's skin, he closed his eyes and clenched his teeth. Why was it that his conversations with Hannah never lasted nearly as long as he wanted them to, but his interactions with Doris never ended quickly enough?

Chapter Five

Hannah was writing on the blackboard when Sawyer and the children arrived the next morning.

"*Guder mariye*, Hannah," Sawyer said, remembering to subdue his voice.

She turned to face them, her eyes crinkling at the corners. "*Guder mariye*, Sawyer. *Guder mariye*, Simon, Sarah and Samuel."

"*Guder mariye*," they chorused.

Each of the children approached her desk, gingerly piling it with the sacks they carried, and then scooted outside to play before the other students arrived. Sawyer placed his two larger sacks on the floor.

"What is this?" she asked in surprise.

"It's for your pantry. I realize your travel into town is limited, and I doubt you had time to shop for enough food for three extra mouths."

"*Denki*," Hannah voiced aloud to Sawyer and then paused to express her silent gratitude to the Lord for His answer to her prayers.

Sawyer quickly said, "I hope you don't receive these supplemental items as an insult—I'm not suggesting you prepare any meals in particular."

"*Neh*, not at all. It's very thoughtful." Amused, she confessed, "But I must say, it looks like enough to fill a silo."

Sawyer chuckled at himself. "My sister Gertrude is the one who manages our purchases. I admit I never pay much attention to the ingredients she buys."

Hannah faltered. "Nothing will go to waste. It's just…"

"Just what?"

"It's just I haven't brought a wheelbarrow to carry it home in," she said with a giggle.

Sawyer threw back his head, laughing aloud. "I suppose I will have to return this afternoon to give you a ride home, then."

Hannah protested that if he came back in the afternoon, it would disrupt his farmwork and defeat the purpose of her watching the children, but he insisted.

"Just this once won't cause a hardship," he asserted. "It would be my pleasure. Truly."

After Sawyer uttered the words, Hannah remained silent, weighing the situation. Her grandfather wouldn't accept groceries from another man, even though she couldn't possibly stretch their menu without the supplemental food. She didn't want him being rude to Sawyer again, but she supposed there was nothing she could do to stop him.

"It would be my pleasure to accept," she finally stated. "*Denki*, Sawyer. I will see you this afternoon, *Gott* willing."

Although she had intended to show the children the hidden bird's nest she'd spotted near the stream on the shortcut home, Hannah was just as glad to be traversing in the buggy. The hot and humid weather still hadn't broken, and the sun beat down on her shoulders. She caught a faint whiff of Sawyer's sweat, which was mingled with the scent of soap and freshly pitched hay. Watching Sawyer's masculine hands loosely holding the reins made her aware of how rarely she'd been in such close proximity to any man except her grandfather.

She needn't have worried about her grandfather's reaction to receiving the groceries, since he was still in his workshop when they arrived home and Sawyer left promptly after carrying the items to the pantry. She shelved them quickly and then devoted her attention to showing the children around the house and small yard.

"After your chores, you may climb the trees, pick the fruit and play games on the lawn," she said, sweeping her hand expansively. "But," she cautioned seriously, waving one finger, "you mustn't disturb my *groossdaadi* or go near his workshop in the backyard."

"Jah." Samuel nodded seriously. "We must mind our manners and obey whatever you tell us, just as we would at school. *Daed* said so."

"Did he?" Hannah asked. While she appreciated Sawyer's instructions, she wanted the children to feel at home. "Well, your *daed* is right. We should always mind our manners. But that's not exactly why you can't go back to the workshop."

"Then why can't we?" Simon asked.

"Because my *groossdaadi* is working very hard and needs to concentrate. If he is distracted, his hands could slip. He could cut himself or ruin what he is making."

"Did he make the big dollhouse?" Sarah asked.

"Jah, he did," Hannah admitted. "He makes toys of all sorts."

"But you're too old for toys!" Samuel exclaimed.

"She is not!" Sarah argued, holding her hands on her

hips. "Remember when she batted the ball at school? It went farther than anyone's, even the oldest boys."

"You aren't minding your manners, Sarah," Samuel corrected her. "You're raising your voice. You'll disturb the *groossdaadi*."

"There, there," Hannah said, clapping her hands together twice to break up their argument. "It's true—the toys aren't for me, as much as I sometimes like to bat a ball. My *groossdaadi* sells the toys to *Englischers* in town. And while we shouldn't raise our voices in anger, my *groossdaadi* couldn't hear us if we did. You see, he is deaf."

All three children looked at her, their eyes as big as coins. Their bewilderment was so innocent, she had the urge to pull them onto her lap and give them the tightest squeeze. Instead, she said, "So it is especially important we don't make sudden movements around him, because he can't hear us approaching. It might frighten him."

"Like sneaking up on a wild animal in the woods," Simon said knowingly.

"*Jah*, a little like that." Hannah nodded, amazed by how accurate the boy's metaphor was. "Yet, although my *groossdaadi* can't hear, he can read lips. If you look at him when you are speaking, he can usually tell what you are saying. He can talk back to you, although sometimes he'll use a loud voice. It might sound as if he's yelling or as if he's angry, but he's not. He just can't hear how loud his own voice is."

"*Daed* uses his big voice sometimes," Sarah confided. "But he says he doesn't mean to. He just forgets. Your *groossdaadi* probably just forgets, too."

"*Jah*, he probably does," Hannah agreed, so grateful for the girl's compassion that this time she did sweep the children into a tight squeeze.

* * *

Hannah was in a rocker on the porch, reading to the children, when Sawyer pulled up that evening. Their hands and faces were scrubbed, Sarah's hair was neatly combed, and they seemed content, if not sleepy. On the way home, they highlighted the afternoon's adventures for him.

"We climbed to the top of the apple tree to pick the five biggest apples we could find," Samuel reported.

"Hannah showed me how to bake them," Sarah said, glowing. "We added a pinch of sugar and a dusting of cinnamon to the top. Those are measurements every baker must know, she told me."

After tucking them into bed, Sawyer retreated early to his own room. His back was aching and he was exhausted, but he grinned from ear to ear; he'd never heard his children as excited about doing chores like baking or picking apples as they'd been when they were doing them for Hannah.

Denki, Lord, for how well the kinner *are adjusting to another change in their lives*, he prayed before easing into bed. *And please keep Sarah from upsetting dreams.* The girl slept soundly through the night without any disturbances, even though a thunderstorm rattled the windows shortly after midnight, and another one blew through right before the break of day.

By the time the children piled into the buggy, the sun had burned off the haze and the day promised to be another scorcher. Still, he was surprised by how withered Hannah looked when he accompanied the children to the classroom door. The dark circles under her eyes intensified their hue, but she appeared heavy-lidded.

"Are you feeling ill?" he inquired.

She looked at him askance, in the familiar manner he'd come to recognize meant she was about to jest. "Do you think I look ill?"

He hadn't meant it like that. "Not at all," he explained. "Just a little tired. I'm afraid one afternoon and evening with my *kinner* may have worn you out completely."

"On the contrary," she protested. "They are one of the most refreshing parts of my day! The thunderstorms kept me awake, which is probably why I'm bleary-eyed. But I am perfectly healthy and my sleepiness will pass. In a few minutes, I'll be as *gut* as new."

"You already are as *gut* as new," Sawyer said without thinking. Then he clarified, "I mean, you needn't apologize for your appearance. That is, your appearance is fine, just fine. Not *just* fine. *Very* fine, I mean. Your appearance is nice. And healthy. Your appearance is healthy."

The more he spoke, the more his ears burned and the more perplexed Hannah's expression grew. He had the sensation of sprinting down a hill; the momentum of his own words was causing him to trip all over himself. He wondered what Eliza might have thought if she had been there to hear his gibberish.

Fortunately, at that moment, Jacob Stolzfus ascended the stairs. "*Guder mariye*, Sawyer," he said. "Hannah, might I have a word with you?"

"Absolutely," Hannah agreed, relief filling her voice. "I'll see you this evening, Sawyer."

Sawyer couldn't get away from the schoolhouse fast enough. What had come over him? He worked the horse into a galloping clip, as if he were trying to outpace his own embarrassment.

* * *

"Did I interrupt an argument? Was Sawyer Plank being rude to you?" Jacob Stolzfus asked protectively.

Hannah quickly denied it. "Sawyer has never been anything but polite and kind to me."

"You were both red in the face," Jacob persisted.

"This weather could make anyone's skin flush," Hannah countered. "What can I do for you? Is Abigail alright? Is Miriam doing well?"

"Abigail is over there, speaking to Sarah beneath the willow," Jacob said, pointing. He puffed his chest ever so slightly when he said, "Miriam is very well. I will tell her you asked after her. But I have come to see you about a business matter."

"A business matter?" Hannah echoed.

"Concerning your *groossdaadi*. I understand Miriam has shared her condition with you, and I would like your *groossdaadi* to craft a cradle for the *bobbel*, a rocker for Miriam and perhaps a chest of drawers, as well."

"Of course," Hannah agreed, although she was surprised by the request. She wondered if Jacob was being charitable because he knew her income would soon cease. He needn't have made such a gesture—she'd have enough money from watching the Plank children to tide them over until she found another way to make ends meet. "But isn't the cradle my *groossdaadi* made before Abigail was born in *gut* condition still?"

"It is. At least I think it is," Jacob replied, a shadow crossing his brow. "After Miriam lost the second *bobbel*, it was too painful of a reminder to keep around. We gave it to her sister-in-law, and as you know, she and her husband and *kinner* have long since moved to Indiana."

"Of course. I will speak to *Groossdaadi* tonight about making the cradle. I know he'll get started right away," Hannah said, sorry she had pressed Jacob about the old cradle. There was a reason topics like this were rarely mentioned, even between long-standing friends. "He will make it nice and sturdy, to hold your bouncing boy, *Gott* willing."

Miriam had confessed to Hannah that Jacob hoped to be blessed with the birth of a boy, so her remark caused a grin to spread across his face. "*Denki*, Hannah."

After he left, it was Hannah who was thanking the Lord for His provision once again. With her income as a nanny and the project for her grandfather, they'd have enough to see them into the winter. *Surely* Gott *will continue to provide*, she thought, and the tiredness she had experienced moments earlier was quickly replaced with such lighthearted energy it carried her through the day.

On the way home, she led the children through the wooded area bordering the fields. Although the jaunt took longer than usual, she figured it didn't matter if she was later returning home, since she had three more pairs of hands helping with the evening chores. Besides, the trees provided shade from the relentless sun, and the stream was a refreshing resting place. As soon as they arrived, the boys capered from rock to rock.

"Samuel, you're splashing Teacher!" Sarah scolded after the boy lifted a large stone and let it drop again.

"He *is* splashing me," Hannah said. "And it's nice and icy cold. Here, feel—"

She dipped her fingers in the water and flicked them at Sarah, who screwed up her face as if she couldn't believe Hannah would do such a thing.

"Be careful—she will tattle on you to *Daed*," Simon accused. "Sarah always tattles."

"Does she really?" Hannah kidded him. "Because to my ears right now it sounds a bit as if *you* are tattling on *her*." With a wink at Sarah, Hannah cupped her hands, lifted a scoop of water and flung it in Simon's direction, dousing him.

Soon, the four of them had squealed, splashed and laughed the afternoon away. Hannah couldn't remember having such fun since she and her sister were children frolicking there themselves.

Sweat soaked Sawyer's shirt and he briefly considered changing it, but his others were just as dirty. The four men tried to keep up with the laundry and housework, and Sarah participated in chores beyond her years, but with three of the men in the fields all day and John doddering on crutches, certain tasks took less priority than others.

As he headed toward Hannah's house, he consoled himself with the thought that they'd only be there for a short season. He was much more effective at hewing wood than at harvesting fields, and he'd be glad to get back to Ohio and his business. He'd be gladder still for Gertrude's return, so their lives could resume as usual. His young sister was not yet the accomplished cook their mother or Eliza had been, but she was certainly more skilled than his uncle.

As the buggy bounced over a dip in the road, Sawyer's stomach lurched. Whatever else had been in the chicken casserole John had served for dinner, it was making Sawyer queasy now. But as he pulled into the lane where Hannah lived, his nausea was replaced by a burst of cheer at seeing Simon and Sarah each holding a handle of a wheelbarrow as they gave Samuel a ride across the yard. Hannah was settled in a rocking chair on the porch, leafing through *Blackboard Bulletin*, a magazine for teachers.

"Hello, Hannah," he said from a distance, removing his hat as the children bounded across the yard to put away the wheelbarrow and then gather their schoolbooks from inside the house.

"Hello, Sawyer," Hannah replied. "Please, *kumme* sit. The *kinner* will be a few moments."

"I shouldn't." He hesitated. "I'm afraid I smell like I live in a sty."

"Not at all," she countered. "You're fine. Just fine."

There it was again, that lilt in her voice and the repetition of the very phrase he had used earlier that caused him to wonder if she was making light or if he'd seriously offended her with his previous comments about her appearance. In either case, it caught him off guard and he didn't know how to interpret it, so he changed the subject to a blander topic.

"I hear we're in for some more big storms, which should break the heat. It sure feels more like July than September."

"It does," she agreed amicably. "But don't be fooled. The days are definitely getting shorter. It won't be long until it's dark by this time of evening."

"Aw, will we still be able to play outside?" Simon asked from the doorway. "It's my turn in the wheelbarrow tomorrow."

"You shouldn't interrupt adult conversation," Sawyer reprimanded. "But *jah*, there's still plenty of time for each of you to have several turns in the wheelbarrow."

"Gut," said Simon. "Because we don't have a wheelbarrow in Ohio."

Sawyer contradicted him. "Actually, Simon, we have two wheelbarrows."

"But it's not the same. It's funner here," Simon argued.

"Funnier," Sarah corrected him.

"More funny," Samuel chimed in.

"Everything is *more fun* when you're playing in a wheelbarrow instead of working with it," Hannah agreed. "Especially if you're playing with people you like. And if you've had a *gut* night's sleep, which is what you need. So, I will see you tomorrow, *Gott* willing, when it will be Simon's turn in the wheelbarrow."

Even in the dusky light, Hannah's infectious smile caused Sawyer to grin back at her, certain now that nothing he said that morning had caused her any offense. In fact, it was likely the opposite was true, and any lingering embarrassment he felt was replaced by a sense of delight.

"My brother and sister-in-law will be going to visit John Plank on Sunday," Doris told Hannah on Friday morning before school began.

Services were held every other Sunday, and this was an "off Sunday," when most families would hold their own worship time together in the morning and then visit other people in the district in the afternoon.

"Our visit is long overdue. We should have gone round when John was first injured. But better late than never," Doris explained. "Besides, with four men fending for themselves during harvest, I suppose they'd *wilkom* receiving an apple crisp no matter when it arrives."

"That's very hospitable of you," Hannah replied, not rising to the bait.

She suspected Doris was more interested in cozying up to Sawyer than she was in the general welfare of John Plank's household, but she quickly dismissed the thought as judgmental. Besides, she felt a bit peaked from the heat. She ducked off the front steps and into the classroom, leaving Doris alone to usher the children into the building.

By the end of the day, she felt no better and the children seemed to be sagging on the way home, as well. They crossed over the stream without stopping to look under stones or attempting to get each other wet. After the boys finished their chore of picking up stray sticks and pulling weeds from the garden and Sarah had swept the porch and kitchen, Hannah suggested they let the chickens out to roam, which was usually a source of great amusement.

"Can we read instead?" Samuel asked, an uncharacteristic whine in his voice, his eyes a paler shade of green than usual.

Hannah deduced Sarah must have been ailing, too, because she didn't tell Samuel to say *may* instead of *can*.

"Jah," Hannah answered, wiping her hand along the back of her neck. "I will bring you a cool drink. I am hot and thirsty myself."

She had just finished slicing a lemon when she heard a gagging cough she instinctively recognized that meant a child was on the brink of getting sick, and she raced into the parlor and shoved a bin under Samuel's mouth. In rapid succession, Simon and Sarah were sick, as well, and although Hannah felt her stomach constrict, she managed to press on, giving each child a tepid bath, fitting them with nightshirts and tucking them into bed. She put Simon and Samuel in the double bed in Eve's old room, and Sarah into her own double bed. Hannah made several trips between the two rooms, wringing cool compresses and arranging pillows before the children were soothed enough to sleep.

Waves of nausea washed over her as she prepared her grandfather's supper, and a wet V formed on the back

312 Amish Triplets for Christmas

of her dress, but she served the meal on time. She could hardly stand the aroma of food, but she took a seat opposite her grandfather to keep him company.

"The *kinner* didn't come today?" he asked loudly as he eyed the empty spots around the table.

"*Jah*, they are here. They got sick," she mouthed. "They're in bed upstairs."

Her grandfather jabbed his fork into a slice of meat and said, "They cannot stay."

Hannah leaned toward him so he would know she was speaking. "*Neh*, they cannot *leave*. They are ill."

The force of her own determination surprised her. Her entire life, Hannah had never spoken back to her grandfather and she wouldn't have contradicted him now if the children weren't sick, but their vulnerable condition ignited a maternal protectiveness she didn't know she possessed. Whether she was running a fever or it was from the strength of her convictions, her face felt fiery and she began to shake so noticeably that she rose, turning her back on her grandfather to rinse the dirty pans until her hands were steady again. By that time, he had vacated the room.

As soon as Hannah opened the door, Sawyer knew something was wrong.

"The *kinner* are fine," she immediately told him, quelling the pounding in his ears. "But they had upset stomachs. I have put them to bed."

"But they are all okay?" Sawyer asked.

"Nothing a *gut* night's sleep won't cure," Hannah assured him. "Some of the other scholars have had this, too. It's a twenty-four-hour flu."

"I am sorry for any inconven—"

"You needn't apologize. I'm relieved they're resting. Since they'd be coming back tomorrow anyway, I think it best they spend the night here. It will save you another trip in the morning."

"I couldn't allow you to do that," Sawyer protested.

"You couldn't *stop* me from doing that," Hannah quipped, her hands on her hips. "The *kinner* need uninterrupted sleep. It's no trouble for me, and no amount of noise would ever wake *Groossdaadi*."

Sawyer could plainly see Hannah looked a bit frayed around the edges herself, although he wasn't about to make the same mistake by mentioning to her how tired she appeared. *"Denki,"* he said, gazing into her eyes. "Would it be alright if I looked in on them before I leave?"

"Of course."

Hannah tiptoed up the stairs and Sawyer followed, trying to keep his boots from clunking through the hall. The boys were lying back-to-back, breathing in unison, even in sleep.

"Gute nacht, Samuel. *Gute nacht,* Simon," Sawyer bade them.

Pushing open the door to her room, Hannah whispered, "Sarah will share her bed with me."

Sawyer peered in at his daughter, who had curled herself around a pillow. "You're aware she sometimes wakes screaming from nightmares."

"If she does, I will comfort her," Hannah promised.

"Of that, I have no doubt," Sawyer replied. "I mention it more for your sake than hers. I'd hate to have her startle you. As the saying goes, it can be a rude awakening."

"I'll be fine," Hannah insisted. "We both will be."

Before dropping off to sleep later that night, Sawyer found himself wondering who comforted Hannah when she was ill. Certainly not that grandfather of hers. Even if he were inclined to help, he couldn't hear her request for a drink of water or a cool compress.

He recalled the many times he had sat on the edge of the bed when Eliza was sick, wishing there was something else he could do to help her.

"Your prayers are most helpful," she would say. "And your presence is a kind of balm. How terrible it would feel to be sick and all alone."

Remembering, Sawyer prayed, *Dear Lord,* denki *for providing someone as competent and kind as Hannah to watch the* kinner, *so I can sleep well knowing they are under her care. Please heal them and keep Hannah from becoming ill herself. And please give them all a sense of Your loving presence, just as You've given me. Amen.*

Chapter Six

It was Samuel, not Sarah, who woke Hannah in the middle of the night. She rushed to his side with a bin and towel, but he wasn't ill; he was merely confused about where he was. The commotion woke Simon, as well.

"I will sit here on the end of the bed until you both fall asleep again," she offered.

"Will you tell us a story?" Samuel asked. "*Daed* sometimes tells us stories."

"What kind of stories does your *daed* tell?"

"Stories about our *mamm*," mumbled Simon. "About how she swept his feet off."

Hannah scrunched her brow. "Swept him off his feet?"

"*Jah*." Samuel yawned. "Because she had a kind heart."

"Such a kind heart that the Lord blessed her with three *bobblin* at once so her kindness wouldn't go to waste," Simon added. "*Waste not, want not*, our *mamm* always said."

"That sounds like a *wunderbaar* story," Hannah replied. "What else happens in that tale?"

But the boys had already fallen back asleep, so she

slipped out of the room, leaving the door ajar a crack. Sarah was sprawled across the center of the bed, so Hannah stretched sideways along the outer edge, careful not to rouse her. Her limbs ached, and as she tried to fall asleep, she thought about Sawyer bidding his children good-night and about the bedtime story the boys indicated he shared with them. How had she ever made the mistake of thinking Sawyer was too forbidding? She had never known a man to be so tender to his children, and she assumed he must have been equally affectionate to his wife. She nodded off, wistfully imagining what it would be like to have a husband like that.

For breakfast, she served the children broth and toast in bed, and by ten thirty, the boys were roughhousing—bouncing on the bed and smacking each other with pillows.

"If you're well enough to wrestle, you're well enough to clean the coop," she said, shooing them outdoors.

Sarah slept in, but by noon she joined her brothers romping on the lawn. Hannah, however, weakened as the day wore on. She held her nose as she fixed supper and excused herself from the room while the others ate. When she heard Sawyer's buggy, she mustered the last of her strength to send the children off before collapsing into bed.

Sawyer was pleased with what he and his cousins had accomplished that Saturday on the farm, but as he guided the horse away from Hannah's home, he worried that their progress had come at too great a cost to Hannah, even if the children were no worse for the wear.

"Hannah served us our breakfast in bed!" the boys reported.

"She helped me write a letter to Gertrude," Sarah informed him.

Sawyer wondered how Hannah had managed, given how sick she looked. Despite his prayers for the contrary, her eyes were a watery blue and her skin sallow. Even her smile appeared feeble. Rationally, he expected Hannah would be fine, but his experience of watching Eliza's condition deteriorate so quickly had made him hypervigilant. He'd learned not to take his loved ones' health for granted.

He reminded himself that Hannah wasn't his loved one, of course. But he did care about her health, and before shutting his eyes for the evening, he prayed again. *Lord, please give Hannah rest today and tomorrow, so she will be well again. Not just for the* kinner's *sake, but for her own.*

The next morning the four men and three children spent quiet time together in Scripture reading and prayer, as was the custom every other Sunday when they didn't meet for church. They sang hymns, and after eating a simple noon meal, the children were allowed to go outside to play quietly. Ordinarily, Sawyer might have enjoyed strolling with them through the meadows, but after their illness, he wanted to subdue their activity, so he remained on the porch, watching as they combed the lawn for grasshoppers.

The week's farmwork had done him in: his eyelids grew heavy, and he leaned his head back against the railing. The next thing he knew, a buggy was pulling up the lane carrying Doris Hooley, her sister-in-law, Amelia, and her brother, James, whom Sawyer had met last Sunday.

"*Guder nammidaag,*" he greeted them.

"*Guder nammidaag,*" Doris sang, holding out a

large rectangular glass dish. "We brought apple crisp for you."

"For everyone." Amelia quickly made the distinction. "We hope we caught you in time for tea."

"I'm not sure John has teacups," Sawyer replied with a chuckle. "But we can put on a pot of coffee. Don't let my cousins see that crisp or it'll be gone before you have a chance to sit down."

He had noticed that despite their superficial disdain for treats, his cousins never passed up any dessert his uncle purchased in town. But it was Samuel, not his cousins, who spied the treat first.

"Apple crisp!" he exclaimed.

"I'm sorry, but none for you," Sawyer said, eliciting cries of disappointment from all three of the children. He turned to Doris to explain. "They were sick last night, I'm afraid."

"That's a shame," Doris said, clucking her tongue. Then she added brightly, "The more for us!"

Sawyer refrained from shaking his head. The woman was candid to a fault about what she wanted.

As the adults gathered for refreshments, Sawyer's uncle apologized for the general state of the house. Amelia politely denied noticing any disarray, but Doris looked around the room and sniffed before saying, "A house needs a woman's touch to make it a home. It can't be easy looking after the *kinner*, harvesting and keeping house."

"Hannah Lantz cares for the *kinner* after school," Sawyer quickly emphasized. He didn't want Doris volunteering her services again. "But when they're here, they participate in chores the best they can."

"She's right," John interjected. "We could use help with mending and laundering. Perhaps a hot meal. I do my best, but it's difficult working one-handed, balancing on a crutch like I have to."

"Of course it is," cooed Doris. "Say no more. It would be a privilege to help a neighbor in need."

Sawyer went silent; it wasn't his home, so it wasn't his place to comment. When the guests were leaving and the crisp was only three-fourths gone, Doris suggested Sawyer save it for the children's lunch the next day.

"What about your dish?" he asked thoughtfully. "Won't you need it for baking?"

"Oh, I'll be visiting a lot more often, so I'll pick it up the next time I'm here," she said, before flouncing to the buggy.

Hannah spent the better portion of Sunday in bed, rising only for Scripture reading and worship with her grandfather and to fix his meals. By evening she felt well enough to pen a letter to her sister.

My dearest Eve,

What a joy to hear about the Lord's blessings to you and Menno! I will pray for all to go well. I relish the thought of holding a baby in my arms, and I know you relish it even more.

I was also pleased to hear Menno's repair shop is flourishing and it isn't necessary for you to make quilts for consignment anymore. It's very generous of you to offer to continue quilting in order to send the income to Grandfather and me, but the Lord has provided for us in another way.

As you recall from my earlier letters, John Plank broke his leg in a ditch. He and his sons couldn't manage harvest season on their own, so recently, his nephew, Sawyer Plank, arrived to help. Sawyer is a cabinetmaker from Ohio who has triplets, Simon, Sarah and Samuel, seven years of age. Although Sawyer is widowed, he has not remarried. I have been hired to bring his children home with me in the afternoon and prepare their supper here. Afterward, Sawyer picks them up. He has been most generous with my salary, and this short-term arrangement should provide Grandfather and me our daily bread until I find other work.

The children are a delight to care for, and they're a big help to me with evening chores. I am teaching Sarah baking basics. Simon and Samuel are so active that sometimes I think I am seeing quadruple instead of just double when they scamper about the yard! Samuel is the tiniest bit stronger and quicker than Simon, but Simon makes up for it by trying twice as hard. Sarah keeps her brothers in line by "correcting" their grammar and scolding them for perceived offenses, although they are never truly naughty. We laugh much of the time we are together and I am sorry to see them leave in the evening.

Sawyer Plank is a very tall man with a solemn face, pensive green eyes and a voice deeper than Grandfather's. Yet despite his size, he is exceptionally gentle with his children and there are times when a laugh breaks through his seriousness, making his eyes dance. He sometimes stammers and is more often than not reserved in nature, but I understand now this is because he is thoughtful, not arrogant. Anyone who doesn't hold a grudge against another for nearly running over his foot with their buggy—as Grandfather nearly did in town the other day—must have a forbearing spirit. Sawyer has certainly been thoughtful in supplementing our pantry, as well, and I appreciate how considerate he is of our situation.

Grandfather's health is well (even if his steering is not!). Our apples are early and copious this year, and I will try the recipe you sent as a special treat for my scholars before I bid them goodbye. As fond as she is of desserts, Doris Hooley does not allow such celebrations in her classroom.

Grandfather and I would like to visit you soon, God willing.

Please remember me to Menno and write again with news of how you are.

Your loving sister,
Hannah

After Doris, Amelia and James left on Sunday afternoon, Sawyer provided the children with sheets of paper for drawing while he wrote letters.

The first was to the foreman of the shop. *Has Vernon's hand healed enough to carry out his daily work?* he inquired.

Then he directed:

If not, assign your duties to him—managing orders, the books and scheduling deliveries to the English; everything except overseeing the rest of the crew. You alone are responsible for their charge, along with performing any work Vernon would do, had he not been injured.

When he had finished addressing matters of business to his foreman, he began a letter to his sister.

Dear Gertrude,

I am thankful Kathryn and the baby are gaining strength. We will continue to ask the Lord's will for them. Remember us to Kathryn and Leroy. John and your cousins also send their greetings.

Sarah's nightmares have decreased, although she still misses you. Samuel and Simon say they especially miss your mashed potato candy on Sunday evenings. The children are faring well in school: Sarah is writing you a letter, as she has mastered the spelling and printing of many small words.

Their schoolteacher is Hannah Lantz and I have hired her to care for them through the supper hour as well as give them their nighttime baths, and she even manages to untangle Sarah's hair without a fuss. Although Hannah is petite in form, she matches the children's vibrancy. They amuse me with stories of their daily escapades together all the way home after I pick them up from her grandfather's house, where she lives. (It is strange she is unmarried, but Willow Creek is a small town and perhaps her suitable choices were few.) She is a fine teacher, too. I concentrate on the farmwork better, knowing her deep blue eyes are keeping careful watch over the children.

The harvesting is as to be expected. We are working as diligently as possible. I am grateful for the strength the Lord provides me in order to help John during this time of need.

I was informed Vernon Mast was injured. I don't know how they are keeping up in the shop, with two fewer men (Vernon and myself) to share the load. God willing, Vernon will be healed and I will make headway here so I can return sooner rather than later.

Your brother,
Sawyer

PS: I miss your Sunday-evening mashed potato candy as much as the boys do, but don't tell your uncle I said that. He's doing the best he can.

"Sawyer mentioned the *kinner* were sick," Doris said on Monday morning. She stood over Hannah's desk eating a doughnut.

"Sawyer is here? I didn't see him arrive with the *kinner* yet."

Doris licked powdered sugar from her fingers. "*Neh*, he's not here. He told me yesterday, when we visited John Plank. They seemed alright to me, though. You have to be careful with *kinner*—they'll feign illness to be excused from their chores."

"I'm wise to the ways of *kinner*, and they were genuinely sick," Hannah snapped. "Not to mention, they had already finished their chores when they became ill."

Doris shrugged. "They seemed fine when I saw them, so I didn't want anyone taking advantage of you. You look a little under the weather yourself."

"I am fine, *denki*," Hannah replied in a milder voice.

The inactivity on Sunday had been helpful; she was all but recovered, although the sight of Doris chewing a doughnut still put her stomach on edge.

"It's time to summon the *kinner* for class," she suggested.

Just as Doris and Hannah exited the building, Sawyer was taking the stairs by twos, a glass dish in his hand.

"*Guder mariye*, Hannah," he exclaimed breathlessly.

"*Guder mariye*, Sawyer," Doris interrupted pointedly before Hannah could answer.

"Forgive my manners," Sawyer mumbled, looking chagrined. "*Guder mariye*, Doris. I've brought your dish."

"I told you I would have retrieved that when I visit the farm tomorrow." Doris pouted.

"I wanted to save you the trouble."

"It's no trouble—I'll be going there anyway," Doris replied. To Hannah she expounded, "I'll be helping with some of the household chores on the farm. Of course, I wouldn't accept a penny for it. I consider it my Christian duty to help a neighbor in need."

Hannah felt her cheeks flame. Whether it was embarrassment because she needed to accept compensation for helping Sawyer's family or the glare of the morning sun, she didn't know, but suddenly she couldn't get out of Doris and Sawyer's presence quickly enough.

"That's very kind of you," she said to Doris, and then she spun on her heel toward the classroom.

The sudden movement caused her such wooziness, she teetered backward. In the split second it took her to become aware she was going to tumble backward down the stairs, she felt Sawyer's strong hands clasp her shoulders, propping her upright.

"Easy does it," he said into her ear, sliding his hands down to clutch her elbows.

Stunned and dizzy, she was in no condition to resist when he steered her inside and settled her into her chair. Using what Sarah referred to as his "big voice," he ordered Doris to bring her a glass of water.

"I'm fine, really," she insisted while the two of them watched her sip the water until it was gone. "It was the heat."

"Then why are you still quivering?" Sawyer asked.

He crouched by her side so he could be level with her face. He gazed so intently into her eyes, she nearly confessed it was the unfamiliar warmth of a man's touch that had unnerved her so.

Instead, she blinked and said, "I'm faint because I haven't been eating enough, perhaps."

"You caught what the *kinner* had, didn't you?" Sawyer asked accusingly. "I don't think you should be here at school today."

Hannah drew herself up to her full height. "Don't be ridiculous," she objected adamantly. "I'm fine. Listen— the scholars are arriving. *Denki* for your concern, but lessons are about to begin. I'll walk you to the door."

Sawyer hung back before following her outside. He knew not to argue with a woman who had made up her mind as definitively as Hannah had. But all the way back to the farm and throughout the day, he thought about her frail form in his arms. She had looked as pale as a sheet.

Finally, he decided that she may have made up her mind, but so had he. When class was letting out, he hitched up the horse and clopped to the schoolhouse. Everyone else was gone, and he knew he could find Sarah, Simon and Samuel inside helping Hannah wash the blackboards.

"Hello, *kinner*," he said. "Hello, Hannah."

"Hello, *Daed*," they chorused as Hannah quickly made her way to his side.

"Is something wrong?" she whispered, her brow knitted.

"Not at all," he faltered, suddenly feeling foolish. "I have an errand to run in town. I thought I'd bring you all home on the way."

"That's very thoughtful," Hannah said skeptically, "but we're in the opposite direction from town. You will have to backtrack."

Sawyer shrugged. "It's no bother."

Hannah tipped her head as if about to expose his falsehood with a joke, but then she seemed to change her mind. "*Kumme*, let's not keep your *daed* waiting," she said to the children.

At the buggy, he took Hannah's graceful fingers in one of his hands and supported her elbow with the other, easing her into the front seat.

"You are being too kind." She laughed breezily.

The sensation of her satiny skin against his caused the tiny hairs along his arms to stand on end. His head spun and his stomach somersaulted so fiercely he wondered if he was coming down with something himself. Yet as he sat beside Hannah, who engaged the children with amusing anecdotes all the way home, he felt anything but sick. Indeed, he felt better than he had in a long, long time.

"I can't eat this." Hannah's grandfather threw the crust onto his plate. "It's tough."

Sarah looked as if she'd been slapped. She had been so pleased Hannah allowed her to help, but in her enthusiasm she'd added too much flour to the bread dough.

You are the one who is tough, Hannah thought.

She held her glass in front of her mouth so her grandfather wouldn't see her lips moving.

"You mustn't pay him any mind, Sarah. He hasn't got all his teeth, so it's difficult for him to chew. This is a fine first effort. If we don't eat it all, I can use what's left for bread crumbs in a stuffing."

"It tastes *gut* if you soak it in your gravy," Samuel said, a kindness that made Hannah want to hug him.

Simon added, "Or dip it in your milk."

Sarah nodded bravely, her eyes brimming.

Hannah remembered all too well how many times her grandfather's cutting words reduced her to near tears when she was a child. She thought she was past being hurt by his criticism, but that evening, after Sawyer and the children left, he approached her in the parlor, where she was patching a tear in his pants.

"I saw him bring you home," he said.

She was so surprised by her grandfather's statement, at first she didn't know what he was talking about. She searched his face for a clue.

"Sawyer Plank," her grandfather explained.

"*Jah*, he said he was running an errand in town," she mouthed. "But I suspect since we had been ill, he wanted to spare us walking in the heat."

Her grandfather jabbed a finger in the air in Hannah's direction. "You are too old to be acting like a schoolgirl being courted home from a singing. Especially with your employer."

He shuffled off to his bedroom without waiting for a reply.

Hannah's eyes momentarily welled, but her hurt was quickly replaced by a sense of fury. As weak as she'd felt that morning, her grandfather's remark sparked a new vigor, and she pricked her fingers so many times she finally tossed her mending aside. She didn't know what offended her more: that her grandfather demonstrated so little appreciation for the fact she was doing her best to earn extra income, which obligated them to maintain friendly rapport with Sawyer, or that her grandfather would begrudge her a ride home after she'd been ill.

However, by the time she'd finished slamming through her evening chores, she was physically and emotionally spent. She sat on the sofa and picked up her grandfather's pants to finish stitching the patch. As she sewed, she realized how threadbare the fabric had become. It made her think of the many sacrifices her grandfather must have made in order to raise her and her sister.

Besides the Lord, who had ever supported her and cared for her for as many years and in as many ways as her family? The nanny opportunity was a blessing, but it was temporary. Soon Sawyer and the children would return to Ohio. As fond as she was of the Plank family, her relationship with them was a way to earn money. Her life was in Willow Creek, where her grandfather was—she was sure that was all he meant to remind her of with his cutting tone.

It was past eleven o'clock when she finally closed the door to her bedroom and knelt beside her bed. *Lord,* she prayed, *please forgive my anger. Thank You for providing for me through* Groossdaadi *all of these years. Please bless him with a gut night's sleep and help Sarah, Simon and Samuel to get the rest they need, as well.*

But it was Sawyer who filled her mind's eye as she lay sleepless in the dark. As humid as the air was, when she recalled his arms bracing her when she stumbled on the steps or his masculine grip as he aided her into the buggy, a shiver ran down her spine. He had treated her as if she was even more precious cargo than her grandfather's dollhouse!

The thought made her feel as giddy as a schoolgirl— and then she remembered her grandfather's words: "You are too old to be acting like a schoolgirl being courted home from a singing. Especially with your employer." She feared her grandfather had hit the nail on the head: instead of behaving like "every bit the woman" Sawyer believed she was, she had been acting like a teenager with a crush, swooning and giggling over his smallest friendly gesture.

She reminded herself that such feelings were fleeting—and soon Sawyer would be fleeting, too. Meanwhile, what would he think if he knew she felt this way? Even from a distance, her grandfather had noticed her juvenile levity. What if Sawyer had, too? Would he think she was too irresponsible and immature to oversee his children? Would he dismiss her as a "desperate Doris"?

She could neither risk losing her nanny job nor could she stand the comparison, so before closing her eyes a final time for sleep, she resolved to behave more appropriately in the future.

Exhausted as he was, Sawyer tossed and turned, wondering if Hannah knew how holding her that morning had affected him. Had she felt his hands tremble? Did she think he was terribly presumptuous showing up to usher her home after school and again taking her by the arm? He hadn't been able to help himself. She seemed so delicate, and no matter how vehemently she objected, Sawyer didn't think she ought to walk in the sweltering weather.

Even toward the end of her illness, Eliza used to claim she felt better than her health implied. Sawyer remembered one time when she patted the bed, gesturing for him to sit with her. Her voice was raspy and her breathing labored. He tried to hush her, but she said it was very important that he listen to what she had to say.

"After I am gone," she began, "there is something I want you to do for me."

Sawyer stood up. "I'll have none of that—" he protested, but she clasped his hand and pulled him back into a sitting position.

"Sawyer, my dear, you must listen and do what I ask," she pleaded. "First, remember me to the *kinner* always."

Sawyer nodded. "I will," he promised. His eyes grew moist, but he couldn't let his wife see how her words pained him.

"I want you to remarry—"

"Neh!" he exclaimed, jumping up and pacing to the window, his back toward her. "Never."

His wife did something then that surprised him—she laughed. From her sickbed, she laughed.

He spun on his heel. "Is this a joke?" he fumed.

"Neh, neh," she softly shushed him. "I couldn't be more serious about anything in my life. It's just that you sounded like Samuel the day we told him he'd eventually grow up and love a girl and get married and move away from us."

Sawyer stood where he was, tears streaming down his face as he stared out the window.

"Sawyer," Eliza continued. "The *kinner* need a *mamm*."

"You're their *mamm*," he argued belligerently.

She continued as if she hadn't heard. "And you need a wife to love you."

"Your love is enough to last a lifetime," he heard himself say.

Eliza coughed several times, and Sawyer returned to the bed to kneel by her side. When she had caught her breath again, she stroked his hair.

"You have so much love to give," she whispered. "You need to give it to a wife." Then, teasing, she added, "Waste not, want not."

"There will never be another like you, Eliza," he cried, burying his head in her shoulder.

"*Neh*, but there *will be* another," she said firmly. "When you find her, you have my blessing, because I know the woman you choose—and the woman the Lord provides for you—will be worthy of your love."

Remembering, Sawyer kicked at his sheets and shifted to his side. He hardly knew Hannah. How preposterous it was to think he might feel a stirring of emotion for her as a woman. Yes, she took good care of the children, but so would anyone he hired in Ohio. And Ohio was where his home was, where his livelihood was and where he was meant to be. This life in Pennsylvania was temporary, and so was the brief kindling of connection he felt with Hannah. It couldn't hold a candle to the steadfast love he'd shared with Eliza during their six-year marriage.

I'm acting like a charmed schoolboy, he thought. He decided he must take care not to confuse his appreciation for Hannah as a hired nanny with any other emotion. From now on, he'd be more mindful that their relationship was built on business and more careful to keep his distance.

Chapter Seven

Hannah's decision to behave in a manner more becoming of a mature schoolteacher and nanny when she was around Sawyer proved easier to practice than she expected. Tuesday through Thursday, Sawyer dropped the children off at school and picked them up with nary a word about anything other than the weather, which remained uncomfortably humid.

On Friday morning, it was Doris who greeted Sawyer at the base of the stairs, so when Hannah saw him there, she returned to her classroom. She figured if Doris wanted to sidle up to him with another apple crisp, she could give it her best effort. He'd probably grumble later that it sat in his stomach like a brick anyway.

She immediately scolded herself for having such stingy thoughts. She had been uncharacteristically peevish for most of the week, and she couldn't put a finger on what was bothering her. She only knew that once the children left for the evening, she hastily finished her chores and retreated to her room to prepare lessons for the following day. She reasoned there was no sense remaining in the parlor; it wasn't as if her grandfather ever initiated a conversation, and he hardly appeared interested in the topics she brought to his attention.

But her cranky mood always vanished when she was with the children, whose wholesome inquisitiveness and entertaining chatter as they walked home from school buoyed her spirit.

"Can we show *Daed* the stream tonight?" Samuel asked for the second time that week.

"*May* we show *Daed* the stream tonight?" Sarah corrected him in her best teacher voice.

"Please?" Simon added.

Hannah hesitated. Over the past few days she had begun to suspect Sawyer was avoiding her as much as she was avoiding him.

"Your *daed* has seen many streams before," she said.

"*Jah*, but this is a special stream," Samuel said.

"What makes it special?"

"It's *your* stream," he said.

Hannah was tickled by the sentiment, but said, "I think after a difficult day of working in the fields, your *daed's* feet are sore and he doesn't want to walk all the way to the stream."

"But that is exactly why we must take him there," Simon contended. "He can take off his shoes and socks and soak his sore feet in the water. It always makes *my* toes feel better."

Hannah chuckled at Simon's logic. "*Jah*, I know it does, Simon. I have to mention to your *daed* that your shoes are pinching your toes. I think you're going through a growth spurt. It's permissible for you to go barefoot now, but later in the fall, you'll need proper-fitting shoes."

"But can we show him the stream?"

"*Jah*, you may," she replied.

If it meant that much to the children, she didn't see harm in allowing them to take their father to the stream. Besides, they knew the way there; it wasn't as if she had to accompany them. She would wait to see how Sawyer reacted to the suggestion. She hoped by that evening any awkwardness between them would have passed and Sawyer would know how sensible she was, despite her temporary lapse in appropriate behavior.

But that evening, it was John Plank and Doris, not Sawyer, who arrived to gather the children.

Hannah was so surprised, she rushed across the grass to the buggy and blurted out, "Where is Sawyer? Is he alright?"

"What a nervous Nellie you are," scoffed Doris. "He's fine."

"The boys had work left to accomplish," explained John. "There may be bad weather tomorrow, so they wanted to finish as much as they could tonight."

Doris boasted, "After I surprised them when I dropped in to cook a hearty meal, they had the strength to complete their work. John and I thought since my horse was already out, we'd use my buggy to pick up the triplets. Besides, as you can guess, John can't get into and out of the buggy without an adult to help him."

Hannah marveled that there was no end to what Doris would do to catch a man's attention. But she doubted her efforts would amount to anything anyway; Sawyer didn't appear interested in her.

After the triplets had been rounded up and the buggy was ready to depart, John snapped his fingers and said, "I almost forgot. Sawyer had a message for you."

Anticipation fluttered in Hannah's chest. *"Jah?"*

"He said if it is raining tomorrow, please don't expect Sarah, Simon and Samuel," John stated. "Although he said, of course, you'd be compensated for the full week, regardless of the weather."

Hannah's cheeks burned. Sawyer's offer further emphasized that their connection was based solely on an employment relationship, and she found it insulting he'd suggest she expected payment for a service she didn't provide.

"Please tell Sawyer I said he might better spend his money on new shoes for the boys—their feet have outgrown the pairs they have now."

She strode toward the house without another word.

Sawyer swatted at a fly buzzing around his ear as he pitched hay in the horses' stalls. He felt as ornery as a mule. Admittedly the yumasetta casserole Doris made was delicious, but he would have preferred eating one of his uncle's unsavory concoctions in silence to listening to Doris prattling at dinner. Furthermore, because of Doris's insistence that she and John pick up the children, Sawyer missed seeing Hannah that evening. If it rained, he wouldn't see her on Saturday, either.

He noticed she'd been out of sorts all week, and he was concerned he had offended her by his behavior on Monday. Or was it an issue of money—perhaps taking care of the children was worth more than he was paying her, especially when they were sick? Did she regret taking on the position after all? At least if it rained tomorrow, she'd have a day to herself. Perhaps that was what she desired.

He resolved to speak to her candidly about it on Saturday if it didn't rain, or on Sunday if it did. Church was scheduled to meet at James and Amelia Hooley's house this Sabbath. The only obstacle Sawyer could foresee was that Doris was sure to be around, since she lived with them, but he was determined to somehow seek Hannah out alone.

Much to Sawyer's relief, by the time he returned to the house, Doris was gone.

"Are the *kinner* in bed?" he asked his uncle.

"Doris said they were asleep before their heads hit the pillow. Hannah Lantz must keep them busy and well fed. They are sleeping better, *jah*?"

"Jah," Sawyer affirmed, grinning. "She is doing them *gut*."

"She is doing you all *gut*," his uncle replied. "Doris was right—a house needs a woman's touch to make it a home."

Sawyer wondered what he was getting at. He shrugged and said, *"Jah*, I am glad I hired her."

"Speaking of that," John said, "Hannah rejected your offer of being compensated if it rains tomorrow and Samuel, Sarah and Simon stay here on the farm. She said your money is better spent on new shoes for the *kinner*."

"She said *what*?" Sawyer asked. "What were her exact words?"

John snorted. "I didn't write them down, man! I only recall that she bristled a bit at the mention of her salary."

Sawyer was flummoxed. Even when he didn't speak with Hannah in person, he managed to bungle his words. He'd have to set it right first thing in the morning.

But when he awoke on Saturday, a heavy rain was thrumming against the roof, thwarting his plans and making for another agonizingly long day without talking to Hannah.

The driving rain did nothing to cool the temperature; instead, the air felt tropical and oppressive. Hannah had just completed her housework when her grandfather asked her to accompany him to town. Although it was pouring, the sky was white, not dark. Hannah figured it wouldn't produce the kind of severe storm that made both her and the horse nervous, so she agreed to go.

Indeed, by the time they arrived in town, the rain had subsided enough for Hannah to dash into the mercantile without getting drenched, while her grandfather visited the hardware store. Once home, she prepared and served dinner and then cleaned and put away the dishes. Afterward, she felt so listless, she baked a triple batch of molasses cookies to bring to James and Amelia's home for church. Usually the family hosting church on a particular week provided the midday meal, but they wouldn't turn away dessert, so Hannah baked enough to feed the entire district.

"Smells *gut*," her grandfather huffed when he entered the kitchen.

She knew from a lifetime of experience that this was his peace offering—a kind word in exchange for a rash of harsh ones. She didn't harbor any bitterness toward him because, as he stood before her, his hands behind his back, she saw him for who he was: a man too stubborn to change, but in need of love just as he was.

"Denki." She smiled. "I have set some cookies aside for you to have with your coffee."

"Here," he said, placing something on the table. "For the girl and her brothers."

It took a moment for Hannah to register what she'd been given: a wooden board, sanded smooth, with two lengths of rope knotted through each end. She realized this was the reason he insisted on going to town today: he needed rope to make a tree swing.

"The *kinner* will enjoy this very much. *Denki, Groossdaadi.*"

Her grandfather grunted and accepted the cup of coffee and plate of cookies she extended to him.

"Their *daed* will have to hang it for them," he said before heading to the parlor. Lest she forget, he reminded her, "And he will need to take it down before they leave. It is only temporary."

Sawyer was relieved when the Sabbath came. His cousins became easily frustrated around the children, and they were especially exasperated when they were cooped up for hours together in the house. He himself felt more and more irascible as the day wore on, the rain a steady deluge against the windows.

"There's no sense in all of us squeezing into one buggy," he announced on Sunday morning. "Besides, my horse needs to stretch its legs."

He left early with the children, intending to speak to Hannah before the services began. He hoped she would be willing to keep an eye on Sarah, Simon and Samuel, since the men sat separately from the women and young children during the services.

But no sooner had he hitched his horse and crossed the yard than Doris appeared out of nowhere.

"*Guder mariye*, Sawyer," she greeted him. "Won't your *onkel* and cousins be coming this morning?"

"*Guder mariye,*" he repeated. "*Jah*, they'll be here soon. We traveled separately."

Sawyer surreptitiously scanned the yard as he was talking to Doris and spotted Hannah far across the lawn.

But before Hannah neared, Doris suggested, "I will watch the *kinner*, so you may go join the other men. They're over there."

Sawyer understood it was customary in this district for the men to gather outside in small groups, usually around the barn, before the services began. Likewise, the women congregated in the kitchen and parlor. At the appropriate time and according to a designated order, the men and women would file into the hosts' meeting room—the Hooleys' basement, in this instance—to worship together. As Jacob Stolzfus signaled to him, Sawyer reluctantly accepted Doris's offer and tramped toward the barn.

A few minutes later, Sawyer took a place on a bench toward the back of the men's section. He hoped Hannah wouldn't think sending the children with Doris was his preference. In fact, he hoped no one thought that, or he'd be the talk of the district.

Yet following lunch, he found out that was exactly what people did think. When he joined a circle of men cavorting in the yard, Jacob commented, "We saw you chatting with Doris this morning and noticed your *kinner* with her, as well. What is the meaning of that?"

"There is no meaning," he stammered. "She offered to oversee the *kinner* during the service and I accepted."

"Are you quite certain about that?"

"Of course I am certain."

"But we have heard her say she has come round to the farm several times recently, supposedly on the pretense of helping with household chores," Jacob pressed. "She's an unmarried woman and you're a widower...yet you still deny she has any designs on you or that you have any interest in courting her?"

In a resounding voice, Sawyer countered, "How many times do I have to tell you, I have no romantic intentions toward that woman? If you must know, I think she behaves more like a silly schoolgirl than a schoolteacher. She is helping my family during a time of need, that is all," he said loudly. "Now if you'll excuse me, I must call my *kinner.*"

"There's no need to call them—they are all right here behind you. I brought them over so I could say hello before I left. So, hello, Sawyer. Hello, gentlemen," Hannah said pointedly, acknowledging the small group of men, who suddenly kicked at the dirt or surveyed the clouds. Then, "I will see you tomorrow, Simon, Sarah and Samuel, *Gott* willing."

She had never felt so humiliated in her life, and she couldn't get away from Sawyer quickly enough. His opinion of her was shameful on its own, but did he have to share it with the other men in her district?

"Hannah, please wait!" he shouted to her, but she pretended to be as deaf as her grandfather as she marched toward the buggy where he was waiting for her.

She was relieved when her grandfather worked the horse into a brisk pace. Back at home, he wandered to his room for a nap and she to the porch to wallow in a good hard cry. She was blowing her nose when a buggy she recognized came up the lane. It was too late to dash inside: Sawyer had already seen her.

"*Guder nammidaag*, Hannah," he called with a friendly wave, as if he hadn't just insulted her and belittled her reputation in front of a half dozen other men.

"Sawyer," she said flatly, glancing beyond him toward the buggy. The children didn't appear to be in it. "Where are Sarah, Simon and Samuel?"

"I left them with my *onkel*," he replied, removing his hat. "Doris said she would see to it he didn't forget to bring them home when he was ready to leave," he joked, but she wouldn't let him wrest a smile from her lips.

He shifted his weight and continued feebly, "Let's just hope she doesn't try to comb Sarah's hair again. Sarah complained she didn't do it as carefully as you do—she said it hurt her scalp—and it doesn't appear as neat, either."

"I'm sure Doris was trying her best." Hannah's temper flared as she rose from her chair. If Sawyer thought insulting Doris was going to distract her from how he insulted her, he was gravely mistaken.

"Of course," Sawyer responded. "It goes without saying Doris did a much better job than I've ever done. I didn't mean to sound ungrateful."

"Just as you didn't mean to sound ungrateful when you said what you said to Jacob Stolzfus and the others after church? *That* certainly sounded ungrateful to me. And mean-spirited, as well."

Sawyer's mouth stretched into a grim line. "I'm sorry. You are right. I said things I shouldn't have."

"Why are you sorry, Sawyer?" Hannah asked, placing her hands on her hips and glaring down at him on the bottom porch stair. "Is it because your words were untrue? Or is it because they were unkind?"

Sawyer kicked a pebble. "They most definitely were unkind. As for being untrue or not... I am sorry, Hannah, but I cannot be dishonest. I do find Doris's behavior silly at times. My own sister Gertrude is half as young but acts twice as wise."

"Doris?" Hannah gulped. Her knees felt as if they would buckle behind her.

"I know she is a friend of yours, and because of that, I don't doubt she has redeeming qualities," he answered, leaping up the stairs to stand in front of her. "But I have only experienced her superficial side. The other men were pressuring me to claim my intentions toward her, of which I have none. Still, I was wrong to say what I said. Please forgive me for speaking out of turn."

As the realization of her mistake washed over Hannah, she struggled to gain her composure. She was so relieved she didn't accuse Sawyer of what she thought him guilty of saying about her—he would have thought her ten times more nonsensical than Doris.

"I understand," she said slowly. "Although I am not certain the situation warrants it after all, I accept your apology. Especially since you came all this way to express you intended no harm."

Sawyer took a step backward and leaned against the railing.

"Actually," he admitted, avoiding her radiant blue eyes, "I came because I was afraid I caused you an earlier offense."

"What offense was that?" she asked, her lips pursed.

Sawyer didn't know how he could answer her question without drawing attention to his behavior. If he hadn't offended her in the first place, he didn't want to point it out now.

Stuttering, he replied, "It's just…I, er… I worry I may have been too intrusive. Taking liberties when I shouldn't have."

"I don't know what you mean," she replied. "But I assure you it isn't the case. I am always happy to see you arrive. You and the *kinner* are most *wilkom*, regardless of whether they are under my charge or you are simply visiting."

"In that case—" he grinned at her "—might you have any cookies to offer your visitor? I heard everyone raving about them at lunch, but I never got around to tasting one before I left."

"Sweets before supper? Tsk, tsk," Hannah said in mock consternation, and they both chuckled. "Please, take a seat and I'll fix coffee."

After the screen door slammed behind Hannah, Sawyer teetered nervously in the second rocking chair, running his fingers through his hair. He was glad he wore the fresh shirt Doris had laundered, and he smoothed the fabric down against his chest.

When Hannah returned, she told him a bit about her sister over the refreshments, and he talked about Gertrude and Kathryn.

"I can tell from the stories they share that the *kinner* adore Gertrude," Hannah remarked. "I hope to be that kind of *ant* to my sister's *bobbel.*"

"I have every confidence you will be," Sawyer stated. He stammered before saying, "You mentioned my being ungrateful…and I, um, I want you to know how much I appreciate it that you are the one caring for my *kinner.*"

"You pay me well," Hannah replied. "Too well, I think. But beyond payment, I am happy to do it. We are, after all, neighbors. For a time, anyway. I'd like to believe we are friends, as well."

"We are indeed," Sawyer declared vehemently, and then he immediately felt self-conscious. "As your friend—as your neighbor…that is, as your friendly neighbor, I want you to know if you are ever in need of *my* help, I hope you will ask me."

"Really?" she asked, laughing in her fetching manner. "Because there is something that would be helpful."

"What is it?"

"I will be right back," she said and collected the dishes. When she emerged from the house, she was carrying a wooden swing. "I'm too short to hang this on the willow, and *Groossdaadi's* balance is unreliable because of his hearing problem."

Sawyer laughed heartily. "I'm definitely the right man for this task."

He retrieved the ladder from the shed, and slight as she was, Hannah's firm grasp held it steady. But even before he ascended the ladder, he felt twelve feet tall.

Chapter Eight

Sarah was so delighted by the swing that when Hannah's grandfather entered the house for supper, she ran pell-mell toward him and wrapped her arms around his waist.

"I pumped so high I nearly kicked the clouds," she yelled, and although Hannah's grandfather couldn't see her mouth to read her lips, Hannah sensed he understood Sarah's elation.

He patted the top of her head and then squawked, "Bah," before loping away.

"Sarah swinged the longest," Samuel complained.

"I *swunged*," Sarah emphasized. "And I gave you both a turn."

Samuel ignored her, saying, "I want a longer turn after dinner."

"Actually," Hannah interrupted, "any *kinner* who don't quarrel during supper time will be allowed to take their *daed* to the stream when he arrives this evening."

"Really?" Simon questioned.

"Really. It's so muggy tonight I think your *daed* might appreciate the cool water."

Sawyer grinned when Hannah suggested it, and the children raced ahead, shouting, "This way, *Daed*!"

Before Sawyer and Hannah had a chance to remove their own shoes and socks, the triplets waded into the stream. Samuel, Sarah and Simon bent down, drawing water in their cupped hands. They formed a circle, their golden heads nearly touching as they studied their find.

"Look, *Daed*, there are bits of gold dust in the water," Sarah gasped.

"I think that must be mica," Sawyer answered, drawing nearer.

"*Neh*, it's gold. Come closer," Simon beckoned.

When Sawyer leaned in to get a look, the children splashed the water toward his face. "Surprise!" they yelled in concert.

He backed away and gave such a hearty laugh that droplets of water flew from his beard.

"Teacher showed us that trick," Simon said, doubling over.

"Oh, did she, now?" Sawyer asked. "Well, we'll see how she likes it." He lifted a handful at Hannah, who kicked water back toward him, squealing.

For the next hour, Sawyer overturned rocks and explored the banks with Hannah and the children, until Hannah heard a rumble.

"A storm is coming. We must hurry back," she warned.

"I think it's still in the distance," Sawyer said, just as a flash illuminated off the water.

"*Neh*, it's here. It's here!" she cried frantically. "Run!"

She swiped up her socks and shoes and then grabbed Sarah by the hand. "Get the boys," she hollered over her shoulder to Sawyer, who already had rounded them up and was close on her heels.

They raced toward the house against the gusty wind that drove the rain sideways into their skin like hot bullets. As they crossed the open field and sprinted up a slope, Hannah's bare feet slipped on the wet grass and she sprawled flat on her stomach on the ground. Above them, thunder crackled and a fork of lightning ripped the sky in two.

"Keep running! Get into the workshop," she urged Sarah. "Don't try to make it to the house!"

"Go!" Sawyer commanded the boys, thrusting his shoes into their hands.

He scooped Hannah into his arms and didn't stop running until he was safely inside her grandfather's workshop. Only then did she exhale, uncertain whether it was thunder or her own heartbeat that was reverberating so raucously in her ears.

Sawyer gently placed Hannah down, but as soon as her foot touched the floor, she winced.

"Wrap your arms around my neck," he said, shifting so she could reach. As he situated her onto a stool, he could feel her fluttering like a bird against his chest.

"Aw, look at this!" Simon stared in awe. The three children were mesmerized by a shelf of toys Hannah's grandfather had made. Sarah stood motionless in front of the dollhouse, her mouth agape.

"You may look, but don't touch," Sawyer instructed them. To Hannah he asked, "May I examine your foot?"

Although the light was waning, when he ran his rough hands over her elegant ankle, he peered into her eyes for a sign of pain. She flinched when a roar of thunder shook the little shed.

"Does that hurt?" he asked.

"Neh," she replied. "It wasn't that. I know I shouldn't be nervous because *Gott* protects as well as He provides, but these storms make me come unraveled."

Oh, so that's why she flinches at loud noises, Sawyer thought. *That, and her* groossdaadi's *voice.*

Sawyer cupped her heel in his hand and examined her ankle once again. "I think you only twisted it," he announced. "It's not even a sprain. It's not swelling."

"I'm so embarrassed," she admitted.

"Why? A twisted ankle can hurt as much as a sprain. You were charging quite fast when it happened. I imagine the pain shot through you like a knife."

"I'm embarrassed by my anxious behavior," she confessed. "What kind of role model am I for the *kinner*, to be afraid of thunderstorms?"

"The *kinner*, I'm sorry to say, aren't paying you any mind," he replied. "They're transfixed by the toys your *groossdaadi* created."

A clap of thunder so startled Hannah that she nearly toppled off the stool. Sawyer clasped her by her shoulders, helping her adjust her balance.

"I'm glad they aren't bothered by storms." She sighed. "I should have outgrown this fear as surely as I outgrew my childhood dresses, but some memories are more difficult to forget than others."

Thinking of Eliza's illness, Sawyer vigorously nodded in agreement. "Did you experience an unusually violent storm as a child?"

"Jah," she said, averting her eyes from his. Her lashes feathered her cheeks as she glanced down, wringing her hands. "A lightning strike brought down the tree that claimed my parents' lives."

"How frightful," Sawyer murmured sympathetically.

After a pause, he nudged her elbow and joked, "But you're safe now. After all, I am the tallest one here. If lightning is to strike, it will strike me."

"Perish the thought!" she exclaimed. Her mortified expression made him laugh so hard that she began laughing, too—as did the children—and pretty soon, the raging storm had passed.

On Wednesday, Hannah's mailbox contained a letter addressed *Sarah Plank, c/o Hannah Lantz*. The return address indicated it was from Gertrude Plank, Sawyer's sister. Hannah was puzzled by why Gertrude would send the letter to her instead of in care of Sarah's uncle. Then she recalled when she was helping Sarah write a letter to Gertrude, she wasn't sure what John Plank's return address was, so she had scribbled her own address on the upper-left corner of the envelope.

She sat in the rocking chair while Sarah stood beside her on the porch. The boys were grateful Sarah was preoccupied with the mail because it gave them an opportunity to push each other on the swing without Sarah counting to one hundred—the maximum number of pushes she allowed her brothers per turn.

My dear niece Sarah,

What a wonderful surprise to receive a note from you! I'm glad your teacher, Hannah Lantz, helped you write it, and I am certain she will help you read this letter from me, as well.

Your initials look beautiful in cursive. I have always liked the letter *S* more than any other letter in cursive, although *L* is also lovely. You are very young to be learning cursive—do you know how to draw any other letters besides *S* and *P*? You will have to write again to show me.

Your aunt is feeling better, and the baby is slowly gaining weight. Her lungs are getting stronger, too. Now she sounds like a bleating lamb when she cries instead of like a mewling kitten. The midwife said she had never seen such a tiny baby before. We are blessed the Lord is increasing her size.

I am cooking for four men here—your uncle and three hired hands. One of them, Seth Lambright, says my meat loaf is the best he's ever tasted.

I miss your smile, and Samuel and Simon's antics. Remember me to your father and tell him I will write to him next.

Your loving aunt,
Gertrude

Hannah read the letter aloud three times until Sarah had it memorized. She bounded down the stairs, waving the page at her brothers.

"Listen," she cried to them. "I will read this letter from Gertrude—she wrote a message for you, too!"

Hannah noticed there was a second sheet of paper folded inside the envelope. It was addressed *Postscript for Hannah*. She unfolded it and read:

Dear Hannah,

I am grateful you are taking such wonderful care of the children. I also appreciate the peace of mind and happiness you have brought Sawyer. He is slow to express his affection, but if you are patient enough to untangle my niece's hair, you have patience enough for him to prove me right.

Sincerely,
Gertrude Plank

Hannah read the note a second time. What a strange thing for Gertrude to write. She didn't recall helping Sarah write anything about her hair, and they certainly didn't mention anything about Sawyer in the letter.

She was warmed by Gertrude's complimenting her care for the children, but she dismissed the notion that she'd brought happiness to Sawyer's life as a sisterly expression of gratitude. It was the kind of thing little Sarah would do—minding her brothers' manners for them.

But there was no need for Gertrude to thank Hannah on behalf of Sawyer; he said as much each time he saw Hannah before school and after supper, often lingering to chat with her about the day's events or else to share a snack together with the children. The week flew by, and before Hannah knew it, it was Saturday—the day Sawyer invited her and her grandfather to come into town with them.

"I'd appreciate your help fitting the boys with shoes," he'd claimed. "This will also save your horse a trip, as I'm sure your *groossdaadi* has errands to run in town anyway."

"And we have a special surprise to share with you!" Simon announced.

"Shush!" Sarah admonished him.

Hannah didn't have any idea what surprise they had planned, but it hardly mattered: she considered time together with all of them to be time well spent, and it couldn't come soon enough.

Sawyer was perturbed. On Saturday morning, he received a letter from his foreman:

Vernon Mast's injury hadn't yet healed, so I switched responsibilities with him as you directed. Unfortunately, Vernon's organizational skills don't match his talents as a carpenter. Subsequently, we missed two important deadlines—both for the Miller & Sons account—and we've botched several regional deliveries to boot.

Sawyer crumpled the paper in frustration and chucked it across the room. As frustrated as he was, he knew it wasn't Vernon's fault. Sawyer had put him in a position for which he was ill-suited, and now Sawyer needed to return to Ohio as quickly as possible to set things right with the customers and help his crew get back on schedule.

He realized that cutting his Saturday working hours in half by going into town wasn't going to speed things up on the farm any, but he had to get the boys new shoes. He was grateful for Hannah's attentiveness—he hadn't noticed how ill-fitting they were until she mentioned it.

He quickly penned a letter back to his foreman, telling him to resume the accounting and scheduling duties. "Prioritize the Miller & Sons orders. Give Vernon whatever woodworking projects he can handle and ask the other men to work late to take up any slack. I will, of course, compensate them for their time," he directed. "When I return, we'll consider hiring another man."

Sawyer hoped it didn't come to that, primarily because he didn't know any other men in his district who possessed the quality of skills the clients expected from his shop. He hated to admit it, but even among the Amish, he found the workmanship of the younger men to be sloppier than the standards he'd been raised to deliver.

His business dilemmas weighed heavily on his mind, especially since his decisions affected the livelihood of families beyond his own. He set his pen down with a heavy sigh and folded the paper into an envelope so he could drop it in a mailbox in town.

When he saw Hannah waving from the porch, a smile decorating her face, he momentarily forgot about his business problems in Ohio.

"It's a beautiful day, isn't it?" she asked as he approached, lifting her chin to scan his face.

Although it was as humid and overcast as ever, he agreed, "A beautiful day, indeed."

Hannah squeezed into the back of the buggy with the children, who sang songs along the way, while Sawyer and Hannah's grandfather took the front seat. When they arrived in town, the old man set off toward the hardware store, while the rest of them entered the *Englisch* clothing shop that carried the kinds of shoes the children needed.

"*Kumme*, Samuel," Sawyer beckoned the boy. "The clerk needs to measure your foot."

"That's Simon, not Samuel," Hannah whispered, nudging him.

"You're right—it is," chuckled Sawyer, lifting Simon's hat and brushing his hair away from his ear. "How can you tell when they are both dressed alike and wearing hats? Even I get mixed up unless I can see which one has the birthmark."

"A mother always knows her children," the *Englisch* salesclerk interjected.

Sawyer recognized that if the clerk assumed Hannah was the children's mother, she must have assumed Hannah was Sawyer's wife, as well. Glancing toward Hannah, he noticed her fair skin was splotching with pink, and she gave him a quick half smile. He couldn't interpret her expression for certain, but she didn't seem to be displeased and neither was he. Although he felt a small pang of disloyalty toward Eliza, Sawyer figured there was no harm done, and he didn't correct the woman's error.

As they were returning to the buggy, the children stopped in front of Schrock's Authentic Amish Shop.

"Look!" Samuel said excitedly, pointing to the window. "A train like the one in your *groossdaadi's* workshop."

Sawyer noticed it had a Model Only sign attached to the caboose. "It looks as if it's not for sale," he noted, just as a short bespectacled man came out of the shop.

"*Guder nammidaag*, Hannah," Joseph Schrock greeted her in Pennsylvania Dutch. Hannah introduced him to everyone in turn.

"I'm happy to see you," Joseph said. "All of your *groossdaadi's* toys sold! A busload of tourists came in and bought up every last one, except the display model, which we kept for future business. Several people asked to order more and have them delivered in time for Christmas. My *daed* was so pleased he cleared an extra space for double the toys and the dollhouse besides! Is Albert in town today?"

"He is," Hannah hedged. "But, Joseph, you know he never goes back on his word."

Joseph's shoulders drooped. "Please, will you talk to him for me?"

"I will try," Hannah agreed, her expression melancholy.

When they had made their way down the street, the children galloping ahead of them, Hannah explained the situation about the toys and her grandfather's promise never to step foot inside Schrock's shop again.

"I feel terrible disappointing Joseph, but when *Groossdaadi* says *never*, there is absolutely no changing his mind."

"But this could be a source of steady income," Sawyer protested.

"*Jah*, but *Gott* will provide us what we need," Hannah said with a sigh.

"*Gott* already *is* providing you what you need," Sawyer argued. "And your *groossdaadi* is rejecting it. What kind of man would rather have you work like a mule than swallow his pride?"

Hannah's temper flared. "Work *like a mule*?" she asked, appalled. Certainly he'd never use such a phrase about a woman who was a mother of her own children. "Is a beast what you'd compare me to? Is that what you think of a woman who teaches other people's *kinner*? Or who cares for them? Is that what you think of *me*?"

"That isn't what I meant at all," Sawyer replied. "It was just a figure of speech."

Hannah turned her head to the side and controlled her voice so as not to upset the children, but she was shaking as she said, "Who are you to criticize the way in which my *groossdaadi* and I run our household? What concern is it to you, Sawyer Plank?"

"It isn't any concern of mine," Sawyer said, gritting his teeth. "It isn't any concern at all. Forget I said anything."

They walked side by side in silence. Tears and fury blurred Hannah's vision so that she walked crookedly, nearly bumping into Samuel, who had stopped in front of the *Englisch* ice-cream shop and was holding open the door for her.

"We're here," he said excitedly.

"It's our surprise for you!" Sarah exclaimed.

Simon gave a little hop. "*Daed* is treating us all to an ice-cream cone, double scoop. They make it homemade here!"

Hannah winced. Her stomach was tied in such tight knots, she didn't know how she could eat, but the children were so pleased with themselves, she couldn't say no. Sawyer asked what flavor her grandfather preferred and then purchased him a dish of maple walnut. Everyone else chose strawberry, in honor of Hannah.

"It's like eating pink snow instead of pink sunshine, isn't it, Hannah?" Samuel asked.

"It is just like that," Hannah replied. "What a *gut* use of metaphor, Samuel."

The youngsters darted ahead as the adults lagged behind, not speaking. When they got to the hitch, her grandfather was nowhere in sight, so the children plopped down on a grassy knoll while Hannah and Sawyer stood waiting at the buggy.

Hannah could barely stomach her ice cream, but the more she prolonged eating it, the more it began to drip. She tipped her head to lick a pink rivulet running down the side of the cone. It was useless; her manners were no better than Doris Hooley's. But what did she care what Sawyer Plank thought of her anyway?

"Hannah," he began, after he had finished crunching the last bit of his cone and swiped a napkin across his mouth.

"What is it?" she asked impatiently, fixing her attention on her ice cream.

"There are two things I need you to hear," Sawyer stated definitively.

"Go on, then." She shrugged, licking her cone in a deliberately indifferent manner.

"The first is that I am very sorry. I didn't mean to insult you or your *groossdaadi*. All I meant was that I would expect a man who cares for you to value you so much he'd do anything within his power to share your burdens, or die trying."

Hannah felt her insides melt as surely as the ice cream she was holding. No man had ever said such a thing about her value to her before. She glanced under her lashes at him, afraid to trust her voice to speak. "And what is the second thing you want to tell me?"

Relieved that Hannah seemed to have accepted his apology, Sawyer gained confidence. He reached forward to touch her face with his napkin. "The second thing is that you have a dab of strawberry ice cream on your nose and another on your chin."

Her laughter was as melodic to his ears as a bubbling brook and twice as refreshing. He readily joined in as she blotted her face with her own napkin.

"Did I get it all?" she asked.

"All but this spot here," he said, cupping her face in his fingers. Her skin was so porcelain and her features so dainty, he felt as clumsy as if he were handling fine

china when he brushed her chin with his thumb. Their
eyes locked for a long moment, and Sawyer felt his
breathing quicken.

"Time to go!" a loud voice shouted behind him, and
Sawyer immediately dropped his hand.

He retrieved the container of ice cream and plastic
spoon he had set on the seat of the buggy and presented
it to Hannah's grandfather, who batted it away. Its contents tipped, landing upside down on the ground.

"Unlike with my granddaughter, my affections cannot be bought," he muttered, climbing into the buggy.

Hannah ducked her head and stepped back. Clapping to get the children's attention, she called them to
the buggy. Sawyer himself felt like a scolded child as
he climbed in after Hannah's grandfather. Oblivious to
the tension, Sarah, Simon and Samuel sang all the way
home. Sawyer half expected the old man to demand
they stop singing out of pure spite, but instead he sat
in stony silence.

When they arrived, Hannah's grandfather trudged to
the house, as the three children spilled from the buggy.
Sawyer immediately directed them back into it.

"Aren't we going to eat supper with Hannah?" Simon
asked.

"Not tonight," he said. "Doris Hooley said she would
come by today and prepare enough for all."

"But she always wants to brush my hair," Sarah
whimpered. "It hurts the way she does it."

"*Kumme*, get into the buggy!" Sawyer called, and
the children obeyed.

"I'm sorry" was all Sawyer could think to say to
Hannah.

"You needn't be," she replied firmly, and he knew
she meant it. "For anything."

He watched as Hannah crossed the lawn. Before disappearing into the house, she turned and waved, calling, "I will see you Monday, *Gott* willing."

Chapter Nine

Hannah never scrubbed the floors as thoroughly as she did when she was angry, and on Saturday afternoon she was so mad, the wood gleamed.

Why did her grandfather have to behave that way? It seemed as if he'd intentionally been trying to snuff out any flicker of happiness she experienced—especially in the company of young men—since she was a teenager, and he showed no signs of stopping now that she was an adult. But why? What had overtaken him, to make him act so hostile toward Sawyer? And how dare he say her affections could be bought—as if she had ever had her head turned by worldly riches! None of it made sense, and she refused to feel guilty for having accepted the rare luxury of a store-bought ice-cream cone—or a kind expression of support—from Sawyer.

For the next hour, her grandfather refused to come out of his bedroom. At first, Hannah was so incensed by his rude display in town that after she fixed supper, instead of telling him it was ready, she turned the pot to simmer and went to retrieve the mail. Among the items in her mailbox was a letter from Eve. She settled into the rocking chair on the porch and ran her finger under the flap of the envelope.

"Dearest Hannah," the letter began.

I know such topics are usually left unsaid, but I must confide that the baby has been kicking and somersaulting constantly! I think it is from this hot weather. I cannot wait to become a mother. I thought no love could be deeper than the love I felt for my husband, but I already love this child with my whole being.

Here, Hannah paused. As happy as she was that her sister was married and with child, it pained her to be reminded of what she hadn't ever experienced and probably never would, if her grandfather's abrasive attitude didn't change. She took a breath and kept reading.

I enjoyed hearing about the Plank children and their father, Sawyer. Is he really as tall as you described, or might he appear head and shoulders above the rest in your eyes for another reason?

Confused by her sister's question, Hannah again stopped reading. Eve had always been closely attuned to Hannah's feelings, and she wondered what she'd written that may have caused her sister to think she saw Sawyer as larger-than-life.

I am glad you and Grandfather have another source of income—as long as he doesn't run Sawyer over with the buggy! How humiliating that must have been for you.

Hannah sighed. Her sister's simple comment showed she remembered what it was like to live with her grandfather's unpredictable behavior. But an uncharacteristic misgiving popped into Hannah's mind: at least Eve had escaped.

Eve closed the letter by writing, "Please pray God provides continued health for the baby and for me."

Again, a bitter thought flitted through Hannah's heart. Why should she ask God for provision for Eve when her sister already had all she could ever need?

She lowered her eyelids and inhaled deeply, willing herself not to cry. With her big toe, she pushed the rocker back and forth, dawdling until she felt composed enough to enter the house and serve her grandfather supper.

Because he wasn't seated at the table or resting in his chair in the parlor, she entered his room and found him lying in bed, feverish, the covers pulled to his chin. His breathing was labored, and he shook from a chill. He looked so infirmed, she immediately was contrite about how furious she had been. For the rest of the evening and through the night, each time she entered the room to change his compress or give him a sip of tea or broth, Hannah knelt by his bedside, praying for him to get well again.

By Sunday morning, his fever hadn't broken, although he dressed and sat with Hannah in the sitting room for Scripture reading and prayer, since it was an "off Sunday," and there was no church meeting that week. Afterward, he stumbled toward his bedroom, and Hannah quickly wrapped his arm around her shoulder and supported his weight as he lumbered down the hall. When she had arranged his pillows around his head, she reached to draw the shades, but he grasped her hand.

"Don't leave me, Gloria," he said, his eyes wild.

That was her grandmother's name. Hannah fretted he was confused from the fever.

"I'll be right back," she mouthed. "I am only going to get you a fresh glass of water."

"Neh," her grandfather pleaded. "Don't leave me."

Hannah blinked back her tears, realizing he was afraid she'd leave him for good, like her grandmother did when she died. Perhaps he feared Sawyer would offer to hire her to go and care for the children in Ohio once her teaching job ended. The children had mentioned having a *daadi haus* on their property—separate living quarters would have made the arrangement appropriate. That must have been why he was unspeakably rude to Sawyer—he was afraid Sawyer had intentions of taking her away from him, leaving him here all alone.

"Groossdaadi," she promised solemnly, looking into his eyes, "I would never leave you."

Satisfied, he closed his eyes and fell into a deep slumber. Hannah pulled the shades, leaving just enough light so she could see to read the Bible, which she did for over an hour. Eventually, she stretched and peeked out the window.

Whom did she expect to arrive for a Sunday visit? Eve and her husband would have let her know if they planned a trip. Jacob, Miriam and Abigail wouldn't drop by because Miriam was limiting her activities. Doris had frequented their home on off Sundays, but it was more likely she was at the Plank farm today, trying to capture Sawyer's attention. As for Sawyer, Hannah felt she'd be fortunate if her grandfather hadn't frightened him away permanently.

She sighed and flipped a page in her Bible. What was wrong with her? Usually she was content to spend a Sabbath resting and reading or in prayer, but today she felt at odds. No wonder her grandfather was concerned she'd abandon him: it was terribly lonely not to be in the company of people who cared about you and whom you cared about, too.

Her grandfather stirred, coughing. She touched his arm—his skin was damp with sweat, and she knew his fever had broken.

"What are you doing here?" he asked in a groggy voice.

"I was making sure you don't feel as lonely as I do," she said. Knowing he couldn't read her lips in the dusky light, she gave his arm a reassuring pat.

"I am hungry," he demanded, and she knew any hint of vulnerability he'd shown was gone. But she'd already made up her mind she'd stay home with him on Monday, just to be certain he was back to his usual grumpy self.

Come Monday morning, it was Doris, not Hannah, who stood at the top step of the schoolhouse stairs.

"*Guder mariye*, Sawyer," she said. "Sarah, Simon and Samuel, you and the other *kinner* will be in my classroom today."

"Did something happen?" Sawyer asked, panic rising in his voice. "Is Hannah alright?"

"You are as much of a nervous Nellie as she is," Doris said with a giggle. "Hannah is fine. It's her *groossdaadi* who is ill. She must have come here early this morning, because I found a note from her on my desk, along with her scholars' lesson plans."

"I see," Sawyer said, feeling both relieved she was alright and disappointed she wasn't present.

"She left a note for you, as well. You'll have to forgive me for reading it—I thought it was meant for me."

Doris extended a folded piece of paper to Sawyer, who snatched it from her grasp.

"Sawyer," it said. "Grandfather has been ill since Saturday evening. He is on the mend, but I want to stay with him to tend to his care. If Doris agrees, might she take the children to the farm after school and watch them there until you are finished in the fields? This arrangement seems best. Hannah."

As soon as Sawyer glanced up from the letter, Doris batted her lashes and said, "I'm happy to bring the *kinner* home from school and tend to their care. I'll cook supper, as well."

Sawyer hesitated. What had Hannah meant by *This arrangement seems best*? It was only for this afternoon, right? Perhaps this one time he should pick the children up himself and take them directly to the farm? But that would mean he'd lose valuable working hours, and they weren't as far along as he'd hoped they'd be.

"Don't be shy." Doris gave Sawyer a nudge while he was silently mulling over his options. "It would be my pleasure."

"Denki," he agreed reluctantly. Then, so there would be no misunderstanding, he added, "I am certain Hannah's *groossdaadi* will recover and tomorrow she will take charge of the *kinner* once again."

But he didn't feel certain at all.

Over a light breakfast on Monday morning, Hannah relayed Joseph Schrock's offer to expand the amount of shelf space her grandfather would be allotted if he'd reconsider consigning his toys at the shop.

"Final means final!" her grandfather brayed, adamant that he'd never again conduct business with the Schrock family.

He puttered out to his shed to work on the cradle for Miriam and Jacob's baby, leaving Hannah to tackle her housework and laundering.

Although Hannah knew the children would be fine with Doris at the farm, and she wanted to prove to her grandfather that her primary commitment was to his well-being, by midday, she was eager to get back to her usual routine at school.

She missed all of her scholars and regretted having even one less day to spend with them before her class was combined with Doris's after harvest ended. Not to mention how much she missed spending the afternoon with the Plank children.

Also, she had to admit—at least to herself—she especially missed the few minutes of conversation she and Sawyer engaged in whenever they saw each other. It never seemed to matter whether they talked about the children's schoolwork, the weather or what they had for dinner, and she derived equal pleasure from watching his forehead crease with thoughtfulness or his eyes sparkle in good humor. Was that the emotion she somehow conveyed in her letter to Eve that made her sister perceive she held an exaggerated regard for Sawyer? Whatever the feeling she had around Sawyer was, Hannah couldn't deny longing to experience it again.

She was so gleeful to return to school on Tuesday she didn't mind at all that Doris jabbered on and on while Hannah wrote sums on the blackboard.

"I am itching to tell you something," Doris warbled. "But you must keep it a secret."

Hannah didn't want to participate in Doris's gossip. "If it's something that's not supposed to be shared, perhaps you shouldn't mention it," she advised.

"But I must," she insisted. "It is too *wunderbaar* to keep to myself. I am being courted!"

"What?" Hannah gasped incredulously.

"*Jah*, it officially happened when he asked me yesterday, after I took the *kinner* to the farm."

Hannah couldn't believe what she was hearing. She knew Sawyer was sorry for the remarks he'd made about Doris, but she never imagined he'd come to think so highly of her that he'd actually court her. She felt as if she had been socked in the gut, but she choked out the words. "How nice for you and Sawyer."

"Sawyer?" Doris jeered. "Who said anything about Sawyer? I'm being courted by his *onkel*, John Plank. What would make you think I'd be interested in that cold fish Sawyer? In fact, he seems more *your* type than mine."

Hannah winced at Doris's crass insult. "I don't think he's a cold fish at all," she retorted. "But I'm not interested in being courted. My responsibility is to my *groossdaadi*."

"One day your *groossdaadi* will die," Doris said frankly. "And you will be past marrying age—or at least, past childbearing age. That's why John and I are so delighted to have kindled a relationship now. Odd, how we never considered each other in the years since his wife died. In a way, if it weren't for his breaking his leg, our courtship might have never occurred. The Lord works in mysterious ways, *jah*?"

"*Jah*," Hannah agreed.

Yet as she moved into the entryway to greet the students, Hannah was pestered by jabs of envy. Why didn't the Lord work in mysterious ways for her? He seemed to provide for everyone else—even providing a match for someone as bold and overbearing as Doris Hooley!

What about Hannah's provision? The one provision she desired so deeply she scarcely could allow herself to admit it, much less to ask for it anymore?

Just then, the children made their way up the walkway, with Sawyer several yards behind them. Watching them approach, Hannah rationalized that she, too, had everything she needed in that moment. Today, she would serve the students and serve God in her role as their teacher. Then she would care for the Plank children as if they were her own. If she was fortunate, she'd have a few extra moments to converse with Sawyer alone. For now, she had her daily bread.

"Teacher!" Sarah gushed. "How we missed you yesterday!"

"Guder mariye," Hannah greeted them, a smile spreading across her face. "I am very glad to see you, too. You may put your books at your desks and go play outside before the bell is rung."

"Guder mariye, Hannah," Sawyer said as the children cantered out the door. "How is your *groossdaadi*?"

"After a few days of rest, he is as healthy as a horse. But he's not any more polite, I'm afraid. Sometimes when he's coming down with an illness, his manners aren't what they should be, and I apologize."

"I'm glad to hear that," Sawyer replied. "I mean, I am glad to hear about the improvement in his health, not about his manners."

When Hannah giggled, Sawyer wasn't sure if it was because he'd bumbled his words or because he'd made a joke—but he didn't care; he just delighted in the sound.

He continued, "You needn't excuse him on my account. I took no offense. I was more concerned that you might have borne the brunt of his...his discontent after we left. So, how are you?"

"I am glad to be back at school," she admitted. Then, with a faraway note in her voice, she said, "I'm glad the *kinner* are coming home with me after school today. I truly missed their presence yesterday. Without them, I felt... I don't know. I guess I might say I was at a loss."

Sawyer was flooded with a sense of warmth. "I was concerned your *groossdaadi* might not have wanted you to care for the *kinner* any longer," he ventured. "I didn't know what I would have done without you."

Hannah scrunched her eyebrows together. "Didn't Doris take *gut* care of them?"

"*Jah*, she did. Very *gut* care," Sawyer immediately replied. The last thing he wanted to do was to inadvertently insult Doris again, especially not when she was within earshot. He lowered his voice. "It's just that she's not..."

When he didn't finish his sentence, Hannah inclined her head to meet his eyes. "She's not what?" she asked. "She's not a *gut* cook?"

"*Neh, neh,*" Sawyer protested. "She made a delicious supper."

"Did you mean she's not kind?" Hannah persisted. "Or that she's not helpful?"

After each question, Sawyer shook his head. His ears were burning, but he didn't know how to change the subject or distract Hannah.

"She's not *what*?" she emphasized again, before impishly asking, "She's not *short*?"

"That's true—she's definitely not short." Sawyer guffawed, savoring the twinkle in Hannah's eye. "And neither am I. But that's not what I was going to say."

"Then what exactly *were* you going to say?" Hannah teased, a saucy smirk on her lips.

He leaned forward, so as not to be overheard. "I was going to say, 'She's not *you*,'" he answered in a husky voice.

Hannah's mouth puckered into an O and her cheeks blossomed with pink. For a change, it was she, not Sawyer, who appeared to be tongue-tied. Before either of them had a chance to say anything more, Doris bustled into the room.

"Hello, you two," she chirped. "You both look as guilty as *kinner* caught with their hands in the cookie jar! You haven't been sharing a secret, have you?"

"Not at all," Hannah responded, giving Sawyer a furtive wink. "Sawyer was just telling me about the *wunderbaar* supper you made the other evening."

"I'm glad you enjoyed it, Sawyer." Doris beamed. "Because as you know, we're meeting at your *onkel's* house for church this Sunday and I have agreed to prepare dinner for everyone. I was about to ask Hannah if she'd help with the dinner preparations, too."

"Of course," Hannah agreed. "It's the least I can do, especially since *Groossdaadi* and I never host because we don't have a big enough gathering room. Sarah will assist me. Now, let's call the scholars in for school, shall we? It's past time."

Sawyer recognized a hint when he heard one, just as he recognized the quality of his exchange with Hannah had crossed the line from *friendly* to *flirtatious*. He hadn't intended for it to happen, but as the buggy sailed toward the farm, he realized he wasn't exactly sorry that it had.

For the rest of the week, temperatures hit record-breaking highs for September. It was so stifling in the tiny schoolhouse that Hannah frequently delivered the lessons outside on the grass beneath the willow tree, where at least there was a small rustle of hot breeze. Yet she hardly minded the unseasonal heat; it gave the illusion that it was still summer. She wanted time to stand still so she wouldn't have to think about harvest ending or saying goodbye to her scholars and to the Plank family. Especially now that Sawyer revealed how special she was to them—in particular, how special she was to *him*.

"He didn't use that exact phrase, but surely that was what he meant. Why else would he have been so embarrassed when he finally spoke the words?" she wrote in a letter to Eve on Thursday after dinner. She had been alternately elated and befuddled ever since her conversation with Sawyer on Tuesday.

In the next sentence, she contradicted herself.

Oh, who am I to think Sawyer Plank has any romantic feelings toward me? He probably only meant I was unique compared with Doris in the way I care for the children, or because of the relationship I have with *them*, not with *him*.

Sawyer and I haven't had another opportunity to speak to each other alone again since Tuesday, as the children have always been close at hand, so I cannot gauge what he might be feeling at this time. I'm afraid I'm better at reading the emotions of children than those of adults—especially men.

It hardly matters anyway, does it? At the end of harvest, Sawyer will return to Ohio and I will stay with Grandfather.

Yet I must confess, my dear sister, I long for a fraction of what you describe between you and your husband. Try as I have to suppress it, it is still something I yearn to experience. I would welcome the affections of a man about whom I feel the same for any period of time, even a brief season.

Please pray that I wouldn't envy those who have what I don't. I know envy is a sin, and I loathe the way I feel when I am envious.

After rereading her words, Hannah deliberated about whether or not to tear up the page. Such intimate romantic matters were seldom discussed, even among sisters. But Hannah didn't know how else to make sense of her emotions since she'd never before experienced feelings like these. She was in such a daze, she didn't hear her grandfather enter the parlor.

"The buggy needs extensive repair," he announced loudly. "I will speak to Turner King about it tomorrow."

"But why? What happened?"

The buggy was old, but as of two days ago, it was operating well. Why would it suddenly need *extensive repair*? When her grandfather left the room without responding, she shuddered.

He must have had a collision when he went to town this week. More likely, he *caused* a collision. She briefly considered tromping out to the garage to see the damage herself, but then decided against it. It was almost dark, and besides, seeing it would only upset her, especially if it was severe. Her grandfather was unharmed, and she assumed the other driver was, too, which was all that really mattered.

Yet her heart sank, knowing the repair costs would far outweigh whatever her grandfather earned for the cradle and rocker he was making for Miriam and Jacob. She picked her pen back up and inscribed a final line:

"And please pray that the Lord will continue to provide for our daily needs, which are abundant."

Usually just the sight of Hannah's lithe form and graceful movements enlivened Sawyer's spirit, but on Friday morning when he arrived at the schoolhouse, his mind was preoccupied with the letter he had received from his foreman the day before. Because of continued mix-ups with recent deliveries, their biggest *Englisch* customer was threatening to terminate their professional association.

Hannah sent Simon, Samuel and Sarah off to carry books and a blanket to the lawn beneath the willow for morning lessons. She then turned to Sawyer, squinting.

"You seem troubled this morning," she said. "Is the heat getting to you, or is it something else? Are you ill?"

She looked so distressed herself, Sawyer found himself disclosing details of the situation he normally would have kept to himself because he didn't want her to fret about his health.

"Oh!" Hannah exclaimed when he had finished. "How terrible! What are you going to do?"

"There isn't much I can do from here," he stated. "As soon as possible, I'll need to return to set things straight again."

Hannah nodded, her blue eyes clouded. "Is there anything I can do to help?"

She appeared so unsettled, he was torn between not wanting to say anything else and feeling as if a huge burden had been lifted from his shoulders simply by telling her what had been weighing on his mind.

"Jah," he replied. "You could pray about it for me, but please don't mention it to anyone else—I don't want John to find out. He's already pushing himself to do

more than he ought to do physically in an effort to help with the harvest. If he hears about this, he'll insist that the boys can handle it from here, and he'll send me home straightaway. I don't think they're quite ready for that."

"I won't say a word," Hannah agreed, and when she solemnly blinked her eyelashes, his knees felt like jelly. "Except to the Lord in prayer. I am certain He will provide a solution. But I'm sorry this has happened."

"And if it weren't upsetting enough," Sawyer continued, suddenly feeling free enough to pour his heart out to Hannah, "I received a letter from my sister Gertrude. She wishes to stay in Indiana a bit longer. She says it's to help my sister Kathryn, who was quite ill after the birth of the *bobbel*, but I suspect it's because a young man there may be courting her."

"Seth," Hannah murmured, a knowing look on her face.

"What?" Sawyer was taken aback. *"Who?"*

Hannah didn't elaborate. Instead, she asked, "Why is it so upsetting that Gertrude is helping your other sister?"

"Because *I* will need her help with the *kinner* as soon as I return."

"Could you hire someone to mind them before and after school?" Hannah inquired. "Look how well it's worked out for me to provide care for them."

"It has worked well," Sawyer admitted. "There's no doubt about that. But it wouldn't work with someone else, not for the long haul. Besides, it's not as if Kathryn really needs help. She has fewer *kinner* than I and a husband, too. Their district is large and there are many young women available for hire. As I said, I suspect Gertrude is only making an excuse to stay there longer because she is interested in a young man. She ought not abandon her family for such frivolity."

"Do you consider a chance at love to be a frivolity?" Hannah asked quietly.

"I don't consider it to be a necessity."

"Perhaps Gertrude does."

"At her age, that is foolishness!" argued Sawyer.

"You remind me of my *groossdaadi*, who always said the same thing to me," Hannah retorted, her chin in the air. "Now if you'll excuse me, I need to get ready for class."

She swiveled and disappeared into the schoolhouse so quickly he didn't even get the chance to say goodbye.

What did I say? he wondered. And how did he manage to bungle the one thing that was going smoothly in his life?

Chapter Ten

Hannah numbly made it through the school day. If ever she had any inkling that Sawyer might feel toward her the way she felt toward him, he had thoroughly shattered it with his remarks. Clearly he thought of her as a nanny only—a very competent nanny, more so than Doris, but still just a nanny.

It took every ounce of determination to focus on the lessons. She was as wilted by her disappointment as the students were by the heat. For the last half hour of the day, she distributed colored pencils and paper for drawing and then sat mindlessly doodling at her own desk, too languid to do anything else.

She was relieved when classes were dismissed and she sent Sarah, Simon and Samuel outside for a moment so she could pack up her paperwork for the weekend. Just as she slid the last folder into her satchel, Doris pranced into the room.

"How can you move about so briskly in this weather? I'm sweltering."

"Lately, I feel as if I'm floating on a cloud," Doris replied. Her singsong reference to being courted by John Plank caused Hannah to feel even more dejected. "You haven't forgotten about making snitz pies for Sunday, have you?" she inquired.

"Of course not," Hannah confirmed. "I have a surplus of dried apples prepared, and Sarah and I will bake the pies tomorrow. I'll send most of them home with Sawyer when he picks up the *kinner* tomorrow evening. However, I will need assistance bringing the rest to the Planks' farm. Our buggy is being repaired, so my *groossdaadi* and I will need a ride to services."

"It's no bother for me to give you a ride to and from the Plank farm," Doris offered. "Although I was hoping you could stay until everyone has left to help with the cleanup. Perhaps Joseph Schrock could give your *groossdaadi* a ride home after dinner, since your house is on his way?"

"Hmm." Hannah hesitated. "I think Turner King might have room in his buggy for *Groossdaadi* on the return trip instead."

"Just remember, you mustn't breathe a word of my secret about John and me to anyone."

Hannah snickered to herself that Doris probably had told most everyone in Willow Creek already anyway, but she agreed not to mention it.

No sooner did Doris leave the room than Jacob Stolzfus entered.

"*Guder nammidaag*, Hannah." His face looked grim.

"*Guder nammidaag*, Jacob. Is something the matter?" she asked. She knew Abigail was playing in the yard with the Plank children, so her thoughts raced to Jacob's wife. "Is Miriam alright?"

"*Jah*, she is alright for now," Jacob confided. "The *bobbel* is alright, too. But the midwife saw us today and advised Miriam to restrict her activities even further.

Which is why I have come to speak to you. We have an important matter we'd like you to consider."

"Of course. What is it?"

"Once harvest is over and your teaching is finished, might you help care for Miriam and oversee the household, including taking Abigail back and forth to school, while I am at the factory? We probably can't pay you as well as Sawyer Plank does, but since you are in need of employment and we are in need of help, it may be an opportune arrangement."

Hannah swallowed hard. She was simultaneously filled with concern for Miriam and Jacob and their unborn child, and with a sense of dread. True, she needed an income, but did God's provision for her have to involve running the household of the woman whose life *she* might have lived if she had agreed to marry Jacob Stolzfus?

Not that she ever wanted to marry him, but that was exactly the point. How was it that she now found herself in a position of overseeing Jacob's household when that was something she deliberately turned down years ago?

"I will speak to my *groossdaadi* about it," she answered. "Please know I am praying for you. Remember me to Miriam."

On the walk home, Hannah was quiet as she thought about Miriam and Jacob. As the children continued their quest to sneak up on late-season turtles in the stream, she perched on the embankment, dipping her feet in the current. She reclined against the grassy edge and noticed a handful of leaves overhead were yellowing around their edges. It may have felt like summer, but autumn was coming. She mused that for better or worse, life was always changing.

As the coolness of the water refreshed her skin, she

felt a sense of rejuvenation washing over her spirit, too. Considering Miriam and Jacob's situation further, she recognized what a blessing it was that Eve and her baby were healthy. She couldn't imagine what a difficult time this was for Miriam and Jacob, especially after all they'd been through.

She asked herself how she could have been so filled with envy for what she didn't have instead of filled with gratitude for what she did. Didn't she just write to Eve, asking her to pray that the Lord would provide their daily bread? And hadn't He done just that? Who was she to request something different, or something more? From this point on, she was going to joyfully appreciate all of His blessings, in whatever form they arrived, for however long they lasted. And if that included a passing crush on Sawyer Plank, she would welcome it with open arms!

With a new vigor, she leaped up from where she was reclining and waded out to join the children.

Sawyer's shirt clung to him like a second skin, and his grimy hair was matted around his forehead. He didn't want to say anything else to upset Hannah, and now he figured he had the perfect excuse for keeping his distance. But when he arrived to retrieve the children, she beckoned to him from the porch.

"*Kumme*, sit." She gestured. "Have a glass of lemonade. You look as if you could use it."

"*Denki,*" he replied. He was relieved that whatever he'd said to aggravate her earlier in the day seemed to have passed. However, he still allowed her to direct the conversation.

She gestured toward the children on the swing. "It was too tropical this afternoon for swinging, so I promised them they could take their turns of one hundred pushes each in the cooler evening hours."

"I see," he acknowledged. After a moment of observation, he pointed out, "Look, it takes both of them to budge Samuel. He is finally gaining weight, thanks to you. They all are."

"It must be the bountiful sweets I feed them at school." Hannah sniggled, so Sawyer knew she was making light.

You're definitely a bountifully sweet teacher, Sawyer thought. Or did he voice the comment aloud? He wasn't sure. The children's blond heads were the only part of them that he could distinguish in the shadow of the willow, and the evening took on a nostalgic glow. He wished Eliza could have seen how big the children had gotten, yet he was grateful Hannah was there to appreciate this aspect of their childhood.

Sawyer didn't want to break the mood, nor did he want to give in to it. Hannah's presence in their family had undeniably awakened emotions in him he wasn't sure he was ready to experience. After a spell of silence, he cleared his throat.

"That's past one hundred!" he called. "*Kumme*, Sarah, off the swing. You need to be up early tomorrow to help Hannah with the baking."

Physically depleted as he was, Sawyer thought he would have dropped off to sleep the moment his head hit the pillow later that evening, but instead he lay blinking at the ceiling.

He wondered what had troubled Hannah earlier in the day and why it so suddenly lifted. Was she prone to moodiness?

He tried to think about what kinds of things caused Eliza to retreat from conversation, but he couldn't recall. Just thinking about his departed wife made him realize his memories of her weren't exactly fading, but they were changing. When he remembered them, they didn't cause as much loneliness as they once did. There were times when he couldn't picture her face as vividly, either. Even Sarah looked more like him than she did Eliza, although every now and then she'd assume a stance or make a gesture that was exactly like something her mother would have done.

His body ached, and he figured he must be overly tired or getting old. Either way, as he drifted to sleep, the only face he pictured was Hannah's.

"Now remember," Sarah said to the boys after their father delivered the children to Hannah on Saturday morning, "you mustn't be underfoot in the kitchen. We have many pies to bake, and you can't be creating a ruckus."

"How could we forget?" Simon complained. "You've been talking about it for days."

"Jah," Samuel chimed in. "It's as if you think you're the only one who does anything helpful for Hannah."

"You're all helpful," Hannah contradicted. "In fact, I have a very important mission for you boys. I need you to run to the coop and gather eggs, or Sarah and I won't have enough for the crusts. Here's a pail and cloth. Please be very careful not to jostle them."

As they shot out of the kitchen, Sarah rolled her eyes and said with a sigh, *"Buwe"*—meaning *boys*—and Hannah had to turn her back so the girl wouldn't see her chuckle.

"Now, now, enough of that," she instructed. Over her shoulder she said, "If you have washed your hands, you may help me measure the flour for the crusts. We'll do that over here as soon as I bring—"

She was about to say "as soon as I bring the sack to the table," but when she turned to face Sarah, she saw the girl was attempting to lift the flour from the counter herself.

"Careful—it's open!" she warned, lunging to assist her, but it was too late. The heft of the sack was too much for Sarah, and as she doubled over trying to balance it, its contents spilled forward onto the floor.

"Oh, *neh*!" Hannah cried.

Sarah managed to keep it cradled in her arms until she reached the table. She hoisted it up the best she could, but at the last second, she dropped it onto the surface. It landed upside down with a plop and a *poof* of white. The powder covered her face and hair, and she stood in stunned silence, blinking.

At that second, from the yard one of the boys screamed, "Run!"

Hannah recognized the level of fear in his voice and bolted out the door and across the lawn in time to see her grandfather chasing something from the chicken coop with a shovel. Simon and Samuel hightailed it toward the porch, which Samuel reached first, but he stumbled on the top step and the pail flew from his grasp. Inches behind, Simon couldn't halt soon enough to keep from tripping over him. A tangle of elbows and knees and broken eggs, the boys scrambled through the door on their hands and knees.

Hannah rushed to their side. "There, there," she comforted them after confirming they were more frightened than injured. "Whatever happened?"

"At first, I thought it was a cat." Simon wept. "A strange black cat with short little legs."

"It had very sharp teeth," Samuel added. "It screeched at us."

"A fisher cat was after the eggs," Hannah's grandfather stated. She was so troubled about the children, she didn't notice him come in. "He got four of the *hinkel* and would have gone after the *kinner*, too."

Hannah gulped. She knew how ferocious fisher cats could be, and she thanked the Lord that her grandfather had been around to ward it off.

"But how did you know?" she asked. He had headed to his workshop earlier than usual that morning—right after he'd told her the astronomical sum Turner King estimated it would cost to repair the buggy. It was impossible for him to have heard either the animal's or the boys' cries.

"Bah, I keep an eye out" was all he said. He left the way he came, sidestepping the broken eggs on the porch.

Sarah called from the other room, "Are Simon and Samuel alright? Remind them not to come into the kitchen—I am still sweeping up the flour, and I don't want them traipsing through it."

"We'll need that broom out here when you're done." Hannah sighed and picked a piece of eggshell from Samuel's hair.

"Why?" Sarah appeared in the doorway, her hands on her hips. "What did those rascals do now?"

When the boys saw their sister's face covered in flour, they rolled on the floor where they lay, laughing and clutching their sides.

"Stop that! Stop that right now!" Sarah demanded, stomping her foot and bursting into tears.

Surveying the situation around her, Hannah honestly didn't know whether to join the boys in laughing or to cry alongside Sarah herself.

* * *

Shortly before Sawyer, Jonas and Phillip broke for lunch, John hobbled to the fields to assess their progress.

"You've made quite a bit of headway. Won't be more than three to four weeks now."

Sawyer was actually hoping to finish quicker than that, but he jested, "*Gott* willing, you'll be back on your feet by then if you don't break your other leg clomping out here to check up on us."

John chuckled. "You go on ahead," he said to Jonas and Phillip. "We old men will catch up with you. By the way, Doris Hooley is in the kitchen—she's fixed us a full dinner. I accompanied her to town this morning to purchase ingredients for the noon meal for the *leit* after church tomorrow, and she'll make those preparations here, too, so mind yourselves not to get in her way."

Doris was there again? Sawyer wondered how many times she'd visited that week.

His uncle interrupted his thoughts. "There's something I want to speak to you about. Something not usually discussed, but this isn't a usual situation. There's no easy way to say it, so I'll come right to the point— I'm courting Doris Hooley."

Sawyer puffed air out of his cheeks. Was John kidding him? Did Jonas set him up to say that as a prank?

"One of the reasons I'm telling you," his uncle continued, "is because she's bound to be here more frequently. Given our age and the fact that I'm not mobile enough to take the buggy to visit her—not to mention, we all benefit from her cooking—it seems easiest for her to come here. I wanted to be sure you're not uncomfortable with that. You understand no impropriety would ever occur between the two of us. I hold Doris's reputation in the highest regard."

"Of course." Sawyer was stumped and didn't know what else to say.

"I know I said she has the reputation of being *desperate*, but that's not how I see her, now that I've gotten to know her. She's made many sacrifices to help our family lately, especially given that the boys are not always receptive to her. *Jah*, she's a terrific cook and she dotes on me, but what I enjoy most is that I can talk to her about things. She offers a perspective only a woman can give. And she makes me laugh, which I haven't done for years."

"I see," said Sawyer, who understood too well what his uncle meant. "Then you have my blessing."

"Denki," John replied. "Now, at the risk of embarrassing you all the more, I'm going to give you a piece of advice."

"If the grass looks greener on the other side, fertilize?" Sawyer joshed, growing uncomfortable with the direction of the conversation.

"Who told you that gem? Jonas?" John howled. *"Neh*, my advice is that you're too young to stay a widower for the rest of your life. You owe it to the *kinner*. Trust me, it only gets more difficult to raise them alone as they grow. But more than that, you owe it to yourself. There's no substitute for the kind of companionship— the kind of *love*—a woman and man share, especially a husband and wife. You know that."

Sawyer did know there was no substitute for that kind of love, which was exactly why he didn't expect he'd find anything quite like it ever again. But perhaps John was right. Perhaps it was time for him to consider marriage for the sake of the children. He couldn't expect Gertrude to live with them forever, and there was no denying how much healthier and happier they were with Hannah in their lives. Granted, he'd known her only a short while, but he and Hannah shared a growing affinity for one another. He wondered if, with more time, she might consider the possibility of an enduring relationship.

As they slowly made their way to the house, John seemed to read Sawyer's thoughts. "If you're considering courting someone, you should ask her soon," he suggested. "After all, you know what they say. 'One of these days is none of these days.'"

"That's interesting advice from someone who's moving so slowly he might as well be going backward," Sawyer joked.

"Hey!" John shouted, swinging his crutch. "I can't help it. I'm injured!"

But Sawyer had already bounded into the house, where Doris had lunch waiting for them.

"Now how are we going to make the pies?" Sarah howled when she realized the boys hadn't managed to salvage a single egg.

Hannah was less worried about the pies than she was about the fact she and her grandfather had only two chickens left to see them through the winter.

"We will borrow some from Grace Zook," she stated calmly. "Simon and Samuel, please run to their house and tell her I need six more eggs for pie crusts for church dinner tomorrow. Grace will be happy to share."

"But what if that fisher cat is lurking?" Simon asked.

"It isn't. *Groossdaadi* scared it off."

"What…what if it's hiding?" he persisted.

"It's not. Her *groossdaadi* killed it," Samuel answered knowledgeably. "With the ax he uses for chopping wood."

"Your *groossdaadi* killed a cat?" Sarah wailed, and a torrent of tears streamed from her eyes.

"Hush!" Hannah raised her voice and clapped her hands. "It was a weasel, not a cat, and *Groossdaadi* didn't kill it with an ax—he chased it away with a shovel. It's gone now, but if it makes you feel better, I will walk with you."

"Can we carry the shovel?" Simon inquired.

"It's '*may* we carry the shovel,'" Sarah corrected.

"Hush!" Samuel ordered her. "You're always doing that. You're not our teacher."

"Kinner!" Hannah exclaimed, exasperated. "I am going to the Zook house myself. Sarah, you are going to finish sweeping up the flour in the kitchen. Samuel and Simon, you are going to scrub the broken eggs from the porch and parlor. When I return, each of you is getting a bath."

Lord, give me patience, she prayed as she trudged through the field. Inhaling deeply, she mused that she suddenly had a new appreciation for her grandfather's mandate that "children should be seen, not heard." Her frustration was short-lived, however; when she spotted a hawk circling above, she wished the children were there to witness it with her, and she hurried home to tell them about it.

"Did her *hinkel* lay enough eggs?" Sarah asked anxiously.

"I don't know. She wasn't home," Hannah replied. "But don't worry—there's still plenty of time. We'll check back in a little while. *Kumme*, get the boys. You all may wash off in the stream. That's more fun than taking a bath any day. I'll carry a large walking stick so Simon doesn't fret about the fisher cat."

The air was so saturated with humidity that Hannah allowed the children to lollygag longer than usual in the water, so by the time they returned to the house, her grandfather was knocking around, grousing about how hungry he was.

She quickly browned half a dozen pork chops, placed them into a glass dish, covered them with onion, Worcestershire sauce and homemade cream of mushroom soup, and then slid them into the oven for baking. After eating, she and Sarah washed, wiped and put away the dishes while the boys helped her grandfather clean his workshop and stack the firewood he split for the autumn.

The third time they journeyed to the Zooks' farm and found no one there, they sat on the grass in the shade before making the trek back home.

Samuel suggested, "Couldn't we take the eggs from the coop and leave a note?"

"Of course not!" scolded Sarah. "That's stealing!"

"It is not!" Simon contradicted. "We'd leave a note. Besides, Hannah said Grace Zook would be happy to share. What do you think, Hannah?"

"I think the three of you have been clucking more than the *hinkel* today!" Hannah laughed. "Come close, so I can give you a big hug beneath my wings."

She lifted her arms and they moved closer to snuggle, despite the heat. She squeezed them so awkwardly that they toppled over into a pile on the grass, laughing like mad. They lay there a long time, their heads touching, telling each other stories about the clouds, until Hannah abruptly sat up.

"Listen," she said. "Doesn't that sound like the Zooks' buggy coming down the lane?"

As drained as he was from laboring in the heat, Sawyer had a hunch Hannah was even more depleted. When he approached their home, he spotted the boys throwing a ball to each other on the grass. Sarah was slumped forlornly on the swing.

"Difficult day?" he questioned Hannah.

"Oh, she's upset because there was a mishap with the eggs," she explained. "We had to borrow from the neighbor, and by the time we had them in hand, it was too late to make the pies for church dinner tomorrow."

"Neh," Sawyer said. "I meant did *you* have a difficult day?"

"Me? Why do you ask?"

"For one thing, I could see from a mile away that Sarah was pouting, which is enough to try even the most patient person's nerves. And for another..." He hesitated. "Either you've gone gray in the past few hours or there was an explosion in your kitchen."

"Ach!" Hannah exclaimed, reaching to touch her hair. "It's flour. I called on Grace Zook looking like this, as well. She never mentioned it."

"She was probably too distracted by the grass," Sawyer joked, pulling a few blades from Hannah's tendrils.

She giggled so hard she started to cough. "I have to admit, we've had our challenges today."

"Did the *kinner* misbehave? I will speak to them if—"

"Neh, they were fine. It's nothing I couldn't handle. I think this oppressive humidity wears on us all, don't you?"

Sawyer wasn't convinced the weather was to blame

for his children's behavior, but he had every confidence that if Hannah said she handled it, the issue was resolved.

"There is one thing I'd like your permission to do, however," she requested. "You know how eager Sarah was to help me bake pies for tomorrow's dinner, and you can see by how readily she just relinquished the swing to her brothers that she's thoroughly disappointed."

Sawyer glanced in the direction of the willow and nodded.

"Would you allow her to stay overnight with me? As soon as you boys skedaddle, she and I will get to work on the crusts. I won't let her stay up too late—I'll just let her complete the first few pies with me. She'll be a big help, and we'll bring her to the service with us in the morning."

"That's very kind of you," Sawyer acknowledged. "But we both know she'll be more of a hindrance than a help. And I don't want your *groossdaadi's* rest disturbed."

"My *groossdaadi* is a sound sleeper—he's deaf, remember?"

"You have so much baking to do before dawn. Sarah is the last person you need distracting you."

"On the contrary, teaching her will help me stay focused on what I'm doing. Please, Sawyer, for me?" she entreated, batting her eyelashes and clasping her hands in exaggerated petition. "Please?"

"How can I say *neh*?" he replied, reveling in their chitchat. "But remember, if you wind up wearing apple slices in your hair to church services tomorrow, I tried to warn you I thought Sarah would get in the way!"

Chapter Eleven

Sarah was so euphoric about being able to spend the evening helping Hannah and then sleeping at her home overnight that she chattered nonstop the entire time they were baking. Hannah didn't mind; it truly did keep her awake, and once they got a rhythm down of measuring, mashing and mixing, they turned into a two-*maedel* pie-making factory. Before long, the aroma of the first pies was emanating from the oven.

"With that fragrant smell in the house, we're all bound to have *sweet* dreams," Hannah punned as she tucked Sarah into bed in Eve's old room.

"The whole day was like a sweet dream," Sarah murmured, settling into her pillow and closing her eyes. "Especially this part, when I got to stay with you."

Hannah was tickled. Only a child who had gotten what she wanted most could ever call this day sweet! But Hannah felt the same way herself—for all of its chaos, she'd prefer this day of "nanny-hood" to the most serene day of solitude. Sarah's remark was so dear it kept Hannah energized as she continued to slide pies into and out of the oven until midnight, when the last one was completed.

In the morning, her grandfather didn't seem surprised to see Sarah at the breakfast table. "You two kept me awake last night with all that baking," he complained.

Hannah wondered how in the world he could make that claim, but Sarah nodded her head knowingly and enunciated in her grandfather's direction. "Next time, we will make something that doesn't smell so loud."

To Hannah's surprise, her grandfather threw back his head and laughed. *"Denki,"* he said. "I'd appreciate that."

Because she would be helping Doris clean up and host until the last person left, Hannah had warned her grandfather she might not return home until evening. So, after preparing and setting aside his supper, she saw to Sarah's grooming. Then the three of them loaded the pies onto large pieces of wood and carried them like trays to the lane, where they waited for Doris to transport them to the Plank farm.

"Guder mariye, Daed," Sarah shouted happily when they arrived and she spied Sawyer hustling with his cousins in their direction. Doris disembarked, taking a board of pies from Hannah's grandfather, who agreed to hitch the buggy in the designated area once they'd unloaded it.

Sarah climbed down next, warning, "Jonas and Phillip, you may carry these but you can't taste them. Don't worry—Hannah and I made a secret extra pie for us to have after everyone else has gone."

"I think you just told the secret, Sarah," Sawyer chided as he helped Hannah with the last of the cargo. "But it looks like you and Hannah made plenty for everyone anyway. You must have been up half the night."

"Not at all," Hannah said as she handed him a pie. "We had a very sound sleep."

"You wouldn't tell me if you didn't, would you?" he teased.

"Are you saying I don't look rested?" she jested back.

"*Neh*, I've learned better than to suggest that!" Sawyer protested, adding, "Even if your hair *is* still coated in flour."

"It is not!" Hannah squealed.

"*Neh*, it's not, but even if it were, it wouldn't matter. *Gott* looks at the heart, not at outward appearances. And so do I," Sawyer said. Turning red, he stammered, "Which isn't to say you're not beautiful on the outside, because of course you are, with or without flour in your hair. What I mean is, it was a beautiful thing you did for Sarah. It meant so much to her. *Denki*."

"It meant so much to me, too," Hannah replied, and although Sawyer used his free arm to assist her down from the buggy, it felt as if her feet never touched the ground.

"*Daed*," Sarah whispered after the lunch dishes had been washed and put away and most of the *leit* had departed. "Hannah said I mustn't fish for compliments, but did you try the pie?"

"I thought it was so *gut* the first time, I tried it twice to make sure I wasn't mistaken," he replied, winking at her before she skipped away to find Abigail.

"What are you doing?" Jonas asked from behind. Phillip was with him.

"Setting up the volleyball net, in case the young people want to play."

"The *young people*," Jonas emphasized, "are leaving to socialize in another district. I'm letting Phillip tag along. We've finished the afternoon milking, so we'll see you later."

Jacob Stolzfus was twisting the other pole into the ground. "Aw, c'mon, almost everyone's gone home. You and Phillip can't leave now! Sawyer and I need at least two more players."

"I'll play," Doris announced from the porch.

"So will I," echoed Hannah.

"I don't suppose anyone would choose either of us to be on their team, would they, Miriam?" John joked in reference to their physical conditions.

"I'm comfortable right here in this rocking chair," she claimed. "I'll keep score."

"Can we play?" Simon asked.

"*Jah*, can we? Can we?" begged Sarah, Samuel and Abigail.

"Sure," Sawyer agreed. "*Kinner* against adults."

"*Daed!*" they moaned, and Sawyer laughed. "Okay, okay, I pick Hannah for my team. And Abigail and Simon. Jacob, you get Doris, Sarah and Samuel."

"You had the opportunity to pick me and you passed it by?" Doris whined, insulted. "Except for you, I'm the tallest person here."

"Hannah may be tiny, but she's mighty," Sawyer replied with a laugh. "I'd choose her every time."

"Let's see what size of a portion you get the next time I make dinner here—it might be tiny, too!" Doris shot back, and everyone cracked up.

After an hour or so of a friendly tournament, Doris and Hannah served leftovers on the picnic table, and then Miriam, Jacob and Abigail said their goodbyes.

"It's almost dusk," Hannah said as she sipped a glass of water. "We should be going, too, Doris, shouldn't we? My *groossdaadi* might be wondering what's become of me."

"I thought you mentioned to him you'd be late?" Doris objected. "I promised the *kinner* we'd watch for shooting stars tonight, and it's not nearly dark enough yet."

Sawyer sensed that Doris's main objective was to stargaze with John, not with the *kinner*, but he decided to take her up on the offer.

"The *kinner* will appreciate that," he said. "Since Hannah is concerned about her *groossdaadi*, I will take her home now and return in time to put Sarah, Samuel and Simon to bed. *Denki*, Doris and John."

Hannah leaped to her feet. "I'll accompany you to hitch up the horses," she volunteered, and the two of them left before Doris could change her mind.

Dusk blended into night as they drove toward Hannah's house, and the darkness created a sense of cozy togetherness. Sawyer didn't speak until the horse stopped in Hannah's yard. There were no lamps glowing from the house.

"It looks like your *groossdaadi* is asleep."

"I think I worry about him worrying about me more than he actually worries," she said and gave a little giggle. "If that makes sense."

"Somehow, it does," Sawyer admitted, reluctant to move. He wanted to delay their parting for as long as he could.

"I should step down," she said.

"Please don't." The words were out of his mouth before he had time to temper the urgency with which he spoke them. "I mean, the boys told me about the fisher cat. Aren't they nocturnal?"

"Primarily, *jah*. Yet remember—I'm small but I'm mighty," she taunted. "You said so yourself."

"Actually, Simon and Samuel said so. They told me all about your ax-wielding abilities."

Hannah laughed. "Their stories are greatly exaggerated, I'm sure. What else did they say about me?"

"What *don't* they say? It's 'Hannah this' and 'Hannah that' all day long. I worry that when we return to Ohio, my poor sister Gertrude will feel put out by their praise of you."

"*Neh*, I hear plenty of *wunderbaar* stories about her, too," Hannah assured him. "Besides, it's not a competition. People care about one another in unique ways and there's room enough for all, especially when love is involved."

Although Hannah was speaking about loving the children, her words caused Sawyer to think of Eliza. Without knowing it, Hannah touched upon the conflict Sawyer felt about being drawn to her. He supposed she was right; people cared about each other in unique ways—their caring wasn't a competition. His interest in Hannah didn't negate the love he'd shared with Eliza, did it?

Hannah continued to speak hesitantly. "In fact, you might be surprised to find Gertrude was relieved that someone else assumed the primary maternal role in the *kinner's* lives for a season."

"What do you mean by that?" Sawyer asked.

"Oh, nothing," Hannah replied. "I've overstepped my bounds. I really should say *gute nacht* now."

As she hopped down from the buggy, she could hear Sawyer following close behind.

"Wait," he said, touching her elbow. "Please tell me

what you meant by that. Are you tired of caring for the *kinner*?"

"*Neh!*" she objected. "Not at all. It's just that…"

She walked toward the swing and sat down before saying anything more. Sawyer played with the ropes overhead, causing her to twist back and forth.

"It's just what, Hannah? Please tell me."

"It's just I know what it's like to be responsible for raising *kinner* when you're barely out of childhood yourself."

"Ah," Sawyer said thoughtfully, letting go of the ropes.

"Please understand, I know that *Gott* calls us to serve one another—that our service to our families is part of how He provides for us. From what the *kinner* tell me, you and your wife served Gertrude by raising her when your *mamm* and *daed* died. She in turn served you and Samuel, Simon and Sarah by helping raise them when you lost your wife."

Sawyer nodded, so Hannah continued.

"I don't regret one instant of taking care of Eve when she was young. I'm honored the Lord gave me that privilege. But after *Groossmammi* died, there were times when I could have benefited from another adult giving me a hand. I do wish, when I was the proper age, I might have been afforded the opportunity to experience the pleasures of being a young adult."

Hannah had never confided these feelings to anyone, and she felt raw with vulnerability, waiting for Sawyer to respond.

His voice was throaty when he asked, "What pleasures do you mean?"

Hannah was glad it was too dark for Sawyer to see the tear trickle down her cheek. "Pleasures such as going to singings. Or walking out with a young man. I mean, there were a few suitors, but I didn't feel strongly enough about them to make it worth battling *Groossdaadi* for permission to be courted. Either that, or they didn't feel strongly enough about me to risk *Groossdaadi's* intimidation."

"I can't imagine that!" Sawyer declared. "Any suitor worth his weight would stop at nothing to walk out with such a fine young woman."

"Denki," Hannah said with a sigh. "But after enough refusals, they gave up on me and I gave up on my *groossdaadi's* behaviors. Time passes, just like that, so here I am, unmarried at twenty-nine."

Fearing she'd said too much, she forced a cheerful note into her voice. "I'm not complaining—if it weren't for my grandparents, especially *Groossdaadi*, who knows what would have become of Eve and me. Most people find him difficult, but I couldn't love my *groossdaadi* more than I do, and I consider it a privilege to care for him and contribute to our household. And although I don't have *bobblin* of my own, I've been blessed to teach the district's *kinner*. Of course, teaching isn't the same as motherhood—that's why it's been especially rewarding to care for Samuel, Simon and Sarah. I've gotten a little taste of what it's like to be a *mamm*."

"You're absolutely certain you're not tiring of it?"

"Of course not!" she insisted. "Now, do me a favor."

"What is it?"

"Give the swing a little push. Actually, give me one hundred pushes, please. That's Sarah's rule—one hundred pushes per turn per person."

"My daughter makes a lot of rules." Sawyer guffawed. He moved behind Hannah and gently lifted the swing, then set it in motion by releasing it. "And my sons *break* a lot of rules."

"You have very obedient, thoughtful, helpful *kinner*," Hannah said, stretching her legs toward the sky. It was as if her muscles remembered the movements from childhood, and she pumped harder to gain more height. "You're doing a fine job raising and instructing them."

"Sometimes I worry because they haven't a woman—an adult woman—present in the household. As you've pointed out, Gertrude is barely out of childhood herself. She is competent with their everyday care, but her judgment is... It hasn't reached its full maturity yet."

Hannah didn't want to pry, but since she had just divulged her innermost struggles to Sawyer, she felt comfortable asking him, under the cloak of night, "Yet, you've not remarried...?"

He stepped around from behind her and walked forward a few paces in silence, his back toward her as he searched the sky. She dragged her feet on the grass until she came to a stop. She was about to apologize for her trespass into such a personal subject when he spoke.

"I never found anyone I'd consider courting, much less marrying. Not in Blue Hill, anyway," he admitted, his voice hoarse. Suddenly, he pointed to the sky. "Did you see that? A shooting star!"

"I did!" Hannah exclaimed, springing from the swing to stand by his side. They allowed the silence to linger as they beheld the sky in awe.

"Well," Sawyer finally said. "I suppose Doris and the *kinner* saw it, too, so that means they can turn in for the night now. I should get back to put them to bed. Let me walk you to the door."

When they reached the porch, Hannah briskly climbed three stairs and then abruptly pivoted so she could be eye to eye with Sawyer, who hadn't begun to ascend them yet.

"As fond as I am of the *kinner*," she said, "I'm glad we had this opportunity to talk alone."

"I'm glad, too," Sawyer answered, his eyes shining in the moonlight. "In fact, you might say I planned it this way."

Overcome with a yearning to prolong the moment, Hannah reached forward and ever so tenderly traced the wound on his forehead. "It's getting better," she whispered before sliding her hand down along the side of his cheek.

Holding her gaze, he wrapped his fingers around her wrist and drew her hand to his mouth. He pressed his warm lips against her open palm once before agreeing, "Much better."

Then he turned on his heel and disappeared into the night.

As he unhitched his horse, Sawyer noticed Doris's buggy was gone. John was sitting alone on the porch when Sawyer got to the house. So much for their private stargazing.

"You're drinking coffee at this hour?" he asked his uncle, who lifted a cup to his lips.

"*Neh*, it's tea," John replied sheepishly. "Doris got me started on this."

"She's left already, I see. Did the *kinner* spoil your solitude?" Sawyer ribbed him.

"On the contrary, we *all* caught a glimpse of a falling star before Doris tucked them in and then left at a respectable hour," asserted John. "Speaking of solitude, you certainly ushered Hannah away from here quickly."

"She didn't want her *groossdaadi* to worry about her."

"Everyone around here knows her *groossdaadi* is a mean old coot. The only thing he worries about is what time his supper is going to be on the table."

"Nobody's all bad," Sawyer said softly. "I was sure grateful he was looking out for my sons when the fisher cat came around."

"Aha, I knew it!" John slapped his good knee. "A man defending Albert Lantz can only mean one thing— you're smitten with Hannah!"

Admitting to himself he had feelings for Hannah was one thing, but acknowledging it to John was quite another, so Sawyer replied, "Of course I'm fond of her. She's my *kinner's* hired nanny, and she provides them *wunderbaar* care," Sawyer replied.

"I'm not talking about your professional relationship, and you know it. Tell me your heart doesn't skip a beat every time she looks at you with those enormous baby blues," John pressed him.

Sawyer's voice cracked as he tried to deny it. "You're so taken with Doris you think everyone else is secretly courting each other, too."

"If you don't want to admit it, fine. I won't force you," John relented. "But mark my words—if you want to capture Hannah Lantz's heart, you better capture her *groossdaadi's* first. She won't do anything without his approval."

"Jah, jah," Sawyer said, opening the screen door. "Enjoy your solitude, John. I'm going inside."

"I'm right. You'll see!" John called, chuckling.

Fifteen minutes later as he lay in bed, Sawyer contemplated how correct John was about Hannah's grandfather's possessiveness—she had told him as much herself. But that was years ago. People changed. Her grandfather couldn't possibly be that controlling now that she was an adult, could he?

As he rolled onto his side, the pillowcase fluttered against his cheek and he thought of Hannah's fingertips against his skin. Even if her grandfather was resistant to the idea of him courting Hannah at first, Sawyer decided he would win his favor. But how? Perhaps with a small gift, something that showed he was grateful to have both Hannah and her grandfather in his children's lives. He could imagine half a dozen presents suitable for Hannah, but not a single idea came to mind for her grandfather. Stumped, he closed his eyes and pictured shooting stars until he fell asleep.

Hannah willed herself to stay awake. She didn't want to slumber, lest at sunrise she should discover she'd dreamed the entire day, from the morning, when Sawyer referred to her as beautiful, inside and out, to the evening, when he kissed her hand—and all of the wonderful moments in between.

But when Monday dawned and Sawyer greeted her at school with a shy radiance about his face as he said, "It is a pleasure to see you, as always, Hannah," she knew her dream was a reality that wasn't about to vanish anytime soon.

Even the clammy weather couldn't dampen her spirits. "We should take a field trip to the stream tomorrow," she announced to her class. "We'll bring sketch pads and study the plant life we find there. We can dip our feet in the water as we're eating our lunches. I'll make a special apple dessert from a recipe my sister sent me. We'll have a celebration before harvest ends. How does that sound?"

"It sounds great!" Caleb acknowledged.

"Jah," the other scholars agreed.

"I think it sounds like a poor idea." Samuel pouted. "I don't want to go."

"But, Samuel, you love the stream," Hannah said.

"I used to, but I don't anymore," he argued. "I'm not going."

Hannah was stunned. Samuel had never talked back to her or refused to participate in a school activity. She quietly dismissed the rest of the scholars for lunch hour, asking Samuel to stay indoors so she could get to the bottom of what was troubling him.

"Samuel, please come to my desk," she requested, and he complied. "Now then, what happened to make you dislike the stream?"

His eyes welled with tears, but he chewed his lip and wouldn't speak.

"Are you frightened of the fisher cat?" she guessed. "Because I don't think he's around anymore. But we will say a prayer for safety before we leave, and I'll carry a big walking stick again, too."

Samuel hung his blond head, and his little shoulders heaved as he cried into his palms.

"Oh, Samuel," Hannah gasped. "When you're so sad, it makes me sad. Please tell me what's bothering you."

"The stream is our special place," he sobbed. "Now you're going to share it with everyone else."

"Oh," Hannah murmured. "And that makes you sad?"

"Jah," he hiccuped.

"But I've seen you share things with your sister and brother and classmates all the time. I thought you like to share."

"I do," Samuel replied, sobbing harder.

"Then why does sharing the stream make you cry?"

"Because pretty soon, I won't be here to share it."

"Oh, Samuel, that makes me very sad, too," Hannah whispered, fighting back tears herself as she enveloped the boy. "But I'm so greedy I want to have as many special days with you as I can before you leave. That way, when you are gone, I can go to the stream and think of you there and I won't be so lonely because I'll have a memory to call to mind."

Samuel's breathing slowed as Hannah patted his back.

She continued, "If you don't want to come to the stream with your classmates, I understand. But I wish you'd come and help me make another memory. Not to mention, you know where all the best rocks are, so I was hoping you'd show the other scholars how to flip them over very carefully to see what's underneath."

"Jah," the boy agreed. He wiped his face with his sleeve and announced valiantly, "I'll carry the big walking stick for you, in case the fisher cat is still lurking. Because your hands will be full with the special apple dessert, right?"

"Right!" She laughed, tousling his hair. "Now scamper outside and tell your friends you changed your mind. They'll be glad to hear it."

After he left, she realized the half-truth of her advice to the boy. Yes, having memories to call to mind *could* help during times of separation—but sometimes the more memories people created together, the greater their loneliness became when they were apart.

As she blotted her desk where her own tears had fallen and pooled, she prayed, *Please, Lord, provide us the comfort only You can provide.* She was going to need it.

* * *

It had taken considerable thought, but Sawyer finally drummed up a couple of gestures that he hoped would put Hannah's grandfather in a better frame of mind when Sawyer discussed his interest in Hannah with him. In conversing with Turner King after services on Sunday, Sawyer had learned about the expensive repairs Albert Lantz's buggy would require. He knew Hannah and her grandfather would be hard-pressed to afford them, so he decided to commission Turner to begin the necessary work.

In this regard, Sawyer's generosity was spurred not as much by an attempt to win the grandfather's favor, but rather by concern about Hannah's transportation, especially into town, or during inclement weather or emergencies. In fact, on Monday when he went to the repair shop, he made Turner promise not to tell Albert or Hannah—or anyone in the district—who paid for the repairs.

"I don't want you to lie, of course, but you can leave the details unsaid," Sawyer suggested. "For all anyone knows, you were compensated from the district's mutual aid fund."

Turner pledged to deliver the buggy to Albert first thing on Friday morning if Sawyer paid him on Thursday evening, which Sawyer promptly did. After stopping by Turner's shop with the payment, Sawyer was off to his second stop: the Hershbergers' farm, where he made a much smaller purchase—the gift he hoped would soften Albert up and show him Sawyer had his and Hannah's best intentions in mind.

His final destination was Hannah's house. Hopping from the buggy, he pulled the crate from the floor.

"*Daed, Daed*, what's in there?" the children asked as they charged across the grass.

"It's for Hannah."

Even from a distance, her smile caused his pulse to race.

"For me? What in the world—"

As he approached her, a fluttering of wings inside the crate gave away the surprise.

"*Hinkel!*" Simon pronounced.

"*Hinkel?*" Hannah repeated as Sawyer set the box at her feet.

"Four of them!" Sarah counted.

"To replace those that were, er, lost," Sawyer explained. Noticing Hannah's expression, he stated, "You're disappointed."

"*Neh,*" she protested. "It's a very thoughtful gesture for you to have picked these up for us. But you must allow me to pay you for them."

"Of course not," Sawyer argued. "They're a gift."

The children had lifted the chickens from the crate and were following them around the yard as they pecked for bugs. Hannah's laughter sounded more nervous than amused, but Sawyer had no idea why.

"Hens aren't the kind of gift a man gives to a woman he fancies, are they?" he finally asked. "It's been so long, I've forgotten."

Hannah's eyes were even more captivating than her smile when she tipped her head and asked, "You *fancy* me, then, do you?"

"I thought that was obvious," he replied. "I actually feel as if we have been courting already. Not in the traditional sense of my taking you home after singings and such, but, you know…"

"*Jah*, I do know, and I agree," Hannah confirmed.

"Despite bemoaning the fact I never had a real opportunity to go through the teenage rites of passage, I actually appreciate it that as adults, we can skip some of the awkward rituals, can't we? The hens were a lovely idea, but you needn't give me a gift."

"I wanted to," he insisted until he saw her face cloud over again. "But if you don't want them, I will take them away."

"I *do* want them. The *gut* Lord knows what it meant to us when we lost four at once. It's just that my *groossdaadi* is such a proud man. He would rather we go hungry than accept a gift."

"That's ridiculous!" Sawyer shouted, and then moderated the volume of his voice. "My *kinner* eat here every evening and all day on Saturday. It's the least I can do."

"Actually, that's not true," Hannah debated. "The least you can do is pay me, which you do handsomely. The hens are beyond generous. I wish I could accept them, but I don't want…I don't want my *groossdaadi* to lash out at you."

"I understand," Sawyer said, although he wasn't entirely sure that was true. How could Albert Lantz be such a stubborn man? It would be one thing if he was the only one who suffered for his pride, but he created hardship for Hannah, as well. "John will be glad to have an extra *hinkel* or two."

Hannah gave his hand a quick squeeze. "*Denki*, Sawyer," she whispered. "I appreciate all of the ways you've been considerate of me."

He felt anything but considerate toward Hannah's grandfather as he reclined in bed that evening. Sadly, he didn't think there was anything he could do to gain his favor. John may have been right after all; Hannah's grandfather was nothing but a mean old coot.

Chapter Twelve

"Yoo-hoo," Doris called, interrupting the coveted moments of conversation Hannah got to spend with Sawyer before the children trickled into the school yard. "What a gorgeous day, isn't it? There's finally a hint of autumn in the air."

"Jah," Hannah replied impatiently. "But I'm sure you're not interrupting us to discuss the weather."

Sawyer raised his eyebrows at her and stifled a laugh.

"Neh," Doris agreed obliviously. "I came to invite you both to visit on Sunday afternoon. I've invited John, as well. Miriam and Jacob won't be attending, as Miriam has to minimize her travel to the bare necessities. But Amelia and James will be home, of course, and we plan to serve a scrumptious supper."

"Denki," Hannah replied, chagrined that she'd been so dismissive of Doris. "I appreciate the offer, but as you know, my *groossdaadi's* buggy is in a state of disrepair, so…"

She let the thought dangle, hoping Sawyer would pick up on the hint.

"I will bring you," he immediately volunteered.

"Of course, the *kinner* and your *groossdaadi* are *wilkom* to attend, as well," Doris graciously offered.

"Actually," Sawyer said, "the boys have been invited on a picnic with Caleb and Eli's family, and Sarah will be spending the afternoon at Abigail's house."

"I will invite *Groossdaadi*," Hannah said, adding, "if it's no trouble for Sawyer to pick him up, as well. But he may decline since you know he rarely goes on Sunday visits."

"Of course I will be glad to pick him up, as well," Sawyer said.

Hannah noticed a curious look on his face when he agreed, and she couldn't help but wonder if he was thinking the same thing, which was that she hoped he chose not to attend. She didn't mean to be unkind, but an afternoon spent with Sawyer and her friends would be an experience she'd treasure—especially riding to and fro alone with Sawyer. She wanted to soak in every last moment with him before harvest ended and he returned to Ohio.

Please, Lord, she prayed fervently, *let me go with Sawyer alone to Doris's house. But if it's Your will to have* Groossdaadi *accompany us, provide me the patience to* wilkom *him as graciously as You always* wilkom *each of us into Your presence.*

To her astonishment, that afternoon when she and the children arrived home after dallying at the stream, she found a note on the kitchen table. In her grandfather's lopsided penmanship, it said:

You should not have written Eve about the buggy repairs—Menno paid for them. Gone to Lancaster. Back on Monday in time for dinner.—Albert Lantz.

If it weren't for his impersonal signature and the implied directive to leave dinner prepared for him on Monday, Hannah might have taken the note to be a forgery. The timing was too good to be true!

"Do you want me to put the water on to boil for potatoes?" Sarah's question broke through Hannah's disbelief.

"*Jah*, please do."

Hannah never wrote to Eve about the buggy, so she doubted Menno had paid for the repairs. Her brother-in-law knew better than to do that. It was more likely Bishop Amos heard of their situation and the repairs were paid for from the mutual aid fund. Poor Eve. Their grandfather would show up unexpected and he'd be on a rampage. That was the last thing she and her baby needed right now.

Yet as Hannah sat wringing her hands over the note, she was overcome with a second realization: she would have the house to herself for the weekend! Not only would she be able to accept Doris's invitation without her grandfather accompanying her, but she decided she'd invite Sawyer to join her and the children for supper on Saturday, as well.

Humming, she rose to cut the potatoes Sarah had been peeling. *Thank You, Lord,* she prayed silently, *for Your most unusual provisions concerning the buggy repairs and my own wishes, selfish as they may have been. Please keep* Groossdaadi *and the cars around him safe. And please give Eve an extra measure of patience this weekend. She will need it.*

Sawyer felt a small pang of guilt as he polished off his second piece of chicken potpie. He hoped Hannah's grandfather believed Menno when Menno inevitably denied paying for the repairs. Sawyer hadn't meant to cause any conflict between them.

But as he surveyed the table, with Hannah blotting her delicate lips with a napkin across from him, and his children hungrily finishing their robust portions, he had to admit to himself, he wasn't sorry that his actions resulted in Albert's absence.

"You're smiling, *Daed*," Sarah noticed. "That must mean you like the potpie I made with help from Hannah."

"What did she tell us about fishing for compliments?" Simon scolded. "Remember? We're supposed to take satisfaction in serving others and not point out our own *gut* deeds."

"Jah," Samuel agreed. "It's like when Hannah serves the apple goodie for dessert. Simon and I aren't supposed to boast about how hard we searched to find the ripest apples without any wormholes."

Sawyer caught Hannah's eye and winked. "At the risk of drawing attention to anyone's *gut* deeds, I will tell you that *was* a delicious potpie, Sarah. Now, let's see if there are any worms in the apple goodie, shall we?"

"Then may we go to the stream?" Samuel asked.

"I don't know if there will be time before dark," Hannah replied. "The days are getting shorter."

"But *Daed* is here. He'll protect us," Simon suggested.

"Please?" Sarah echoed.

"Jah, I'll protect you," Sawyer repeated. "Please?"

"I know when I'm outnumbered." Hannah giggled. "Alright, then, leave your dishes on the table and let's go now before the bats come out."

But by the time they got to the stream, the sun was on the verge of setting, so Sawyer forbade them to go wading. "We ought to get back to the farm. You're visiting your friends after we have our home church services tomorrow. You need a *gut* sleep."

"I wish we could stay overnight here," Simon hinted.

"Jah," agreed Samuel. "Sarah was allowed to stay overnight, but we didn't get a turn."

"You did, too!" Sarah protested. "Don't you remember?"

"We were sick. That doesn't count," Simon said. "You got a turn when you were sick and another when you were well."

"Stop your squabbling," Sawyer chided them. "You are not staying overnight."

Samuel suggested, "You could stay, too, *Daed.* You could sleep in Hannah's *groossdaadi's* bed."

"Then we could have breakfast and our family church worship time together here, since we're sort of a family," Simon proposed.

"Jah," Sarah agreed. "Hannah's our sort-of *mamm.*"

"Gott must love us a lot to give us our *mamm* and also a sort-of *mamm* like Hannah once our *mamm* died," Samuel reflected. "Doesn't He, *Daed*?"

Sawyer was startled by the insightfulness of his son's remark, which showed that while he'd never forget his mother, his heart was open to loving Hannah, too. Samuel's words caused Sawyer to remember Hannah saying when love was involved, it wasn't a competition—there was room enough for all. It was growing clearer to him that a space was expanding in his own heart, too.

"Gott's love and provisions for us are abundant, indeed," Sawyer resolutely confirmed. "But you heard my answer. We are not staying here overnight. Now run up ahead before I tickle the silliness right out of you."

Beneath pastel pink and vibrant orange clouds, the

children bounded up the hill. Sawyer glanced sideways at Hannah and noticed she was biting her lip.

"I'm sorry if anything the *kinner* said embarrassed or…or bothered you," he stammered. "Despite your best efforts to teach them modesty and discretion, I'm afraid they still tend to say whatever they feel."

"A little candor can be refreshing," Hannah replied. "Especially when it comes from the mouths of babes. I fear it's *you* who was bothered by their remarks."

"On the contrary," Sawyer stated. His knees went weak as he gazed into Hannah's eyes. He dearly wanted to kiss her rosy pink lips, but he was afraid if he moved, he'd scare her off, like a bird.

"A bat!" Sarah shouted from the hilltop.

"It is not—it's a sparrow," Samuel argued back, just as loudly.

"*Neh*, it's an owl!" claimed Simon.

"Are you certain you don't want to keep my bickering brood overnight? They're yours for the taking," Sawyer joked, and he and Hannah laughed breathlessly all the way up the hill.

Hannah didn't mind washing the dishes on her own; it gave her something to do while she daydreamed. She felt guilty, knowing her pleasure was coming at such a cost to her sister, and she could only imagine the scenario that must have been unfolding at her home. But Eve got to experience married life alone with her husband daily. She had only the tiniest glimpse of that for one weekend, and as Simon would have said, it was her turn!

She didn't know what warmed her heart more: Sarah claiming, *Hannah's our sort-of* mamm, or the look Sawyer gave her when he denied being embarrassed by the

sentiment. She fell asleep replaying every aspect of the
evening in her mind, as clearly as if she were watching
the scene take place with figures in the dollhouse her
grandfather made.

Come morning, she was surprised by the slight
chill in the air, and she thought to warn her grandfather to wear long sleeves. Then she remembered he
wasn't home. She read Scripture and spent time in quiet
prayer before fixing a second cup of tea. She'd never
noticed how quiet it was there before. As the rocking
chair creaked back and forth, she contemplated whether
this was what it felt like for her grandfather to be deaf.

She was ready and waiting when Sawyer arrived at
three thirty. Before she could cross the lawn, he had
stepped down and was heaving a potted plant from the
buggy. Its lavender spray was so wide it nearly eclipsed
his face as he ambled toward her.

"Russian sage!" she exclaimed. "And it's already in
bloom for autumn."

"It's a perennial, you know," he said awkwardly and
set it down on the porch. Then he glanced at it and
back at her. "I was right. It reminds me of the color of
your eyes."

If the three children weren't watching from the
buggy, Hannah might have embraced him and never
let go.

"Denki," she said. "It's lovely."

The children prattled about the day's upcoming
events as they journeyed, much to Hannah's amusement. Sawyer dropped them off at their respective locations with warnings to mind their manners and a
reminder that he'd be back after supper time but before
dark to pick them up.

"After all, it's a school night," Sawyer joked as he

and Hannah traveled alone down the lane. "I've heard their teacher is very strict."

"Oh, *neh*!" Hannah bantered back. "That's the *other* schoolteacher you must be thinking of. I'm the sweet one. I even have thimble cookies to prove it," she said, holding up the container she'd been carrying on her lap.

When Sawyer laughed, Hannah wished she could bottle the sound, so she could loosen the lid and listen to it anytime she wanted—especially after he returned to Ohio. She pushed the dreaded thought of his departure to the back of her mind.

"Why did you sigh just now? Did you forget something?" he asked as they pulled into Doris's lane.

"Neh," she answered. To herself, she thought, *I'm memorizing every part of this by heart.*

"Wilkom!" Doris called, flapping her hand. *"Kumme* around to the side. We're playing lawn croquet."

Hannah waited for Sawyer to unhitch the horse so they could join the group together. Amelia and Doris were settled into lawn chairs, but James and John were taking practice shots knocking the croquet balls through the hoops.

"John!" Hannah exclaimed. "Doris and Sawyer didn't tell me you got your cast off! When did that happen?"

The men stopped playing, and John limped over to where Hannah was standing with Sawyer. "I just got it off on Friday. The *Englisch* doc was surprised it had healed so nicely. He said most Amish men try to put too much weight on it too soon and it ends up needing to stay in the cast longer than not."

"So essentially what you're telling us is that you're lazier than most Amish men?" Sawyer joshed.

"Neh," John replied and took a friendly swing at him. He teetered on his good leg, and Doris jumped up

to offer her arm to steady him. "What I'm telling you is that I couldn't have healed so quickly if it weren't for this lovely woman here."

For the first time in all of the years she'd known her, Hannah observed Doris blushing shyly and averting her eyes.

"*Denki*, John," she said demurely.

"In fact—" John cleared his throat "—it's no secret, since you've all been told by either Doris or me, that we've been courting. But what no one here knows— well, no one except for James, because I spoke to him about it before making it official—is that Doris and I are getting married."

By now, Doris was beaming, her head held high. "It's being published soon in church—even though John has been married already, I still want to follow the tradition of announcing it as a first-time bride. John told his sons last night, and we've already begun our meetings with the deacon. But other than those people—and now you—no one else knows. So please don't tell them."

"Who is there left to tell?" Sawyer quipped, and everyone laughed good-naturedly.

"That is *wunderbaar* news," Hannah managed to say. "When do you intend to hold your wedding?"

"The first Tuesday in November," Doris chirped.

"So soon?" Amelia questioned.

"It can't be soon enough for us," John said. "Doris has waited her entire life to marry. It's been five years since I buried my wife. We are past our youth, and we believe we're acting in wisdom, in accordance with the blessing *Gott* has provided us."

"The wedding day can't come quickly enough," agreed Doris. "There is only one obstacle we hope you will help us with, which is partly why we're confiding in you."

"What's that?" Amelia asked.

"We didn't have time in advance to plant an extra celery patch, and I don't need to point out how important celery is to the wedding meal!"

"I will save you every last stalk from my garden," Hannah pledged, before giving her friend a hug. "You'll have a surplus of creamed celery to share with your wedding guests and plenty left over to decorate the tables beside."

While the women were cleaning the supper dishes and James went to milk the cows, John said to Sawyer, "You know, the doc said I'll be up to speed in a week. Maybe not one hundred percent, but enough that the boys and I can manage what's left of harvesting by then."

Although he'd been champing at the bit to return to Ohio to sort out the problems at his shop, Sawyer suddenly found himself wishing he had more time in Willow Creek. His mind reeled with the discussions he needed to have and the arrangements he needed to make with Hannah before he left.

But he said, "I'll help out through Saturday, then. We'll spend the Sabbath resting and leave first thing on Monday morning."

"I can't thank you enough." John choked out the words, his tone unusually serious.

"Nothing you wouldn't do—nothing you *haven't done*—for me," Sawyer said.

"Even so, it's humbling to have another man do your work for you. But Doris kept reminding me what a sin it is to be prideful and to refuse help from others. I'm indebted."

"You're not indebted—you're family."

The moment the last supper dish was done, Sawyer suggested that he and Hannah should leave in order to round up the children.

"Is it that time already?" Hannah's brow was furrowed, as if in disappointment.

"I don't want them to wear out their *wilkom*," he stated definitively.

After bidding their good-nights, they rode in silence before Sawyer pulled down a dirt lane.

"The Stolzfuses' house isn't this way," Hannah said, "although I can see why you'd be confused. That fence looks similar."

"I'm not confused. I turned here on purpose," he admitted, bringing the horse to a halt at the crest of the road, which opened to a magnificent field alive with birdsong and overrun with late-blooming wildflowers. "I wanted to spend a few moments with you alone, if that's alright."

"It is," she said, and they got out and ambled over to the fence.

Sawyer sat on the railing so his face was level with hers. Hannah's profile glinted with the light of the sun hanging low in the sky as she looked out over the field.

"Some of the leaves are beginning to change," she observed about a stand of trees in the distance.

"Jah," Sawyer agreed, briefly glancing over his shoulder in the direction she was pointing, but he only had eyes for her.

He pulled a tall piece of grass and used the tip of it to tickle Hannah's ear, causing her to giggle and swat it away. When she did, he clasped her hand, caressing her silky skin with his thumb as he spoke.

"So, you knew about John and Doris courting, too?"

"I did," she said. "Although the wedding news is a big surprise."

"Do you think it's too soon?" Sawyer had to know.

"Ordinarily, I might say *jah*, but John made a *gut* case for their getting married sooner rather than later. They are of a mature age, they're like-minded in important matters, such as family and beliefs, and they genuinely care for one another. But even if all that weren't true, who am I to judge what the Lord provides for someone else?"

Sawyer felt his mouth go dry, and he wiped the corner of his lips. "I agree," he concluded solemnly. "I couldn't have said it better myself."

She gave his hand a little tug before mentioning, "We should go. It's getting late."

But it's not too *late*, he said to himself, his thoughts elsewhere. Now that he had confirmed Hannah wasn't opposed to a brief courtship, he felt encouraged about asking her to become his wife. But first, knowing Hannah wouldn't leave her grandfather, Sawyer needed to come up with a plan to convince him the move to Ohio would benefit him, too. He mulled over his options as they journeyed to gather the children.

"How were your visits?" he asked them.

"We had a *wunderbaar* time with our friends," Samuel said, and Simon agreed.

"I had a *wunderbaar* time with my friend, too," Sarah claimed.

"How about that—so did I!" Sawyer trumpeted.

"Me, too," Hannah stated, giving Sawyer a gentle nudge. "I'm glad the Lord provided us all with such special friends."

* * *

"I'll see you bright and early tomorrow morning, *Gott* willing," Hannah called from the porch as the buggy pulled away.

Before she crossed the threshold to the house, she sensed something was different, the same way she could perceive when a storm was about to break. *My* groossdaadi *is back*, she thought.

Sure enough, a voice from the dim parlor yapped, "While you've been gallivanting who knows where, I've been sitting here hungry. After such a long trip, this is the *wilkom* I receive in my own home?"

Hannah turned on the gas lamp and faced him directly. She knew it was futile to remind him he wasn't expected until Monday, and she doubted Eve would have sent him off without enough food to feed him for a week.

"I'm sorry. I was visiting Doris Hooley. I will prepare your supper now."

"And ruin my sleep by eating so late?" he grumbled. "*Neh*, don't bother. I am going to bed."

Hannah bit her lip, but the tears came anyway. Try as she did to hold on to every good memory of the blessed weekend she had just experienced, she was crushed by the reality that it was undeniably over. Soon her relationship with Sawyer and the children would be over, too, now that John's leg had healed and he no longer needed Sawyer's help. She thought she'd be content to experience just a fraction of what it would be like to be married with children—but instead, it had made her all the more aware of how wonderful it was. It had increased her longing tenfold.

She sat on the sofa a long while, sobbing into her arm, and she might have spent the night like that, were it not for a brilliant flash of lightning illuminating the window beside her. She leaped to her feet and moved to sit in her grandfather's chair beneath the lamp. She hadn't noticed it before, but he must have placed an envelope on the end table. *Hannah*, it was labeled in Eve's flowery penmanship. Sniffling, she tore it open.

"Dearest Hannah," it began. "Aren't the rocking chair, chest of drawers and cradle Grandfather made for us a most handsome set? We are so grateful."

Hannah was surprised. She knew her grandfather had spent an unusually long time working on the Stolzfuses' furniture, but she had no idea he was really working on an additional set. He must have been paying attention to her during mealtimes when she told him about Eve being with child after all. She read on:

What a surprise it was to have Grandfather show up here unannounced, ranting about Menno paying for his buggy repairs. It took some convincing before he believed we didn't know anything about the matter, and we imagine the church was responsible for this generous act of charity. (Had we known, we would have contributed; in the future, you must share your struggles with us. We will find a way to help that doesn't offend Grandfather's sense of responsibility.)

Despite his antics, I was—and I write this sincerely—very glad to see him, because I've missed him in his own way, although I would have been much gladder if you had been present, as well. You see, while I've written that there is nothing like the bond between a mother and child, or between a husband and wife, there's also nothing like the love between sisters.

As your sister, in response to what you wrote in your last letter, please allow me to express my advice and my hopes for you. By now, your Sawyer Plank may have made—*should* have made—his intentions toward you clear. When a man is interested in a woman, there should be no guessing. His actions and his words should unequivocally reflect the intentions of his heart. There should be no guessing, no interpreting, no doubting how he considers you. It should be clear in everything he does and says. (Likewise, the same is true of a woman's consideration for a man.)

If that is the case with Sawyer, then I will pray God will somehow work a way to allow you more than just a "brief season" of sharing your mutual love. I want this for you as much as you want it for yourself, dear sister.

Your loving Eve

Hannah was really bawling now, but her tears were… not joyful, exactly, but hopeful. She hoped to marry Sawyer more than she'd ever hoped for anything in her life, and she decided if he asked her to become his wife, she'd agree, no matter what her grandfather wanted. She'd do everything she could to persuade him to accompany her, but if he refused, that was his decision to make, not her fault to bear.

A dull roll of thunder sounded in the distance as she climbed the stairs. *Lord,* she prayed beside her bed, *thank You for my sister, Eve. Please keep her and the* bobbel *healthy. Thank You for bringing* Groossdaadi *home safely. And if there is any possible way Sawyer*

*and I might share a future together, please move Heaven
and earth so it may come to pass.*

After he'd tucked the children into bed, Sawyer
scribbled a quick letter to Gertrude:

Dear Gertrude,

I trust this letter finds you and Kathryn's household healthy? I especially pray for the strength
and size of the baby.

We're grateful the Lord has healed John's leg,
and the children and I will return to Ohio on Monday, God willing.

A little birdie told me a young suitor named
Seth might have captured your attention, which
is certainly understandable at your age, but I hope
he will not keep you from returning to Blue Hill
soon? The children have much to tell you, and so
do I. (I hope there will be surprising new devel-
opments to report.)

Remember me to Kathryn and her family.

Your brother, Sawyer

After he sealed the note into an envelope, Sawyer
turned in to his room for the night. Kneeling beside his
bed, he prayed, *Lord, You have indeed given me someone very special in Hannah, just as you did with Eliza.
Now I ask that Hannah's* groossdaadi *will be willing to
allow her to marry me. And I ask for Your guidance in
knowing how to approach him about it so the move is
acceptable to him.*

As he turned down the lamp, Sawyer imagined the

daadi haus he owned. Not much smaller than Albert's own home, it would offer Albert all the privacy and independence he wanted, yet would still allow Sawyer and Hannah to check in on him as needed. But, although older Amish in-laws frequently lived in such houses, Sawyer knew Albert would see it as charity. That man had no sense of humility or gratitude.

Sawyer punched his pillow and suddenly recalled John's words: *it's humbling to have another man do your work for you.* Perhaps that was how Hannah's grandfather felt. Didn't he say his affections couldn't be bought? It dawned on Sawyer that he shouldn't have tried to give him gifts. He should have valued the contributions Albert could make.

He immediately knew what the solution to his dilemma was: he would ask Albert to work in his shop. The man's hearing was gone, but his craftsmanship was still keener than most, and Sawyer desperately needed the help. He felt convinced that once her grandfather had a stake in moving to Ohio, nothing would stand in the way of Sawyer and Hannah becoming husband and wife.

Chapter Thirteen

Hannah woke early to prepare her grandfather a bigger breakfast than usual.

"I found Eve's letter," she mouthed. "She was very pleased with the furniture."

"Bah," he muttered, and she dared not ask him any other questions about his visit. For now, there was no need to say anything about the buggy repairs, either.

"That storm cooled things off last night, but it's shaping up to be hot again," she said, but he wasn't watching her lips, so she gave up conversing with him and set about making his dinner instead.

"Your eyes are...overcast," Sawyer stated when he greeted her in her classroom. "Did the storm keep you up last night?"

"*Jah*. We're probably in for some more tonight. The incoming autumn air makes for an unstable atmosphere."

"I couldn't sleep for imagining you last night, all alone," Sawyer said. Almost immediately, he turned a deep shade of crimson. "I mean, because I know how electrical storms rattle you so. At least tonight your *groossdaadi* will be home."

"Actually, he is already home. I was surprised to find he'd arrived while I was out visiting."

"Oh," Sawyer said somberly. "Did he confirm that Menno paid for his buggy repairs?"

Hannah giggled. "*Neh*, but according to a letter my sister, Eve, sent me, he must have put on quite a display interrogating them. They finally persuaded him they knew nothing about it."

"I see. So, is he well rested from his journey?"

"*Jah*, but why would you ask abo—"

"I knew I could find you here," Doris announced. "The two of you are always clucking away like hens. If I didn't know better, I'd think it was *you* who were betrothed!"

Hannah noticed Sawyer's jaw tense.

"What may we do for you?" she asked impatiently.

"I wanted to inquire if Sawyer will be bringing his younger sister to the wedding as well as the *kinner*. I heard from John she might still be in Indiana. My understanding is your eldest sister and her family most likely won't be able to attend, due to her weakened condition?"

Sawyer rubbed his forehead as if he had a headache. "I'm not certain, Doris," he said with a sigh. "Can't the answer wait a bit? We'll be heading home in a week and I can send John a letter once I've assessed the situation then, okay?"

"Of course," Doris gushed. "I only want them to know they're all invited."

"You're leaving in a week?" Hannah repeated, her heart pounding in her ears. "I knew John's leg had healed, but I thought you'd at least stay through the end of harvest."

"I was going to talk privately to you about that,"

Sawyer murmured quietly. Then, glancing at Doris, who was still hovering within earshot, he quickly added, "Because I wanted to prepare the *kinner* to say their farewells."

Hannah's mind whirled. Sawyer was leaving, just like that, as if their time together—especially these last few days—had meant nothing to him. And all he cared about was how his children felt about saying goodbye to her as their nanny, not how he felt about their parting. Not how *she* felt about it. She'd thought he valued the confidences they shared. She'd believed he saw her as strong and beautiful. That he considered her special as a woman—as "every bit a woman." The way he held her hand…the way he *kissed* her hand…the way he asked her opinion about Doris and John getting married so soon… She thought it was all leading up to one thing. What else was she to think?

Hannah recalled what Eve had written in her letter about how a man's actions and words should unequivocally reflect the intentions of his heart. Until that moment, Hannah had believed that everything Sawyer said, no matter how awkwardly it may have been expressed, reflected his true intentions. But his actions showed her where his heart was: in Blue Hill, Ohio. Now that the opportunity presented itself, he couldn't say his goodbyes quickly enough.

"Excuse me," someone said from the doorway. "May I speak with Hannah?"

"Jacob," Hannah acknowledged. "I'm sorry, but school is about to begin and I need a moment to prepare. If you're here about the arrangement we discussed, I'd be pleased to care for your household when my teaching assignment ends."

"*Denki*, Hannah," Jacob replied. "Miriam will be thrilled to hear this news, and so will Abigail."

"It's my pleasure. Now, everyone, please scoot. I have sums to prepare."

She turned her back before her eyes overflowed with the tears that had been gathering there.

Sawyer snapped the reins, and the horse took off. Hannah's disappointment was nearly tangible. He hadn't meant to spill the news he was leaving like that. His intention was to propose to Hannah once he'd spoken to her grandfather. Then they could work out the details together concerning the wedding and relocating. He didn't think about what he'd said before he said it—he just wanted to give a quick answer so Doris would leave. If she weren't always butting in, this never would have happened.

He had hoped to wait until Hannah's grandfather was rested from his trip and in a fairly reasonable mood. But now, as the horse trotted along, Sawyer realized he had to act with extreme urgency, and he redirected the animal toward Hannah's home.

He expected to find Albert in his workshop, and he tried to think of how he could enter without startling him. But when he arrived, Hannah's grandfather was sitting on the top step of the porch, sipping coffee as if he'd been expecting Sawyer all along.

"*Guder mariye,*" Sawyer said when he positioned himself at the bottom landing, where his mouth was nearly at the same height as Albert's eyes.

The grandfather nodded but didn't reply.

"I'll be brief," he mouthed carefully. "I want to marry Hannah."

No sooner had the words left his mouth than the old man shook his head.

"Neh," he uttered. *"Neh."*

Sawyer wasn't dissuaded. "I want her to move to Ohio with me. I want you to come, too. I have a *daadi haus* for you to live in. I need another man in my shop. It isn't charity—I've seen your work. I need someone like you on my crew."

"This is my home. *That* is my shop." The man gestured, shouting. "Hannah is *my* granddaughter."

"I care for Hannah and so do my *kinner*," Sawyer shouted back. He wanted the grandfather to see the intensity in his features, even if he couldn't hear it in the volume of his voice. "I want to be her husband and for her to be my wife."

"Neh, never!" her grandfather cried.

Sawyer's expression crumbled, but if there was one thing he resolved, it was that he wouldn't break down in front of Albert Lantz.

"But why not?" he questioned. "Why not?"

The grandfather stood and tossed the remains of his coffee cup onto the potted Russian sage, the hot spray narrowly missing Sawyer's shoulder.

"Never," he repeated evenly and then shuffled into the house, letting the screen door slam behind him.

"Ach!" Sawyer yelled and punched at the air.

When that did nothing to defuse his ire, he kicked the railing. To his astonishment, it splintered and cracked like a toothpick from the force of his fury, dangling crookedly from the side of the porch.

That is how you have trampled my heart, Albert Lantz, he thought as he sped away.

"You're later than usual," Jonas remarked when he

strode into the barn a few minutes later. "And you look like a raging bull."

"Don't start with me," Sawyer warned. "I need your toolbox. I'll be back in the fields whenever I get there."

When he returned to Hannah's home, her grandfather was already beginning to repair the damage he had done.

Although the words were bitter on his tongue, he mouthed, "I'm sorry."

The old man nodded and they worked together on the repairs. As Sawyer had already observed from the toys Albert created, he was a skilled carpenter, and the finished result was so seamless, one might have never guessed it had been broken.

"Albert, please," Sawyer started to say.

"Never means never," the grandfather replied, and Sawyer knew he meant it, just as definitively as he'd meant it about never doing business with the Schrock family.

Sawyer took hold of his sleeve to get his attention. "Listen, this isn't about marrying Hannah. It's about the toys you made. I want to buy them. All of them."

He would resell them in Ohio. Meanwhile, as he journeyed toward the farm with the dollhouse in the second seat and a box of trains beside him, he took small consolation in knowing the money he paid for the toys would help see Hannah and her grandfather through a few months this winter, God willing.

"You look awful," Doris commented at lunchtime. "Are you ill?"

"I feel awful," Hannah said. Her stomach was doing flips and her head was buzzing, but it was the cavernous ache in her heart that hurt more than anything. She couldn't bear the thought of facing Sawyer that evening. "I am afraid I need to go home. Would you mind taking over my class and watching the Plank *kinner* after school?"

"Of course not. It gives me another opportunity to see my betrothed!"

Hannah managed to slip away before Doris could see that her words triggered a torrent of tears. She numbly marched along the meadow route home, crossing the stream without stopping to dip her feet. Although it was a muggy afternoon, she felt chilled to the bone. Ascending the incline behind the house, she decided to stop at her grandfather's workshop to let him know she was home early, but that she intended to nap before preparing supper.

She slowly pushed open the door so as not to startle him, but as her eyes adjusted to the light, she realized he wasn't inside. The fragrance of the wood shavings filled her nostrils, reminding her of the evening she ducked inside the workshop with Sawyer and the children. She shut her eyes and recalled his hands moving over her ankle as he gingerly examined it for an injury. She shuddered and pushed the memory from her mind.

Spotting the rocking chair her grandfather was working on for Miriam, she traced the smooth curve of the wood along the arm. On the floor beside it was a matching cradle. But something was missing. Something wasn't—

Scanning the room, she realized there were no toys on the shelves. The dollhouse was gone, as well. Did her grandfather take them to sell in Lancaster? It would have been unlikely, but she supposed it was possible.

Inside the house, she found him sitting at the kitchen table, finishing the dinner she'd prepared for him.

Before he could make a single demand of her, she put both hands on his shoulders and mouthed, "What have you done with the toys?"

"I sold them to Sawyer Plank."

"All of them?" she questioned incredulously.

"Including the dollhouse. His *kinner* are spoiled, are they not?"

"I'm ill and I'm going to bed," she responded and fled the room.

She barely unlaced her shoes before collapsing into bed. She wondered why in the world Sawyer wanted all of those toys. Were they really for his children? She didn't think he was the kind of father to lavish material goods on them, but what did she really know of his character? Until that morning, she actually thought he had intentions of asking her to marry him.

What a fool I've been! She wept into her pillow. She thought she was more than a nanny to his children, and more than a trifling flirtation to him. How could she have been so wrong? She'd finally allowed herself to believe that it wasn't too late and she might actually receive her heart's deepest desire. She'd finally allowed herself to *admit* her heart's deepest desire. Come to find out, she wasn't anywhere close to having what she so desperately yearned for.

"Is one weekend of bliss all I get?" she shouted in frustration. "It isn't fair. It just isn't fair!"

She slept through the afternoon and evening. When she felt a hand on her shoulder the next day, she pushed her grandfather's arm away. She didn't care about teaching now. She didn't care about watching the Plank children. She just wanted to sleep. Rather, she only wanted someone to rouse her from sleep to tell her this had all been a bad dream.

"I will make your breakfast in an hour," she said when her grandfather returned a second time. "I need more rest. I'm sick."

"I brought you eggs," he said and set a plate on the nightstand before leaving the room.

Hannah shifted to a sitting position. Her grandfather usually did kind things like that only when he felt guilty, but she was hungry enough not to care what had panged his conscience. She ate the eggs and half of the piece of burned toast and then got dressed.

The clock said ten thirty; plenty of time to get to school and relieve Doris from the burden of teaching her class a second day. No matter how despondent she felt, she had a responsibility to her scholars, and once her class ended, she would regret missing any time with them.

"I can feel the sun beating down on my skull right through my hair," she said when she saw her grandfather on the porch. He was sanding the railings, but she didn't question him about it. "I'm taking the shortcut to school. I feel better now—I think the eggs helped. *Denki*."

"I will see you tonight, *Gott* willing." He continued scratching the wood smooth.

Hannah grew so sweaty on her way that when she arrived at the stream, she removed her socks and shoes to maneuver through the deepest water instead of using the stepping-stones. She had reached the opposite embankment when a man's voice called, "Hannah, wait!"

Hannah's expression was even icier than the water he was slogging through, but neither stopped Sawyer from rushing to her side.

"What are you doing here?" she asked, bending to lace her shoes.

"I was waiting for you. I had a hunch you might come here at some point."

"And if I hadn't?"

"Then I would have come back each day until you did," Sawyer exclaimed. "Listen, Hannah, I need to talk to you. It seems you're angry, and I can't return to Ohio knowing you're upset with me. Are you?"

"Did you buy my *groossdaadi's* toys for your *kinner*?" she asked, avoiding his question.

"Er, *jah*," Sawyer stammered. "I mean, *neh*."

"Which is it?" she asked, shooting him a penetrating look. "*Jah* or *neh*?"

"I bought the toys," he admitted loudly. "But not for my *kinner*."

"Then why?" she asked, standing akimbo. When he didn't answer, she threw her hands in the air and began stamping through the grass.

"Wait!" he called, hobbling barefoot after her, his shoes and socks bundled in his arms. "I bought them to resell in Ohio. They'll garner a high price there, and I wanted you and your *groossdaadi* to have enough income to see you through the winter."

She whipped around and shrieked, "Your financial responsibility toward me ends when I stop caring for the *kinner* and you return to Ohio."

"You are as prideful as your *groossdaadi*, Hannah Lantz!" Sawyer hollered back as he tossed his footwear beside him. "I didn't purchase the toys out of responsibility or obligation. I purchased them because I care about you."

"You care about me? You care about me?" Hannah

sobbed. "Not like I care about you, Sawyer Plank. I thought… I actually thought—"

"You thought what?"

"I thought you might be the Lord's intended for me." She wept, falling to her knees and burying her head in her hands.

"Oh, Hannah," Sawyer murmured, crouching down beside her. "I wanted to marry you, too. I had it all planned. I offered your *groossdaadi* employment in my shop. I told him I have a *daadi haus* he can occupy. I pleaded with him, but still he refused."

"Why?" she asked, intensely scrutinizing his face. Her eyelashes were damp with tears as she asked again, "Why?"

"I don't know," Sawyer moaned. "He wouldn't say."

"I mean why did you want to marry me?"

"What kind of question is that?"

"A direct one. Why won't you give a direct reply?"

"You already know why I want to marry you." Sawyer sighed. "We truly care for each other, and the *kinner* are clearly as fond of you as you are of them. We're responsible adults who are old enough to know what we want and who try to obey *Gott*. And we're like-minded in the ways that matter most…especially in our beliefs about family and the Lord. You said these same things about Doris and John not two days ago!"

"I'm not talking about Doris and John. I'm talking about you and me," Hannah stated quietly, a note of resignation in her voice. "You mentioned caring for me. What you didn't mention—what you've *never* mentioned—is *love*. You once told me you thought love was a frivolity, not a necessity. I thought perhaps you were referring to the kind of romance teenagers engage in, but now I'm not so sure. Tell me, Sawyer, is love a necessity for marriage, or is it just a frivolity?"

Sawyer's head was swimming, and he felt as if he might keel over from the blistering heat. "What does it matter?" he asked with a sigh. "Your *groossdaadi* already irrevocably refused to allow it to happen."

"It matters," she said, straightening her posture and rapidly blinking droplets from her eyes as she beheld his face, "because even if my *groossdaadi* had said *jah*, I wouldn't marry a man who doesn't love me with his whole heart, the way I love him. I wouldn't marry a man who can't even say the words!"

"Hannah—" Sawyer began, but his voice was too raspy to be heard.

"I will honor my commitment to care for the *kinner* for the rest of the week," she said before walking away. "But you'll forgive me if I don't engage in idle small talk when you drop them off or pick them up."

She headed toward the school, and Sawyer stumbled back to the creek, where he dipped his hand to drink again and again, trying to fill what felt like an unquenchable thirst.

Hannah managed to make it through the afternoon without weeping in front of her class, but once home, she removed herself from the children's presence to blot her eyes. She keened forward and backward on her bed, willing herself to stop crying. It was one of her last days with Sarah, Samuel and Simon. She didn't want them to remember her as tearful and blotchy-faced.

There was a knock on the door.

"Hannah?" Sarah asked. "Would you brush my hair? Doris Hooley wanted to do it because she said I look unkempt, but I told her I wanted you to do it."

"Of course. Sit here beside me. You're getting old enough to brush the ends yourself now. Don't you remember the secret trick I showed you?"

"*Jah*, but *Daed* said we would be leaving soon, so I wanted to get in all the brushing with you I could," Sarah sniffed.

"Shh, shh," Hannah said. "If you fuss, you'll make me cry, too."

"If I write to you, will you write to me?"

"*Jah*."

"Can I come to visit?" Sarah pleaded.

Avoiding the question, Hannah corrected her, "*May* I come to visit?"

"Of course you may!" Sarah giggled gleefully until Hannah did, too.

But a few hours later, Hannah lay in the same spot, sobbing her heart out again. She hadn't cried that hard since her *groossmammi* died, or her parents before that.

She wondered if this was how Jacob Stolzfus felt when she told him she held only a sisterly affection for him. But this was different, wasn't it? She'd made it clear to Jacob on several occasions she was interested only in a friendship with him. Sawyer, however, asked her grandfather for her hand. He led her to believe he felt about her as she felt about him, didn't he?

As she wept, lightning flickered and the curtains danced as the breeze picked up. She raced to shut her windows. As the skies let loose a deluge of rain, Hannah wept a spate of tears, until another day dawned, hot and dry.

"You look miserable," her grandfather said when he finished his breakfast. "You're too old to be staying up half the night from a little lightning."

Hannah walked to the sink under the pretense of washing dishes.

"And *you're* too old to be making such unkind remarks!" she replied with her back turned, thrashing a dishcloth over the pots in the sink. "How dare you complain about what I look like? *You* have always tried to squelch every fragment of joy I've ever experienced. *You* are responsible for this frown I'm wearing, *Groossdaadi*. Because *you* have wanted me to wind up like *you*—a miserable, lonely, bitter old coot."

The combination of the scalding dishwater, her fiery temper and the broiling sun made her hotter than ever by the time she reached the stream. She removed her shoes to wade across, and as usual, the chilly current soothed both her mind and body.

Lord, please forgive my wrath, she prayed before continuing on her way. *Keep* Groossdaadi *safe this day. And if I should see Sawyer, please give me the grace to speak to him as I would want to be spoken to myself.*

When Sawyer came down for breakfast, he found Phillip alone at the kitchen table, drinking from a mug.

"Is that coffee or tea?" he asked.

"Coffee, of course," the teenager sneered, sounding more like Jonas than like himself. "My *daed* is the only one who started drinking tea."

Sawyer poured himself a cup of the strong, dark brew. "*Jah*, tea's not for me, either. I wonder what other changes Doris will try to bring to this household."

"She can try to make as many changes as she wants," Phillip spit, "but she's not *my* wife and she's not *my* mamm, so I'm not required to do a thing she says."

Catching the resentment in his cousin's voice, Sawyer realized Phillip was only nine or ten when his mother died. Old enough to remember, but not necessarily old enough to comprehend.

He carefully suggested, "You know, your *daed* will never forget your *mamm* or the love they shared together."

"I know that," Phillip said with a snicker. "You don't have to talk to me like I'm a *bobbel*."

But Sawyer needed to speak what was on his mind for his own benefit as much as for Phillip's. "But your *mamm's* no longer here, and whether your *daed* remarries or not, nothing will bring her back."

Phillip rose and poured his coffee in the sink, but he didn't leave the room.

"No one will ever replace your *mamm*, not in your eyes, nor in your *daed's*. And I don't think Doris intends to try. In fact, I think it would be wrong to expect her to—even though I know she cares deeply about you and your brother, not unlike a mother might. But Doris and your *daed* have a unique relationship, one that's different from what your *mamm* and *daed* shared."

Phillip feigned a yawned, but he seemed significantly cheered.

"One more thing—you're right that you're not required to do what Doris wants you to do. But since you care about your *daed*, you should remember that he suffered unimaginable grief when your *mamm* died. If he's blessed enough to find a woman worthy of marrying again, you might consider honoring him by honoring that woman, too. And when you do, you shouldn't feel a bit guilty about it, because that's how your *mamm* would have wanted you to behave," Sawyer suggested.

After taking a swallow of coffee, he added, "Of course, that doesn't mean you need to start drinking tea."

"Jah, jah," Phillip agreed. "End of the lecture, Bishop Sawyer?"

"End of lecture. Now you go on ahead. I'll be out in a few minutes."

Sawyer pressed his palms against his eyelids, trying to block out the image of Hannah's pained face when he refused to say the words he knew she needed to hear. If only he'd had this conversation with Phillip earlier, he would have been more prepared to express himself to her. He knew his love for her to be true all along, he just didn't give it voice. He agonized that he was so inarticulate, always stuttering and stammering!

But what did it matter in the end? Her grandfather said he would never approve of their marriage. Hannah had to live with him for the rest of his life—it was better she should blame Sawyer for not loving her than to spend her daily life resenting her grandfather for forbidding their union. At least in time, Sawyer hoped she would forgive and forget him.

A shudder racked his body as he said aloud, "Even though I will never, ever forget her."

Chapter Fourteen

"The sky looks ominous. Would you and the *kinner* like a ride home?" Doris asked at the end of the day.

"*Denki*, but because of my absences, I need to catch up with my lessons," Hannah answered. "I've heard thunder growling all day, but so far, the clouds haven't erupted. If it begins to storm, we'll stay here until it passes."

After an hour of playing outdoors, the children traipsed into the classroom, sticky and panting from the heat.

"Will we have time to stop at the stream on the way home?" Samuel asked.

"I don't see why not," Hannah said. "As long as there's no lightning. Why don't you sit down and cool off for five minutes, and then I'll be ready to go. I'll even spoon the very last of my strawberry preserves from the jar for you to have on bread."

"Mmm," Sarah hummed after they'd been served. "It tastes just like pink sunshine, remember?"

"I remember."

"Why aren't you eating any, Hannah?" Simon noticed. "Are you terribly sick, too, like our *daed*?"

"What?" Hannah's ears perked up. "I just saw your *daed* drop you off this morning. What makes you think he's ill?"

"He told us on the way to school," Samuel said, hanging his head.

"*Jah,*" Sarah confirmed. "He said he was terribly lovesick. That's what he said."

"Oh." Hannah gulped. She suddenly remembered what Grace had written about Sawyer being slow to express his affection, and her eyes moistened. *Was I too impatient with him, or did the* kinner *misunderstand something he told them?* "Do you know what *lovesick* means?"

"*Jah*, it means having a kind of sickness only grown-ups can get. *Daed* said it happens when you have love to give to a special grown-up but they don't want it anymore," Sarah answered.

Samuel added, "*Daed* told us love is like having too much strawberry ice cream. If you don't share it with someone else, if you keep it all inside, you get sick. You get lovesick."

"And since *Daed* has so much love inside, it's making him extra terribly lovesick," ended Simon.

"I see," Hannah said, crossing the room to the window so the children wouldn't see the tears escaping her eyes.

She blinked several times as she peered into the school yard, trying to clear her vision. Finally, she rubbed her eyes with her fingers and realized she wasn't imagining it—the distant sky actually was tinged with green. But there was no thunder. In fact, she'd never heard such silence. Not a leaf was stirring.

As if to challenge the notion, a tremendous gust abruptly lifted the branches of the willow tree and a cacophony of thunder reverberated overhead. The room went dim as instantly as if someone had doused a lamp and then just as suddenly was illuminated with a succession of brilliant flashes. Sarah screamed a piercing wail. Hannah barely had time to shut the windows against the barrage of hail bombarding the panes.

"Kumme!" she urged the children. "Under my desk, now!"

The children curled into balls on the floor, with Hannah shielding Sarah beneath her chest and the boys under each arm. *Please, Lord, shelter us with Your mighty strength. Please, Lord, shelter us with Your mighty strength*, Hannah prayed repeatedly as the atmosphere churned and cracked above them. The lightning was so scintillating and constant, Hannah could see it even as she squeezed her eyelids shut. The windowpanes popped like gunshot, and the force of the gale caused the desk to rattle like a train. Hannah tightened her grasp around the children.

"Hold on!" Although she was just inches from their ears, she had to shout to be heard over the ruckus. "Hold on tight!"

Such tremendous claps and clatters filled the air, she couldn't discern what was happening inside the schoolhouse and what was happening outside it. In fact, she didn't know if there *was* an inside anymore—it sounded as if the walls and roof had been fractured clear away from the building. Hannah tucked her chin to her chest against the dust and debris the wind was sweeping toward them in every direction.

There was a formidable splintering before *wham!*— something above boomed so forcefully that Hannah felt the floorboards jump before she and the children were engulfed in complete darkness.

* * *

Sawyer, John and the boys made it to the house just as the squall broke out, large pellets of hail bouncing off the grass as they ran.

"This is twister weather," John said breathlessly to Doris, who was in the middle of supper preparations. "The animals knew it before we did. I had a hard time getting your horse into the stable, but eventually he settled down."

"You're soaked, poor things," she said, handing them each a towel. A bolt of lightning cracked nearby, causing her to leap. "My, my. I'm not even afraid of storms, and this one is making me jittery. I hope Hannah isn't too nervous alone at school."

"You think Hannah and the *kinner* are still at the schoolhouse?" Sawyer asked in consternation. "Wouldn't they have left a long time ago?"

"I can't be certain," Doris stated, her pale skin fading to a lustrous shade of white, "but she had lessons to prepare. She said if a storm arose, they'd wait it out there."

"I have to make sure they're alright."

"Sawyer," John protested, grabbing his arm, "you can't go out in this. The horses are already spooked and will run off the road. The Lord will keep Hannah and the *kinner* safe. We'll go when it lets up."

"Neh," argued Sawyer. "I have to get to them now."

"I'll go with you," Jonas volunteered.

"Me, too," said Phillip. "*Daed*, you should stay here and make Doris a cup of tea. It looks like her nerves are frazzled."

By the time they'd hitched the horse to the buggy and set out for the schoolhouse, the storm had traveled at a good clip from the southwest to the northeast. They witnessed lightning forking from the bruised clouds to the horizon, but the sky overhead was already brightening. Steam rose from the ground, and the air had a metallic smell. The fields were blanketed in hail like snow.

As they neared the school, Sawyer was sickened by the sight of the damage: trees were uprooted and toppled, fences smashed and strewn, and a cow lay on its side in a field. He was grateful Jonas had the foresight to bring a couple of pairs of handsaws; more than once he and Phillip had to hop down and clear a path through the fallen trees. Sawyer realized this part of the town was the hardest hit. But nothing could have prepared him for the shock of seeing the schoolhouse.

One side—the side where Doris held her classes—remained relatively unscathed. Hannah's side, however, was nothing more than a heap of rubble, pulverized by the weight of the giant willow. Gasping in horror, Sawyer shouted, *"Neh!"*

When the noise finally abated, Hannah wiggled her fingers and her toes. In shock, she thought strangely, *I must be alive.*

"Sarah? Simon? Samuel?" She tried to call their names, but her mouth was dry.

The space was too tight for her to shift her body, and she was crouched in utter darkness. Nearly overcome by a wave of panic, she attempted to take a deep breath. It was then she felt the most marvelous movement beneath her chest, and subsequently each of her arms fluttered, too, reminding her of chicks hatching from their eggs. The children were stirring!

"Are you hurt? Are you hurt?" she repeated. "Wiggle your fingers and toes. Tell me if you are hurt."

When all three children confirmed they were fine,

Hannah burst into prayer. *"Denki,* mighty Lord, for Your provision!" she sang. *"Denki, denki, denki!"*

"Is the storm over?" Sarah asked. "May we get out of here now?"

"It's very crowded," Simon whimpered.

"And dark," Samuel admitted.

"The storm *is* over," Hannah said carefully. "I know it's dark and crowded in here, but we'll get out soon. You see, the wind blew quite a few branches and pieces of wood down on top of us. As soon as your *daed* and the *leit* come, they will lift the debris up and we will climb out."

"Are we trapped?" Sarah asked, and Hannah could feel her body quiver.

"Trapped? *Neh,* we're *cozy,*" Hannah replied. "This desk saved our lives! And do you know what? My *groossdaadi* made this desk many, many years ago when my *daed* was just a boy your age. My *daed* used to hide under it in the workshop. He pretended it was a cave."

"We can pretend it's a cave!" Samuel suggested.

"Jah," Hannah encouraged him. "When people are in caves, they like to pass the time by telling stories. Let's think back to the first day you came to school in Willow Creek and tell all of the stories we can remember about our time together."

"Like the time we caught the giant toad?" Simon asked.

"Or when we played that gold dust trick on *Daed*?" Samuel wondered.

"How about when we made snitz pies?" Sarah questioned.

"Oh, my," Hannah said. "Until this storm struck, I

don't think there was ever a bigger mess than on the day we made snitz pies!"

"Jah," agreed Sarah. "Now, that was a real disaster!"

The four of them began to laugh so hard they shook.

"Hey! You're wiggling me like jelly!" Simon shouted, which made them laugh and wiggle all the more.

Sawyer had jumped from the buggy before he'd brought the horse to a complete halt. He sprinted up the stairs of the schoolhouse. The door to Hannah's classroom oddly stood standing, but the rest of the wall and roof were skeletal at best. The space once occupied by neat rows of desks was covered with thick willow tree branches, piled at least a dozen feet high. Fearing no one could have survived it, Sawyer retched at the sight of the destruction.

"Kumme," Jonas said, grasping his shoulder from behind. "They're not here. They probably left for her *groossdaadi's* house before the storm broke."

Holding on to the possibility as a ray of hope, Sawyer turned to accompany his cousin when he heard it: giggling. He'd recognize the sound anywhere; it was the sound of his children's happiness. It was Hannah's wind-chime laughter.

"Hello! Hello!" he shouted frantically. "Are you there? Are you hurt?"

"We are here," a faint voice responded. "We're fine, but we can't get out!"

Tears sprang to Sawyer's eyes, and he didn't bother to brush them away as he scrambled over the willow branches. "Where are you? Call out again!"

"Under Hannah's desk!" came several voices in unison. "Front of the classroom!"

"We're coming!" he shouted back, using his loudest volume. "We hear you and we're coming!

"They're on the other side of this tree," Sawyer directed. "It's too high to cross. We have to come at it from the other side."

The back wall had collapsed forward, but Sawyer was able to determine the location of Hannah's desk by memory. He, Jonas and Phillip began heaving the wreckage over the side of the foundation to the ground below, assuring Hannah and the children as they worked that they'd have them out soon.

"Cover your heads," Sawyer yelled when all but the last layer of pilings had been removed. "Some of this wood might shift when we pull the desk away. On the count of three—"

Sawyer and Jonas tipped the desk at an angle so the foursome had room to escape. Samuel and Simon sprang to their feet, but Sarah's and Hannah's muscles were cramped from being in the same position for so long and the men had to help them stand.

After embracing his children in a tremendous bear hug, Sawyer instructed, "Jonas, grab the boys' hands. Phillip, you take Sarah. I've got Hannah."

His heart thudding like mad, he lifted her into his arms and placed her gently into the buggy. Her face was streaked with grime and her eyelashes were thick with dust, but he thought she was a most beautiful sight.

He asked again, "Are you sure everyone is unharmed?"

"We're fine," she confirmed, "but I must see if *Groossdaadi* is alright."

As they charged toward her home, Hannah was appalled by the extent of the damage. Her stomach lurched several times, realizing her grandfather would never have heard the storm coming. She bit her lip and begged, *Please, Lord, let him be safe.*

When they crested the hill leading to her lane, her worst fears were realized: even from a distance she could see the chimney was all that remained standing of her house. The horse stall was smashed, as was her grandfather's workshop. The willow was stripped of its leaves, and the swing dangled like a flag of surrender from a top branch.

"Neh! Neh!" she moaned, scrambling over the children to leap from the buggy while it was still in motion. *"Neh!"*

"Hannah, wait!"

But Hannah ignored the voice. She ran to her grandfather's workshop and numbly began flinging pieces of wood from the pile. *A miserable, lonely, bitter old coot.* Those were the last words she'd spoken to him.

"Hannah, wait!" the voice said again, in her ear now.

Sawyer wrapped his arms around her waist and pulled her off the pile of debris, but as soon as he set her down, she bolted for the wreckage again. She had to get to her grandfather. He could be buried beneath the rubble, as she and the children had been. He wouldn't be able to hear her coming. She had to get to him. She had to let him know she was coming, that she'd never leave him.

This time, Sawyer restrained her arms as he embraced her from behind. She kicked him and wept hysterically. "Let me go! Let me go!" she yelled. "I have to get to my *groossdaadi*. Why aren't you helping me save him?"

"That's what I'm trying to tell you," Sawyer stated emphatically. "Your *groossdaadi* is alive. He returned in his buggy behind us just now. He said he was delivering a cradle to Miriam Stolzfus when the storm struck."

Sawyer loosened his grip on her, and she slowly shifted to see if he was telling the truth. Although it was dusk, there was no mistaking the stooped figure shuffling in her direction.

"Hannah!" her grandfather called. "My Hannah! I thought I'd lost you!"

Hannah's knees knocked, and her breathing was hard and fast. *"Groossdaadi,"* she whispered. Then the ground seemed to come up from behind to clock her in the head.

She woke in a room where she'd never been and shaded her eyes against the glare of white morning light.

"Hannah, it's me, Doris Hooley," a familiar voice greeted her. "You're at the Plank farm. You had a fall and bumped your head. It probably hurts and you may experience a bit of confusion for a few days, but you're going to be fine."

"My *groossdaadi*—"

"He is fine, although I must say he has a huge appetite. I think he ate four eggs for breakfast!" Doris chuckled. "The *kinner* are fine, too, to your credit."

"Neh, to the Lord's credit," Hannah murmured, suddenly flooded with fragments of recollection about what happened the day before.

"You may stay in bed, or if you can manage it, join us downstairs. I believe you're better suited for one of Amelia's dresses than for mine, so this morning I brought you one to wear. Sarah offered to brush your hair for you if I deem it *unkempt*," Doris said with a chuckle. "And the washbasin is freshly filled."

Hannah felt as if every bone in her body ached, and

her mind was slightly addled, but she was so eager to see everyone, she dressed and hobbled downstairs.

"Guder mariye!" the children whispered.

"Doris said we have to be quiet because your head might hurt still. Does it, Hannah?" Simon asked.

"It hurts a little," she said, "but do you know what might make it feel much better?"

"If I fix you strawberry preserves on toast?" Sarah suggested.

"I was going to say *three hugs*, but now I think I'll say *three hugs and strawberry preserves on toast*!" she said, and the children readily complied.

"Hannah, *kumme*," her grandfather said from the porch.

He patted the swing and she sat down, positioning her body not only so he could read her lips, but so she could take a good look at him. She felt as if she never wanted to let him out of her sight again.

"Do you feel better?"

"Jah," she answered. "Much better. Safe and sound."

As the two of them sat watching the birds flit about as if their world hadn't been turned upside down the day before, Sawyer ambled up the stairs and lowered himself into the spare chair.

"Guder mariye, Hannah," he greeted her. "We were all worried about you."

"Guder mariye, Sawyer. I am fine, *denki*."

"He wants to marry you," Hannah's grandfather announced in his characteristically bold manner, motioning his thumb toward Sawyer. "He has a *daadi haus*. I could work in his shop. You should consider saying *jah*."

Hannah closed her eyes. After all they'd just been through, her grandfather hadn't changed a bit. He still wanted to control her life, based on his own desires.

Even more disappointing, Sawyer hadn't tried to convince her to marry him—her grandfather had done it on Sawyer's behalf, just like his children had told her how lovesick he was. Shouldn't these sentiments come from Sawyer? If he truly loved her, why didn't his words express what was in his heart?

"Neh," Hannah refused, and Sawyer's heart sank.

She squinted in her grandfather's direction, but her words were clearly intended for Sawyer. "You want me to marry him because our house and all that we own is gone, but even that's not reason enough for me, *Groossdaadi*. There are other things we can do. You can stay with Eve and Menno. I will live at Miriam and Jacob's and care for their *bobbel*. After that, we'll figure something out. The Lord will provide."

Her grandfather spryly leaped to his feet. He clasped Hannah's shoulder with one hand and Sawyer's with the other.

"I may be deaf, but nothing gets by me. I saw some time ago that the two of you love each other, and I was selfish to stand in your way. I didn't want to end up alone, but the *gut* Lord showed me yesterday how wrong I was to think I could hold on to you forever. For that, I am sorry, Hannah. I truly am."

Pausing, he took out a handkerchief and blew his nose.

"You are right. The Lord will provide our daily bread, whether or not you marry this man. If you don't want to marry him, don't marry him. That is your decision to make, not mine. You have my blessing either way," he said and then retreated into the house.

"Your *groossdaadi* is right," Sawyer said, leaning forward in his chair to brush a tendril of hair behind

Hannah's ear. His voice was husky as he declared, "I do love you and I have loved you for some time. I just haven't expressed it aloud to you until now. I love you in a way I've never loved anyone before, and I always will."

Hannah's eyes, so soulful and blue, scrutinized his face. *She always seemed able to see right through me. She must know I'm telling the truth*, he thought.

Dropping to his knees, he pleaded as much as proposed, "Hannah Lantz, will you be my wife?"

Her eyes widened and she lifted her hands to the top of her head. Her lip began to quiver as tears streamed down her face, but she said nothing, neither turning away nor drawing near. His lungs began to burn, and he felt as if he couldn't get enough air. Unable to bear the silence, Sawyer closed his eyes. As he was wishing the ground would swallow him up, a butterfly alighted on his cheek.

Then he realized it wasn't the beating of a butterfly's wings against his skin; it was Hannah's eyelashes fluttering.

"Jah, jah," Hannah repeated, laughing and crying at once as she pressed her cheek against his. Sawyer wasn't certain whether she was delirious or ecstatic.

"Do you mean *jah*, you will marry me?" he asked, half question, half exclamation.

"Jah, I will marry you, Sawyer Plank," Hannah replied, nodding vigorously. "I love, love, love you!"

Standing, he picked her up, twirled her around, and then he kissed her softly on the lips once before setting her back on the ground.

With her brothers in tow, Sarah stepped out onto the porch at that moment carrying a plate of toast.

"Daed," she scolded, "you mustn't get too close to

Hannah. That is how germs are spread. She'll catch your lovesickness."

"Neh," her father told her. "Hannah cured my lovesickness. I'm over it for *gut!*"

Epilogue

"*Denki* for hosting us this Christmas," Doris said as she cut slices of caramel pie for the adults to enjoy with their afternoon tea. "I've never been to Ohio before."

"I hope you'll come often. After all, we're family now." Hannah beamed. "Besides, it's the least we could do after you allowed us to get married at your home in November."

"*Schnickelfritz!*" Doris exclaimed. "Where else would you have wed? Where would your relatives have stayed? Your house was thoroughly destroyed."

"I suppose we could have gotten married next autumn, but we didn't want to wait a moment longer than we already had—we were following your example," Hannah teased back.

"You don't think I was being too *desperate*?" Doris asked.

"*Neh,*" replied Hannah. "*Gott's* timing is perfect."

So were His provisions. As she prepared hot chocolate for the children, Hannah thought about how abundantly the Lord had provided for her, especially during the past autumn. John had allowed her grandfather to live in his home until he moved with Hannah to Ohio, and meanwhile he'd kept busy helping rebuild the schoolhouse.

Hannah had stayed with Miriam and Jacob, assisting their household as they ushered their healthy son into the world. Given the extenuating circumstances, the deacon had been very accommodating in meeting with Hannah and Sawyer as many times as necessary in order for them to marry in November.

Who would have thought the very kind of storm that was the source of so much loss and grief when Hannah was a child would ultimately result in so much gain and joy now that she was an adult? She sighed and filled the mugs as Gertrude scurried into the room.

"Oh, you've finished already! I was coming to help," the young woman said.

"You've already helped me in more ways than you know," Hannah replied, placing her hands on Gertrude's shoulders. "I've long meant to say *denki* for the postscript you wrote me on Sarah's letter. The part about Sawyer not being quick to express his affection helped me when I was filled with doubt."

"I should say *denki*, as well. I sense your influence in some of the freedoms Sawyer has allowed me as of late."

Hannah smiled warmly, lifting the tray of mugs. "Speaking of my husband, I heard him call me a moment ago. I'd better go see what he wants."

She stopped at the threshold of the gathering room to behold the scene inside: her grandfather was using blocks to construct a trestle for the wooden trains he'd made Samuel and Simon for Christmas. Their cheeks were rosy from helping him clear a path in the snow from his *daadi haus* to their back porch, and now the trio worked together in wordless cooperation.

"Make sure your railroad tracks don't run through my yard, please," Sarah requested from where she was seated on the floor nearby. She fingered the miniature table Hannah's grandfather carved for the dollhouse he'd presented her the day after Christmas, when the Amish traditionally exchanged small gifts.

The best gift I've received is to have all these loved ones in my family, Hannah marveled as she scanned the room.

"*Kumme*, sit with me." Sawyer gestured to the empty spot on the love seat after he had taken her tray and set it on a side table, which was modestly decorated with an evergreen centerpiece and candles. "We didn't want to start dessert without you."

"But first you must open the gift I brought," Eve insisted. "Here, Menno, could you please hold the *bobbel* while I give them their present?"

Eve deftly passed little Joshua to Menno, her face aglow.

"Motherhood certainly agrees with you, Eve," Hannah noticed.

"Funny you should say that," Eve replied as she handed her sister a large package wrapped in bright green paper and tied with silver ribbon. "Menno and I were just commenting to John and Doris how much we think motherhood agrees with *you*."

Hannah modestly dipped her head, but she was delighted to her core. When she lifted her chin again, she caught Sawyer's eyes sparkling with pride.

"It certainly does," he agreed.

"Aren't you going to open it?" Doris prompted.

Together, Hannah and Sawyer tore off the paper to discover the most beautiful wedding quilt Hannah had ever seen.

"Eve!" Hannah exclaimed, but she was too choked up to say anything more.

"All of my life, you've been like a *mamm* to me," Eve said. "Now I get a small chance to be like a *mamm* to you—the quilt is something I imagine our *mamm* might have given you as part of your dowry."

"But how could you have made it so quickly, especially with a new *bobbel* to care for?"

"I've been working on the quilt for years, Hannah," Eve explained. "I never stopped believing and praying that the Lord would provide you the desires of your heart, as well as your daily bread."

As Doris served the pie, Hannah interlaced her fingers with Sawyer's beneath the quilt and whispered, "Eve is right—through my new life with you and the *kinner, Gott* has provided both my daily bread and blessed me with the deepest desires of my heart."

"And our life with you," Sawyer murmured into her ear, "is sweeter than a dream."

* * * * *

WE HOPE YOU ENJOYED THIS BOOK!

New beginnings. Happy endings.
Discover uplifting inspirational
romance.

Look for six new Love Inspired
books available every month,
wherever books are sold!

Love Inspired ®

Save $1.00

on the purchase of ANY
Love Inspired or
Love Inspired Suspense book.

Available wherever books are sold,
including most bookstores, supermarkets,
drugstores and discount stores.

Save $1.00

on the purchase of ANY Love Inspired or Love Inspired Suspense book.

Coupon valid until February 28, 2020.
Redeemable at participating retail outlets in the U.S. and Canada only.
Limit one coupon per customer.

52616512

Canadian Retailers: Harlequin Enterprises Limited will pay the face value of this coupon plus 10.25¢ if submitted by customer for this product only. Any other use constitutes fraud. Coupon is nonassignable. Void if taxed, prohibited or restricted by law. Consumer must pay any government taxes. Void if copied. Inmar Promotional Services ("IPS") customers submit coupons and proof of sales to Harlequin Enterprises Limited, P.O. Box 31000, Scarborough, ON M1R 0E7, Canada. Non-IPS retailer—for reimbursement submit coupons and proof of sales directly to Harlequin Enterprises Limited, Retail Marketing Department, 22 Adelaide St. West, 40th Floor, Toronto, Ontario M5H 4E3, Canada.

5 65373 00076 2 (8100)0 12434

U.S. Retailers: Harlequin Enterprises Limited will pay the face value of this coupon plus 8¢ if submitted by customer for this product only. Any other use constitutes fraud. Coupon is nonassignable. Void if taxed, prohibited or restricted by law. Consumer must pay any government taxes. Void if copied. For reimbursement submit coupons and proof of sales directly to Harlequin Enterprises, Ltd 482, NCH Marketing Services, P.O. Box 880001, El Paso, TX 88588-0001, U.S.A. Cash value 1/100 cents.

LICOUP47016R

He reached out a hand, meaning to shake hers, but she
grasped his and held it. Looked into his eyes. "Reese, I'm
sorry about what happened before."

He narrowed his eyes and frowned at her. "You
mean...after I went into the service?"

She nodded and swallowed hard. "Something
happened, and I couldn't...I couldn't keep the promise I
made."

That something being another guy, Izzy's father. He
drew in a breath. Was he going to hold on to his grudge,
or his hurt feelings, about what had happened?

Looking into her eyes, he breathed out the last of his
anger. Like Corbin had said, everyone was a sinner. "It's
understood."

"Thank you," she said simply. She held his gaze for
another moment and then looked down and away.

She was still holding on to his hand, and slowly, he
twisted and opened his hand until their palms were flat
together. Pressed between them as close as he'd like to be
pressed to Gabby.

The only light in the room came from the kitchen and

the dying fire. Outside the windows, snow had started to fall, blanketing the little house in solitude.

This night with her family had been one of the best he'd had in a long time. Made him realize how much he missed having a family.

Gabby's hand against his felt small and delicate, but he knew better. He slipped his own hand to the side and captured hers, tracing his thumb along the calluses.

He heard her breath hitch and looked quickly at her face. Her eyes were wide, her lips parted and moist.

Without looking away, acting on impulse, he slowly lifted her hand to his lips and kissed each fingertip.

Her breath hitched and came faster, and his sense of himself as a man, a man who could have an effect on a woman, swelled, almost making him giddy.

This was Gabby, and the truth burst inside him: he'd never gotten over her, never stopped wishing they could be together, that they could make that family they'd dreamed of as kids. That was why he'd gotten so angry when she'd strayed: because the dream she'd shattered had been so big, so bright and shining.

In the back of his mind, a voice of caution scolded and warned. She'd gone out with his cousin. She'd had a child with another man. What had been so major in his emotional life hadn't been so big in hers.

He shouldn't trust her. And he definitely shouldn't kiss her.

But when had he ever done what he should?

Don't miss
The Secret Christmas Child *by Lee Tobin McClain,*
available December 2019 wherever
Love Inspired® books and ebooks are sold.

www.LoveInspired.com

LIEXP1019

Looking for inspiration in tales
of hope, faith and heartfelt romance?

Check out **Love Inspired**® and
Love Inspired® **Suspense** books!

New books available every month!

LIGENRE2018R2